Aphrodite's War

www.rbooks.co.uk

Also by Andrea Busfield

Born Under a Million Shadows

Aphrodite's War

Andrea Busfield

Doubleday

LONDON · TORONTO · SYDNEY · AUCKLAND · JOHANNESBURG

TRANSWORLD PUBLISHERS
61–63 Uxbridge Road, London W5 5SA
A Random House Group Company
www.rbooks.co.uk

First published in Great Britain
in 2010 by Doubleday
an imprint of Transworld Publishers

A CIP catalogue record for this book
is available from the British Library.

ISBN 9780385618458 (hb)
9780385618229 (tpb)

Addresses for Random House Group Ltd companies outside the UK
can be found at: www.randomhouse.co.uk
The Random House Group Ltd Reg. No. 954009

The Random House Group Limited supports the Forest Stewardship
Council (FSC), the leading international forest-certification organization. All our
titles that are printed on Greenpeace-approved FSC-certified paper carry the FSC logo.
Our paper procurement policy can be found at
www.rbooks.co.uk/environment

Typeset in 13/16.5pt Garamond by
Falcon Oast Graphic Art Ltd.
Printed and bound in Great Britain by
Clays Limited, Bungay, Suffolk

2 4 6 8 10 9 7 5 3 1

Mixed Sources
Product group from well-managed
forests and other controlled sources
www.fsc.org Cert no. TT-COC-2139
© 1996 Forest Stewardship Council
FSC

Dedicated to 'Mamma' Erato Hajisavva
and the loving memory of 'Papa'
Varnavas Hajisavva

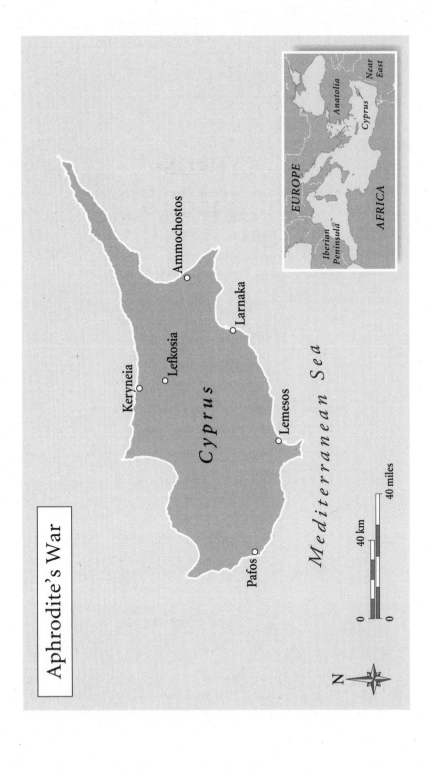

Aphrodite's War

CYPRUS

1955

The General Assembly,

Considering that, for the time being, it does not seem appropriate to adopt a resolution on the question of Cyprus, decides not to consider further the item entitled 'Application, under the auspices of the United Nations, of the principle of equal rights and self-determination of peoples in the case of the population of the Island of Cyprus'.

United Nations Assembly Resolution 814 (IX),
17 December 1954

1

Dhespina was preparing the ointment for Mr Televantos's piles when the old man came running, holding his stick in one hand and the seat of his pants with the other.

'It's Loukis!' he wheezed, coming to an uneasy halt in the garden room, his face flushed with discomfort.

'What about him?'

'He came bursting through the door with a mad crazy look in his eyes and he collapsed right in front of me. Like a rock. Bang! Fell to the floor harder than a dead man!'

Dhespina dropped the jar she was holding, grabbed two metal buckets from under the table and ran to the house. She found the wooden door open and her son sprawled on the floor, whimpering. His face burned red and his black hair was curled wet with perspiration.

'Mamma . . .'

'Don't worry, Loukis. Mamma's here. Mamma's here, son.'

Gently, Dhespina picked up her youngest child and carried him to his bedroom, where she closed the shutters to protect his frightened eyes from the light.

It had been a long time since Loukis had suffered an

attack of the terrors, the first coming eight years earlier after their dog Apollo died. Dhespina's father had been the same way, plagued throughout his life by something stronger than his mind could cope with, and she now used the same tricks her mother once taught her to soothe Loukis's pain: a cloth, cold as ice, another warm as summer. The cold calmed the child's fever and the warmth eased the pressure building inside his head.

Despite everything her own mamma and the island's plants had taught her, Dhespina knew there was no cure for the terror; it was an illness that came from the soul, not from the body. From past experience she also knew that once the cloths had weaved their spell her son would drift into sleep and dreams would take up his care, leading him away from the darkness that had rendered him half-conscious.

Carefully, so as not to disturb him, Dhespina moved from the bed to return the warm cloth to the bucket wafting rosemary. Thankful for the plant's narrow leaves and pale-blue flowers that were available all year round, she kissed the cloth before dropping it back into the water. She then reached for the fabric soaking in the cold bucket and placed it upon her son's forehead. At the sudden change of temperature, Loukis's lashes flickered. He was as pale as a ghost and shadows danced upon his slim, shirtless body from the light of the candle sitting next to the statue of Apollo which his brother had carved so many years ago.

With a mother's love, Dhespina worked into the evening wiping the red from her youngest son's cheeks. Soon the terror would loosen its hold completely and by morning his creamy brown complexion would return.

Mikros Lykos. Little Wolf. That's what Georgios had called him when he first set eyes on their fifth and final child. For Loukis had come into the world with dark down covering his back, and four tiny teeth stabbed through his gums. He also arrived with a head of the fiercest black hair, and eyes glinting like coal. '*Mikros Lykos,*' Georgios had whispered, and Loukis had cocked his head. He seemed to take hold of his father's words and decide to keep them.

In that moment, with the blood of birth still shrouding their son, Georgios and Dhespina recognized there was something not only hairy about their fifth child, but also peculiar. Not in the same way as Nicos's twin Marios, whose gentle nature made up for his slow learning, but rather an extraordinariness they would later struggle to cope with.

'Artemis must have been passing on her way to the hunt when he was conceived,' Georgios joked as he stroked Loukis's soft little cheeks. 'The breath of her wolves lives on in our son.'

At the time, Dhespina smiled at the image of the wild goddess having blessed their child, but the fun of her husband's words gradually lost their magic as the years drifted by and Loukis moved from baby to toddler and from cot to floor without showing the faintest inclination to stand on his feet. Until the age of three, their youngest son refused to do anything but crawl, and Dhespina found it alarming. Inevitably, her older boys thought it hilarious, and they noisily encouraged their brother to nip at their ankles. But outside their home, the child's oddness brought pitying looks from their neighbours, who assumed, not without some justification, that Dhespina had given birth to another idiot. However, Marios – afflicted as he was – had been upright by fourteen months, and Dhespina sensed that it wasn't that her new son was unable to do the same; it was simply that he was unwilling. From the moment his black eyes stopped rolling in his head, Loukis showed scant interest in anything his family urged him to do, preferring instead to ignore them completely and chase after the dog, Apollo, on his hands and knees.

'He'll stand when he's ready,' Georgios assured his wife when she brought up the subject once again during dinner.

'It's not just the standing, Georgios. Loukis doesn't try to speak much either. It's not normal at his age. Really, it isn't.'

'You worry too much, Dhespo. All our sons are healthy and strong and *Mikros Lykos* is of the same blood. One day he will stand up, just like the rest of them did, and he will race around the house, get into your precious pots and pans, break your crockery and ruin the clothes you sew for him, and you'll be wishing he was back on the floor messing with the dog again!'

'His name is Loukis, Georgios! He is not a little wolf, he is a little boy, and the more you call him Little Wolf the more chance there is that he'll grow into a big one. Now stop it. I beg you.'

Georgios sighed in husbandly defeat. His wife was a creature of chaos; a confliction of inner strength and emotional imbalance, and right now she was teetering on the edge of an episode. He rose from the table to return to the workshop he'd built, next to the oleander-covered den where his wife made her mixtures. He knew he shouldn't, given Dhespina's current vulnerability, but he couldn't help himself, so before he reached the door he bent down to Loukis, who was resting on the warm belly of Apollo, and he growled. The toddler looked up and smiled at his father. To Dhespina's mind, it looked nothing short of conspiratorial. She shook her head and offered a prayer to the Virgin Mary.

As Georgios headed out of the house, Apollo got up, arched his back in a stretch, and followed his master. With his pillow taken away, Loukis lazily roused himself and padded after them both.

'Oh, Mother Mary,' Dhespina moaned. Her son hadn't just crawled out of the house; he had swung his little hands out before him in a definite padding motion. Her flesh and blood was imitating the family dog.

'He'll be peeing up a tree next,' she muttered.

Although she tried to deny it, Dhespina realized she only had herself to blame. After all, she had been the one to insist that Apollo be brought into the house rather than kept chained to the tree like every other hunting dog in Cyprus. She had been the one to override the protests of her husband in order to indulge the peculiar whims of her son, the one to permit the softness of her heart to dismiss the reason in her head. But when she woke every morning to find her boy already up and waiting by the door, what else could she do? Yes, she had picked him up, kissed him on both cheeks and tried to distract him with breakfast, but the attentions he returned were tolerant rather than affectionate, and as soon as she turned the door handle to allow the sun into their home, he struggled to be released from her arms. Back on the floor, he was off; crawling down the pathway to sit with Apollo. Even when it rained, and the wind and the wet demanded the door be locked shut, Loukis would sit before it, willing its hinges to snap open. He never once complained; it wasn't in his nature. He just sat there; saying nothing. In the end, Dhespina lost patience and convinced herself that she had no option but to bring the dog into the house. Naturally, the twins, Nicos and Marios, then demanded their goat be given the same privileges.

'As soon as Athena allows you to sleep on her stomach and pull on her tail, as soon as she chases the flies from your face with her tongue, then you can bring her in – and not before,' replied Dhespina, who was subsequently forced to watch her boys wrestle the poor animal to the ground until Athena, who was never the easiest of goats, kicked one of them in the head. She forgot which one now.

'That goat's as dumb as a Turk!' Nicos had shouted in fury, and his father flew at him.

'Leave that talk for the schoolyard!' he ordered, before grumbling about the 'damn Church' and walking back to his workroom to mould leather into shoes.

As the months dragged by and Loukis continued to deny his species, it was, finally, her friend Elena's child Praxi who took control of the situation, in a way none of the adults had so far managed to do. Born fourteen months before Loukis, she had always found the boy intriguing, and one day, after watching him slide along the floor, going nowhere in particular, she eased herself from her mother's lap and walked over. Crouching in front of him, she wiped the long fringe from her eyes before taking his cheeks in her tiny hands and looking at him sternly.

'Walk now, Loukis,' she ordered. 'Walk!'

Loukis looked to Apollo for guidance, but the dog was preoccupied with an ant running through the hairs circling his anus.

'OK,' he sighed, in a very definite, very breathy groan, like a stubborn old man bowing to the inevitable.

As the adults looked on with amusement, followed by gasps of astonishment, Loukis grabbed hold of a table leg and pulled himself to his feet. He wobbled a little before finding his balance, but his legs proved surprisingly strong and ready for the challenge. Praxi then took him by the hand, and together they went to play in the garden, closely followed by Apollo.

For the next two years, boy, girl and dog were inseparable, and it was only when a snake bite took Apollo away that the three of them became two.

As they buried the dog, beneath the orange tree that cried blossom upon his tiny grave, Loukis didn't say a word. His four older brothers all shed a tear, and Praxi was inconsolable. In fact, so terrible was her grief that her mother had to take her home, where she spent the next two days in bed, refusing all food. But Loukis, he never wept. He simply stood by the grave and stayed there long after the rest of the family had returned to the house. Later that evening, when he was called for his supper of cheese and warm milk, he declined to come inside, and Dhespina left him to handle his grief in the way he found natural.

By the time the sun had set and the moon had taken command of the sky, the twins were finished with crying and were busy flicking marbles at each other. As Dhespina washed the evening's dishes, she watched her eldest son, Christakis, work on his tribute to Apollo. Her second boy, Michalakis, was in his room studying, and her husband was snoring loudly in a chair by the stove. Suddenly, from outside, there came the most unholy noise, and Dhespina smashed a plate in alarm. Remembering her youngest remained outside, she ran into the garden. There, she found Loukis crouched on the dog's grave; his neck was stretched to the sky and he was howling to the moon above him. A terrible anguish contorted his beautiful face, and every pain in the world seemed to pour from his throat in a desperate, animal cry that all but broke his mother's heart. He howled like the wolf they had made of him – and his mother could do nothing but stand and watch as she waited for the moment to pass.

The next day, fearing more talk from their neighbours, who had already found Loukis a source of gossip due to his slow walking and sullen refusal to play with their sons, Dhespina told her child that, in Cyprus, it wasn't considered appropriate to howl at the moon, especially now he was five years old. He was a boy, after all, and not a wolf. She asked him to agree to her words, but though Loukis looked at her carefully, he said nothing. Two days later, he suffered his first attack of the terrors.

Watching him now, some eight years later and paralysed by a different pain, Dhespina felt ashamed of having been the one to turn him into a human being who locked in his tears until they built up and pounded at his skull to escape. And yet, her shame was placated by a certain pleasure; it was the satisfaction of knowing her son needed her. Although the demons that paled his sweet face and tortured his chest in great gasps of breath stabbed at the very core of her, she cherished the opportunity to reach out and be the one to save him. Loukis had been such a distant creature all his young life, and moments like these, when he physically searched for her touch, were as rare and as beautiful as a rose in winter. And may God strike her down for saying it, but she loved the boy's helplessness and the feeling that, if only for the shortest time, she was his world. Loukis was her son and she loved him – God knows how she loved him – but she had never owned him. It was a truth she had recognized almost from the beginning, when her belly stood huge and hard, and Praxi reached out with her baby arms and laid claim to her son. Demanding to be pulled on to Dhespina's lap, the child wrapped herself around the bump hiding Loukis and she couldn't be moved until sleep came to take her. While Praxi was near him, her baby lay still, and Dhespina sensed his happiness.

All the women taking coffee – Dhespina's sister, Lenya; Praxi's mother, Elena; and their neighbour Mrs Germanos – had giggled at the time, and Elena had joked that, if Dhespina's child turned out to be another boy, his marriage was all but arranged.

'If it's not painted in our coffee cups, it's written in the stars,' she predicted, and the rest of them agreed she was most probably right.

Of course, in Cyprus, even the brightest star can lose its way in the dark.

As Loukis fell into sleep, Dhespina took hold of the buckets and quietly closed the door behind her, leaving the boy's dreams to continue her work.

Now that her first son, Christakis, was living with his wife, and Michalakis was in the capital, Lefkosia, working for the newspaper, the twins had moved into their own room, and for the first time Dhespina was grateful for the space her older sons had left behind them. Boys were territorial and became increasingly irrational the taller they

17

grew. There would have been hell to pay if the twins had been forced from their beds to make way for 'Mamma's favourite' and, right now, Dhespina's bones felt old and her head was sore from thinking. A fight with petulant teenagers was the last thing she needed.

'Don't worry, Mamma, Loukis will be fine,' Marios assured her when she finally joined the rest of her family in the front room. He reached out his hand, and she took it with a smile before placing a kiss on his forehead.

'You should have let him howl when he wanted to,' accused Nicos, but he was joking and his brilliant smile took the sting from his words.

'Yes, and maybe I should have let him grow into a real wolf and eat you!' Dhespina retorted. Her twins, identical to look at in every way, were worlds apart in their manners: one soft and considerate; the other harder and mischievous.

'By the way,' Georgios interrupted, 'old Televantos is still in the garden room cushioning his arse on our pillows.'

Dhespina threw her hands to her hair. 'Mr Televantos! Why didn't you tell him to go home?'

'He wouldn't budge. He insisted he had to wait for his cream.'

'Mother of Mary,' Dhespina laughed, and disappeared out of the door.

Coming to the den, with its shelves burdened by jars of dried herbs, bottles of vinegar, pickled pig's ears, plant roots and pans, she found Mr Televantos snoring loudly, his back resting against the wall and his bottom relieved by two large pillows Georgios had obviously taken from their bed. Dhespina took the jar she had hurriedly left on the counter and finished filling it with the ointment of marigolds and butcher's broom she had prepared.

Gently, she shook the old man awake.

'Mr Televantos. Your medicine.'

Startled, her neighbour looked around, bewildered and blinking, until he remembered where he was and his reason for being there.

'Really, you should tell Mrs Televantos to cook you more vegetables.' Dhespina smiled at him.

'It doesn't matter what she cooks. It always tastes like hell,' he grumbled, wincing with pain as he manoeuvred himself from the floor.

'That may be so, but it might ease your condition.'

'Little Dhespo, my condition, as you put it, is both a curse and a blessing. If it wasn't for these troublesome veins, my wife would have me dead in a week. The woman is insatiable.'

Dhespina raised her eyebrows. Mr Televantos was quickly sailing through his seventies; it was hard to believe his wife of the same age possessed the stamina – let alone the inclination – to pursue her age-mottled husband in such a way.

'Here, let me help you.' Dhespina took the old man by the arm as he struggled to regain his feet. She passed him his stick and the jar of ointment, which he put in his pocket.

'Let's hope the British don't arrest me on the way home.' He laughed. 'They probably think haemorrhoids are the latest explosives brought in from the motherland.'

'I think you'll be safe enough, Mr Televantos. The troops will be drunk in their barracks by now.'

'Yes, of course, you are right.' The old man chuckled. 'When they're not stealing other people's countries, they're usually pickling their *poulloues* with warm beer.'

With that, the old man tapped his stick to the front of his head in farewell and hobbled awkwardly down the path he had run up some five hours earlier.

After watching him go, Dhespina put away her pots and utensils then lightly kissed the photo of her mother that hung on the back of the door before returning to the house. As she neared, she noticed the shadow of a girl crouched at the front gate.

'Praxi?'

The shadow got to its feet and moved into the moonlight. With her large eyes and fragile legs, the girl looked pretty as a fawn.

'Mrs Economidou. Is Loukis all right?'

'Yes, child, he's asleep. Have you been here all this time? Why didn't you come into the house?'

Praxi's lips quivered, and huge tears welled in her eyes, quickly rolling down her cheeks. 'I couldn't come in. I feel so guilty,' she cried. 'It's all my fault, you see. My death is killing us both.'

Dhespina instinctively moved forward to take the girl's hands. 'What on earth are you saying, Praxi? Your death is killing you both?'

'Oh, Mrs Economidou, it's too sad, both of us so young. We could hardly believe it either, but it's true. I'm dying, Mrs Economidou, there's no use in denying it. That's why, for the past two days, me and Loukis have been hunting for the perfect place where I can be buried and rest in eternal peace. Today, we decided on a patch of ground under St Hilarion's Castle that's sheltered by a pistachio tree. We both love the place so much, and the spirit of the mad monk will always protect it, and Loukis agreed it would be the perfect spot for my grave. And though I knew he was sad, he didn't say anything, and so I guessed he had come to terms with my passing. But I must have been wrong, Mrs Economidou, because now it seems my illness is going to claim your son too, and I can't bear it. I'm so sorry . . . really I am . . . I never meant to take away your Loukis. Not yet, anyway. It's all too terrible, really it is. And I wouldn't blame you if you wanted to take my life now, while you still can.'

The girl collapsed in Dhespina's arms, her strength broken by great, heaving sobs.

'Praxi, stop it! Come on, child, enough of this nonsense. Why in God's name do you think you're dying?'

Praxi gulped for air and tried to calm herself. It was difficult, but Mrs Economidou deserved an explanation.

'It's . . . well . . . it's been two days . . . and still the blood keeps on coming. It won't stop and I've done everything I can think of; I've put cloths inside to heal the wound, and Loukis brought me medicines from your workroom, but still it comes down and now I've also got the most terrible diarrhoea. It's quite clear, Mrs Economidou, that my insides are being eaten by cancer.'

Dhespina saw the terror in the girl's face and it killed the laughter rising inside her.

'*Mikri mou*, you're not dying! I promise you that. You're growing, that's all. You're becoming a woman, Praxi. And you've no doubt got diarrhoea from the medicines Loukis shouldn't have given you. Here, come with me. It's time you had a talk with your mother.'

Dhespina took the girl's hand and dragged her down the pathway to Elena's house, further inside the village.

*

Christakis was big and he was blond – both unusual traits for a Greek – and though his mother had continually shaved his head when he was a child, in order to banish the bad luck that superstition insisted would find him, his hair grew back no darker than before and he continued to be charmed. He had a beautiful wife, a lovely new son and he was happy. He didn't have an important job in the city, not like his brother Michalakis, but he was slowly making his name with a talent that had reached even the ears of the British commander-in-chief of Middle East Land Forces. Four months earlier and to his great surprise, an army Land Rover had pulled up outside his shop and a soldier dressed in khaki shorts revealed that his boss wanted a table and eight chairs.

'Make it as grand as you like,' the soldier beamed, and Christakis nodded. As he had never paid much attention to English lessons while at school, he had no idea what the freckle-faced private was saying, other than it involved tables and chairs. Still, he shook the soldier's hand and thanked him for the work. He figured a British commander in charge of so many troops would expect something sturdy and grand, and he wouldn't disappoint him.

As soon as the soldier drove away, Christakis took hold of his pencil to sketch designs of delicately carved aprons hanging above boldly proportioned legs fashioned from the finest walnut wood. He would provide the kind of craftsmanship a big military man and his wife could be proud of. And he would have done as well, if EOKA hadn't blown up the good commander's house the very next day. Hours later, the soldier returned to Christakis telling him to forget the furniture and knock up some door frames instead. Although it wasn't the most challenging of commissions, the carpenter

agreed to take the job, even though he knew there would be mutters of collaboration. The truth was he needed the money – if only to pay the taxes the British had brought with them.

Christakis entered the coffee house and joined his father in the corner where he could be found most mornings before lunch, putting the world to rights with his friend Stavros.

'The paper, Papa.' Christakis slapped *The Voice* down in front of him. It had arrived in the morning post from Lefkosia and Michalakis had a small article on page six, something about pottery. As supportive as Christakis was of his younger brother's efforts, he didn't think it was destined to become the major topic of conversation among the men of the village. Since the British governor, in all his wisdom, had stamped his iron fist on the heads of the people, Lefkosia had erupted in fire and fury, and that's all anyone could find the energy to talk about these days.

Bar the clashes in 1931, when rioters set fire to Government House, the British had ruled the island in relative peace since 1878, but now church bells were rallying hundreds to the streets in protest against laws which brought detention without trial, stop-and-search insults and six months in jail for possession of firearms. When the new laws were passed, the capital raged at the news; buildings burned and British troops answered with tear gas and bullets. Now, it seemed there was a riot taking place every other week; fifty-seven Greeks had been arrested so far. In a few short months, the governor had managed to transform Lefkosia into a war zone.

'The occupiers haven't a hope of quelling the uprising

with these measures,' Georgios stated flatly as the hysterical commentary of Radio Athens echoed around the café, spitting furious indignation.

'What other option do they have?' Stavros asked, leaning forward in his chair, his large belly straining above the belt of his pants. 'You Greeks form a terrorist organization . . .'

'It's not a terrorist organization,' corrected Christakis as he took his seat to join the two men. 'EOKA fights for our freedom; for the freedom of Cyprus and our union with Greece.'

'OK,' Stavros conceded. 'Your "freedom fighters" then, they say they will fight for the "liberation of Cyprus from the British yoke", they smuggle in dynamite from Greece, bomb government offices, police stations, power plants, hotels – and even attempt to kill the governor himself while he's watching a film at the cinema in Ammochostos – and you expect the British to capitulate and give everything up? Has history not shown you what they are capable of? You are but boys, and you are boys playing with fire.'

'No one's playing with anything, Stavros. This isn't a game, it's serious. This is about our rights as a nation.'

Christakis waved to the *kafetzi*. 'Coffee, medium,' he ordered, and continued. 'We are tired of the occupiers and, though I may not agree with all of their ways, EOKA fights for us. Cyprus rightfully belongs to Greece, everyone knows that, and our hearts beat to her rhythm.'

'And those of us who aren't Greek?' demanded Stavros. 'What about our hearts, that don't, won't and never will dance to the Greek drum? This EOKA leader of yours – Grivas – he said they would take Cyprus with blood if they have to. Well, the blood is pouring, Christakis, and I tell

24

you, it will keep pouring until this country of ours drowns in a red sea of her own making.'

'Hush now, old friend.' Georgios placed a soothing hand on Stavros's knee. 'It won't come to that. We won't let that happen. The world won't let that happen.'

'You say that, Georgios, and God knows I want to believe you, but I see disaster hurtling towards us with the speed of a bullet. The world has already washed its hands of this problem; the United Nations won't even discuss it. And I tell you, this war against the British will spread like a cancer through our island and it will eat away at our two communities. Look at us! Look at my people. See how the Greeks already think of us! In a matter of years we have gone from being Muslims to being Turks. This is just the start, you mark my words.'

Georgios looked at the old man, who had been as much a part of his life as his son sat next to him. He didn't want to give credence to his prophesy, but he was uneasy. Stavros had been his father's friend, and he was the only Turk Georgios had ever sat at a table and shared coffee with. The others – well, they kept to their own shops and their own side of the village. In fact, hadn't it been his own father who had originally given Stavros his Greek name, to fool the priest into allowing him to take his place as best man at his wedding? It was a name that had followed him through the last four decades of his life to where he was now: a Muslim Turk in all but name, drinking Greek coffee in a Greek coffee house. If he looked around him, Georgios could count on two fingers those who would remember Stavros's birth name – and that would be Stavros and himself. This friendship they shared was one born of

25

coincidence, and it was an anomaly. The island, whether they chose to accept it or not, *was* divided. It had always been divided: by history, by religion and, ultimately, by differing dreams. Even the towns had multiple personalities: Greek, Turkish and now British. Where else in the world could you find three names for one place? Lefkosia or Lefkoşa or Nicosia; Lemesos, Leymosun or Limassol; Ammochostos, Gazimağusa or Famagusta. The list went on and on.

'You know, Georgios,' the old man continued, as if reading his thoughts. 'We have a crisis of identity on this island. We, the Muslims, think of ourselves as Cypriots and *then* Turks. But your people, they will always be Greek first and Cypriot second, and that is why Cyprus will suffer in the end: because your eyes are locked on the past while the rest of us are looking to the future.'

Loukis sat on the ground and waited. It didn't take long for the window to open.

'Mamma says you're not dying after all and that you're actually having something called a period.'

'Apparently so,' confirmed Praxi, leaning over the sill to get a better look at her friend. He was sat with his back to the wall, and his hands picked at small blades of green pushing through the gravel. 'The bleeding's supposed to stop tomorrow, but it might be the day after, and you know what?'

'What?'

'It will come back next month and the one after that and the one after that for the rest of my damned life – well, until my teeth fall out and I grow hair on my chin. That's what

26

Mamma tells me. Really, it's pretty disgusting, if you ask me. I'm going to hate being a woman.'

Praxi sighed and rested her head on the window frame. The summer sun had turned the wood warm and it felt good on her skin.

'Will your mamma let you out again when this period finishes, or are you a prisoner now as well as a woman?' asked Loukis. He was feeling restless and uncomfortable for reasons he couldn't understand.

'Who knows? But she says that from now on I have to start playing with girls my own age because of the danger I'm in. She's even invited Maria Germanos for lunch, which will be scintillating . . .'

'What danger are you supposed to be in?' Loukis looked up, but Praxi's face was hidden from him and he could only see her long hair hanging from the window.

'From men,' she replied. 'Now I'm a woman I'm in constant danger of being attacked. Men are like animals, Mamma says. They sniff you and pull you, and given half the chance they will throw you to the ground and stick their tongues in your mouth as well as their *poullou* in your *poulli*. If that happens I'll have a baby and I'll be shamed for ever and I'll never find a husband.'

'That's bullshit. And, anyway, what husband are you hoping to find?'

'I don't know.' Praxi laughed. 'Whatever husband Saint Anthony has planned for me!'

Loukis got to his feet.

'Where are you going?'

'I don't know – maybe to find myself a wife. It's boring here. And you're boring me.'

'Hey! That's not nice, Loukis! I can't help being a woman. It's not that I want to be one. Take that back!'

Loukis looked up and straight into Praxi's chocolate-brown eyes.

'No,' he said finally and turned away.

'Take it back, Loukis, you pig!' But Loukis was already at the garden gate, and he had no intention of taking anything back. If she was a woman she could learn to handle him the way his mother did.

As Loukis turned the corner, Maria passed him, obviously on her way to Praxi's for lunch. She was considered to be the prettiest girl in the village and, though Loukis saw the truth of it in her face, he found her spoilt and difficult, like a child with too many toys.

'*Yassou*, Loukis,' she greeted, holding her hair in her hands to stop the wind from tugging it.

'*Yassou*,' he returned.

'Where are you going?' she asked, forcing him to a halt.

'As far away from women as I can possibly get,' he told her, and carried on his way. If he'd bothered to look back, he would have seen Maria watching him all the way to the junction until he turned right, and out of her sight.

With no particular place to go, nothing to do and no one to do it with now that Praxi's virginity was in mortal danger, Loukis wandered towards the Turks' side of the village. He found it much like the Greek side but with more Turks in it. Unnoticed, he slipped into the fields belonging to his father's friend Stavros. It was said they had shrunk in size over the years since the Greeks clawed back the gifts of the Ottomans, but they were impressive nonetheless and the old man was generous with the wealth he had left, allowing

Loukis to hunt snakes on his land – an act of vengeance he had taken up in memory of Apollo as soon as his father had permitted him to pick up a gun.

Slowly, because it was hot and he was bothered by change, Loukis wandered through the orange trees, which were starting to show the fruit his mamma said the ancients called 'golden apples'. He moved onwards, deeper into the farmer's property, stooping under carob branches that dripped flat pods filled with the shining brown seeds that Stavros fed to his animals and his wife made into *pekmez* syrup. Then further ahead, beyond the huge olive grove, its fruit about to change from green to black, he noticed a large truck dropping off four British soldiers. They were setting up a checkpoint, and Loukis walked in their direction, curious and in need of distraction.

'*Yassou*,' greeted one of the soldiers as he came near.

'*Yassou*,' replied Loukis. 'What are you doing?'

'Looking for Black Mak's bad guys,' another soldier informed him. 'You're not one of them, are you?' The others started chuckling.

Loukis shrugged and walked off.

Half an hour later, though he hadn't been intending to go there, he wound up at Keryneia harbour. For some reason, the place was crawling with British soldiers, marching in and out of carob warehouses, turning over crates and kicking at boxes. Loukis saw Yiannis Christofi leaning against a wall, drinking cola and smoking a cigarette. Though Yiannis was five years older than him, Loukis went over, because there was no one else around and he had gone to school with his brother Michalakis.

'What's going on?'

Yiannis started laughing. 'You haven't heard yet?'

Loukis shook his head.

'Last night, sixteen EOKA escaped from the prison.' Yiannis nodded his head towards the castle dominating the far corner of the harbour. Hundreds of years ago, it had defended the island from Arabs. Now the British used it to defend themselves from Cypriots. 'The boys jumped from the wall using knotted bed sheets. The British are furious, useless buggers.'

Yiannis offered him a cigarette. Loukis had never smoked before and he didn't even like the man, but he took it anyway.

'Where's your girlfriend today?' asked Yiannis. 'You two are usually joined at the hip, aren't you?'

'She's ill,' replied Loukis, refusing to rise to the bait.

'Too bad. She's a nice-looking girl. How old is she now? Fifteen?'

'Fourteen.'

'But coming on fifteen, eh?'

'That tends to be the natural order of things.' Loukis stubbed the cigarette out under the heel of his shoe and moved away. His brother Michalakis had once thumped Yiannis. He couldn't remember why, but he guessed he had probably deserved it.

2

There were few things in life that made Loukis genuinely laugh, but Aphrodite was one of them. Unlike the rest of the island's donkeys, which clopped through rocky fields on four hooves, this one picked her way along the landscape in leather shoes – fashioned and fitted by his own father. When Aphrodite was much younger, Stavros called on Papa's skills when he realized his donkey's refusal to come out of the barn had less to do with obstinacy and more to do with weather. Despite his initial amusement, Georgios took the request seriously and took out his tape to measure the animal. In his workshop, amidst the teasing of his sons, who placed orders for goat saddles, dog sandals, cat gloves and fish jerkins, he created two pairs of bowl-like boots, made from the strongest tanned leather, with a small buckle at the back to keep them in place. His work finished, he helped Stavros shoe his donkey, and after some reluctance she left the barn without being pulled, her grey head held high and her ears facing forwards.

'They call it mysophobia,' Stavros explained as he loaded Aphrodite's back with baskets of oranges. 'She has a fear of the dirt. It started in the autumn, when the rain turns the ground to mud, lasted through the winter, grew into spring and, eventually, into summer. She's a typical woman – she won't go anywhere if she's not properly dressed.'

Stavros patted the old girl's neck and reached for the melon juice his wife Pembe had brought him. Even though she had tried to cajole Loukis into taking a glass, saying it was good for his kidneys, the boy insisted on Coca-Cola.

Loukis had been helping Stavros on his farm for the past three months, ever since his brothers accidentally closed down the school. In a moment of mischief, no doubt instigated by Nicos, the twins had daubed blue paint on a white wall. Their words read, 'We want to join with Greece even if we have to eat stones!' The British, who were already convinced that every Greek school was a breeding ground for terrorists, shut the place down the very next day, along with 418 others that had been rendered useless by demon-strating students and Greek flags that refused to be lowered.

Georgios, who valued education even above a skilled trade like his own, was furious. And his temper wasn't improved by the slaps of solidarity he received whenever he visited the coffee shop. To the men of the village, Nicos and Marios were nothing less than patriotic heroes. The priest even congratulated them in his Sunday sermon, saluting resistance against the oppressors by the 'glorious sons of Georgios, of Cyprus and of Greece'. Practically apoplectic with rage, Georgios had ordered the last of his school-age sons to learn the error of their ways through hard labour. Until the British relented and reopened their classroom, all three of them would have to find jobs. Loukis was livid, not only because it was grossly unfair that he should be punished for the sins of his brothers, but also because it was at school that he saw most of Praxi. Following the arrival of her period, she was forced to spend her evenings in womanly contemplations with Maria, or any other girl with budding breasts that her mother dragged back to the house. For this reason, and no other, Loukis looked to Stavros for work rather than following his brothers to Keryneia, where they found jobs in the warehouses hugging the harbour. At least in the village he would be closer to Praxi.

As Stavros was turning older and fatter by the day, and because most of his family had drifted south, been married off, or disappeared to Turkey, the farmer agreed to pay him one Cyprus pound a week to help with whatever seasonal harvest his fields were surrendering. It was hard work, but Loukis tasted the salty sweat on his lips, watched the sun browning his skin, and felt the weight of the baskets expanding his arms, and he enjoyed it.

Looking up, he quickly downed his Coke. On the road, he could see Praxi coming, dressed in green and swinging a leather bag behind her. Inside would be fresh bread, a jar of black olives, and a cake of goat's cheese. Stavros noticed her too, and he winked playfully at Loukis.

'Off you go then,' he said. 'I'll see you after your lunch.'

With the sun slowly warming the sea after winter, the two friends decided to eat at the beach. Praxi was wearing a sleeveless dress that pinched at her waist. It daringly skimmed the wrong side of her knees, and Loukis realized she was significantly taller than she had been last year. A flash of blue lace caught his eye.

'Are you wearing a bra?'

'Yes, Loukis, that's what women do, don't you know. Why? Do you want to see it?'

Praxi giggled and Loukis blushed, which made her laugh all the harder. The girl was in high spirits because she felt different, and beautiful and, more importantly, she was free. Ever since the British had kicked Archbishop Makarios out of Cyprus, her mother had been felled by religious indignation and womanly tears, which meant she was too preoccupied to guard Praxi's virtue with the same suffocating intensity she had set out with eight months previously.

Makarios was the island's spiritual and political leader – and he had been charged with indoctrinating young Greeks with anti-British propaganda as well as encouraging them to join EOKA. According to Loukis's brother Michalakis, the archbishop had been on a collision course with the British ever since the funeral of Charalambous Mouskos. Charalambous had been Makarios's cousin, but he was also a member of EOKA, and he was killed in a shoot-out with the British in Troodos. The service was conducted by Makarios and, because the British anticipated trouble, they posted troops around the church. When the funeral was over, and torrential rain failed to disperse the mourners, the soldiers fired tear gas into the crowds to force them home. Makarios called it an act of sacrilege and 'a dark stain on the history of the British occupancy', and everyone agreed with him.

In Loukis's house, the shameful disrespect shown by the occupiers had special significance because it was the first major report Michalakis got into his newspaper. His mamma was so proud she cut out the article and stuck it on the wall, next to a photograph of the archbishop.

The new governor, Sir John Harding, wasn't quite as impressed as the Economidou family, and three months after the funeral he exiled Makarios to the Seychelles. When the crime was reported, the island responded with riots. Soon after, a British policeman was gunned down; a Turkish officer lost his life; an Englishwoman and her child were shot at; former neighbours came out fighting in the village of Vassilia; shops were trashed and looted; and a bomb was secreted under Harding's bed, but failed to go off.

According to Michalakis, who often had to talk about such things when he came to visit his mamma and papa, Cyprus was on the brink of civil war. Not that it seemed to have spread to their village. From what Praxi could see, the only uprising taking place was being carried out by little old women throwing stones at patrolling soldiers in retaliation for the exile of Makarios.

'I know I shouldn't say this,' said Praxi as they tumbled down the sandy cliff to the edge of the sea, 'but my life has got a whole lot better since Archbishop Makarios left Cyprus.'

'And mine,' agreed Loukis. 'How long do you think your mother will be in mourning?'

Praxi unpacked the picnic bag. 'Who knows? Probably for the rest of her life – or at least until they let Makarios come back.'

'I can't see that ever happening.'

'No. Me neither.'

Praxi handed Loukis some bread, but she held tight when he reached to take it. Her eyes were serious, and Loukis felt her breath on his lips.

'Do you think we are at war, Loukis?'

He held her stare. In the brilliant sun, with the clear waters of the Mediterranean tickling stones of blue and green near their feet, the troubles seemed so far away they belonged to another place. But he had listened to his father and Michalakis talking; and they seemed convinced that the troubles would only get worse unless Britain relented and gave Cyprus to Greece.

'I don't know, Praxi,' he said honestly. 'The adults seem to think so, but I have no idea where we're all heading. Personally, I don't get all this burning desire to be part of Greece.'

'But we *are* Greece!' Praxi shrieked, letting go of the bread and reaching for the cheese. 'Greece is our mother, and we must, we simply must, be reunited with her. How would you feel if the British marched into your house and told you that you'd never be with your mother again? That's the way you have to think of it, Loukis. You can't go around the village saying you "don't get all this burning desire to be part of Greece". You sound like a Turk!'

Loukis gave up and kicked off his shoes. As he removed his shirt and unbuttoned his trousers, he knew the only thing he needed in his life was sat next to him. Anything more was confusion.

He ran into the water and dived into the sharp cold of the sea. Seconds later, Praxi came running after him.

Far from daylight and the salty breeze of the harbour, the office sweated under a single yellow bulb. The air was clogged by stale cigarette smoke and, with its disorderly jumble of stacked invoices and boxes, both its atmosphere and appearance were depressing. Nicos took a seat on the far side of the table. He knew why he had been summoned; earlier that morning he'd lost his temper and the target of his fury was currently at home nursing a broken nose.

'I can't have fighting in my warehouse,' the manager told him, inserting a Chesterfield under his broad moustache and lighting it. 'Do you have anything to say in your defence? Any excuse you'd like to give?'

Nicos thought about it and shook his head. The manager closed his eyes for a second to demonstrate his disappointment.

'You know I can't let this go unpunished. You broke a man's nose. Is there really nothing you want to tell me, perhaps a reason for your outburst?'

Nicos appreciated the older man's perseverance, but he remained silent. He knew when to keep his mouth shut, even when his actions were justified. Marios hadn't been interfering, he had simply been curious when he picked up the box and it rattled. But as he looked inside Costas came running over, pulling him roughly by the hair and calling him a stupid *vlaka* who should mind his own business. Nicos, who had been at the other end of the warehouse, was floored by the hurt and incomprehension on his brother's face and a red mist descended. No one called his brother a retard, and before he could collect his thoughts, he had charged across the floor, leapt at Costas and slammed his fist into his face. There was a sickening crack followed by blood. Behind him, he heard Marios crying.

'I understand from the foreman that you were sticking up for your brother,' the manager continued and then paused, waiting for Nicos to confirm what he had heard. 'Well, if that is the case, I admire that, and in a way I respect what you did. However, this is a place of work, not a playground or a boxing ring. Therefore, consider this a formal warning.

Today, you keep your job, but if I have to speak to you again you're fired. Understood?'

'Understood,' agreed Nicos.

The manager rose from his seat, signalling the teenager to go, and Nicos returned to the warehouse, relieved but little surprised. He was under no illusion as to why he had been dealt with so leniently. Now he'd have to make sure Marios understood as well. If his brother let slip about the guns he'd discovered, they wouldn't be looking for new jobs, they'd be meeting the hangman.

'You'll never guess what they've started calling your boys.'

'Who?'

'Pretty much the whole village, that's who.'

'I shudder to think,' Dhespina told her sister.

'They're calling them the Dighenis brothers – after the Five-finger Mountains!'

Dhespina smiled. She could see the logic in the comparison. According to legend, Dighenis – the giant Byzantine hero – escaped the Arabs by leaping from Asia Minor on to North Cyprus. As he landed on the island, his five fingers grabbed hold of the mountains and left their mark there for all eternity. Although her five sons might not be legendary heroes beyond their own home, they were all uncommonly tall. Even Loukis, who at fourteen had long towered over her, was creeping ahead of his father with every passing day.

'I think it suits them,' Lenya declared, popping into her handbag the tincture Dhespina had concocted from the red berries of the chaste tree.

'Are you still wearing the pants at night?'

'Night, morning, afternoon; they're never off, apart from

38

when we're doing the obvious, of course,' Lenya laughed. 'Andreas is going insane. He's started calling me *dolmades*!'

Dhespina gasped. No woman in her right mind should allow her husband to compare her to vine leaves stuffed with rice. The pants were designed to keep in awkward sperm, and they were particularly effective following sex, everyone knew that, especially if the woman kept her legs in the air. Granted, they were ugly, but in some cases they were a necessary evil, and certainly nothing to be ridiculed.

'It's OK,' assured Lenya. 'I know Andreas is only joking. He loves me completely.'

'But still . . . *dolmades*?'

'Oh, don't worry. When the pants and your medicine do their trick he'll see it's been worthwhile.'

Dhespina smiled. It wasn't easy for Lenya; three years married and still no children. No one could understand it, least of all Lenya, who was healthy and strong and who, as a girl, had watched their mother's silver cross circle above her palm to predict the birth of two daughters. Some years earlier, Dhespina had been dizzied by the prospect of five boys. The cross was never wrong.

'Are the twins behaving at the warehouse?' Lenya asked, breaking into her sister's thoughts.

Dhespina raised her eyes. 'So they say, but you know the twins, they're thick as thieves. If they'd burned down Keryneia Castle I'd be the last to find out.'

'You're not wrong there, Dhespo. Honestly, I pity the woman who ends up married to Nicos!' Lenya winked and, though Dhespina smiled back, because no offence was intended, she was stung by her sister's words. Not because she thought Nicos would make a perfect husband – on the contrary, he was a storm of light and darkness, with a devil's charm. She couldn't see him easily bowing to the will of any woman. No, the reason Dhespina felt hurt was because they were talking about the twins, not just Nicos, and by denying Marios, Lenya must assume he was never destined to marry. That might very well be the case, but it was nothing Dhespina was ready to accept or even think about. Marios was as big and as strong and as handsome as any of her sons, but a child lived within his head and it would never leave him. As the years turned her boys into men, Dhespina couldn't bear to imagine how Marios would react once Nicos did settle and marry. Her baby would be left to face the world on his own; one half of a life that had always lived as two.

'OK, Dhespo, the night calls.' Lenya grabbed her sister warmly and kissed her goodbye, blissfully unaware of the anguish she had caused. As the door closed, Dhespina turned her attention to the jumping potatoes boiling on the stove.

At the other end of the village, Michalakis had picked up his father from the coffee shop. Together they walked past the church, the village bakery and the small convenience store, whose lights had long gone out. Curfew was nearly upon them, but Michalakis was in no mood to hurry; the start of summer had turned the air warm, and he breathed in the scent of jasmine, relieved to be out of the capital, with its closed spaces and stench of mistrust.

'You're doing well,' his father noted, tapping a rolled copy of *The Voice* on his son's shoulder. 'Yet another front-page story. You'll be the editor next.'

'If they don't close us down,' Michalakis responded, half-joking.

40

Since a state of emergency had been declared, a number of pro-EOKA newspapers had been silenced. Even the transmissions of Radio Athens were intercepted and blocked. There was so much going on in the country, but the more that happened, the fewer avenues remained open for journalists like him to tell people. As a result, rumour had become gospel, and the flames of a just conflict were spreading into something darker and less honourable.

Once they reached home, Michalakis knew how the conversation would go. His mother would lay the table and they'd eat until they were full and his father pulled out a bottle of wine. Their talk would then turn to politics, and his parents would look at him for news and insight. What could he tell them? Only the truth as he saw it: that the island they loved was turning into a coffin. Grenades were being thrown into bars used by soldiers – most of them boys hardly any older than he was; bombs were exploding in military bases; planes were being blown up; there were pitched battles in Ammochostos; and fire fights breaking out in the cool of the Troodos Mountains. English mothers were losing their sons, and Michalakis couldn't help but pity them as he wrote endless reports of young men crippled and killed, their limbs shredded by bullets, their intestines mashed by shrapnel, their blood spilt and seeping into Cypriot soil. He had no time for politicians and their posturing and games, but the soldiers – he didn't hold any special grudge against them. He knew many had simply taken advantage of earning a few extra pounds in their pay cheques. He doubted whether any of them cared less whether Cyprus remained sovereign property or Greek. But they were here and they were dying.

And it wasn't just the British. Every week Greek mothers were mourning sons drawn into a fight masterminded by a handful of men now in exile or in hiding. Grivas, with his rhetoric and patriotic demands, was throwing more and more boys to their deaths, and the more who died, the more followed them; joining a cause that had long mislaid its reason. The battle for *enosis* – the island's union with Greece – had lost its simplicity. It was no longer about ridding the island of the occupiers, it was about killing all those who stood in the way of the grand idea, be they British, Turkish or Greek. The conflict had broken its boundaries and was running untethered along the length and breadth of the island.

'Hundreds have been arrested,' Michalakis told his parents as they relaxed after their meal and discussed the continuing crackdown. 'Even members of the communist party. The British are killing any form of dissent.'

'And they've deported our teenagers, don't forget them,' Georgios added, pouring more wine into their emptying glasses.

'I heard they were jailing kids for carrying stones,' Dhespina said. 'That can't be true, surely?'

'Well, that's what the law allows,' admitted Michalakis.

'Bloody ridiculous,' spat Georgios.

'Shameful,' agreed Dhespina. 'Jailing our kids, fining our villagers and putting nooses around the necks of our young men. The British deserve everything they get.'

Michalakis looked up from the table and his eyes fell on the growing number of articles fighting for space between family photos and pictures of saints. Near the window he saw his latest front page: the hanging of EOKA fighters

Andreas Demetriou and Michael Karaolis. They were the first members of the organization to have received the death penalty, and Andreas had remained defiant to the end, telling his killers, 'I am sorry I will not be able to see our Cyprus free. However, I am not frightened of death, because life is worth nothing in slavery.'

'What I don't understand is why we keep killing our own,' Dhespina muttered as she uncorked another bottle for her men. 'Like that lay preacher who was shot dead in Kythrea.'

'He was a traitor,' Michalakis told his mamma. 'That's what the gunman told the congregation. Traitors and informers – they're as much a target for EOKA as the governor's soldiers these days.'

'EOKA shouldn't be shooting Cypriots,' Dhespina stated firmly, and moved from the table to put the dishes drying by the sink into their cupboards.

Michalakis and Georgios shared a look but said nothing. They had already spoken of the spreading conflict on the way to the house. The British were being backed into a corner, and they were exploring other options; relying increasingly on the support of the Turkish minority. To the anger of the Greeks, the Turks were joining the police force in huge numbers. Now, when one of them was killed, it was no longer an attack on the ruling authority but an attack on the Turkish. The British were splitting the two communities like never before. In January, a Turkish police sergeant had been killed after giving evidence at the trial of several EOKA members. In response, Turkish Cypriots had formed their own resistance unit – demanding fifty Greek lives for every Turk killed. In little over a year, the struggle for *enosis* had mutated into a fight for survival – and one of terrible vengeance.

Maria was sweating, and the more they walked, the more annoyed she became with the heat and with heels that lodged in rocks and threatened to turn her ankle. They were supposed to be going *together* to St Hilarion's Castle. Not that you'd know it if anyone could see the three of them; she'd fallen so far behind she could no longer hear them talking. They were so ungrateful! If Maria hadn't agreed to chaperone, there was no way Praxi could have escaped her mother to spend time with Loukis. Yet when she had politely asked them to rest for a while, Praxi acted cross and irritated.

'I told you not to wear those shoes!' she practically shouted, and Maria struggled with tears, because she was hot, she was tired and it was bloody unfair.

'Hold on, Praxi,' Loukis had relented. 'Maria, come and rest a minute.' He led her by the hand to a large boulder. In exasperation, Praxi had thrown her arms in the air and carried on walking. A minute later Loukis had followed, and Maria was on her own, again.

By the time she got to the roadside, where the two of them were sat on the grass waiting, she was finished. Her lovely shoes were scuffed, and her face and neck were wet. The end of summer was coming, but the days still burned hot, and she hated it.

'I can't go on,' Maria insisted as she collapsed next to them. The castle was still miles away, hanging above their heads like some damn vulture of death. St Hilarion's gave her the creeps. Her mamma said it was named after a monk who had lived there in ancient times, when the mountain was stalked by demons. Because the old monk was deaf, he couldn't hear them trying to terrify him, so the demons got bored and moved away, leaving the old monk in peace. Now, looking at the crumbling ruins bearing down on her from above, Maria was certain St Hilarion must have been dumb as well as deaf. Why anyone would want to live so far away from civilization was beyond her. When she had agreed to spend the day with Praxi and Loukis, Maria had assumed they would go to Keryneia to walk along the pretty harbour, where the wind kept her cool and the young men turned to whistle at her. But no, Praxi insisted they climb to the castle and, as Loukis only did what Praxi wanted to do, they had set off, a little before lunch. Right now, Maria wished she had just left them to it, but then she would have been forced to keep out of sight so as not to give them away and she would have grown bored. Besides, it was a chance to spend time with Loukis. Although he was a little serious, Maria thought he was to die for – something that might very well happen if they forced her to walk any farther. Really, they shouldn't even have been there; her mamma would go spare if she found out she was traipsing up the mountain where the British woman and her driver had been killed just a few weeks ago, and she said as much when she fell to the ground, exhausted. But Praxi just laughed.

'It's not funny,' Maria insisted, annoyed that Praxi was trying to make her look silly in front of Loukis. 'It's dangerous now. EOKA are fighting everywhere.'

'They're not likely to shoot three Greek schoolkids, are they?'

'Ex-schoolkids,' corrected Loukis.

'OK, not on purpose, no,' Maria conceded. 'But they could easily kill us by accident. What if the occupiers suddenly come by and they all start shooting? Everyone knows there are EOKA hiding in the mountains.'

'Then we've got an armed escort, haven't we?' Praxi lay back on the grass, and Loukis gave a small laugh. Maria's face darkened. Since the two EOKA boys had been hanged, the spring had marched into summer and the war taking place in Lefkosia and other cities around the island had finally found its way to Keryneia. Last month a bomb had gone off at the Customs House, for goodness sake! EOKA men had even captured the police station next to the prison, stealing a load of guns and bullets. Then, a few days ago, they had executed one of the area's boys, and that was sure to mean more trouble. Nowadays it seemed that every time Maria turned on the radio there was some catastrophe to worry her parents, and she couldn't stand it. She was scared. Praxi might want to act the tough guy just to impress Loukis, but Maria was a girl, and she liked being one. And some day soon, when Loukis matured enough to fit the body he had grown, he would see Maria differently, and then Praxi wouldn't feel so special or superior.

'Well, I think we're being incredibly foolish,' she stated.

'For God's sake, Maria, don't you have any understanding of the situation at all?' Praxi stood up, her hands on her hips and fire in her eyes. 'EOKA are fighting the occupiers not only for our union with Greece but to save all Cypriots. The British train their dogs to bite us to death; they torture our people by hitting their genitals; they kick men in the belly in a way that leaves no mark; they burn them with red-hot irons and use drugs to make them confess. Innocent Greeks,

Maria! Being tortured in their own country by people who have no right to be here! And your pretty face won't help you if they arrest you for being Greek; they pierce women's breasts with needles and stretch their bodies on ice. The British are monsters! It is them you should be afraid of, not EOKA!'

'And how exactly do you know all that, then?' Maria challenged.

'From the leaflets Yiannis Christofi gave me!'

Loukis looked up. 'When did you see Yiannis?'

'Oh, I don't know – a month, two months back, when you were busy in Stavros's fields. He drove by with . . .'

'He's got a car?' Maria's tone suddenly changed to one of interest. Most boys she knew were on donkeys – or bicycles, if they managed to get a permit from the British.

'Yes, some heap of junk . . .'

'Did you speak to him?' Loukis asked.

'Who?'

'Yiannis, that's who.'

'Of course I did.'

'What did you talk about?'

Praxi looked confused and shook her head. 'I don't know, nothing much. He asked me to some dance in Keryneia . . .'

'He asked you to a dance?' Loukis got to his feet. 'And what did you say?'

'Look, Loukis. What does it matter, he was just handing out his EOKA leaflets and making small talk.'

'It matters.' Loukis's face grew dark, and Praxi's words slowed. Maria smirked at her friend's discomfort.

'I said I'd think about it.'

'Fine, well, you think about it then, Praxi. Come,

Maria. I'll walk you back along the road. It's easier that way.'

Maria jumped to her feet and followed Loukis, who was already striding away.

'Loukis! Don't be such a child!' Praxi shouted, causing him to stop and turn. As Maria caught up with him, he took hold of her hand and continued.

As summer shrank from the island, bringing dark clouds that draped their bellies along the limestone spikes shielding Keryneia, Britain shifted a number of troops from Cyprus to Egypt to deal with the Suez crisis, and Praxi continued to punish Loukis for leaving her alone on the mountain. She let Yiannis take her to the dance, which was so boring she was glad her mother had insisted on her being home by 6.30 p.m., and when Loukis still refused to apologize, she employed all the tricks she had learned from the women of the village when they wanted to chastise their men; a little prim courtesy and a lot of disinterest. But because Loukis was as stubborn as Praxi was, he ignored her.

Dhespina watched the whole carry-on from her position on the edges of her son's life and worried that it would bring on an attack. However, Loukis remained untouched by the terrors and continued to work on Stavros's fields during the day and cloud the house with his presence at night.

Georgios came in from his workshop. He looked at his son, who was apparently engrossed in the copy of *The Voice* which Christakis had dropped off that afternoon, and swapped a look with his wife. She shook her head and he shrugged.

'Where are the twins?' he asked.

'Out of our hair for the night,' Dhespina answered. 'They had to deliver some boxes to Ammochostos port, and because of the curfew they'll be staying over at the foreman's house. I said that was OK – it is, isn't it?'

'Yes, of course,' Georgios agreed, 'they're not children any more. And if the job requires it, they should go.' He turned on the radio. The voice was Greek but the agenda was English.

. . . Tens of thousands of people have taken to the streets in Hungary to demand an end to Soviet rule. It started as a peaceful rally, and ended with running battles between police and demonstrators, in which shots are said to have been fired. The demonstrators are demanding that the former prime minister be returned to power. Other demands include free elections, freedom of the press, and a withdrawal of Soviet troops . . .

. . . In Home News; a British soldier has been killed in a callous attack in the village of Lefkoniko. The nineteen-year-old was drinking at a public fountain following a game of football. A pre-planted bomb exploded, killing the soldier and wounding five others. The latest attack by EOKA was condemned as another cowardly act of murder carried out by the terrorists . . .

'Oh, turn it off, Georgios, I can't bear it.' Dhespina slammed the oven door shut and brought the lamb to the table. Every day it was the same: nothing but fighting and death. Now a nineteen-year-old boy, the same age as Michalakis, had been blown to pieces as he quenched his thirst after a football match. Not a fight or an ambush, just a harmless game.

Dhespina pulled the meat from the bone and demanded

Loukis put the paper away. As she filled their plates, the radio's revelations hung in the air and, despite her efforts to block out the report, she saw the dust of the explosion covering the wounded and a young man with everything to live for lying motionless on the ground, his guts ripped from his body by a bomb planted by her own people. It was just too awful, and as a mother it pricked at her conscience. By the time Loukis returned to the newspaper, the *kleftiko* she had cooked lay untouched on her plate.

The next day, the pictures Dhespina had formed in her mind of the soldier playing football continued to drag her down and worry her spirit. She felt nervous and distracted, and a terrible sense of foreboding consumed her. No matter what she did, she couldn't take her mind away, and it kept pulling her back, time and again, to the boy on the ground, mutilated beyond recognition, dying by a fountain whose water flowed red. Without her boys around to fill the house, Dhespina's footsteps echoed in the emptiness, and after trying and failing to enjoy the rare peace, she went to the den to make herself an infusion. As she took a pan from the shelf, she sensed him arrive.

Hurrying back to the house, she saw his knuckles poised at the door. He saw her and stopped. He was the manager of Vassos Trade Suppliers in Keryneia. He was sorry, he said, and she could see that he was. It was terrible, he told her. They were all shocked, every one of them, and as he stumbled over his words Dhespina's heart pounded. As her body weakened, its blood took up the rhythm and its deafening beat swallowed his words. It was the soldier, the one from the football match. They came into town. There was anger and chaos. They wanted revenge. They descended on Ammochostos with heavy boots that kicked at doors. Wood splintered. Women screamed. The people were terrified, but the hate, there was so much hate. They were thrown into trucks, one by one, lying on top of each other, crushed and suffocating. There was a house. Her boys were inside. They came to search and they came to destroy. Marios didn't know. He was scared, but he was brave. He tried to defend the lady, but they pushed him against the wall and punched him in the stomach. He was brave, so very brave. Nicos leapt and the butt of a gun hit him in the face. Between the eyes. There was a crack. Was it the gun or the floor? His head opened. His life poured out. There was nothing they could do and the man was sorry. He was truly, very sorry. And he wept.

3

They came to take the body in the early afternoon.

Heavy clouds hung over the village, threatening rain from a sky that reflected the colour of their clothes, and it was how it should be: the sun was gone, her son was gone.

All night she sat with him, her eyes fixed on the casket, silently reaching for his presence, willing him to wake, to open the lid and tell her it was OK; it was just a joke, and he was sorry. But he didn't, and this wasn't how she wanted to remember him; in a box, cold and lifeless, her beautiful son dented and taken by hate. How could she have let this happen – to her own flesh and blood; to the baby that raced from her womb to beat his brother into the world; to the boy who chased the sun and filled their lives with light? How could he be gone? Overnight, the world had turned hideous, devoid of any reason or hope, and the force of it suffocated her. In less than four decades, she had gone from girl, to wife, to mother, to *miroloi* – a woman dressed in black. It was too soon. It wasn't right. She shouldn't be here, she shouldn't be doing this, *why are they making her do this?*

Dhespina's legs gave way and she crumbled into the arms of Christakis.

'No, please, please . . . just a few more minutes, I beg you, please . . .' Blinded by tears, she grabbed for the box as they moved him, but her hands were weak and her son slipped from her grasp. If only they would give her more time. Just a few days, that's all she needed, just a little space so that she could do something, she knew she could find something, there had to be a way; something to stop him going, to keep him here, here with his family, with the people who loved him, who needed him. The plants – they had their secrets. Surely they would help her; an ointment perhaps, or a mixture of herbs and perfumed water, anything to stop his cheeks from sinking, to keep him whole, to keep him here – oh God, to keep him with her.

'No, please! Please, don't take him. Not yet . . . Nicos! My son! Please, my son! Don't take my son!'

Christakis and Michalakis stood either side of their mother, two giant pillars protecting her from the grief trying to crush her. Although the boys had long ago become men, it was their first outing in the shoes of their parents, and they bore their own pain with a quiet dignity that impressed the villagers watching behind them. As the priest poured olive oil into the grave and took the soil from its four edges, Marios wrapped an arm around his father, whose shoulders trembled with tears he could no longer control. Georgios felt the compassion in his son's embrace, and he was humbled. By rights, he should have been the one giving comfort, but his strength had deserted him and he surrendered to his son's care. To the right of the family, Loukis faced the grave, standing with them, but alone. His back was straight, his eyes unblinking as he watched the earth being thrown upon the open casket and into his brother's face. Praxi left her mother's side and stepped forward to take hold of his hand. Though Loukis didn't look, his fingers tightened around hers, and she wept for him, because she knew he wouldn't.

After the service the mourners took their solemn procession back to the family's home to take comfort in the *pariorka* – bread, olives and wine – but Praxi and Loukis slipped away from the sadness that had come to engulf his family. Hand in hand, they left the village.

Crossing the Keryneia road, they walked up rocky steps they had trodden a million times before, climbing higher and higher until St Hilarion's Castle cast its shadow upon them. Finally, they stopped under the pistachio tree they had once chosen to shelter Praxi's own resting place. Neither of them said a word, because there was nothing to be said. Praxi felt Loukis's pain as if it were her own. Nothing could repair the damage that had been done to his family. Nothing could bring Nicos back. All she could do was be there for him. So when Loukis dipped his head into his hands, she gently took his fingers and placed them on her face. Without thinking, she brought her lips to his and breathed her love into him.

As the wind pulled at their hair the rain began to fall, dripping down their faces to dance on their tongues, and the smell of the earth rose from the ground and smothered them. Cyprus answered their loss with a tenderness that whispered in the wind, and she kissed the two of them with tears of her own.

Under the monk's castle, Praxi and Loukis took their pain and fought it together with hungry lips and clumsy hands.

They searched for a reason in the curves and shadows of their bodies, and when he moved inside of her Praxi answered his urgency with abandon. There was no more fighting, no creeping fear, or the Church feeding her mamma's condemnation; only the hammering of their hearts and the steam of their breath. Praxi kissed Loukis's face and cried unashamedly, not out of grief or discomfort, but because she loved him, and in the confusion of their devotion they were no longer just Praxi and Loukis but something different and stronger. They were together, and it was the way it should be.

Marios felt the wood under his fingers and smiled. He had done a good job; using the file to smooth the rough edges just as Christakis had demonstrated.

'Lovely work,' his brother agreed when he walked over to show him. 'A few more of these and I'll teach you how to plane a board using a trick with chalk to make sure the surface is level.'

'I'd like that,' Marios told him, and went back to his place at the window. It was a lot lighter in the shop than in his father's workroom, and he much preferred it. Although he didn't like to say no to Papa, he didn't really want to spend the rest of his days making shoes for village people, or even donkeys. It was the leather; it smelled funny and it felt dead in his hands, not like wood. At least an old tree can be brought back to life; be made into something new and quite beautiful. But leather, it always looked dead, no matter how clever his papa was.

In the first few days after Nicos was killed – because his father needed him and because nobody wanted him to go back to the warehouse – Marios had tried really hard to be a shoemaker. But then his papa broke down and made it impossible. As he moved closer, to show Marios how to punch a hole into the leather, his fingers began to tremble. In a heartbeat the tremors took over his body, like something invisible was shaking him, until they forced the water from his eyes and he had to drop the tools he was holding to grab the table instead.

That's when Christakis walked in. He took one look at their father and asked Marios to wait outside. About twenty minutes later, his brother emerged and told Marios he would be learning woodwork from now on, if he was happy with that. And of course he was. It wasn't so depressing in Christakis's workshop; no one cried or made jokes they didn't believe in, they just worked. All morning, his brother would chisel and carve – leaving curls of golden wood in his wake – and Marios would concentrate on the tasks he had been given. At lunchtime, Christakis's wife Yianoulla would appear carrying baby Angelis in one arm and three plates in the other. Together, in the sunshine, the brothers would devour the meal she had prepared, and Angelis would play on his father's lap, pulling fiercely at his moustache and laughing. Now and again Yianoulla roasted potatoes that melted on the tongue, and once she even made ice cream. But mostly it was cheese and bread with some olive oil to wet it. Yesterday, though, Christakis had told Yianoulla she would have to stop chasing after them, on account of her getting so fat with the baby inside of her, but she just laughed and said it was her job to look after her men.

Marios thought his sister-in-law was nice, and she was pretty, and he hoped for her sake that when she finally gave birth it would be to a little girl and not to another boy. Cyprus was dangerous for boys. They grow up and die.

By about four o'clock, Christakis would tell Marios to go home, which was helpful, because the sun still hung in the sky, whatever the season or weather, and that gave him time to walk to the village and visit Nicos before seeing his parents. Although Nicos was dead, he hadn't actually gone anywhere, because Marios could feel him. He figured this was due to them being cracked from the same egg, but he also thought it might be because he still listened. When he sat by the grave to tell Nicos about his day and all the things he had learned, he heard his brother's questions and he answered them truthfully. Tonight he would speak about Christakis's promise to show him how to plane wood well. Nicos would like that. He'd be very impressed.

Really, it was a shame his parents no longer felt Nicos, because if they did it might end their tears and stop them growing old. It seemed to him that their papa had shrunk over the past weeks, becoming slow and unsure, and the morning after Nicos was laid in his new bed, their mother woke up with a line of grey in her hair that ran along the side of her face. Nobody mentioned it, which Marios found strange, but he was too scared to say anything in case they all started crying again. But when he told Nicos he heard him laugh loudly in the ground, and he decided to forget about it. Now when he looked at his mamma he didn't see the grey streak any more; he heard Nicos's laughter.

Yiannis lowered the car window and stuck his head out.

'*Yassou*, Loukis. I was very sorry to hear about your brother. Nicos was a good boy; a good Greek.'

57

Loukis paused on the roadside. His eyes narrowed with irritation at the man's unwanted presence and the laws of decency that compelled him to accept the bland commiserations on offer.

'I promise you, the occupiers will pay for what they did,' continued Yiannis.

'How very comforting,' Loukis sneered. He moved closer to the car and deliberately placed his hands on the roof, forcing Yiannis to withdraw.

'Now, tell me,' he demanded, 'what exactly do you propose to do? Blow up the British, gun them all down or perhaps leaflet them into submission?'

'Steady on.' The older boy laughed, in case Loukis was joking, but the sound came out feeble and strained. Loukis raised an eyebrow and stared. Not sure how to react, Yiannis put his foot on the accelerator and revved the engine. The Economidou boys were hard work, and he'd had enough of playing the nice guy.

'Listen, kid, you don't even know the half of it,' he said darkly, or as darkly as he was able to, and drove off.

Loukis watched Yiannis disappear down the road, which was little more than a track. The hairs on his neck were up and anger coloured his cheeks. The Chevrolet had come from Praxi's house, and against his best efforts to deny them, his head crowded with conversations between the pair. He heard dull flattery, Praxi's giggles and invitations to dances. As his jealousy took hold it orchestrated music from a gramophone, and he watched hands that weren't his sweating within hers; they led her around a dance floor, resting occasionally at the small of her back, touching her playfully, forcing her in, and bringing her breasts to press against his chest.

In a heartbeat Loukis would snap the man's neck. But it wasn't just Yiannis gnawing at his patience; for more than a week Praxi had been hiding herself. Loukis understood that she was trying to protect them, but it felt like a punishment. After the day on the mountain, they had come together only twice more before she shrank from his touch and constructed barriers out of excuses. Loukis's blood was pounding in his veins and he could hardly stay his hands, but as the intensity of her grief for Nicos eased, Praxi's guilt filled the void, causing her to pull away and enforce rules on their lives that belonged to other people, not them. Loukis ached to shake her by the shoulders and shout that the rest of the world could go to hell as far as he was concerned, but he couldn't even get near her; Praxi's shame and moral fever had sent her scurrying for Maria. Everywhere he and Praxi went, the Germanos girl came too, twirling her hair and dragging him into discussions he had no interest in taking part in. Now she was here again; staring at him from a stool as, behind her, Praxi struggled with an axe.

With her papa dead and her mother still nursing the loss of the troublesome archbishop, it was left to Praxi to prepare the logs for winter and, whereas a few weeks earlier Loukis would have stepped forward to take the axe from her hands, he now stood his ground – frozen by Maria's presence and his own bristling anger. Praxi hadn't noticed him arrive, and she was talking about Yiannis.

'He really does think he's something special, doesn't he?'

'He wants to be your boyfriend,' Maria stated, all the while looking at Loukis, mischief playing in her eyes and a smile dancing upon her lips.

'I tell you, hell will freeze over before I make that man my boyfriend! He may impress *you* with his car, Maria, but Yiannis would drive me crazy with all his talk of EOKA this and EOKA that.' Praxi slammed the axe down, almost splitting the log in two, but not quite.

'You know that if Yiannis does open that café in Keryneia like he says he's going to do then he would be quite the catch – a man of business and all that.'

'*If* he opens a café . . . I mean, where's he going to get the money from? Honestly, you shouldn't believe everything that braggart tells you.'

'All right then – if not Yiannis, who do you want to be your boyfriend?'

Praxi paused and fiddled with the axe, working it free of the log she was trying to halve. She really didn't want to be having this conversation right now, especially not with Maria. She could hardly think straight these days; everything was so muddled and uncomfortable.

'Come on,' Maria encouraged, staring directly at Loukis. 'Who do you want to be your boyfriend? What about Loukis?'

'Oh, grow up, Maria. Loukis is a friend, nothing more. He's just a boy, for God's sake!'

Praxi wielded the axe above her head and brought it down with a crack, sending splinters flying past her feet. Even as she spoke she hated herself, because it sounded like a betrayal. And if she had turned around, instead of balancing another log in front of her feet, she would have detested herself even more.

Loukis turned his back on Maria and walked away.

*

It was near midnight when Mrs Economidou came banging at the door as if the devil himself were chasing at her heels.

'Loukis?' she demanded of Praxi, barging past her and searching him out with her eyes. 'Have you seen Loukis?'

Praxi admitted, with some guilt, that she hadn't seen him for a couple of days.

'He hasn't come home and I don't know where he is,' Dhespina gasped. 'I just found some money on the table when I came in from the den, and I didn't think anything of it, guessing Georgios must have left it there for some reason, but it wasn't his or Marios's. Therefore, it could only belong to Loukis, but I can't ask him about it because he's nowhere to be found. I have to find him, Praxi! He hasn't been home all night. I've got to find him!'

Praxi's mum Elena came rushing forward to take her friend in a tight hug, cooing her into calmness.

'Shush now, don't worry, Dhespina, we will find him. Don't worry. There will be an innocent explanation for all of this, I'm sure. Come, Praxi, get your coat on, child.'

Praxi took her jacket from the peg and slipped it over her nightdress to follow the women out of the house. Her mamma had hold of Mrs Economidou's shoulders, and she was struggling to wrap her woollen shawl around them both as they walked deeper into the village, calling out Loukis's name all the while.

As they approached the heart of the community, with its small cluster of shops, there came the rumble of engines. Suddenly headlights clicked into life, breaking the darkness and temporarily blinding them. Shielding her eyes, Praxi saw the silhouette of a man approach them. As he neared, she recognized his soldier's uniform. He was followed by two others carrying heavy-looking guns. Amusement painted their pale faces.

'Good evening, ladies,' the man said, affecting a commanding pose. 'Now would one of you speak English by any chance?'

'I speak English,' Praxi volunteered, stepping forward.

'What is he saying?' asked her mother.

'He's asking if we speak English,' Praxi told her.

'English!' Dhespina retorted. 'I would rather cut out my own tongue!'

The soldier in front of them coughed and Praxi turned her attention back to him.

'Well, young lady, perhaps you might like to tell me what you are all doing out at this time of night – well after curfew?'

'We're looking for someone,' Praxi told him.

'What's he saying?' Elena asked.

'He's asking why we're out after curfew,' her daughter answered.

'Curfew! Damn their curfew! This is our country and we'll go where we damn well please at whatever time we damn well like!' Dhespina started walking again, roughly brushing past the soldier, who instinctively grabbed hold of her arm. He immediately regretted it.

'Take your hands off me, you son of a whore!' she shouted, fire raging in her eyes. The soldier instinctively recoiled.

'What did she say?' he asked Praxi.

'She called you a son of a whore,' she replied.

'*Dolofonoi!*' Dhespina screamed, now wildly addressing the rest of the soldiers. '*Dolofonoi!*'

'Now she's calling you murderers,' Praxi helpfully continued.

The soldier looked embarrassed. Lights were snapping on in the houses nearby, and he really didn't need this. In a few weeks' time he would be free of the bloody country and preparing for Christmas in his own home with his own family; the last thing he wanted was to get caught in a riot sparked by two mad old bints and some slip of a girl.

'Get back in the vehicle,' the soldier ordered his two comrades, who were becoming visibly anxious as more house lights switched on.

'Right you are, sarge.'

As the soldiers retreated to their Land Rovers, Dhespina spat her hate at their backs. '*Dolofonoi! Dolofonoi!*' she screamed, and she continued screaming until they bumped and growled their way out of her sight.

When the last of the vehicles vanished, the villagers crept out of their houses to investigate the commotion.

'It's Loukis, he's missing,' explained Praxi to the small, curious crowd, causing a few of the women to hurriedly cross themselves and tut in sympathy.

'But I only saw him this afternoon,' Mr Televantos piped up.

'Where?' demanded Dhespina, tearing herself from the arms and kisses of the other women. 'Where did you see Loukis?'

'He was on his way to Keryneia, by the looks of it. I'll tell you what though, he was in a fearsome mood. His face had such a scowl on it, dear Dhespo, he looked quite the villain. Of course I tried to get him to chat a while, but you know what Loukis is like – no offence intended – he's never been

63

the easiest of boys. Anyway, he said the strangest thing, and I couldn't work it out at the time . . . still can't really, I even asked Mrs Televantos what she thought and she had no idea either . . .'

'What did he say, Mr Televantos?' Dhespina's voice cracked with irritation.

Mr Televantos nodded. 'Yes, sorry, Dhespo. He said, now let me think, what was the exact wording he used . . . ah yes . . . he said that I was to tell all of those who needed to know that he was on his way to become a man. It was very odd, if you don't mind me saying so, yes, very odd, indeed.'

4

The priest was little surprised when he found Loukis waiting for him in the chapel. After the atrocities of
Ammochostos, the black-robed messenger of God and
EOKA had half expected at least one of the Economidou
boys to come calling, and Loukis did nothing to dispel the
priest's assumption that his sudden interest in *enosis* was
stimulated by the murder of his brother. He ushered the boy
into the back room – for guidance and assistance.

With small nods, Loukis dumbly accepted the platitudes
on offer and kept his face placid as holy endorsements of
violent resistance bounced off stone walls. Having shied
away from religion, the priest's proximity and intensity
made him itch with discomfort; he had never possessed
much patience for the preaching of the Church, and less so
the older he grew. Loukis believed in what he could see; in
the strength of the wind, the force of the sea, the light of the
sun and the glory of the moon. He desired no stories to
explain their existence or to excuse their natures, and he
hardly required the services of a priest who promoted the
gun with one hand while damning sins of the flesh with
the other. However, circumstances being what they were, he

did need this particular priest to organize his passage, and therefore he contained the irritation pulling at his temples and continued to do so throughout the night and into the morning until they reached the outskirts of Skylloura, where he was led into a curtained room at the back of the altar of another small chapel. In the half-light of the chamber, another priest stood waiting for them, along with three teenage boys whose feverish eyes betrayed their solemn expressions. On a seat in the corner sat a man dressed in a worn jacket and muddied trousers. He got up as they entered.

'Finally – let's get on with this,' he growled.

Taking centre stage in the small gathering, the man gave a tired speech that touched on the struggle for *enosis* and how the archbishop's exile had fanned the flames of revolt into the fire of conflict. He then called on the boys to swear their allegiance. Loukis took his turn dispassionately, opting to avoid the theatrics he had just witnessed.

'I swear not to disclose to anybody, under any circumstances, however hard I may be tortured,' he repeated, 'secrets concerning individuals, arms, hideouts, the funds or the activities of the organization. I swear not to take advantage of the organization's money, to obey without dispute the orders of my superiors, and finally to dedicate with all my strength and even my life to the success of the holy aims of the organization.'

When he finished, the priest blessed him, and the other boys patted him on the back, demonstrating a kinship that was lost on Loukis. The man who had sworn them all in also shook his hand; he was EOKA's district officer, he said. Dark circles hung under his eyes, and tension lined his forehead.

Loukis guessed he was probably younger than he looked – a similar judgement reached by the EOKA man after Loukis informed him of his age. Despite trailing a year behind the other boys present, he was a head taller than anyone else in the room, and though his frame was still slight, it was starting to break the mould of his youth.

'Pity you're so young,' the EOKA man said. 'We can't let you pick up arms until you're seventeen, and I trust in God that the struggle will be over before that day comes around.'

The priests both nodded their heads in agreement, and less than twenty-four hours after turning his back on the life he had known, and those he had loved, Loukis became a member of Cyprus's resistance force.

In the Bedford bus on the way to Lefkosia, the district officer offered Loukis the window seat, but not his name, and as the sun heated their skin through the dirty glass the man relaxed and warmed to his newest recruit. They had left the other boys back in Skylloura. Loukis didn't ask why, but the district officer divulged the information anyway.

'There's no denying their passion for the cause, but they're young so we'll start them out making and distributing leaflets, plus a little slogan painting. If they show an aptitude for it, and they manage to avoid capture, we'll train them in other irritation tactics and, finally, militarily. It's the way we do things. Your case is a little unusual, given your insistence to be out of the area and our current predicament, so we'll put you to use in Troodos.'

'What predicament?' Loukis took the cigarette being offered and lit up.

'In the past few months we've taken a hammering. Suez gave us a breather, but now the troops are coming back and, earlier this month, one of our smuggling rings was rumbled in Lemesos.'

'Actually, that's always puzzled me – where do you get your weapons from?'

'From a variety of sources,' the man admitted. 'From Greece via the parcel post or couriers – we also salvaged ammunition from ships sunk off the coast during the Second World War, and there are supplies from raids on police stations and bases. Others we manufacture ourselves, using explosives sold in our own shops. But none of this should concern you at this stage; I imagine you'll be used as a courier between the mountain cells, taking messages, food and whatever other necessities they might need to various drop-off points.'

Loukis listened, intrigued. The resistance was far more organized than he had realized.

'So what's the set-up?' he asked.

'What, in terms of whom you'll report to and such?'

Loukis nodded.

'Well, it's fairly standard,' the district officer told him, flicking the dandruff from his shoulders as he spoke. 'Members operate from safe houses or hideouts and most cells are made up of between five and ten members. The Central Headquarters is mobile so as to avoid detection by British intelligence, and all orders are communicated by hand. As I said, you'll probably form part of the chain. If this struggle continues and it works out for you, I guess you'll eventually be promoted to assassin, if you've got the stomach for it.'

The man turned to look at Loukis, who felt his scrutiny and replied with silence. The district officer seemed pleased.

'EOKA thrives on secrecy,' he continued. 'It is the most crucial element in the organization's survival. A lot of you boys, like the three we've just left behind, have your hearts in the right place, but hearts are easily made proud and in many cases it causes loose tongues. It's always better to keep silent; that's the trick to being a real part of the resistance. When you get to Troodos, you'll meet with the district officer there, be assigned to a cell and given a codename; this will be between you, your commander and his cell members. No one else will ever know your name unless you divulge it, and if you do that just one time you effectively double your chances of being betrayed, unmasked and caught. Always keep your silence, boy, and trust only those in your cell.'

Loukis thanked the man for his advice and turned to the window, mulling over their conversation as he took in the view: behind them, the mountains hiding Keryneia and the northern coastline were quickly shrinking into the distance as the bus travelled deeper into the flat plains leading them to the capital. Although Loukis still had no burning desire to be part of Greece, his blood was hot and it needed a release. He loved this country, with its jagged peaks, sandy shores and rocky plateaus and, for now, that would be reason enough.

In the confusion of Lefkosia, the district officer bid Loukis farewell, giving him a little petty cash for a bus ticket to Alona. From there he would be met by another EOKA member and taken to a safe house.

'Good luck,' said the district officer, clasping Loukis's arm in a rough embrace. He then disappeared into the heaving mess of the capital's crowds. Four months later, Loukis heard he had been arrested by the British and hanged at Lefkosia's Central Prison. His body was buried in an unmarked grave. He was twenty-four years old.

When Loukis arrived in Alona he was met by a bear of a man who was not only huge but ridiculously surly. His reticence to engage in any form of conversation made Loukis's own gruffness seem positively girlish, and their journey, mostly by foot along rough, rocky tracks, was difficult and awkward. Pressing on, deeper into the woods, Loukis was passed on twice more to strangers, who offered varying degrees of camaraderie, until eventually he reached his new home: a small cottage lost in the thick of the pine forests that dressed the slopes of Troodos. The man of the house was Demetris Thedosias – and he was a sergeant in the Cypriot police force.

'There are about twenty of us in EOKA,' Demetris informed him as they settled down to the *kleftiko* dinner his wife Lella had prepared. 'I don't know who the others are – that's the way of the organization; only those who need to know, know. Obviously, having you with us is something of a risk, but you've been vouched for, and it is our duty – and our pleasure, mind – to do what we can to help you while you need us. Saying all that, if you betray us, the little woman here will cut off your *polloi*.'

'Demetris!' His wife shouted in mock horror.

'I'm only joking!' her husband protested. 'The lad knows I'm joking!'

And Loukis did.

Demetris was a large man in every way; passionate about his food, his girth matched the size of his heart, and hefty hands punctuated his easy conversation with thunderous claps. Lella, though quieter than her husband, was equally round and just as jovial, with a mother's impulsiveness for displays of affection, suddenly planting kisses on Loukis's cheeks that caught him off guard until he grew accustomed to the woman's warmth. From the moment Loukis stepped foot through their door, the couple accepted him without question and with a generosity that humbled him. He was made to feel part of their family, which indeed he now was, to all intents and purposes. On the day Loukis arrived, the three of them sat long into the night concocting their story and arguing over the finer points and details that Loukis was told could make the difference between freedom and arrest. He was their nephew from Keryneia – St Andrew's Street, to be precise. His widowed mother, Lenya, was Lella's sister and she had become worried her son was getting caught up with the wrong crowd. As a last resort, amid much soul-searching and tears, she had sent him to his aunt and uncle to keep him on the right side of the law until the troubles subsided.

'From now on, this story is your truth,' Demetris told Loukis in a rare moment of seriousness. 'Believe in it and live it. For our part, Lella and I won't ask anything about your real circumstances, because what we don't know can't muddle us. Sticking to your story, night and day, is important, Loukis, I can't stress that enough. As a policeman, I get visitors here all the time; sometimes EOKA, sometimes colleagues in the force, sometimes the British themselves. When they come they will all be curious, so keep to your story – and continue acting like the sullen teenager you are, that's probably your best defence!' Demetris started laughing and Lella clucked at him reproachfully, grabbing Loukis's face in her chubby hands and planting another hot kiss on his cheek.

For the best part of two weeks, Loukis stayed with

Demetris and his wife, helping Lella with her chores, taking tours with the police sergeant so as to find his feet in the area, meeting with their neighbours and sullenly greeting, as advised, their police friends. Then one afternoon, as Loukis sweated in the winter sun, chopping wood in the yard, a teenager approached the cottage. Lella noticed him arrive and threw Loukis a reassuring look before disappearing into the kitchen.

'Brother,' the boy greeted him, 'we're going for a walk.'

Loukis dropped the axe and followed. Pushing their way wordlessly through the wet ground of the forest, snapping twigs and branches in their wake, the pair emerged from the trees to join the road leading to Pano Platres.

'We've a note to drop,' the teenager explained, stopping to catch his breath. He was shabbily dressed, and the skin on the left side of his face was paper thin and mottled with violent red scars.

'I can't tell you who it's for and I can't tell you what's written on it, so don't even ask.'

'OK,' replied Loukis.

'You're not even curious?'

'Not enough to ask.'

'Good, because I couldn't tell you even if I wanted to – which I don't, by the way.'

Loukis shrugged; it seemed his 'brother' was intent on securing his credentials as the lead man in this, Loukis's first EOKA operation. As they ambled along the asphalt road, a British convoy rumbled past them. The vehicles at the front and rear both had their windscreens folded to the bonnet, on top of which stood a small wall of sandbags. The trucks were fitted with pitched roofs covered with layers of chicken wire.

72

'That's to make the grenades roll off when we throw them,' revealed the EOKA boy as the trucks roared past. 'They've also got sandbags on the floors to stop our land-mines. We still get a few of them though.'

'Have you killed many British?' Loukis asked.

'Enough to send a message to their parliament and their Queen,' the boy sneered, and carried on walking.

About four miles into their journey, the teenager's back suddenly tensed as a roadblock loomed ahead. Three soldiers in heavy jackets stood guard; they were all smoking, and when one turned in their direction, the other two followed.

'The buggers have seen us,' the EOKA boy stated need-lessly. 'We can't make a run for it, otherwise they'll start shooting.'

'We could always turn back if you're worried,' Loukis sug-gested, but the teenager appeared offended.

'I'm not worried – who says I'm worried? Come on, stop dawdling!' He marched purposefully ahead, and Loukis surmised that if the British hadn't been interested in them before, they soon would be, given the EOKA boy's angry determination. Unsurprisingly, the three soldiers stopped them as soon as they came within earshot.

'Going anywhere interesting, lads?' one of them good-naturedly asked as another came close and ordered them to raise their arms so he could pat down their pockets.

'What's it to you?' the boy demanded, and Loukis's heart sank.

'I'll tell you what it is to me, son,' replied the soldier, stubbing out his cigarette and taking a firm hold of his weapon. 'We're in charge here, this is a checkpoint and you can be as belligerent as you bloody well like, but you'll answer the damn question and you'll answer it civilly.'

Loukis watched the boy's reaction with interest; in his enthusiasm to show off, he had created quite a dilemma for himself. Would he stand his ground and face a beating or would he back down and lose face in front of the new recruit? Loukis stepped forward.

'Sir, forgive my friend's impatience, but we've come a long way on a matter of some urgency.' The teenager threw Loukis a hostile stare.

'Is that right, young man? And what exactly would this matter of urgency be?' As he spoke, the soldier kept his eyes trained on the EOKA boy's face.

'Girls,' replied Loukis matter-of-factly.

'Girls?'

'Yes, we're on – what do you call it in English?' He paused for a second to search for the phrase he already knew. 'A promise! Yes, we're on a promise . . .'

The soldier relaxed the weapon in his hands.

'Well, why didn't you say so?' he asked. 'No wonder your friend here is in such a rush.'

'He's probably messed his pants already,' another of the soldiers joked.

'On your way then, lads,' the first soldier told them. 'And do us a favour: if you find any other willing girls in the village, come back and tell us, will you? We're dying up here!'

'Will do,' agreed Loukis.

As the soldiers parted to let them pass, the teenager sidled up to Loukis and aped the soldier in Greek. ' "We're dying up here! We're dying up here!" Of course they're dying up here – we're the ones killing them.' He fired a short, humourless laugh in their direction. 'Anyway, quick thinking on the girls, I like that. I had the situation covered, of course. I just like to bother them a bit, but good work nonetheless. We'll make an EOKA man of you yet. I'm Stelios, by the way.'

'Loukis.'

'Yeah, I know. I was given your details this morning. They've obviously got some of them wrong though, they told me you were fourteen.'

'I am.'

'Holy Mother of Mary! What do they feed you on in Keryneia?'

'Pig's ears and snails mainly.'

'I can't stand snails . . .'

'They're not too bad, if they're cooked. Raw they can be bland.'

'Raw?' Stelios turned to look at Loukis, his nose wrinkled in disgust. 'Oh, you're joking, right?'

'Right,' agreed Loukis.

'Still, you're damn tall for your age.'

'It's a family thing. I'll be fifteen in just over a month, if that helps.'

'In truth, it doesn't make much difference,' Stelios told him. 'You still won't be able to shoot the buggers who killed your brother. He was murdered in Ammochostos, right?'

'Yes.'

'Well, for what it's worth, I'm sorry about that.'

Loukis thanked him.

'And I'm also sorry for all of the stuff earlier; to be honest with you, Loukis, all this letter-delivering is for kids, but I was told to show you the way, and I couldn't exactly say no . . . "Obey without dispute the orders of my superiors", and all that.'

Loukis recognized the line from the oath he had recently taken. 'I don't suppose you've got any of the organization's money we can take advantage of, have you? I'm starving.'

Stelios snorted good-naturedly and attempted to rest his arm on Loukis's shoulder. Being much shorter, he ended up settling for his back. At the next village they came to, he stopped at a shop and bought a slab of bread and two bottles of cola.

'You know, the British use these in their fight to oppress us Greeks.' Stelios lifted the Coke bottle to the sun, catching its rays in the thick green glass. 'On riot patrol, they leave them in the back of their trucks to cook in the sun. Then, when there's trouble, they grab a few bottles, give them a shake and lob them in front of the protestors. When they hit the ground, they explode like grenades, covering the area in a thick carpet of glass. It's a pretty neat trick, actually.'

Loukis agreed that it was.

Once Stelios stopped playing the hard man, Loukis found him oddly engaging and as they chatted the journey away, the boy's scarred face became increasingly animated. He now shared his knowledge of the organization with none of the reservations that had previously clouded his conversation. Stelios had been in EOKA a little over a year, he said. He loved the life and he lived for the cause, but it was a commitment fraught with danger and disaster. He'd lost two friends so far, one to the hangman and one to an electricity pylon during an act of sabotage. His Troodos commander was currently on the run from the British.

76

However, Stelios insisted that Hermes himself would have trouble catching him. The commander's name was Gregoris Afxentiou and he had a £5,000 reward on his head. By all accounts, he was the most competent of the EOKA leaders and commanded not only the loyalty of his men and the admiration of all Greeks, but also the grudging respect of the British trying to capture him. Loukis acknowledged that he had heard of him; Afxentiou had been the leader of the Keryneia mountain group for a while and the word locally was that he once refused to execute a traitor because the man's wife had just given birth. Furthermore, after he relocated to Troodos, his cell's hit-and-run campaigns were so successful, he became Britain's most wanted man.

'He's probably as famous as Grivas now,' Stelios stated, pride written all over his face, and Loukis agreed that he probably was.

Stelios explained that, with the occupiers giving chase, it was next to impossible for arrangements to be made for Loukis to meet Afxentiou, which was why it had taken this long for him to be permitted to make contact. However, the day was coming, Stelios assured the younger boy, and in the meantime he could still be an active member. There were three others in his cell, a couple of old-timers, who had seen their fair share of fighting, and a part-time girl called Toulla, who had as much courage as the men but better breasts. Loukis couldn't help smiling at the observation, but then Praxi sprang to his mind, and his face fell dark.

'I guess you'll be delivering messages, like we're doing today,' Stelios continued. 'But I'll have a word and try and get you on some of the irritation operations as soon as possible. That's where the real fun is to be had.'

Loukis thanked him. 'So what happened to your face?' he asked.

Stelios self-consciously touched his scars. 'The occupiers did it,' he said. 'In the summer, Grivas was on the run in the mountains, and the British were on to him. Then the fire broke out. You must have heard about it.'

Loukis nodded. Michalakis's newspaper had been full of it. It had been an inferno that had destroyed practically half of the forest.

'It was impossible to outrun the fire,' said Stelios. 'The trees were exploding like shells in the heat and gales were fanning the flames to the sky. I was coming from Kykkou at the time and I suddenly found myself trapped. The fire took us all – Greeks, Turks, even British soldiers. I heard them you know, the soldiers; they were exploding in the flames. It was the ammunition catching fire in the bandoliers they wear around their waists. When the flames caught them, they literally blew up, their guts ripped out by their own ammunition. Obviously, in the chaos, the fight was forgotten; we were all running for our lives from a fire that outpaced us at every turn. Everywhere the flames jumped ahead of us and trees as hot as burning ash fell into our path. The heat was so intense it sucked the air from our lungs. In all honesty, Loukis, I was prepared to die; I couldn't see a way out. Then, as this wall of fire closed in, some local foresters caught sight of me and waved for me to follow them up a hill. As I chased them, that's when the tree cracked in a ball of flame and crashed into me. Where the strength came from I still don't know, but I pushed myself out of those flames and ran for my life, with my clothes and hair on fire. Seeing me, a forester ran back – he was a Turk, funnily enough – and he slapped the flames eating at my head and my jacket. The pain was excruciating, I can't tell you, but that man risked his life for me and dragged me to an already burnt-out patch of ground. Together we sat there as the fire roared around and past us. In the heat I lost consciousness, I'm not ashamed to say it. When I woke up I was in a clean bed and I was alive, but my face was burnt beyond recognition.'

'Jesus,' whistled Loukis. 'But how was it the fault of the British?'

'They started it,' Stelios said, his eyes bright from the anger and pain of his memory. 'In their operation to get Grivas, they strafed the area with mortars and heavy machine guns. The summer drought had made the trees tinder-dry and the slightest spark would have ignited a fire, let alone the barrage of bullets the British rained down on the area.'

'And what happened to Grivas?'

'He escaped.' Stelios shrugged. 'They say he's now hiding in a safe house in Lemesos, which must be nice for him.'

Praxi slapped Maria with such force that the welt of her anger remained on the girl's face for three days. If her mother hadn't come tearing out of the house to wrestle her away, she was sure she would have killed her.

Praxi had long suspected Maria had an eye for Loukis, but she dismissed her friend's ambitions for the romantic stupidity it so blatantly was. Maria carried in her heart the picture of a boy who didn't exist. She was taken by Loukis's looks, but she hadn't the slightest understanding of what lay beneath them. She didn't know Loukis at all. She didn't even recognize the animal he was. When his lips clamped shut, bolting in his words, Maria thought him moody and mysterious; when he took her hand that day as they walked from the castle she mistook the gesture for an act of tenderness. But her childish teasing and amorous games had broken the boy's heart, and right now Praxi hated Maria with a passion matched only by her own self-loathing.

A stupid moment, that's all it had taken, a second's weakness brought on by her own tangled emotions, moral shame and fear of being discovered. If only she had been honest and brave enough to stand up to Maria's questioning. If only she had admitted her love for Loukis, swallowed her embarrassment and told of her passion: the way he turned her blood to hot oil; how it raced through her veins when she felt him draw near; the way her skin tingled at his slightest touch; how her dreams were filled with dancing pictures of his eyes and his smile; how she would give up her life for him. But she had said none of those things. She had lied. After privately loving him, she publicly denied him, and in doing so she had ruined both their lives. Praxi couldn't believe it had come to this. It should have all been so simple: next month they would have begun courting; they would have got engaged; married; had children; and lived happily ever after. Now she had no idea when she would next set eyes on him. She only knew it wouldn't be any time soon. Loukis had run from her to become the man she had called for. And because God punishes the guilty, it would be too late when he forgave her and came back. There wasn't any time left: she had seduced him in grief, renounced him in fear, and now she was undone.

*

The note was left a mile outside of Pano Platres, under a rock at the foot of a small shrine. Before they left, Stelios took a match to the candle to alert local EOKA men that a new missive had been laid.

By the time the boys had retraced their steps, the army checkpost had gone and the day's light had been taken by the night. They parted company on the road with brief plans to meet up again soon, and Loukis plunged into the blackness of the woods. When he emerged on the other side, he found an Austin Champ parked at the gate of his safe house. Inside, Demetris was drinking tea with a British soldier. It was bitterly cold, but the fireplace stood dark and the men's hot breath clouded their talk.

'Ah, my nephew Loukis arrives – about time too.' Demetris got up and motioned for him to step forward. 'This is Major Harvey from British Intelligence. He's come to offer his Christmas greetings – no gifts, mind.'

The man got to his feet with a smile. He was thick set with rich brown hair and a fearsome moustache.

'It's nice to meet you, Loukis.' The army man offered his hand.

'You too, Major.'

'You speak English then, how excellent.'

'Well, I am a product of the English school system,' Loukis pointed out.

'Yes, quite,' the major replied and returned to his seat. 'So how are you finding it here? A little boring I imagine, what with your cousin being away and only having the old man for company.'

'Less of the old,' Demetris moaned, mock offence paining his face.

'Well, you're hardly a teenager, old boy,' the major replied, 'and your nephew here must be climbing the walls after the excitement of Keryneia. If your own lad was still at home, he could at least offer young Loukis some company, although I guess Costas must be a few years older, isn't he?'

'A couple of years,' replied Loukis, noticing Demetris's smile slip from his lips. 'However, you need to work on your memory or your intelligence, Major; my cousin's name is Kypros not Costas.'

'Ah yes, Kypros,' the major laughed. 'How strange of me to forget.'

'It's probably your age,' Demetris gently ribbed him, visibly relaxing again.

'Yes, you're right. Well, I can't stay here all night. We've got terrorists to catch, even on Christmas Eve.' The British man got up and handed Lella his cup. 'Thanks for the tea, Mrs Thedosias and, Demetris, we'll talk again soon, yes?'

'Of course,' replied the police sergeant, 'it's always a pleasure having you visit. Although next time, bring a drop of that Scotch you've got tucked under the dashboard!'

Demetris walked his guest to the gate and watched him drive off. When he returned he made straight for the fireplace.

'Damn, that was close.' He pulled the grate away from the hearth and removed the iron chimney guard. Seconds later, two men emerged, patting black soot from their clothes. They wore smiles on their grubby faces and rifles slung over their shoulders.

'Now let's start that bleeding fire,' Demetris ordered, clapping his monster hands together. 'It's cold as hell in here.'

Unbidden, Loukis went outside to gather some logs. When he returned, the two men were warming their hands with tiny cups of hot coffee, Lella was bringing meat and potatoes to the table, and Demetris was briefing their guests on the good major. Loukis made up the fire, took a seat and waited for an explanation. Instead he got a history lesson on school curricula.

'It's true what you told the major – you are a product of the English school system,' Demetris commented, dipping his bread into the meat gravy swamping his plate. 'For you, this struggle of ours is no doubt a combination of wishing to be free of the occupiers' rules and your own private revenge, but to the old school, to people like me, the struggle goes much deeper; it's about fulfilling our destiny. When I was a boy, we were taught one thing: to believe in a future with Greece, our motherland – and all our lessons prepared us for that.

'When the British took Cyprus from the Ottomans, our people believed that reunion would soon become a reality, and at first it wasn't so bad – the British took only our money – but as time went on they dug their heels into our island and worked to supplant the mother we yearned for. Like farmers killing a tree they began by cutting off our branches and pouring oil on to the stubs; those branches were our schools, Loukis. The British brought in a common curriculum for both our communities, and the teaching of Greek became just another language – nothing to do with our mother tongue. Greek history became part of the general history of the Balkans, Greek maps were banned, along with pictures of Greek royals. No longer was the Greek national anthem taught or Independence Day celebrated. Soon the

Greek flag was forbidden – in fact, anything that bore the blue and white colours of Greece was outlawed. Therefore, you see, Loukis, EOKA's fight has never been about greater rights or opportunities; it is a struggle for our union with Greece, for the realization of the one thing our history has prepared us for. Over the years, the British have worked to rob us of this future, but they cannot win; they will lose in the end, because you cannot deny a man his destiny.'

When Demetris finished, his eyes shone glassy with emotion and, for the first time, Loukis understood that the policeman wasn't aiding EOKA out of fear or loathing for the British; he was compelled by a simple sense of fate. His patriotism flowed from the blood of ancestors long dead, and his determination to realize their dreams was hewn from the gravestones of an ancient history.

Demetris's passion for Cyprus and his love of her mother Greece made Loukis feel ashamed of his own motives, but even so, deep within his soul he knew there was nothing the old man had said that would ever change them. As far as Loukis was concerned, Cyprus was his country, and he loved her, but his mother was the woman who had spilt blood to give him life, and the cause that he fought for started and ended with a girl.

After the meal, both Demetris and Lella removed them-selves to the kitchen. Before he went, the policeman had placed a heavy hand on Loukis's shoulder, signalling him to stay put. The boy did so, and he looked at the two remain-ing men expectantly, waiting for them to take lead of the conversation.

'I'm Antoniou and this is Harris,' the man directly opposite finally informed him. He was small and wiry, with a sharp face half-hidden by a flat cap. The other guy, Harris, had a line of dark moles on his left cheek. They looked like muddy tears, but his brown eyes sparkled with good humour and honesty.

'You will also come to know us as Xanthus and Balius,' Antoniou continued.

'Which one of you is Xanthus?' Loukis asked, and Harris grinned.

'I'm Balius,' he said. 'I take it you know why we're telling you this, then.'

'Yes,' Loukis confirmed.

'Good,' interrupted Antoniou. 'We don't have much time.'

In the space of twenty minutes, the two 'old timers' from his cell explained their methods of communication. Every morning, they instructed, at differing times, but early enough not to lose the day, he should make his way to the village. Occasionally, on the tree by the village well, he would see some wool snagged on the second lowest branch; this was the signal that he was needed. When he saw the sign he was to head immediately to the group's hideout. Stelios would reveal its whereabouts the following morning. Loukis was to meet him at 8.40 a.m. outside the coffee shop, when most of the villagers would be in church.

'I take it we don't need to tell you to keep your mouth shut about all of this?' Antoniou inquired brusquely.

'No, you don't,' Loukis replied calmly.

'Good. Then we'll see you when we need you.' The two men downed their glasses of *zivania*.

'And Loukis,' Antoniou added, 'on matters of duty you will hereby be known as Echion, OK?'

'Fine,' agreed Loukis, and after Demetris had checked the coast was clear, the two men disappeared into the night.

The next morning at the café, Stelios was perturbed.

'Let me get this right,' he moaned. 'Your codename is Echion, as in one of the *spartoi* who rose from the teeth of the dragon of Ares?'

'I guess so,' replied Loukis vaguely. 'Why? What's your name?'

'Priapos.'

'Priapos? What's wrong with that? He was a fertility god, wasn't he?'

'Yes, he was,' affirmed Stelios, 'but he was also so incredibly ugly his own mother threw him out of the house.'

As Yianoulla helped serve the food, she paused for a moment, confronted by two extra plates battling for space on the long table.

'Nothing for Nicos,' Dhespina prompted her.

'And Loukis?' her daughter-in-law asked.

'He'll have what the rest of us are having. The dead can't eat, Yianoulla, but the missing will never lose their appetite.' Dhespina took her seat, cradling her latest grandchild in her arms, and Christakis glanced at his wife, urging her with his eyes to do as his mother wished. On his lap, Angelis sat crying.

'Marios, I must say this is a lovely piece of work.' Georgios ran a finger along the edge of a wooden board that was saving the table from an oven-hot meat dish. Marios beamed with pride, and Christakis patted his back in recognition of a job well done. The mats had been Marios's own idea; after watching the plank ends pile up in a corner, destined to end their days as firewood, he asked if he could make something of them. As Christakis found no reason not to let him try, Marios got to work; sawing and sanding the leftovers into a collection of square and rectangular boards. As his confidence grew, he etched designs on his creations, carving shapes into the wood that were drawn from his imagination. The result was a collection of rather fine place mats, with an abstract quality that caught the eye of several customers who had come into the shop.

'I'm going to try door-stoppers next,' Marios informed his father.

'That's a fine idea, son. It's always the little things in life that get neglected, and yet they tend to be of the most use.'

As he spoke, Georgios felt a lump rise in his throat. It was funny the kind of things that set him off these days. Marios had genuine talent; a God-given gift that had somehow lain dormant. Of course, it took the loss of one son to allow the other to find his path, but who knows? Maybe Marios would have arrived there anyway, even with Nicos by his side. There again maybe he wouldn't have done. But the point was he had got there and Georgios was more proud than he could possibly say.

'So, Michalakis,' Georgios said, pulling himself away from the melancholy creeping to take him, 'any news from the big city?'

'The only news I want to hear from Lefkosia is that my son has finally found a woman to marry,' Dhespina interjected.

'Archbishop Makarios will be back in charge before the day comes that this bachelor gets married.' Christakis laughed, and Michalakis nodded in agreement.

'He's right, Mamma. Christakis has already bagged the best-looking girl on the island, so anyone I bring home is bound to be a disappointment both to you and to me.'

'Michalakis, you're making me blush!' Yianoulla's face lit up with a broad smile. Because her husband was unwittingly mean with his compliments and the weight of the baby still clung to her stomach, the young woman appreciated her brother-in-law's words, even if they were made in jest.

'Michalakis is absolutely right,' Georgios confirmed, seizing the chance to keep the air light, 'and I think that deserves a toast!'

'Why, because I'm right for once?' asked Michalakis. 'Or because Yianoulla is a beautiful woman?'

'Because you are right, as always, because Yianoulla is beautiful, as always, and because God has blessed this house with intelligence and good looks!'

Georgios filled their glasses, and even though Dhespina's heart was beyond cheer, she played along with the game because her family needed her to. Throughout the day, they had conspired to chase away the sadness eating at her bones, and she was grateful for their attentions. On Christmas Day, of all days, she needed their care.

During morning mass, Dhespina had prayed with the feverish intensity that infects the near-hopeless; she begged God to show His mercy and bestow upon her a miracle, and she kissed the saints that they might convince the Almighty to come to her aid. But the door remained closed to the vision she asked for, and she was forced to carry her anticipation to Nicos's grave.

As they emerged from the church, and despite their differing faith, Stavros and Pembe joined what was left of her family. They prayed for the soul of her dead son with hands that wiped at their faces and opened to the heavens. Dhespina thanked them for their efforts and though no miracle came, the day remained young and she refused to give up hope.

Shortly before lunch, Elena and Praxi came calling. The girl looked awkward and sickly, and Dhespina invited them to stay to eat. However, Praxi cut her to the quick by insisting she had to go and ready herself. She had a meeting with the rich boy Yiannis, and the betrayal Dhespina felt on behalf of her missing son strangled her into silence. Elena whispered that her child was handling her grief in her own way, and though Dhespina nodded, she wasn't convinced. She hadn't seen sorrow written in the girl's eyes, she had found distance. This wasn't Praxi, or at least not the Praxi she knew. This was some kind of changeling; a cold spirit gazing from the eyes she had always known, and always loved. Dhespina didn't think she could ever forgive the girl.

Once the roast had been devoured, and the wine and conversation had trickled to a stop, Christakis and his family left for their home in a flurry of sweet kisses and hard hugs. Not long after, Marios and Michalakis retired to their beds and Dhespina finally took the two untouched plates from the table.

'Here, Dhespo, let me do that.' Georgios gently reached for his wife's hands, but she elbowed him away with barely contained anger.

'I can clear a table, Georgios!' She spat the words with a harshness that shocked her husband, but he no longer had the stomach for a fight, so he bowed his head and walked away. Though Dhespina ached to follow and rain apologies upon him, she was frozen by disappointment. She had somehow convinced herself that Loukis would return to spend Christmas with his family, and in the days leading up to it, she had played the scene over and over in her head; imagining the tears and the anger, the questions and answers, the upset and the sweet comfort of having him home. But his place remained empty, no word came to reassure her, and it was as if she had lost him all over again.

Forcing herself into action, Dhespina tipped Loukis's plate over the bucket. As the cold potatoes slipped into the mess that would be eaten by their goat, she suddenly caught the meat, overwhelmed by an urge to take something to Apollo. She realized it was close to sacrilege, but her God had done little to help her so far, and so she carried her son's dinner to the small mound of earth beneath the orange tree.

Under the moon's light, the lamb looked ugly and obscene in her fingers, its wrinkled skin pitted by lumps of white fat, and she worried she should have come earlier, when the flesh was still warm and the scent of its taste would have alerted the dog's spirit.

'Apollo, please take care of him,' she whispered.

She bent down to place the meat on the grave, but as her hands touched the soil they flinched at its hardness. The dog would be nothing more than a collection of bones; a fond memory turned to dust. How could he ever bring back her child? Dhespina's knees hit the ground, and the towering grief of her helplessness came crashing upon her in a wave of utter desolation. Her bones shook with a low, plaintive wail that boiled from her stomach.

Moaning, she rocked on the ground until the rhythm of anguish grabbed her by the throat and pushed her cries into the silence that had been left by her sons. Shattering the calm of the night, she wailed with a terrible fury until she yielded to instinct and allowed her misery to melt into a long, mournful note. She howled to the moon just as her son had done before her, because the blood that coursed through his veins was also her own.

As Dhespina's torment echoed through the valley, bringing goose bumps to the arms of their neighbours, Georgios came running for his wife. At his touch, she screamed as though her very skin was on fire, but he remained holding her until she could struggle no more and the wind took her cries and swept them away.

Across the snow-covered peaks, along the frozen soil of the plains and up to the evergreen forests of Troodos, the wind took Dhespina's grief and unleashed it among the leaves of the trees. They delivered her message in a shivering whisper.

In his bed, Loukis woke in a cold sweat.

When the spring sun arrived to warm the earth, the anger that had claimed Loukis began to loosen its grip. Instead of seeing Praxi wielding an axe as she sliced open his heart, he felt the heat of her skin and the softness of her lashes playing on his cheek. He remembered the sparkle in her eyes as she teased him and the warmth of her lips where she kissed him, and as the island stretched from sleep he smelled her presence in the heady pine of the forest, the scent of the flowers and the musky grains of the soil. His birthday had been and gone and, with every passing day, he stepped closer to forgiveness. When he returned to claim her, he knew he would be ready and she would see that he was. All his anger and frustration would be buried with the boy and the girl they once were, and they would meet a new world together, as man and wife. Of course, crippled as Loukis was by an inability to see beyond his own horizons, he had no under-standing of the chaos he had left behind him or of the monstrous ramifications of his sudden departure. He had no idea that the only girl he had ever loved had opened her legs to another man in order to claim him as the father of their baby, and he had no knowledge of the hurried wedding that had taken place between a groom pale with shock and a bride white with sickness. And because Loukis had no awareness of any of this, he was able to sit under the brilliant sun and fill his head with hazy dreams of his future with Praxi.

'What's the matter with you?' Toulla came shuffling through the gate.

'What do you mean?'

'You're smiling,' she said.

'I'm just enjoying the sunshine, that's all. Here, take the weight off your feet; we can't have a woman in your con-dition standing around.' Loukis rose from his chair to offer it to the EOKA girl. She patted her stomach carefully, and shook her head.

'If you wouldn't mind, dear Loukis, I'd rather get going and deliver this "baby" of ours.'

Loukis laughed. She had a point. Homemade bombs had a tendency to be temperamental.

'Come then, my love. The child will not wait for ever.' Loukis took her arm and they walked out of the garden. He enjoyed his missions with Toulla; she was easy company, with a dirty laugh and a straightforward manner. She said what she meant and she meant what she said. He liked that. It felt honest. Although she wasn't particularly pretty – her nose was large and her lips too thin – she was attractive in her way, with an earthiness that made up for her looks. She also had fantastic full breasts, just as Stelios had claimed.

'The British still think they've got Afxentiou surrounded at Machairas Monastery,' Toulla told him as they laboured up the hill to the main road.

'Well, that's at least one piece of good news,' Loukis replied. Over the past two months, the resistance had been battered by a series of offensives. Some seventeen hideouts had been uncovered, flushing out scores of their men. Afxentiou himself had been wounded in battle and had sought refuge among the priests. Thankfully, by the time the occupiers caught wind of his whereabouts, he had already fled. Now, Loukis and his cell were helping with diversionary operations to keep the heat off the district commander. At night they severed telephone lines and set fires to draw the soldiers away. And the bombs Stelios now made, which Toulla carried strapped to her belly, were left at designated dropping points to keep the fugitive and his men supplied.

'Afxentiou got a message out,' Toulla continued as she waddled along the road. 'He said that, no matter the size of our misfortunes, we will not retreat. He said we should throw ourselves into the fight with greater determination than ever. He said "our faith in victory is unshakeable."'

'To be honest, Toulla,' Loukis replied, 'I'd be happiest right now if the only thing unshakeable was your stomach.'

The girl started giggling. She liked Loukis. He didn't fill his talk with grand statements or flowery speeches like some of the other boys. He simply did what was asked of him and

took all developments, good and bad, with a calm accept-
ance. He made her feel safe. Although Toulla tried not to
show it, she was often paralysed with fear, not least when she
had explosives strapped to her body. She was petrified
the bombs would go off accidentally, or be triggered by the
rough hands of a disrespectful soldier. But Loukis was a
giant of quiet control, and he helped her to forget her fear.
Whenever they came across a British patrol he acted with
such an easy affability that they quickly dismissed any
suspicion they had felt.

'Hold on.' Loukis pulled gently at Toulla's arm as they
came to the village. On the tree by the well was a clump of
wool, apparently snagged on the second to bottom branch.
'Are you seeing what I'm seeing?'

'Ah-ha.' Toulla nodded. 'I guess we'd better abort the
mission and get to the hideout.'

'What about the "baby"?'

'I suppose it must come with us,' she grinned.

As the two of them headed up the track that wound itself
around the steep slope away from the village, they caught
sight of Stelios. His head was cast downwards, and he
walked with heavy legs.

'It's OK,' he said, as he neared. 'I'll save you the bother of
climbing any further.' The boy paused to deliver his
message, but his breath was abruptly taken by tears.
Struggling to put a lid on his emotions, he blurted out the
reason and slumped to the ground.

'Afxentiou is dead,' he told them.

As Stelios sobbed unashamedly, Toulla's legs crumbled in
shock and Loukis quickly moved to take the weight from
around her waist. The two friends reached for each other

and wept. Unable to match their grief, Loukis distanced himself and buried the explosives under a large rock, noting its position to recover them later.

'Come on,' he said finally, stirring the pair into action. 'Let's head back to the village.'

By the time the three of them entered the coffee shop, news of Afxentiou's death was already passing among the men gathered there. Some of their faces were wet with tears.

'The occupiers were led to Afxentiou's hideout,' Stelios told them in a hoarse whisper. 'They surrounded him – helicopters and everything. When they ordered him to come out he refused, and so they threw a grenade into the cave. He answered the bastards with more of his own. Next, they brought fifty gallons of petrol and drowned the area before setting it aflame. But because God protects the just, the rain came and killed the fire. The occupiers then used plastic explosives to blow the roof off the cave. Even that failed. However, it meant they could throw petrol into the cracks and turn the hideout into a fireball. For good measure, they also threw more grenades at the entrance and pummelled the place with bullets. Not even Afxentiou could survive that mauling. He died yesterday.'

As he finished, Toulla crossed herself and added to Stelios's tears. Although Loukis suffered no such sense of devastation, he thought the commander's death was a damn shame and was sorry he had never got the chance to meet him.

Afxentiou, a farmer's son from Lysi, had been the closest it got to the mythical heroes of ancient Greece, and in the days following his death, an eerie silence hung over Troodos, as if even the birds could no longer find the heart to sing.

But as grief turned to anger, what was left of the EOKA mountain gangs fell under a new command, and the fight took on a fresh urgency and determination. Afxentiou had fought to the death, and EOKA would not forget his sacrifice or betray his courage. A little over three weeks later, Loukis was dispatched on his first bombing mission.

As he was a novice, Stelios came with him, hiding his jam-jar creation of high explosives and bolts in a hollowed-out melon. 'Basically, there's the fuse wire, then the det cord, followed by the detonator itself,' he explained. 'You don't light the det cord, because it goes up instantaneously, and the fuse wire by itself isn't hot enough to ignite a detonator. So, we light the fuse when we get close to the target, throw it, hoping it lights the det cord on the way, the det cord then ignites the detonator, which goes pop and sets off the explosives and . . . *boom!*'

'Well, as long as it doesn't go pop and boom before we get to the target,' Loukis muttered.

'Sadly, I can't guarantee that, my friend.' Stelios steadied himself with a branch to avoid falling. With the occupiers primed for revenge attacks, the pair could no longer risk bluffing their way through checkpoints, so they moved gingerly through the forest, edging around precipitous drops that often appeared from nowhere. Thankfully, they knew the area fairly well, because the police station they were heading for was an irritation favourite; every few weeks they crept through the undergrowth to cut the landline to the local infantry battalion. They would then bind the break with regulation army tape stolen by an EOKA sympathizer. It meant that a signaller, with an escort of riflemen, would have to make his way along the cable, checking each of the previous repairs until he found the latest cut. It was a job that took Loukis seconds to complete and the British hours to fix.

'What's with all the bell ringing?' Loukis asked, hearing the frantic peals coming from the village a few yards below them.

'No idea. But take a look at this.' Stelios handed him a leaflet he had plucked from a nearby tree. It was written in Greek, but the hand was British and the tattered paper promised 'Rewards for Arms'. Loukis read the list aloud: '£100 for a Bren gun or mortar; £50 for a Sten gun; £40 for a rifle; £30 for an automatic pistol; £20 for a revolver; and £10 for a sporting gun.'

'Hell, if I handed in all the weapons dotted about this island I could *buy* Greece, let alone be joined with her,' noted Stelios. As the station was around the next bend, he took out his matches. According to the plan, once the fuse was lit, they would have just enough time to tear around the corner, lob the bomb through the window and leg it to safety.

'You know, I've now made so many of these beauties I can practically do it with my eyes closed,' bragged the older boy, showing no hint of anxiety as he set fire to the fuse. Unfortunately, his feet proved less steady than his nerve, and as he spoke the earth shifted beneath him. Flailing wildly to regain his balance and save himself from the ten-foot drop below, he reached with his free hand to catch a branch. But in his panic, the melon was sacrificed. Before Stelios could stop it, the bomb jumped from his hand to land on the tree roots below. The boys stared at it in stunned horror. Slowly, the yellow ball nudged forwards and began to move. As it continued its journey, picking up pace as it bounced down the rocky ravine, Loukis and Stelios scrambled after it.

'Jesus!' cried Stelios.

They tore down the slope, snagging their clothes on thorny branches and ripping their hands on sharp stones as their feet slipped beneath them, following the melon's terrifying trip until it disappeared over a wall built to keep the forest back. With a dull thud, it fell on to the road below. Nearby, four small children were playing marbles. Noticing the fruit come unexpectedly into their play area, a tiny girl in a yellow dress with a matching ribbon in her hair got up from her knees and walked towards it.

'No!' screamed Loukis and Stelios in unison, and the surprised girl recoiled as they jumped in front of her with torn clothes and wild eyes. Loukis was first to the melon and he picked it up quickly, throwing it as far as he could, away from the children, who were now crying in shock and incomprehension. Less than a second later, there was an almighty bang, and Stelios jumped on the youngsters to cover them. As the explosion echoed around the stone village, a cloud of dust reared ahead of them, and they looked up to see a priest, stunned and dazed, emerging from a smoking porch.

'Scarper!' Stelios commanded, and he and Loukis ran for it, not daring to apologize or even look back.

Considering the enormity of their mistake, the pair ran straight for the rendezvous point they had been told to go to after completing their mission. It was an old barn, long forgotten by anything larger than rabbits or snakes.

'Let me get this right,' Antoniou said stiffly after the two boys burst into the hideout to sheepishly reveal their error, 'we send you to bomb a police station, and instead you take out the local church?'

'Yes,' confirmed Stelios, 'that would be correct.'

'And did you happen to notice that the bells were in full peal?' asked Harris, trying hard to stifle his amusement.

'Well, now you mention it, we did comment on that, didn't we, Loukis?'

'Yes, we did, Stelios.'

'And do you have any idea why the bells were ringing?' asked Harris.

'Well, no,' Stelios admitted.

'I'll tell you why they were ringing,' continued Antoniou. His eyes were serious and his tone was deliberate, as if he were addressing a couple of idiots. 'Today is one of the brightest days in the history of Cyprus – and of Greece and EOKA. You see, boys, the British have backed down in the face of a popular uprising, and all over this island Greek Cypriots are savouring the sweet taste of that success and the anticipation of their future freedom. *Today*, gentlemen, the bells were ringing because our colonial rulers are about to free Archbishop Makarios. And what did you do to celebrate this very fine occasion?'

'We bombed a church . . .' muttered Stelios.

'Yes,' agreed Antoniou, his eyes wide with disbelief. 'You bombed a church.'

5

The Keryneia-bound bus was unusually lively, with passengers reciting old commentary from Radio Athens and gaily embroidering the facts of the archbishop's release with their own colourful fancies.

'Neither Middle East oil, nor Western defence, nor Turkish opposition shall deter the Cypriots' claim to determine their present and their future,' one man stated authoritatively, repeating Makarios's speech to the other travellers onboard.

'He was greeted like a king,' a woman near to him sighed. 'Our own archbishop, the pride of the motherland.'

'That he was, Mrs Papadopoulos, that he was,' the man agreed.

'I heard they threw flowers at his feet and rained kisses on his fingers,' a woman behind them added, 'and they carried him through the streets on a silver chariot.'

'My nephew was in the crowd,' an old man informed them, touching the cross hanging from his neck. 'He said he'd never seen anything like it; the city was awash with a river of tears and a crippled boy leapt to his feet as Makarios drove by.'

'Oh, merciful Lord,' the women muttered as one, and a few of them cried into their hankies at news of the miracle.

As Michalakis listened to the passengers' excited chatter – and their fantastical adaptations – he glanced at the two Muslims sat quietly at the back. They were motionless in their seats, their eyes concentrated on their laps. The journalist recognized their anxiety – the riots and arson attacks in the capital had made everyone tense – but this was no gathering of rabble-rousing patriots; the Greeks on the bus were mainly old women accompanied by their elderly husbands. They were far too immersed in their own happiness to pay attention to the minority who weren't.

Almost a month had passed since Makarios escaped the Seychelles, yet talk of his liberation continued to echo around the island, growing ever grander with every retelling. The account on the bus was largely correct; finally released from his thirteen-month imprisonment but banned from returning to Cyprus, Makarios was driven through Athens in a white Cadillac convertible, like the all-conquering hero his devoted subjects believed him to be. His triumphant procession was greeted by the hysterics of women and the cheers of men, who thronged walkways, climbed rooftops and hung from balconies to get a glimpse of the great man. Flowers had indeed been showered upon his car, although Michalakis had heard no reports of miracles taking place, and the streets were decorated with banners and painted signs demanding *enosis*. For the Greeks, the archbishop's release was welcomed as the precursor to the end of an epic struggle. However, Michalakis wasn't so convinced. Cyprus was currently a mess of political aspirations, inter-communal suspicion and sprawling violence. Britain had grown tired of both the conflict and the recriminations flying at home and abroad, and now sought to disentangle herself by advocating tripartite talks with Greece and Turkey to find a solution. However, Makarios refused to entertain any negotiations that didn't include him, and the Turkish government remained fiercely opposed to any consultation that did include him. Therefore, even though Grivas had ordered a ceasefire to coincide with the archbishop's release, the prospects of a settlement looked as distant as ever. Without the restraining influence of Makarios, the EOKA campaign had turned bloody and brutal, and when it stoked the fires of inter-ethnic violence, it added impetus to Turkey's demands to divide the two communities for their own safety. As a result, there were now not only Greek calls for *enosis*, but Turkish calls for *taksim*. In short, the island had reached an impossible stalemate: the British were looking for peace in self-government, the Greeks would only consider union with Greece, and the Turks were demanding partition. Michalakis was only twenty years old, but the horrors of the last two years had taken their toll and the sights he had seen and the stories he had heard had aged him beyond imagination. He was tired, and he longed for the peace he had known as a boy.

Leaving the bus at the harbour, Michalakis made the final part of his journey on foot. As he neared his home, he saw his mother at the gate bidding farewell to a striking young woman. Her black hair was long, and it shone in the fading sun. Even from a distance, he could see that she was uncommonly beautiful.

'Who was that?' he asked.

'The Germanos girl, Maria. She comes every day, hoping

for news of Loukis. I think she's a little in love with him.'

Michalakis felt a pang of disappointment at his mother's words, and the shock of it almost made him smile. He wasn't prone to such weakness, and its sudden appearance stirred his interest all the more. If he found the time, he'd try and happen across the Germanos girl, and see if she was as good as she looked.

Inside the house, the air was heavy with his mother's concoctions, and there was the hunched form of a woman hovering over the dining table. Her head was lost in a bowl of steaming, perfumed water and her hair was covered by a black headscarf. As Michalakis coughed, she started with a jolt and looked up, quickly wiping the moisture from her face. It was Praxi's mum, Elena.

'Oh, Michalakis, welcome home,' she greeted, getting to her feet to kiss him. He bent down to allow her. 'What a wonderful surprise. How is your job going? I must say we are all so very proud of you.'

'The job's going well – it's busy and tiring, but it's never dull,' he replied honestly. 'How's your Praxi?'

As the words escaped from his mouth he immediately regretted them.

Elena shot Dhespina an apologetic look and hurriedly mumbled some well-rehearsed phrases about married life and the blessings of God. Feeling the heat of embarrassment rise up his neck, Michalakis said he was glad her daughter had found a good man to marry – not believing she had, but rather because he was unsure how else to recover from the blunder. His mind hadn't ventured beyond making pleasantries, and his thoughtless inquiry had inadvertently dragged up the poor woman's shame. A shotgun wedding was the nightmare of every Greek mother, and the sleepless nights Elena had subsequently endured had scratched claw marks in her face.

Michalakis had been as shocked as anyone when he had heard about the wedding, partly because of its regrettable speed and the complication of his youngest brother, but mainly because Praxi had married Yiannis Christofi. Ever since his former classmate had surprised him with a kiss and Michalakis had surprised him with a punch, Michalakis had assumed he was *omofulofilos*.

'Where's Papa?' he asked.

'In his workroom,' his mother replied, and Michalakis took the chance to escape the sorry atmosphere he had created.

'It's a crying shame, all right,' his father acknowledged when his son explained the awkward conversation that had just taken place. 'God knows how Loukis will take it when he comes back.'

'If he comes back,' Michalakis responded, and his father shot from his seat and clipped him around the ear. 'Hey!' he protested.

'You deserved that,' his father responded, and went back to resoling Mr Televantos's shoes.

'I was only making a point. We've heard nothing from Loukis for more than six months.'

'It doesn't mean he's not coming back,' his father insisted. 'Your mother would feel it if the boy wasn't returning, and she doesn't.'

'Well, let's hope she's right.'

'Have you ever known your mother to be wrong?'

'Not that I'd ever tell her,' Michalakis grumbled, and Georgios chuckled. His wife was indeed a formidable creature. For more than two decades, her ferocious temper, as well as the lazy swing of her round hips, had kept him tantalized. While her friends had wilted under the onslaught of middle age, Dhespina had grown more curious, more alive and more beautiful with each passing year. In truth, Georgios was in awe of his wife, which is why when grief came between them it hit him in the stomach with the force of a truck. After Nicos died and Loukis disappeared, they were somehow lost to each other. Thankfully, his wife's lunatic episode at the dog's grave had changed all that; allowing Georgios to wrestle her in the dirt of their garden and win back the woman he married, albeit greyer than before and a little more muddy. Their lives had irrevocably changed, there was no running away from it, but Dhespina was once again making her mixtures and ruling the house with quiet determination. And at night she brought her softness to their bed like she had always done. Although they continued to carry the heartache of loss in their breasts, they now shared that terrible burden together, and not as two souls separately chasing the same ghosts.

Yiannis woke up thirsty and alarmed. As he blinked away the storm that had swept through his dreams, his head continued to rattle with the sound of wind-battered doors. Searching the room, he saw the shadow of his wife pulling at a cupboard. Yiannis sat up and followed her with his eyes, watching her glide to the wardrobe, where she opened the wooden shutters and closed them again with a bang. She turned towards the bed and crouched low, as if to look underneath it. She then moved towards the bedroom door, and Yiannis got up to stop her.

Looming over her tiny frame with its distended stomach, Yiannis felt ugly and huge, like a monster holding a nightingale captive. In the twilight, his wife looked as pathetic as a child, achingly fragile and vulnerable, and the sight of her stirred emotions in his chest he had yet to fathom. Although Yiannis was still waiting to feel the warmth of their marriage – and even though the swell of her belly physically repulsed him – he knew he could find a way to love his wife, if only she'd let him.

'Praxi?'

She turned to his voice, and Yiannis realized that, while her body was awake, her eyes were glazed with sleep.

'What are you looking for?' he asked softly, taking her carefully by the arm to stop her from leaving the room.

'I can't find him,' she answered. Her voice sounded distant, like a dying echo.

'Who, Praxi? Who can't you find?'

She cocked her head to one side, looking at him and through him. 'Loukis,' she replied. 'I can't find Loukis.'

'OK, I've finished.' Stelios put down his pen with a flourish.

'I'm nearly there,' Toulla informed him, scribbling furiously on the pad in front of her.

'Me too,' agreed Loukis, who was bereft of ideas and weary of trying to find them.

Since EOKA had silenced its guns, the three of them had been burning with boredom in the heat of another summer, and Loukis was almost jealous of their leaders' temporary escape to the south coast. Despite the peace, Antoniou and Harris remained on the run, having shunned a British offer of amnesty.

'Be ready,' Antoniou had ordered them in their last meeting. 'We are honouring the truce to aid Makarios in his political endeavours, but the British are slippery and the Turks devious dogs, so this may change at any moment. Keep alert, keep your eyes on the tree, keep your mouths shut and may God keep you all safe.'

With that, the two men had disappeared into the undergrowth, leaving their less conspicuous protégés twiddling their thumbs. With no telephone lines to cut, no bombs to throw and no guns to run, the three friends decided to work for *enosis* by writing hate letters to Governor Harding. Stelios had got the idea from his mother, who had been busily penning resistance for the best part of two years.

'What have you got then?' Toulla asked Stelios.

'I think you'll like it,' he grinned. The boy gave a theatrical cough and climbed on to his stool:

'Dear Governor Harding, I would like to take this opportunity to congratulate you on the most excellent campaign of genocide you have waged against the innocent Greek Cypriots of this nation. Not since Genghis Khan has one man been so deserving of the title "psychopath". In order to fill the coffers of your bloodthirsty queen, you have ripped out the hearts of a million mothers and fed your worm-riddled stomach with the flesh of our brave heroes. It seems you find the greatest happiness in your inglorious attempts to vanquish the righteous, to chase them before you, to rob them of their wealth and to see those they hold dear bathed in tears. You have committed mass murder, dear Governor, with a smile on your lips and evil in your heart. Along the length and breadth of this beautiful island, you are despised beyond compare, and one day your fatuous head will be wrenched from your shoulders and it will fly from the catapults of those you would murder. You are a blood-stained ogre, Governor Harding, whose hands drip with the blood of your victims.

Yours sincerely, Mrs T.'

'Oh well done!' Toulla applauded loudly. 'That really is one of your best!'

'Why thank you, comrade. So, what have you got?' Stelios stepped down from the stool and folded his letter with inky fingers.

'Oh, it's not as good as yours,' Toulla answered modestly. 'But here you go . . .

"Governor Harding, you think yourself to be a military genius, but your prowess on the battlefield is derived from the nightmares of tyrants. Like Tamerlane, you have descended on Cyprus hoping to wield absolute power, with no care for justice or humanity. Your armies have swept through our island like a plague. Your only purpose is to loot and to strike terror into the hearts of innocent Greeks, and like Tamerlane you hope to wipe out our brave men and build your ivory towers with their skulls. But you will never succeed because . . ."

That's as far as I've got, sorry.'

'So far a very fine letter,' Stelios approved. 'I especially like the tower of skulls.'

'Thanks, my grandfather told me about that. I was think-ing of saying something about Harding using human spleens as a cloak, with buttons made of eyeballs. What do you think?'

'Oh, I'd definitely add that,' agreed Stelios. 'It doesn't

have to be factual, just hateful. Right, Loukis, what have you got?'

Loukis's heart sank. 'It's not finished,' he mumbled.

'Neither was mine,' Toulla reminded him. 'Just read what you've done.'

'I'd rather not.'

'Oh come on, Loukis, it can't be that bad,' Stelios encouraged.

'OK,' Loukis sighed, 'but it's short.'

'And no doubt very sweet,' Stelios added.

'I don't know about that.' Loukis wiped at the sweat building on his forehead and started:

'Governor Harding, you are a pig. You will die. In a sty. You pig.'

Loukis looked at his friends.

'Is that it?' Toulla asked.

'Yes.'

'Oh,' said Stelios.

Christakis thundered into the coffee shop and slapped *The Voice* on the table. The headline screamed 'Turkish plan to steal half of Cyprus', and Georgios frowned in response. Stavros leaned away from the newspaper in a futile effort to ignore the confrontation brewing.

'How is Marios doing?' he asked.

'Marios is fine, he's doing well,' Christakis muttered, and pointed an angry finger at the newspaper before them. 'Have you seen this? Can you believe it?'

The two older men kept silent. They didn't need to read the article, because the radio had been broadcasting its contents all morning; The Turkish Cypriot leader Dr Fazil Küçük had announced that Turkey wanted a section of Cyprus that would give their people, who made up just 18 per cent of the population, 50 per cent of the island. The Greeks were incandescent with rage.

'You know, when I was a child, Greek boys used to taunt me with songs on the way to school – "Little Turk, little Turk, your eyes are like sewers,"' Stavros told Christakis.

'They were just childish torments,' the carpenter replied gruffly.

'Perhaps,' Stavros continued, 'but what of their mothers, who used to tell them that Turks were no better than barbarous dogs who smelled bad because they weren't baptized? Oh don't get me wrong, we were no angels, my own aunt used to insist that you couldn't even trust the shadow of a Greek man; that they were all devil-minded from the poison they were fed in Church. But what I'm trying to say is, Christakis, there is an inherent dislike between our two communities and there has been violence – on both sides, I know – but if the Greek dream is realized, what becomes of the Turks?'

'They will continue to be a part of this island, as they have been for the past three hundred years,' insisted Christakis. 'But to wilfully conspire to cut themselves off and take with them our homes and our land is an un-forgivable exploitation of our problems.'

'But these are also our homes and our land,' Stavros reminded him. 'There is an old song that goes, "If I squeeze this soil, Turkish blood comes out, if I excavate this land, Turkish bones come out, oh what these Turks have endured." Believe it or not, Christakis, your Turkish neighbours are frightened of you, sitting terrified in their own homes, and there is a growing section of opinion that only partition can bring them peace of mind.'

'I don't believe anybody seriously thinks separation is the answer,' Georgios stated flatly. 'What we've got here is nothing more than political sabre-rattling.'

'I think you're right,' Stavros admitted. 'Personally, I don't think partition will solve our problems either, but didn't your own EOKA man Grivas once say, "When water and fire become intimate friends and when Hell and Paradise unite, then and only then shall we be the sincere friends of the Turks"?'

'Pay no heed to Grivas,' advised Georgios, washing the last of his coffee down with water. 'The colonel's time has been and gone. This is Makarios's game now. He's the man to sort out this sorry mess.'

Marios made his way to the cemetery walking on clouds. Before today, he had never given babies much thought, but when he found Praxi in the street – her legs wet and her husband out cold on the cobbles – he ran for the doctor and decided to hang around to see how it happened. Two hours later, a baby's cry overtook the screams of its mother, and the doctor came out of the house, smiling widely and telling them the baby had come into the world with the speed of a thunderbolt. He then set about bandaging the cut on Yiannis's head.

When Marios crept into the room, he saw Praxi sat up in her bed, looking more beautiful than he could ever remember. She held a bundle of blankets at her bosom, and hidden inside was the tiniest creature Marios could ever have imagined, with raw-looking skin, sharp black eyes and a head of fine, fluffy hair of the fiercest black.

'What is it?' he asked.

'It's a she,' Praxi smiled, placing a soft kiss on her little girl's head, 'and her name is Elpida.' As Marios cradled the baby, at Praxi's insistence, he agreed she couldn't have chosen a better name if she had searched the entire world, because *elpida* meant 'hope'.

'I guess she's hoping the kid doesn't grow up to look like her husband!' Nicos joked when Marios arrived at his grave-side to tell him the news.

'I can't see much danger of that happening,' Marios replied. Yiannis was not as fair as their brother Christakis, but his hair was a dull brown and his eyes a light hazel.

'The baby is too dark,' explained Marios. 'She looks more like Praxi, or even one of us.'

'Ooh, Marios, what have you been up to?' teased his dead brother and he blushed.

'Shut up, Nicos, you donkey!'

Immediately regretting his words, Marios kissed the head-stone and said 'sorry' before making his way home.

When Elena heard her grandchild had arrived, she grabbed the small bag of clothes she kept ready at the door and went running for the town. On the way she passed Stavros in his fields and, when she revealed why she was in such a hurry, he ordered her to jump on his new tractor. Elena was aghast at the attention their journey might bring, but her legs had grown old and so she thanked him for the ride.

On route to Keryneia, Stavros did his best to make small talk over the hellish rumble of the engine without touching on the fact that the baby was more than a month early, and Elena was grateful for his consideration. God knows she had kissed her lips sore trying to appease every saint under the sun so that they might delay the birth and restore some level of propriety to her daughter's tarnished reputation. Everyone knew first babies often arrived late, and she had prayed that this one would cling to the womb and allow Praxi to complete nine months of marriage. However, because the sinner cannot go unpunished, the baby had barely held on for seven months and now her daughter would pay for her immorality with a child cursed with the sickly constitution of the premature.

In front of the coffee shop that her son-in-law had yet to open, Stavros helped Elena down from the tractor. She thanked him for his kindness and rushed up the outside staircase to her daughter's living quarters. As she entered the bedroom she was surprised to see the windows pulled open. The sick needed quiet and darkness – bright sunlight wasn't going to help anyone, least of all this tiny baby.

In a corner, Praxi was placing her child into a cot after feeding. Yiannis greeted his mother-in-law with a kiss and left the women to talk while he attended to his business downstairs. As soon as the door shut behind him, Elena moved to the wooden cradle. When she neared, she caught her breath with dismay: her granddaughter was the picture of good health, with eyes bright and alert and cheeks round and plump. Like a bell ringing in Elena's head, the full truth of Praxi's dishonour came crashing upon her, and she stepped away from the cot to deliver a stinging slap on her daughter's face.

Praxi took her mother's violence without a word, allowing

only a single tear to fall in response to the attack. Elena then grabbed her in a fearsome hug and sobbed into her hair, because after setting eyes on the baby she fully comprehended for the first time the enormous sacrifice her daughter had made in order to protect her own child.

6

The creaking chorus of crickets stopped abruptly every time the boys moved. With the half moon blanketed by clouds, the air sat heavy on their chests and colluded with the dark to heighten their fear.

'What about snakes?'

'What about snakes?' another voice mimicked in a high-pitched whisper.

'I'm serious. What about snakes?'

'Don't be such a woman.'

'Right, so you're not worried about being bitten and having your leg cut off?'

'They can't cut off your legs, they're snakes; they don't have hands.'

'Not the snakes! The doctors! I heard they have to amputate if the poison takes hold.'

'You'd be dead before we could get you to a doctor.'

'Oh, that's a comfort . . . I hate snakes.'

'*Will you not shut up?*' The boy crouching ahead turned to hiss at the two lagging behind. Toni was tense to the point of snapping, and the bickering following him through the undergrowth was tearing at his patience. Beneath the sweat-drenched shirt he wore, his heart hammered with anxiety, and his weapon slipped between fingers wet with nerves. He had come a long way since taking the oath in Skylloura's dim chapel, but he was now out of his district and well out of his comfort zone.

'Shush!' he suddenly commanded, stopping dead in his tracks, only to be rear-ended by the lad behind.

'What is it? What have you heard?' the boy asked nervously.

'Shush, will you!'

Reacting to the sound of something unknown, the three of them simultaneously hit the ground with dull thuds. Some way ahead of them, dry twigs crunched to the rhythm of footsteps.

'Oh God,' prayed the boy with the snake phobia. 'How many do you reckon there are?'

'At least two,' assessed Toni. He dragged his hands down his trousers to dry them and aimed his gun roughly in the direction the noise had come from. The boys were taking dynamite and detonator charges to a drop-off at Keryneia. If caught, they faced the death penalty. Toni was only seventeen years old, but he planned to live for at least seventeen more.

'Who goes there?' he barked in Greek as false courage took charge of his fear. In reply, the footsteps stopped and the crickets hushed their song. The boys looked at each other. The whites of their eyes shone bright.

'Do you think it's the British?'

'I hope not,' Toni whispered.

As they strained to see through the black, gnarled branches of the olive grove, the footsteps started again.

'Who goes there?' Toni demanded again, but this time fright grabbed a hold of his throat and it pushed his voice higher. Sweat dripped from his forehead and fell stinging into his eyes. As he moved to wipe his face, fallen branches and dead twigs snapped ahead of them, growing ever louder and suddenly rushing towards them. In sheer panic, the boys opened fire. Amid the light and explosions a hellish scream shattered the night and the boys roared forward, pressing wildly at their triggers, spitting bullets before them. In the confusion, adrenalin attacked their vision and they burst through the olive grove blinded by fear and desperation. There was nothing they could see and no longer anything they could hear above their own guttural shouts and terrified challenges. But as they broke into the clearing, their yells rapidly subsided and the three of them came to a bewildered halt. The clouds drifted across the moon, allowing a shard of brilliant light to fall upon the corpse of their enemy, and the boy afraid of snakes vomited noisily. In front of them lay an elderly donkey; its grey coat red with fresh blood. Weirdly, on its hooves were cups of battered leather that looked something like shoes.

The next morning, Stavros stumbled upon the murder and the sight of it all but ripped out his heart. A note of apology had been left in the old girl's mouth; it read 'Mistaken identity. Sorry. EOKA'. Taking his spade to the dirt, the farmer cried bitter, uncontrollable tears.

'Even the British don't shoot donkeys,' he shouted to his wife Pembe, and he buried Aphrodite in the ground along with his hope.

*

The aircraft flew over their heads for the second time that morning, breaking the peace of the mountains with its twin engines and Tannoy system.

'What on earth are they saying?' Toulla asked, craning her neck to the sky.

'I think they're asking us to give up,' Loukis informed her. The EOKA ceasefire was in its fifth month and the British had taken to aerially bombarding fugitive members with promises of safe conduct if they surrendered. A couple of men had taken advantage of the offer – only to find themselves fodder for the occupiers' propaganda campaign. The majority of fighters continued to ignore the amnesty out of loyalty, suspicion or embarrassment.

'Do you ever think of getting out?' Loukis asked.

'No! Of course not,' the girl replied, turning back on to her stomach. They were lying on a patch of dry grass in front of Stelios's home, waiting for him to be released from his mother's chores. 'Why, are you thinking of leaving?'

Loukis shrugged noncommittally, but he was restless and feeling the pull of home – and of Praxi. The proximity of Toulla's curves only reinforced his creeping need to reclaim the life he had known.

'So, what makes you stay?' he asked.

'My brother,' the girl answered. The certainty in her voice demanded an explanation, and Loukis waited. Toulla had never spoken about her family before, but then again, neither had he.

'He was arrested by the British,' she continued, more haltingly. 'After torturing him for weeks on end they finally let him go, but his life was pretty much over.'

'Why? What happened?'

'He killed himself,' she stated flatly. 'He was eighteen years old when the British picked him up, and their Special Branch monsters beat him with everything they had. They stuck pins into his flesh and burned him with cigarettes in order to get him to confess to so-called crimes he never committed. Most of the time, they kept him naked in his cell and bound his hands and feet together. Now and again they would put wet cloths over his face to suffocate him. Apparently, others had it worse. My brother said one man in his cell was routinely attacked by another Cypriot; a crazy man under the pay of the British. He was a lunatic, and he laughed and cried in the same breath as he raped his victims with broom handles and danced upon their broken bodies. Every day my brother spent in that hell hole, he believed he would be next. When he was finally released – because he was no one really, just a boy caught with a message – he was unrecognizable to us, his own family, and at night he would wake our house with his screams. It was horrendous, Loukis, ugly and terrifying. You can't imagine what it was like. Anyway, one day, two months after his release, my brother just gave up. He couldn't shake off his fear and he couldn't move forward. My father found him hanging from a tree in our garden. After we buried him I vowed to do everything in my power to make those bastards pay for what they did to my brother and to my family. And I tell you, Loukis, I won't stop until they leave our island or we wash our soil with their blood. Let their families feel the pain we lived through, and continue to live through, let them try and find a way to carry on after death comes knocking at their door.'

Toulla broke down in tears and Loukis reached out to comfort her. At his touch, the girl crawled into his arms and buried her mass of curls into his neck.

'I'm sorry,' she wept. 'I'm sorry to cry like this in front of you.'

'No, I'm the one who's sorry,' Loukis whispered. And he was. He hadn't meant to drag up Toulla's tears. He had only been curious. Therefore, when she raised her head and climbed to his lips, he felt somehow responsible and unable to stop her. But even as he responded he shut down. Loukis had been there before, in grief and in tears, and though he stirred at the heat of her body, he had nothing to offer the girl but his own pent-up desire. He knew he could never give Toulla what she wanted. It simply wasn't in his power. Loukis wasn't blind, he had caught her looking at him during the long, idle days they shared together and he realized she engineered ways to be in his company when Stelios was preoccupied. And because he liked her, and in some ways even admired her, he couldn't lie to her.

'I'll never love you, Toulla,' he said as their lips parted.

'I know,' she admitted and cried even harder.

Elpida gurgled with delight every time Yiannis dipped his huge face into the folds of her blanket, and Praxi smiled fondly at their play. Although her husband continued to struggle with the noxious secretions her daughter expelled, sometimes with such violence it caused his face to pale and his throat to convulse, he was completely devoted to the child. Within weeks of her birth, woollen toys from the widows' cooperative fought for space in Elpida's cot and a rocking horse had been ordered from Christakis's work-shop, even though the baby was years away from appreciating the gift. Now, watching him nibble at her daughter's fingers as they reached for his mouth between half words and hums, Praxi wondered what it was that shaped his tenderness. With no blood to bind them, Yiannis's attachment to her daughter was curious and a blessing. Whether it was born out of ignorance or human instinct to protect, Praxi possessed neither the wish nor the courage to find out, but if Yiannis suspected the dark-eyed girl in his arms wasn't his, he never voiced it, and Elpida's face lit up whenever he took hold of her.

'Back to your mother,' Yiannis finally told the tot. As he handed her over, Elpida's face crumbled. Praxi took her daughter to her breast and rocked away her tearless protests.

'Will the coffee house be ready on time?' she asked.

'If the supplies come in,' he told her, laughing. He then kissed his wife's hair and headed downstairs.

Such cursory affection was as physically demanding as Yiannis ever got after the birth, and his lack of insistence for anything more only increased Praxi's determination to be a good wife to him. She didn't understand what motivated her husband, but she had almost grown to like him. He held her carefully before he fell asleep, and though his hands occasionally wandered over her breasts, there was never any urgency to his touch. It was almost as if he felt compelled to do something and a quick stroke was all he could manage. Since their marriage they had made love a handful of times, but his apprehensive explorations usually ended in humiliated apologies. Even her initial insistence that he take her – and save her – had been a pitiful duplicate of the ferocious love she had experienced, but it hardly mattered, because it was enough to complete her intent.

Praxi was certain her husband didn't desire her, but she realized he appreciated her. He often asked her opinion about matters of business and he seemed to genuinely value her input. And though sometimes she caught him looking at her, when she returned his gaze she found no hunger in his eyes, only a sad gratitude. Praxi didn't love Yiannis, and she never would, but she cared for him in a way she hadn't counted on when she had deceived him into taking responsibility for her downfall. And though her husband was often foolish and his brash comments rang hollow in considered company, his heart seemed intrinsically good and she vowed to compensate him for his ignorance with loyalty and kindness.

'No matter what happens, you make sure you take care of that man,' her mother demanded, days after Elpida's birth, when Yiannis had left them alone to take charge of the furniture arriving downstairs. They both knew what, or rather who, Elena was alluding to, and Praxi dutifully promised that she would never do anything to hurt her husband or disappoint her daughter, which is why, when Dhespina turned up and dipped her fingers into Elpida's mouth – hunting for tiny teeth – Praxi blocked the truth begging to be released.

'I recognize your child,' Dhespina told Praxi.

'Then you will also recognize my child has a loving father, a good home and a chance of a decent life,' Praxi replied coolly, and Dhespina left the flat with tears in her eyes.

When Dhespina arrived home, she headed straight for the den to put a pan on the boil. Adding a handful of dried rose petals, she stirred the water and breathed in the aroma. Although the scent gradually calmed her nerves it failed to soothe the pain of certainty that tightened her chest.

'Praxi's child belongs to Loukis,' she later informed her husband, before Marios joined them for dinner.

'Has she said so?' Georgios asked carefully.

'No, but the child's the spit of our son and, more than that, I feel it.'

Georgios sighed. He couldn't deny that his wife's proclamation made sense: Praxi's sudden interest in the Christofi boy; the hurried wedding; the premature birth. However, he knew beyond doubt that it was not their place to interfere, even if Elpida was indeed their grandchild.

'A feeling is not enough to destroy three lives,' he told his wife as gently as he could. 'If there is a truth to come out it will find a way, but it is not up to us to force it into the open. Promise me you won't do anything rash.'

'What can I do?' Dhespina asked, her voice breaking with emotion. 'If I say what I know to be true I curse my own granddaughter. May God forgive me, but I could kill Loukis right now!'

Georgios moved to embrace his wife. As he pulled her into his arms, Marios walked through the open door, loudly dropping his bag on the floor.

'Not you two as well,' he grumbled.

'What do you mean, not us two as well?' Georgios asked, letting go of his wife.

'Michalakis is at the gate mooning over Maria.'

'Is he now?' Dhespina inquired, thankful for the new intrigue that had arrived to take her mind from her thoughts.

'Yes, he is,' Marios confirmed, picking at the kebab waiting on the table. His mother slapped his fingers. 'Nicos says hello, by the way.'

'Hello, Nicos,' Dhespina and Georgios returned, sharing a sad smile as they did so, just as Michalakis walked through the door, a rare joy lighting his face. 'God, I'm starving!' he announced.

'Michalakis!' Dhespina cried. 'How many times . . .'

'Sorry, Mamma,' he apologized. 'You know, for a woman who creates more potions than a witch, you can be oddly pious when it comes to invoking the Lord's name.'

'A witch,' Marios giggled. 'That's a good one. So, have you finished with your girlfriend, then?'

'If you mean have I finished talking with Maria, then yes, that would appear to be the case, seeing as I'm now here looking at your hairy face.'

'I know which view I'd prefer,' Georgios interjected, and Dhespina pushed at his head as she moved to the kitchen to fetch the salad.

'So are you staying for the dance tomorrow?' she asked.

'No, I'm on the late shift. I need to be back before three.'

'Thank God for that – you spend more time here than you do in that room you waste your money renting,' his father stated.

'Georgios!' Dhespina shouted from the kitchen, reprimanding him for the blasphemy of wishing their son away.

'Sorry, Dhespo.' Georgios gave his sons a wink. 'So, what will you be working on tomorrow?'

'A couple of features, possibly the rise of Turkish resistance or the recent attacks on the trade unionists.'

'Is there any real Turkish resistance?' Georgios asked in surprise. 'I thought it was merely tit-for-tat rioting and arson attacks rather than a movement.'

'It is largely,' Michalakis admitted, 'but one Turk was

killed and three others seriously wounded a few weeks ago in an explosion at a house in Omorphita. The theory is that the men were making bombs with the idea of using them against Greeks should EOKA become active again.'

'Not more bombs . . .' Marios muttered. 'What is it with this place?'

'It's only a theory,' Michalakis assured his brother, patting his arm, but Georgios caught his eye and raised an eyebrow in question. Michalakis shook his head in answer.

'Is EOKA likely to become active again?' his mother asked, now joining them at the table.

'The British think they might,' Michalakis told her. 'They've recently discovered what they are calling "possible evidence" of preparations; large quantities of cartridges have been found near Lefkosia, plus a number of other small weapons caches, and in Pafos they found pipe bombs.'

'Active or not, EOKA are still shooting donkeys,' Marios added glumly.

'That was an accident,' Georgios assured his younger son.

'Tell that to Mr Stavros,' he replied.

'Here, pass me some of that kebab,' Michalakis ordered his younger brother. He was tired of talking and hearing about death. There was more to life, and right now much of it revolved around a young woman not a stone's throw from where he was sat. With the ceasefire holding, Michalakis was finding more time to make the journey home, and although he'd been so far stuck at polite conversation, if the island remained quiet he could possibly take some proper time off to pursue Maria in the way a woman like her needed to be pursued.

Unfortunately for Michalakis, the following day he

returned to Lefkosia only to find himself attending a hurriedly assembled press conference that soon kissed farewell to any thoughts of a vacation.

In front of a bank of reporters and photographers, the British chief of staff revealed apparently unequivocal evidence that EOKA was planning to resume operations. With his fair moustache bristling with indignation, the brigadier told of documents discovered in a mountain hide-out revealed by a surrendering EOKA commander. The papers outlined plans that included the blowing up of a major power plant, an attack on a police station and the assassination of a number of traitors.

'Altogether more than one hundred specific persons are known to be on EOKA's list for assassination if and when terrorism is resumed,' the brigadier informed the press. Michalakis filed his report with a sense of despair and utter irritation.

Lella was struggling with a sack of spuds when Loukis and Stelios spotted her waddling up the lane. Running to catch her, Loukis bent to take charge of the load and felt his shirt rip in response. The cool autumn wind blew through the split.

'It appears we may need to buy you some bigger clothes,' his 'aunt' noted with a grin.

'Do me a favour, Mrs Thedosias,' Stelios implored, 'buy him some new trousers while you're at it – the ones he's wearing are tight to the point of obscene!'

'It has been noticed,' Lella chuckled. 'Poor Demetris is starting to feel quite inadequate in his own home.'

'People! Please!' Loukis protested.

It was fast coming up to a year since Loukis had fled his home so that he might become a man, and even though his only major EOKA operation had ended with minor damage to a Greek church, he felt the achievement of his purpose in the broadness of his body.

'Now, can I interest you boys in a cup of coffee and a glass of *zivania*?' Lella asked.

'You can indeed, Mrs Thedosias,' Stelios replied. 'You can indeed.'

Loukis smiled. He liked Stelios a lot, much more than he could have imagined after their first encounter, but his speech had inexplicably become littered with dandified repetitions, and he had started smoking a pipe. He could only imagine how his brother Christakis would react should he and Stelios ever meet.

As Lella boiled up the coffee, the friends took a seat on the porch to catch the last of the warm sun. Taking out his pipe, Stelios mentioned that he thought Toulla might have designs on him.

'She's always hanging around my house these days. She never used to come around so much. What do you think?'

Although Loukis knew why the girl was occupying her time in such a way, he told Stelios that women were a mystery to him and he wouldn't know if she was interested or not.

'It's puzzling,' Stelios said. 'I used to think she was more interested in you.'

As Loukis searched for a way to respond without divulging the girl's embarrassment, Demetris arrived, rubbing his large hands together with news of an announcement.

'Harding is out!' he shouted.

'The governor?' Loukis asked in surprise.

'The very one.'

'Well, that's a pretty little development,' Stelios noted, packing his pipe with tobacco. 'A very pretty development, indeed.'

Loukis shook his head and continued. 'Why? What's happened?'

'The details are a little sketchy,' Demetris said, pulling up a chair to join them in the sun, 'but with Makarios refusing to do business with the swine that exiled him, there's a new governor on his way. His name is Sir Hugh Foot, he's the current governor of Jamaica.'

'So, the archbishop might be returning to us?' Stelios asked. His eyes were watering, and Loukis couldn't be sure whether it was as a result of the news or the smoke clogging his vision.

'It's early days, but there's certainly more chance of that happening with Harding out of the way,' Demetris informed him.

Pausing to thank his wife for the coffee she handed him, the policeman explained that, after the Brits' sobering experience at Suez, all thought of reasserting their dominance in the region had been forgotten, and Cyprus was no longer deemed essential to their plans. As governor, Harding had become identified with a policy of repression and if Britain hoped to negotiate a political settlement, he had to go. Sir Hugh, by all accounts, had enjoyed a success-ful career as a diplomat and he was favourably remembered on the island for the time he spent there during the Second World War. The man was liked by both Greeks and Turks.

'If the British are looking to salve the open sore they have made of this place, the appointment of a new governor is a step in the right direction,' Demetris informed them. 'Makarios is playing the political game – calling for self-determination after a period of self-government – and as long as we can contain the Turks' demands for *taksim*, we might see an end to this conflict, and the beginning of our future with Greece.'

Demetris slurped the last of his coffee before bringing his meaty hands to slam against his upper arms. The sun was starting its slow descent towards Pafos and stealing away the day's heat.

'Mother Mary, there's a nip in the air,' the policeman muttered to no one in particular. 'Feels like winter is on the way.'

As if in answer, the branches around them creaked in the breeze. Demetris got to his feet and ushered the boys inside the cottage, where the smell of pork and wine instantly flared their nostrils.

'My Lord,' Stelios sighed, 'is there anything more pleasing than Lella's *afelia*?'

'I could think of a couple of things,' Demetris returned, unleashing a shriek of embarrassment from his wife, still working in the kitchen.

'Why of course,' Stelios joined in, 'your good lady is also famed for her wonderful *sheftalia* and sumptuous *stifado*.'

'I wasn't limiting myself to the kitchen, boy!'

'Oh good God,' mumbled Loukis, 'any more of this and I'll be losing my appetite.'

'More for your friend then,' Demetris laughed. 'I take it you'll be joining us, Stelios?'

'I wouldn't miss this glorious assault on my salivary glands for the world,' the boy replied. He moved to the fireplace, where he tapped the dottle from the heel of his pipe into the grate.

By the time Stelios had cleaned his plate and exhausted his welcome, night had fallen and the afternoon breeze had grown blustery. With his collar turned up to ward off the chill, he entered his home shortly after 9 p.m. He closed the door, emitting a contented belch, and went in search of his mother – to eat the meal she almost certainly would have prepared him and to reveal the promising change of governor.

As Stelios devoured his mamma's meatballs in a state of near ecstasy, outside the rough wind slipped into a storm and unleashed a cacophony of howls as it pushed between gaps of masonry and wood. As the squall span across the mountains, it came to rest momentarily atop the capital, whipping the debris of daytime high into the night sky. Against the ancient doors of the mosque once known as St Sophia's a discarded leaflet slapped wetly upon the wood. Headed 'Bulletin Number One', the scrap of paper announced the formation of *Türk Mukavemet Teşkilatı* and called on every Cypriot Turk to 'stand by for instructions'.

7

Armed with sticks, bricks, paving slabs and firebombs, the snarling mobs surged through Lefkosia. Windows were smashed. Shops were set on fire. Families were left terrified. And after two nights of intolerable violence, barbed-wire barriers were erected to separate the two sectors.

The next day, Michalakis walked through the misery of the city's shell-shocked neighbourhoods. Glass crunched under his heels; gutted stores revealed blackened stomachs through windowless frames; doorways bore the stains of piss and excrement; and two lorries lay on their sides, like huge metal beasts poleaxed by hate. A day later the new governor toured the damage. By then the glass had been swept away and the windows boarded up. He spoke to Greek and Turkish shopkeepers, whose terror-filled stories were almost identical. Only their blame differed. Greeks had rampaged through the Turkish quarter, Turks had stormed the Greek. Both sides had sought to destroy the other with missiles and fire.

Three days later, the United Nations General Assembly ended its twelfth session with thirty-one member states voting in favour of a Greek resolution to entitle Cyprus to self-determination without delay. However, twenty-three states rejected the motion and twenty-four abstained. The vote was therefore indecisive, and the island remained under colonial rule with one community demanding *enosis* and the other calling for *taksim*. Nothing had changed. The world had considered the situation and walked away.

'My word, Marios, that is beautiful!' Praxi held up the mobile and peered closely at the wooden shapes. They were obviously meant to resemble some kind of creatures, but for the life of her she couldn't make out what.

'Do you recognize them?' Marios asked. He had been working on Elpida's Christmas present for nearly a month. The idea had come to him at Nicos's grave, like most of his best ones.

'Well . . .' Praxi ventured, 'this one here looks like a lion . . .'

'Yes! Exactly right,' Marios shouted with glee, taking the mobile from Praxi's hands. 'The lion is Christakis, because he is the leader and he's yellow.'

'OK,' Praxi nodded, smiling at his apt association.

'And this one here is an owl, and it represents Michalakis, because he's wise like an owl and he's always reading books. Then, the angel is Nicos, because he is dead and in heaven. The sheep, well, that's me, because Nicos says I always used to follow him like one, and the wolf is Loukis, because that's what he was born as. Now, Elpida will never have to be afraid at night, because she has five brothers to look after her – in this life and the next.'

Marios placed the mobile on the table and looked at Praxi proudly. Unable to stop herself, she burst into tears and hugged him tight. It wasn't the reaction Marios had been expecting, but when Praxi pulled back and he saw the smile on her face, he relaxed.

Bereft of the skills to sift sense from sentiment, Marios was often knocked dumb by the strangeness of women; when they were angry they pretended they weren't and when they were happy they cried like babies. Take the other night, when it was announced on the radio that the new governor had released a hundred prisoners as a present to their families – his mamma had wept as if the British man had just told the world he had taken the men out of their cells and shot them all.

'Praxi, do you think Loukis will come home this Christmas?'

'I don't know,' she replied hesitantly, turning to Elpida to stop him reading the hope in her face. 'Why do you ask?'

'I was just thinking that maybe Loukis was a prisoner in one of the governor's jails and maybe that's why he's stayed away for so long. And if that's what happened, maybe he's now free and he can finally come back to us.'

'Maybe,' Praxi replied, 'but don't pin all your hopes on him coming home just yet. Loukis will return when he's ready. I'm certain of that.'

'Yes, I suppose he will,' Marios agreed. 'He's a devil-minded creature all right.'

Praxi laughed. 'He sure is, Marios, but it doesn't stop us loving him.'

That evening, as Praxi tied the mobile to a beam above her daughter's cot, she let her fingers run over the shapes until they came to rest on the wolf that was Loukis. She bent forward and kissed it.

'Happy Christmas, my love, wherever you are,' she whispered.

To mark the Feast of Epiphany, Demetris and Lella presented Loukis with a pair of roomy trousers and two new shirts, one blue and one grey. He thanked them for the gift and apologized for returning their kindness with empty hands. A month later, the couple surprised him with a razor on his birthday, and the policeman showed him how to scrape the hairs from his chin after taking a soapy brush to his face to smooth the blade's passage. Loukis, though grateful, was taken by guilt as the policeman lifted his chin and pulled at his nose, because it was a ritual into which his father should have rightly initiated him. By the following month, the razor stood idle; not out of any sense of family betrayal, but rather because EOKA had ordered a boycott of all British goods, and creamy soap bars were now off the shopping list.

'It's certainly a pain in the rear, this shaving business,' confirmed Stelios as they waited for Toulla at the coffee house. 'Personally, I'd love to let my whiskers grow, but the problem is they don't take well where the burns are, so I'd only get half a beard anyway.'

Loukis looked at his friend's face and found it hard to imagine that the soft skin on his good side was much troubled by whiskers either.

'Does it still hurt?' he asked. 'You know, the burnt side?'

Stelios shook his head. 'No, not really. I have to stay out of the sun a bit more, but it's not exactly sore. In fact, seeing myself in the mirror is as painful as it gets. And it really doesn't help hanging out with Cyprus's answer to Victor Mature.'

Loukis frowned in good-natured pain at the comparison; he didn't know about looking like a movie star but he recognized he came from a family noted for its good genes. Christakis – though devil-cursed with dirty blond hair – had grown into a giant of a man, with an easy smile that seemed to impress the women of the village; Michalakis was nearly as tall, but less broad and with sharper features; and Marios was blessed not only with height but also with straight teeth and doe eyes. He was perhaps the most handsome of them all, just as Nicos had once been.

Out of all of his brothers, Loukis believed he resembled Michalakis the most, which he also recognized was no bad thing.

'At last,' Stelios said, rising to his feet as Toulla approached.

'Sorry, gentlemen,' she greeted. 'I had a heck of a job getting away.'

'No problem, there's enough of the day left . . . just.' Stelios picked up the two empty sacks by his feet. 'We'll catch you later, then,' he told Loukis, and Loukis nodded.

'Good luck,' he told them.

'Thanks,' responded Toulla. She flashed a shy smile before taking Stelios's arm and walking away.

Stelios and Toulla were on a mission ordered by Antoniou and Harris, who had reappeared on the scene four days earlier, after Governor Foot had dismissed all calls for *enosis* in the wake of the UN's disinterest. In the cemetery near Pano Platres, under the dirt covering the bones of Harris's great-grandfather, there was a small stash of revolvers, a rifle and some boxes of ammunition. Antoniou wanted them brought to the hideout, and Stelios readily agreed to play the

135

part of strolling lovers with Toulla to bring the cell's bounty back home. Just in case any British soldiers failed to fall for the ruse, Stelios had been furnished with a carton of Woodbines – in blatant defiance of the EOKA boycott, which would suggest that the two of them were in no way sympathetic to the 'terrorists'.

Because Stelios had become an incorrigible pipe-smoker, he generously gave a couple of tabs to Loukis who, unwilling to budge from his warm place in the sun, lit one up, savouring the taste on his tongue and enjoying the punch it brought to the back of his throat. As he watched the smoke snaking on the breeze, he relaxed into his seat and allowed himself to think of Praxi and whether she had a fancy for Victor Mature. In all the years he'd known her, she'd never mentioned the movie star, but everyone changes, given enough time, and Loukis had been hiding himself for more than a year. In his absence, perhaps she had grown fat – or painfully thin. Maybe she had run to the Church or fallen for the Americans' rock'n'roll. Or perhaps nothing had changed and she remained glued to her window, waiting for his return. The only thing that Loukis could be sure of was that time had allowed him to change for the better; he was a touch taller than he used to be, his body was much stronger and, mentally, he felt he had turned a corner.

When he had left for the mountains, Loukis had never stopped to think about how long he would be gone; he had simply wanted to escape – to lose himself for a while in a place where no one knew him so that he could find enough space in his life to allow him to catch his breath and think clearly. Now, his thoughts were no longer cluttered and so he found his mind drifting back with increasing regularity to a place cooled by the sea, where the scent was honeysuckle and citrus rather than heavy pine, and where the rocks of the mountains held his feet steady and the shingle of the shore tickled and slid through his toes. Right now, he longed to go back, to feel once again the sun on his chest and watch waves, glittering with light, wash over his body. He yearned for everything he had known and, above all of that, he yearned for the woman he loved. He was nothing without Praxi, just a ghost playing with time. And even though he was taller and he approved of the way his chest had expanded along with the muscles in his arms, he still felt less than half the person he used to be. Praxi was more a part of him than his own flesh and bones; she was his heart. It was hard to believe he could have lasted so long without her, and he wondered if her fingers reached for him in the night the way his did for hers.

Stavros sat on the fallen tree, his fleshy face in his hands. The world was turning too fast and the old man could hardly make sense of it any more. Earlier this week, he had visited Gönyeli, after learning that his nephew had fled there with his family, unable to cope any longer with the terrors of Lefkosia. They took flight from a predominantly Greek area to seek sanctuary in a village that was wholly Turkish. So great was the family's fear, they closed the door of their home, leaving everything in it apart from a few cases of clothes and a handful of keepsakes. Naturally, Stavros had initially directed his anger at the Greeks for ruining the life of the family, but in the days that followed, he became dismayed by the actions of his own people too. As the island's two communities turned their backs on each other, the only common ground that remained was one of hostility, and the troubles were spinning out of control, creating a spiral of atrocity and counter-atrocity. In the chaos of conflict, the Turkish Information Centre was bombed and Turkish Cypriots took to the capital's streets armed with cudgels and metal bars. Shouting 'Partition or death!', they attacked police cars, burned buildings and looted shops in the old quarter. As factories and offices were set ablaze, four people lost their lives and scores more were injured.

Two years ago, Stavros's wife used to dream of the cymbals and flutes that had sounded on her wedding day and the beautiful white horse that had carried her on a cloud of red ribbons. Now she dreamt of men holding guns, of dead donkeys in her orchard and her home withered by flames. When Pembe awoke trembling in the night, her husband had no words to comfort her. How could he insist that she was only being foolish when, during the day, he suffered the same visions?

Hopelessly wrapped in his own agonies, Stavros failed to register the presence at his side until he heard a polite cough. He removed his head from his hands to see Georgios sat next to him. His neighbour handed him a silver flask and the farmer thankfully accepted the warmth of *zivania*.

'We haven't seen you at the coffee house for some time,' Georgios commented. 'We were getting worried.'

'Worried about me or worried that you'd have to pick up your own bill?' Stavros tried to joke.

'In truth, a little of both.' Georgios laughed gently. 'Come let me pay my debt to you, old friend. This is no time to be sat on dead trees.'

Although Stavros hardly felt up to the walk – or the

company of Greeks – he got to his feet. Perhaps a trip to the coffee house might shake the depression hanging on his shoulders. And maybe this time he wouldn't have to clean the spit from his shoes – a passing comment from one of his own kind who had disapproved of his last visit.

As the two friends strolled down the lane, they did their best to step around the politics destroying their country, opting instead to talk about the weather and the price of potatoes, but as they neared the village square it became apparent that something had happened to cause fresh agitation; none of the older men were playing cards and hands were waving in the air in heated discussion. Stavros and Georgios took their customary position in the corner of the coffee shop. When the *kafetzi* brought over their drinks, Georgios asked for details.

'Eight Greeks were murdered yesterday near the village of Kioneli,' he replied. 'It seems the security forces rounded up thirty-five men from Skylloura and Kontemenos and then released them again.'

'What? In Kioneli?' Georgios asked incredulously. 'That's at least seven miles from their villages.'

'It was a plot!' screamed Mr Televantos, picking up the thread of new conversation. 'The British did it on purpose, because they knew the Turkish heathens would slaughter our boys given half the chance. Well, they did it all right. Ripped them apart like savages.'

'Well, what do you expect from the Turks?' joined in the farmer Fotis.

'I say we go over there and give them a taste of their own medicine,' suggested Kostas, the bus driver. 'Remember what Katalano once said? "We, the brave Hellenes, should form an alliance, being united in one, and let us make turn round the doggish and infidel Turks like a kebab on a spit!" '

The men in the coffee house whooped and applauded the bus driver's remarks, and Stavros rose from his chair. Georgios put out an arm to stop him, and as he did so Mr Televantos suddenly appreciated, through his tearful indignation, the terrible insult they had caused.

'Hey, Stavros! Sit down, man. We're not talking about you – you're practically one of us,' he told him.

The farmer turned slowly at his words. The room had gone quiet, and all eyes were upon him. Where earlier there had been confusion in his mind, Stavros was now filled with purpose and fire.

'My name,' he told them loudly and deliberately, 'is Mehmet. And for close to seventy years I have lived in this village and counted many of you here as my friends. And right now, I tell you, I am ashamed to even call you neighbours . . .'

'Now hold on,' interrupted Kostas.

'No, you hold on, Kostas Mavrommatis!' the old man fired back. 'For three hundred years the Ottomans ruled this island. Did they persecute you in all that time? No – not in a way that they didn't also harass their own people. Did they threaten to roast you on a spit as if you were animal meat? No, they did not. Did they, in fact, treat you equally, if not always fairly? Yes, they did. And did they not allow you to follow your own religion? Yes, they did.

'But of course, all of this counts for nothing in the face of the so-called Grand Idea. You Greeks, you all talk so loudly about this island belonging to the motherland – well, tell me, when was the last time you felt the glory of her caress on these shores? Since time began, Cyprus has been batted between consecutive invaders. First, the Phoenicians and then your Greek-tongued Achaeans; following them you were ruled by the Assyrians, the Macedonians, the Egyptians, the Persians, the Romans, the Byzantines and Saracens. But when the British came to set up their camps in 1878 this island belonged to the Ottomans – yes, us Turks! We leased this island to the British, have you forgotten that? And then in 1914 the British annexed the place and stole Cyprus right from under your Greek noses. So, I tell you, if anyone has a right to feel aggrieved, and if anyone has a legal claim on this island, it is my people, the Turks. But of course you cannot see that, none of you can, you are so blinded by your own versions of injustice. But worse than that, you no longer choose to see those that have lived among you for hundreds of years as people, but as animals. Well, listen to me. I am not an animal waiting for you to slaughter and quarter and roast on a spit. I am a human being. I am a man built of flesh and blood. I have parents and grandparents and great-grandparents buried beneath this soil and I have children breathing this air. I am a Cypriot Turk and, like you, I have a heart and a soul. More than that, I have a right to life. Do you hear me? I have a *right* to life! And my name is Mehmet Kadir.'

Stelios leaned against the stone wall, packing his pipe. His scarred face was serious.

'You know, I never thought I could kill a Turk, even if I was ordered to,' he said. 'I mean, it's only because of that Turkish forester that I'm even here today. But now, after what they've done, I wouldn't think twice.'

Loukis was listening to his friend, but as he didn't agree he felt no need to reply. In his head he remembered Stavros's wife, Pembe, and the way she superstitiously emptied a bowl of water after him whenever he left her home – a wish for travellers to go and also to return again. It was hard to reconcile the image of the woman he knew with the savagery that had taken place in Larnaka. And no matter what Stelios might say, Loukis found no reason to blame the old woman for the sins of her brothers.

According to the reports filtering through, a Ford Consul had been dumped outside the city police station. A dark liquid oozed from its doors, and the vehicle, unsurprisingly, caught the attention of officers. When they went to investigate, they found the remains of three butchered Greek Cypriots. The men had been hacked to pieces and their penises cut from their bodies and jammed inside their mouths – a barbaric rite meant to stop their souls from entering into heaven.

'Come on, let's go and get something to eat,' Loukis muttered, and he marched across the road and into the wood, with Stelios scrambling after him. More than ever before, he felt the weight of his decision to return home, and some time this weekend he'd have to let everyone know that he was going.

As the trees thinned on the slope to Demetris's house, the boys suddenly stopped in their tracks.

'What the hell?' whispered Stelios.

There were four Champs outside the gate and four soldiers stood guard. Loukis and Stelios crouched low in the undergrowth. Minutes later, Demetris emerged from the house, blood on his face, his hands shackled behind his back. He was pulled to a vehicle by the British major Loukis had met not long after he arrived. Closely following them was Lella; her hands were free and they held the sides of her face in shock.

'Not my wife!' Demetris shouted, as he realized the British were taking her too. 'I tell you she had nothing to do with any of this! Let her be, damn you!'

'Watch your mouth,' the major ordered through gritted teeth and pushed the policeman into the back of a Champ. Lella was taken to a separate vehicle. Behind her, a number of soldiers followed. Their uniforms were dirty with black soot and their arms held bundles of rifles.

Loukis rolled on to his heels in anguish and dismay. The couple had been good to him – and the British major would be aware of that fact. As sure as the sun comes up, the hunt would now start for Demetris's missing nephew.

There was no possible way Loukis could return home as a Wanted Man.

8

Within weeks of finding himself homeless, Loukis's skin was ingrained with a filth impervious to water and his hair itched with grease and grime. His discomfort was further exacerbated by guilt – at being free whilst those who had sheltered him languished behind bars – and by days that were spent either in complete idleness or exhausting flight on the wing of a rumour.

The British, who had seemed but a minor irritant when Loukis had a roof over his head, transformed overnight into an ever-lurking presence. Every halt of birdsong and crack of branch seemed to signal his imminent arrest. His muscles were tense to the point of snapping and his neck ached from the creeping cold of draughty sleep.

Although EOKA had resumed its activities, Loukis and his cell were in no condition to launch any assaults. Following the occupiers' steady decimation of the Troodos network, they were largely engaged in matters of recruitment. Dodging checkpoints and patrols, the men spoke of glory and commitment while Toulla employed her considerable charms to cajole potential volunteers, but the going was tough. The shooting of a British woman had caused national revulsion, and there was a growing reluctance to embrace the cause.

The radio had named the victim as Catherine Cutliffe. She had been shopping with her daughter Margaret in Ammochostos when two youths opened fire, shooting the older woman in the back. They hit her twice more as she lay bleeding on the street. A German lady was also gunned down. She was critically but not fatally wounded. By some miracle, Margaret escaped unhurt. Reports revealed she had been due to get married and, when the attack happened, she had been carrying her wedding dress in her arms.

Following the murder, the Mayor of Lefkosia offered a £5,000 reward for the capture of the killers. EOKA immediately denied it had played a role in the execution, and the Greek Foreign Minister claimed the crime was the bloody handiwork of a spurned ex-lover. The mountain folk in Troodos were not wholly convinced, and Loukis and his comrades remained a band of five.

During the harsh winds of November, Stelios attempted to relieve the boredom of their inactivity by disclosing his bomb-making skills to Loukis; Toulla kindly shared her mother's cooking; Antoniou and Harris imparted pearls of hardened wisdom; and the occupiers almost stumbled upon one of the gang's hideouts. Whether it was God, good luck or the soldiers' carelessness, their heavy boots lumbered over and around the tunnel's opening but the occupiers remained unaware that they were in touching distance of three wanted men. During the commotion, Harris thrust a gun into Loukis's hands and, after their hearts had returned to their normal rhythm, the weapon became as much a part of his outfit as the clothes rotting on his back.

Although Loukis had always struggled with the idea that killing a man was somehow a patriotic act, he held no such reservations when it came to his own survival. If he was forced to save himself, he had no qualms about shooting his way out of a corner or dying in the process. And during the long, interminable nights as a fugitive, there were times when he almost prayed for an ambush, if only to put an end to the uncertainty. However, when winter dug her claws in and snow fell upon Troodos, his life became oddly more bearable, because the men had to rely less on their wits and more on the hospitality of known sympathizers. Therefore, instead of freezing in a cave or deserted barn or forgotten outhouse, they were given rooms in friendly homes, they were fed until they were full and they had motherly women queuing up to wash their lice-crawling clothes.

'It gets easier once you're into your second year and you know what to expect,' Antoniou assured him. 'When I first went on the run I was filled with all sorts of romantic ideas, and I was wholly prepared to die from the bullet of a soldier's gun. Of course, it gradually became apparent that I'd be more likely killed by boredom or cold.'

'Or your cooking,' Harris interrupted. Earlier that month, Antoniou had boiled up a chicken he had stolen. As well as being tasteless, it had subsequently exploded from the men's arses with the force of a grenade. The barn they had been hiding in was declared a disaster zone, and once they were able to move again, they evacuated the place, after covering their disgrace with fire.

'I tell you what gets me the most though,' Harris continued. 'It's the lack of women.'

The three men laughed and nodded in agreement.

'Seriously,' he insisted. 'Here we are, fighting for our beloved Cyprus, to all intents and purposes national heroes, and yet the only nightly company I've had for as long as I can remember has come with a small arsenal of weapons and two testicles! God knows what I'd give to hold a naked woman in my arms, to feel her tender kiss on my lips and the lively thrust of her hips.'

'I'd second that,' murmured Antoniou. And though Loukis wasn't averse to the idea of female company, he kept quiet. The three men were currently stark bollock naked, watching their clothes dry in front of a roaring fire. It was neither a conversation nor a situation he was entirely comfortable with.

Dhespina nodded as Georgios went to lift the untouched plate.

'Athena or Apollo?' he asked with a grin.

'Athena,' she answered and continued washing the dishes.

For the third Christmas in a row, Dhespina had waited for her youngest son to come home, and for the third Christmas in a row, he had failed her. But even though sadness never abandoned her, the occasion was becoming almost bearable thanks to the chaos created by Christakis's growing brood.

'This is what happens when you don't have a radio in your house,' Michalakis warned Marios as Yianoulla, heavy with a third child, wrestled her two little boys.

'Hush, Michalakis!' Dhespina reprimanded.

'It's nothing to do with the radio,' Christakis cheerfully informed his brother. 'It's simply the difference between wielding a pen and wielding a chisel.'

147

'Christakis!' Yianoulla shrieked, and the three brothers and their father laughed out loud at the sensibilities of the women.

Although there wasn't one person around the table who didn't wish for the front door to burst open and for Loukis to appear, a form of happiness had nonetheless returned to the house, and that Christmas a miracle did in fact pay them a visit – and it came in the blooming figure of Dhespina's younger sister. With faces rosy with delight, Lenya and her husband informed the family that she was finally pregnant.

'Congratulations!' Dhespina squealed, grabbing her sister in a water-tight hug.

'Oh, well done,' Georgios beamed, patting Andreas firmly on the back.

'Do you own a radio?' inquired Michalakis.

'No,' Lenya admitted, 'it stopped working three months ago.'

'And I rest my case!' Michalakis swept his hand before him as he performed a theatrical bow. His mother was stood near and she pushed him on to the floor.

The next day, and no doubt spurred on by the virile victories of the men in his family, Michalakis called on Maria. When he knocked at her door, Mrs Germanos seemed pleasantly gratified by his interest in her daughter, and she encouraged the two of them to explore their new friendship in the air outside. Shyly the pair agreed it was a most splendid idea, and they made their way along quiet country lanes, going nowhere in particular as they talked themselves into dead ends.

From their halting conversation, Maria formed the impression that Michalakis was extremely clever but also a little dour. However, because he was older and therefore more sophisticated than any of the other boys who had tried to court her – and he had the unmistakable look of Loukis about him – this made him rather appealing. In turn, Michalakis quickly established that Maria's opinion of the world bordered on vacuous, but in truth it didn't matter. He had never set eyes on a lovelier creature and, instead of being irritated by her inane chatter, he found her ignorance innocent and charming.

As the mountains behind them changed from purple to black, the couple arrived at Keryneia harbour and, lured by a warm light, they entered a café that had recently opened there. Inside, the room was cosy with a fire casting orange shadows upon brick walls, and on small, intimate tables, single candles glowed brightly. Maria was impressed. Michalakis was self-conscious.

Behind a tall wooden counter, Yiannis was counting money from a till. When he looked up, he locked eyes with Michalakis, and his cheeks burned with shock and embarrassment.

'I don't believe it!' From a corner table Praxi jumped to her feet and ran across the floor to throw her arms around Michalakis's neck.

'Praxi *mou!*' he replied, kissing her fondly on both cheeks. 'You look beautiful.'

'And you are more handsome than ever,' she laughed. 'And shame on you, Michalakis. Why on earth has it taken you so long to come and see us?'

'I really don't know,' he told her honestly, 'but I promise to make more effort in the future. You have a very fine place here. Congratulations.'

Praxi smiled with real pleasure at the compliment; the candles had been her own idea. When she loosened her grip on Michalakis she lazily glanced at his date. 'Maria,' she greeted.

'Praxi,' her old friend returned.

'And who is this adorable creature?' Michalakis asked, oblivious to the coolness between the two women. He approached the pram Praxi had left. 'Surely this can't be little Elpida?' Bending down, he picked up the child, who squealed with delight. Level with his face, the toddler placed her hands on his cheeks and gazed adoringly into his eyes. Michalakis kissed her sweetly on her nose, and Praxi's heart swelled.

'So, what can I get you both?' she asked.

'I'll have a Keo beer,' Michalakis told her. 'Maria?'

'Coca-Cola,' she replied. She moved to a table by the window, forcing Michalakis to hand back the child and join her. When he took his seat, facing away from the room, Maria flashed Praxi a look of womanly triumph.

'Do you know the story of winter?' Toulla asked.

Loukis shook his head. It was a lie, he knew full well about the myths of Persephone, but being in Toulla's company had become a rare pleasure, and he didn't want to do or say anything that might discourage her.

'Well, according to legend, Persephone was the daughter of Zeus and Demeter, the goddess of the harvest,' Toulla explained. 'Persephone was very beautiful and everyone loved her – even Hades wanted her. Then, one day, when she was collecting flowers on the plain of Enna, the earth suddenly opened and Hades rose up from the gap and abducted her. None but Zeus and the all-seeing sun, Helios, noticed. Broken-hearted, her mother wandered the earth looking for her daughter, until Helios revealed what had happened. Demeter was so angry that she withdrew herself in loneliness, and the earth ceased to be fertile. Knowing this couldn't continue, Zeus told Hades to release Persephone. Hades grudgingly agreed, but before she went back he gave Persephone a pomegranate. When she later ate just one seed, it bound her to the underworld for ever and she had to stay there for one-third of the year. The other months she stayed with her mother. When Persephone was in Hades, Demeter refused to let anything grow, and that's how winter began.'

'Nice story,' Loukis commented wryly, 'and typically tragic.'

'Then it's rather like life, isn't it?' Toulla sighed. Her wild hair was hidden under a hat and her strong face was pinched with cold.

'I know I shouldn't say this, but I'm getting heartily sick of all this nonsense,' she muttered, digging her hands deeper into the pockets of her coat. 'Everything is such a struggle. Honestly, I hate it. When I decided to dedicate myself to our liberation, I never dreamt it would go on this long. Do you know we're coming up to four years? I mean, when will it all end? Really, I'm so utterly fed up. There's no finish in sight for our fight, and in the process I'm becoming an old maid.'

Loukis looked at Toulla. He had no idea how old she was. Perhaps eighteen? Nineteen? She was certainly old enough to have married and collected an armful of children.

'You're not an old maid,' Loukis reassured her. 'You're a vibrant, beautiful young woman.'

'But I'm not vibrant or beautiful enough for you, am I?'

Toulla tried to laugh, but they both recognized the hurt in her question so Loukis ignored it.

'Did Stelios tell you that he's asked me to marry him?' she suddenly inquired.

'No, he didn't,' Loukis admitted, not a little surprised by the revelation. His friend had been in high spirits back at the hideout, but Loukis had assumed it was from nailing the timer mechanisms he'd spent the best part of the day fiddling with. 'So, what did you tell him? Are you going to marry him?'

'I don't know. I told him I'd think about it.'

'Do you love him?'

'What's love?' she asked.

Loukis knew exactly what love was, and he was sorry the girl had chosen to answer his question in such a way. Stelios was a good man, and he deserved a woman who truly loved him, not one who agreed to be his wife simply because he was second best in a limited pool of options.

'Oh, hell!' Toulla shouted, stopping in the lane and patting her pockets. 'I've left my purse in the den.'

'OK, no problem, we'll go back. We can't get much in the way of supplies without it.'

'Don't worry. You wait here,' she insisted. 'I'll run back. I'll only be a couple of minutes.'

Loukis shrugged and, as Toulla dashed up the hill and into the trees, he rested himself by a small, broken wall. Although the day was bitterly cold, he had jumped at the chance to escape the claustrophobic prison of the hideout. Before he left, Antoniou had warned him not to accompany Toulla all the way to the village and he had promised he wouldn't. But he could at least try and catch some of the sun's warmth on his face a part of the way. He looked at his feet as he waited. Mud, wet from melting snow, had made a mess of his shoes, and he picked up a stick to poke at the clumps clogging his soles. As a chunk broke free, splattering against the crumbling wall, a mighty bang filled the air and Loukis dropped the stick.

Pushing himself from the wall, he ran up the hill in the direction of the explosion. As he stumbled and slipped on the wet ground, he prayed under his breath to a God he scarcely believed in. It had sounded like a bomb, but it didn't necessarily mean . . . it could have been anything . . . he hadn't seen any British . . . there were farmers . . . they had bangers . . . bangers to scare the crows.

He crashed headlong into the wood, branches whipping at his face and pulling at his jacket as he raced to the hide-out. Within seconds, the den was in his sight; the bushes hiding the entrance had been blown away and dying smoke wafted from the hole. Crouching low, he dipped into the opening. The stench of burning flesh instantly smacked his senses. In the dark, he stumbled across Toulla lying motion-less on the floor. Her eyes were wide with surprise and her mouth hung open. Bolts and nails had torn great holes into her flesh. As Loukis stepped over her, the horror of what he next saw hit him hard in the throat and he was forced to swallow the taste of his own vomit. On the chair where Stelios had been playing with his bombs, there remained only the bottom half of a torso and a pair of twitching legs. His chest, arms and scarred face had been blown away and were now plastered along the damp walls of the cave in a grotesque pattern of blood, muscle and bone. Opposite Stelios, Harris's eyes flickered to a close as the metal shard

153

that protruded from his windpipe took the last of his breath.

'Loukis?'

He turned wildly, in search of the voice among the debris of death. At the far end of the cave, Antoniou shivered in the dark. His leg was shattered, and his face was pitted with shrapnel.

'Antoniou, Jesus . . .' Loukis moved towards him.

'Get out!' the man commanded, summoning what was left of his strength as his body convulsed and blood spat from his mouth. 'Run! Go! There's nothing you can do. The occupiers . . . they will come. Run!'

Loukis went to approach the man he had come to consider a friend. His body trembled with shock.

'Get out!' Antoniou screamed again. And Loukis turned and fled.

As he thrashed his way through the wood, he was blinded by the horror of what he had seen: Toulla's striking face stuck for ever in a mask of deathly surprise; Antoniou disfigured and dying; Harris twitching to an end; and Stelios. Dear God, Stelios. The boy's trousers had been ripped from his amputated legs by the force of the blast, but his feet still wore the shoes his mother had bought him for his last birthday, like some last ghastly joke. Loukis retched. And he ran. His head pounded with blood, and the terror began its descent. He felt his skull slowly being crushed by a vice of excruciating grief, but he kept on running, not seeing, just moving. Behind his eyes, his brain hammered its incomprehension and his chest began to heave with agony and effort. He couldn't breathe. God help him, he couldn't breathe. He had to run, but he couldn't breathe. And then he fell, and he tumbled on the ground as the world span into a blur and

154

tree roots stabbed through his clothes and into his skin. Then he was still.

Somewhere, far away, he heard voices. But the world had gone dark and the hammering in his head drowned out everything but the screams coming from his mouth.

In a small cottage within a village Loukis used to call home, Dhespina woke with a start. Georgios turned on the pillow.

'What is it, Dhespo? What troubles you?'

'It's Loukis,' she said. 'He's coming home.'

9

The doors were always locked, apart from one, and it pushed open with creaking hinges. Inside, the scene was forever the same: amongst the dark liquid, muscle and glinting shards of bone, an eyelid would blink or a toothless mouth would curl in a scream. Scattered upon the floor were pulsing organs disconnected from bodies he had known, and he would have to walk away. Outside, the corridor led him to a hall with more doors, but they were always locked, apart from one, and the door would fall back on creaking hinges and his friends would reappear: mutilated, bleeding and dead. Loukis knew he was dreaming, therefore he felt no panic. But he couldn't wake up. His body pulled at him, weighing him down, and his stomach had turned in on itself. But he couldn't escape. He was trapped. Now and again a woman approached and soothed him. Her skin was hard but her touch was soft and, in the background, he heard bells ringing.

When sleep finally lost its hold, Loukis saw that he was lying on a bed, under a knitted blanket, and he was naked. A wood fire warmed him, and by the window the silhouette of an old woman stood on a small carpet. Her arms were folded in front of her full waist. After a few seconds, they fell to her sides and she knelt, bringing her face to the ground. Sitting back on her heels, she moved her head to the right and then to the left. She leaned forward and brought her breath to the floor again. The woman was performing the Muslim prayer, and Loukis was puzzled as to how he happened to be naked in the home of a Turkish Cypriot he had no memory of.

'You've finally come to join us then?' the old woman asked as she folded the prayer mat and saw him looking at her.

'Where am I?'

'In Pano Platres,' she replied. 'Rest yourself and I'll get you some food. You must be starving.'

Over a stew of potatoes and old chicken, the woman revealed her name was Havva Husseyin. Her husband was long dead, and her sons were in Lefkoşa. They were good boys. Not like some.

'How did I get here?' Loukis asked. The woman shook her head and her shoulders bounced with quiet laughter.

'Oh, now that is a pretty tale,' she told him. 'The British brought you here. I bet you'd like that!'

Havva explained that, three days earlier, she had seen Loukis 'fall from the sky' and into the path of a military vehicle.

'You were in a frightening way,' the old woman continued. 'All ripped up, with bleeding hands and scratches covering your face, and the soldiers didn't know quite what to make of you. Furthermore, you were making the most terrifying racket, but lucky for you, none of it was obviously Greek. Anyway, you looked lost and I decided to save you. I

157

told the soldiers you were my lunatic grandson and they carried you here.'

'Why?'

'Well, I couldn't very well carry you myself. Look at the size of you!'

'No,' Loukis tried again. 'Why did you decide to save me?'

'Oh, I see. You know, I haven't the faintest idea, maybe because I felt sorry for you.' Havva got up and pulled back the curtains. 'It's true you have the body of a man, but I see you're no more than a child and, as a mother, I suppose you touched me in a funny sort of way. I don't know what happened to you, or what you'd done to get yourself in such a state, but my conscience told me I couldn't walk away and that's why you are here.'

Loukis was confused and yet touched by the old woman's kindness. He didn't know what to say, except thank you. Exhausted, he fell back into sleep.

Over the following days, as Havva fed the strength back into him, Loukis surrendered to her care and listened to her stories and memories of her childhood in one of the country's many mixed villages. She presented him with no harrowing tales of hardship or ethnic injustice, only happy recollections of a time when life was simpler, and her easy talk helped ease his own pain.

'So, who's Praxi?' she asked on the third day of his convalescence.

Startled, Loukis opened his mouth to speak, but nothing came out. The old woman explained herself. 'When you were asleep, and in between calling for your mamma, you shouted the name Praxi. Is she your girlfriend? Or even your wife?'

Loukis replied that she was neither. 'Not yet anyway,' he added.

'Well, maybe you can rectify that.' Havva smiled warmly.

'Yes,' he agreed, 'when the island is free.'

'Oh my!' she exclaimed, slapping at her cheeks. 'In all the excitement of having you wake I clean forgot. The war is over, child, if that's what you're waiting for. Yes, the war is over!'

Havva dragged her chair closer to better report the extraordinary developments that had taken place, and which Loukis struggled to accept. None of it made any sense. It seemed too quick, too easy. He had fallen asleep and the island had woken.

'No, it's true,' Havva insisted. 'The Greek and Turkish Prime Ministers came to an agreement with the British somewhere in Europe, and then in London they met with your Archbishop Makarios to sign a document to bring an end to colonial rule. The British will keep two bases, but the country will get its independence with both Greeks and Turkish Cypriots sharing power. Really, I was surprised when the bells didn't wake you. They were ringing for a good twenty minutes. At the time nobody had the vaguest idea what all the fuss was about until the radio brought the news. Cyprus is free, Loukis!'

Listening to Havva's excited chatter, Loukis could barely contain his anger. If everything the old woman said was true then his friends had died only days away from the freedom they had fought for. Loukis recalled Toulla and her need to avenge her brother's death, and how just minutes before she lost her life she had despaired of ever seeing an end to the struggle. He thought of Antoniou and Harris, and their thirst for liberation and hunger for women. And he remembered Stelios, with his florid conversation and sweet-smelling pipe.

'Do you know what day the EOKA campaign started?' Havva asked, as if reading his thoughts.

'1955,' Loukis replied glumly.

'No, I asked for the day not the year.'

Loukis shook his head.

'It began on April the first,' the old woman informed him, a sad smile pulling at her lips. 'April Fool's Day.'

'How apt,' confirmed Loukis, and he walked out of the room and into the sun to see what freedom tasted like.

With the struggle apparently over, and his friends undeniably gone, Loukis remained one more day at Havva's home, helping her as much as he could with the chores around the house that needed a man's hand. With a hammer and nails, he fixed a wonky leg on her main table; he chopped wood for her fire; greased the hinges on all of her doors; and he swept the winter debris from the porch. He then kissed the old woman gently on both cheeks and bid her farewell.

Havva cried when he left, but she hid her face in a scarf and Loukis missed seeing her tears. Carrying only the clothes on his back – which Havva had lovingly washed and mended – Loukis made his way along the main road, certain he would meet a British checkpoint on his travels. Instead, the most challenging obstacle he encountered was a herd of frisky goats.

As the morning slipped into the afternoon, he dipped into the trees sloping towards a small house on the outskirts of a typical Cypriot village. In the garden, he found

Demetris sat on an old wooden chair. As the former police sergeant span around, Loukis saw that the left side of his face was torn by scars and his eye bore the milky-white sign of blindness.

Demetris immediately leapt to his feet and grabbed Loukis in a warm embrace. Tears filled his eyes, both good and bad, and he called for Lella, who came running from the kitchen to rain kisses upon Loukis's face. Since he'd last seen them, the couple had lost the soft fat that used to cocoon their bodies and they seemed not only smaller but much older.

That night, after a plate piled with potatoes and roasted lamb, Loukis slept in his old bed, and in the morning he joined Demetris in the bathroom so they might shave together one last time. Throughout his short stay the couple never spoke of their ordeal and Loukis never asked them about it. He knew too well that some memories were best left forgotten. After a breakfast of cheese and bread, Demetris stuffed a handful of Cyprus pounds into Loukis's pocket and made him promise to return one day. Loukis swore that he would try. The old man then drove him to Alona, where he took a bus to the capital.

In Lefkosia, Loukis was stunned to see posters of Makarios adorning the walls and streets fluttering with the blue and white flags of Greece. Gone was the sullen resentment that once breathed so heavy on the capital, and Loukis was scarcely able to make sense of the change. The world had turned bright with the speed of a light switch.

Boarding the packed bus to Keryneia, Loukis had further difficulties finding a seat. He eventually ended up at the back, squeezed between a large woman and a small man holding a chicken.

'Nice hen,' Loukis commented.

'Isn't she?' the man beamed.

From the conversation of the other passengers, Loukis quickly learned that Archbishop Makarios had returned to the island the day before, in a glittering triumphal procession. His homecoming marked the climax of a week of jubilant celebration that had seen thousands converge on the capital to greet the release of nine hundred political prisoners. For the first time since he had left Pano Platres, Loukis started to fully accept that the struggle he had inadvertently involved himself with was over. With a smile creeping across his face, he watched the mountains protecting Keryneia looming ahead of him, and he battled to contain the excitement flickering in his gut.

At Keryneia, Loukis left the bus and chose the picturesque coastal route to carry him home. The late-afternoon sun remained warm, and as he walked he allowed himself a moment of contemplation to wonder at the beauty of its rays as they danced upon the waves. Unable to resist the invitation, Loukis discarded his clothes and ran into the freezing springtime waters that shocked his skin and caused him to catch breath. Beneath his feet, the rocks felt achingly familiar and he crashed into gentle waves knowing there was no greater place on earth.

Sated, Loukis walked back to shore, where he noticed a striking young woman sat on the shingle watching him. She had hold of his clothes, and her eyes twinkled with happiness and mischief.

'Maria,' he greeted her as he neared. She held out his clothes for him to take but didn't immediately release them.

'Loukis,' she returned. 'I hardly recognized you at first; you've grown so much.'

'Anywhere in particular?' he asked, and she dropped his trousers in embarrassment.

'We've missed you,' she told him, as he dressed with his back to her. 'Where were you all this time?'

'Away,' he said, and walked off.

As Loukis climbed the sandy slope towards fields owned by farmers he'd known all his life, and maybe some he no longer did, he passed the olive groves belonging to Stavros. Although he searched in passing, he saw no sign of the old man, nor of his donkey, Aphrodite, and so he continued onwards, ducking beneath the branches of trees that seemed to have shrunk in his absence. As he turned the corner to his home, the first sight he saw was that of his mother sitting on a stool in front of the door.

'I knew it!' she shrieked. 'I knew it! I knew it! Georgios, come quickly! Your son has come home!'

Loukis ran forward and swung his mother in his arms. She felt light as a feather, and she squealed like a teenager at his fun. Coming to a stop, she tenderly touched his face and planted two longed-for kisses on his cheeks. She then took his hand and pulled him inside the house.

'I felt you coming,' she excitedly told him. 'Of course, your father thought I was talking nonsense, but I felt you, Loukis, and I've been waiting for you on that stool for the past two weeks, waiting for you to prove him wrong and me right. See, Georgios! Who's a crazy old woman now?'

Georgios leapt from his position by the stove and pulled his son firmly into his chest. As he pushed Loukis away again he took hold of his face and kissed him hard on the cheeks and forehead.

'My God, boy, we've missed you,' he said, sniffing with emotion. 'Where the hell were you all this time?'

'Not now, Georgios,' Dhespina ordered. 'We've plenty of time for talking. Right now, I just want to enjoy having my son home without looking for the whys and wherefores of his absence.'

Loukis looked at his mother, and she read the gratitude in his face. Shaking her body free of its paralysing happiness, she set about celebrating her son's return in the traditional Cypriot way; with good food and warm wine.

As she prepared their dinner, Dhespina helped her son get to grips with everything he had missed. She revealed Lenya's baby joy, that Christakis had another new son, that Marios was getting to be quite the carpentry genius, and told how Mr Televantos's piles had grown particularly irksome following the exertions that had come with the island's liberation.

'You should have seen him, the silly old fool,' Dhespina laughed as they sat down to the table. 'He was dancing like a teenager and eating like a horse. Of course, the next day he could hardly move, but the smile never left his face, even as he waited for his medicine.'

'I'm going to have to burn those cushions of ours,' Georgios grumbled. As he reached for a second bottle of wine, the front door burst open and the towering form of Christakis exploded into the room, quickly followed by Marios and Maria.

Loukis got to his feet to greet his brother and as he did so Christakis punched him hard in the face. The big man then pulled him from the floor by the scruff of his shirt and all but squeezed what was left of the life out of him.

'Good to have you home, brother,' he told him in a voice gruff with sentiment.

When he let go, Marios walked over and grabbed Loukis just as tightly, but with none of the violence of their older brother.

'I've missed you, Loukis,' he said.

'I've missed you too, Marios,' replied Loukis honestly.

Rubbing his battered chin, he picked up a chair which had been upended by the force of Christakis's affection and rejoined the table. His brothers also pulled up their own stools and filled their plates as Georgios filled their glasses. Maria went to sit on the stairs. Half an hour later the room was further complimented by the arrival of Stavros and Pembe. As always, the couple enlivened the gathering with their peculiar playfulness, but Loukis saw something lurking behind their eyes he couldn't quite catch, and it reminded him of how long he had been gone. Time had not stood still, that much was evident. Suddenly restless, he got to his feet. He was tired of waiting.

'Where are you going?' his mother asked.

'Well, if the woman is that bloody-minded that she won't come to me, I guess I'll have to go to her. I'm off to see Praxi.'

At his words all conversation stuttered to a halt. Loukis felt the prickle of suspicion creep along the nape of his neck.

'What's the matter?' he asked. 'What's happened to her?'

He looked at the solemn faces before him, and a collage of horrors invaded his mind, triggered by those he had witnessed in Troodos. Panic took hold of his throat. 'What is it?' he demanded.

Dhespina got to her feet.

'Son, Praxi no longer lives in the village, she lives in Keryneia . . .'

'Is that all,' Loukis sighed, half laughing, but his mother hadn't finished.

'She lives in Keryneia with her husband, Loukis. Her husband and her baby . . .'

Loukis felt his breath snatched away and he leaned on the chair to steady himself. His stomach churned with nausea. He shook his head. 'No. No, I don't believe you, she wouldn't do . . .'

'She's married, Loukis.'

Dhespina reiterated the fact with a quiet force, and she paled as she watched the words slowly sink in to crush her youngest child.

In his chest, Loukis felt his heart break. He couldn't breathe. The room rushed inwards, stealing his sight. He felt sick and his body staggered under the force of his mother's words. Every hope he had ever cherished fell out of him and a black emptiness moved in, an impossible weight come to pull, to drag, to drown, until the wave of realization of all that he had lost swelled again and exploded. With a roar of despair he kicked at the table in front of him, sending it crashing to its side. His rage unleashed, he grabbed the nearest chair and swung it wildly above his head, bringing it smashing upon the floor. His hands grasped for anything they could find and he hurled plates and glasses against walls he could no longer see until he felt himself trapped and unable to move. Christakis was behind him, pinning his arms to his side. In fury, Loukis snarled and kicked, but there was no escape. Christakis was too strong and he

166

refused to let go. Together they wrestled in the room, their feet slipping on the wet mess of the floor. Despite Loukis's strength, Christakis kept his hold, and the more he fought, the tighter his brother squeezed him until the fit of his anger gradually dissipated and the blur of the room shifted back into focus and he saw his mother's terrified face staring back at him. She was crumpled on the floor, and blood poured from a cut on her left cheek.

'Oh God, no . . .' Loukis whimpered when he saw what he had done.

Although Christakis continued to hold Loukis, the strength had vanished from the younger man's legs and he was no longer containing his brother but keeping him up. With his arms still bound to his side, Loukis strained his neck forwards, reaching for his mother.

'Leave us,' Dhespina quietly ordered.

She got to her feet, and the vice-like grip of Christakis slowly yielded to let Loukis fall into her arms. Around them, the room emptied, and as soon as the door closed Loukis collapsed. And he cried.

Dhespina gently placed her son's head on her lap and she caught each and every one of his tears.

10

Elena worried that Praxi was teetering on the edge of hysterical. Her daughter had always been highly strung. She was, without doubt, the product of her father, God rest his soul. There was never any calm to him either and in truth it wore her out, right up to the moment he dropped dead in their bed from cardiac arrest. Similarly, Praxi had developed into a nightmare of hyperactivity that often bordered on the wild, and even though she was a mother herself she remained prone to the dramatics of her childhood and her genes. Elena passed the brandy she had poured to numb her daughter's nerves. The girl was shaking with such violence she found it alarming, but someone had to tell her the boy was back in the village, and better it came from her.

Praxi tipped the brandy down her throat with a haste Elena thought shocking. 'I have to see him,' she whispered.

'You'll do no such thing.'

'I have to.'

'And what will you tell him if you do see him?' Elena asked sternly. Her daughter parted her lips to speak, but no answer came and she saw it was hopeless.

'Oh, Mamma!' she shouted, and flung herself back on to the bed.

'Don't be so silly, Praxi. Get up.'

'How can I?' she implored. 'I'm nineteen years old and I'm as cursed as a widow. I swear I have nothing to live for.'

'You have your daughter,' Elena tutted.

'I have *our* daughter.'

'Now, hush yourself! I won't listen to any more of this foolishness. Do you hear me? You were old enough to get yourself into this situation and you are old enough to live with it. You have a fine home and a good husband who thinks the world of both you and Elpida, and you'll thank him for that with a wife's loyalty.'

'A wife's loyalty.' Praxi laughed. She couldn't remember the last time there was anything wifely about her relationship with Yiannis, bar the washing of his clothes. 'Oh, don't worry. I know my duty, Mamma. You don't need to remind me.'

Praxi turned on the bed and Elena – unwilling to give audience to any more of the girl's histrionics – marched out of the room, taking her granddaughter with her. 'Come, child, let's go and see your papa.'

The door shut behind them with a bang, and Praxi curled herself into a ball, relieved to be alone. After all these years, Loukis was home. He was so close she could smell him, and her skin crawled with frustration. Although their childish love had grown distant, the sweet affection they once shared had mutated in the memory of their last touch, becoming something more powerful, much crueller and adult. Praxi yearned not for the boy she had known but for the man she had briefly met. She ached to feel his lips upon her own and her love for him crushed her.

She dragged herself to her feet and poured herself another brandy. The liquid brought fire to her throat and burned in her chest. She filled another glass and drifted over to the window. Below her, Yiannis was clearing tables. As he picked up the dirty glasses he balanced Elpida on his hip, and Praxi realized that any normal mother would have been gratified by his attachment. However, it only added to her despair, and she moved back to her bed. Closing her eyes, she attempted to lose herself in dreams of her own making. She desperately needed the comfort of a happy ending, if only in her imagination.

As Praxi tried to settle on an image of an older Loukis, a few miles from where she laid the reason for her restlessness fought a similar battle. However, Loukis wasn't attempting to conjure up pictures in his mind but straining to block them. Losing the battle, he paid a visit to the man he used to call Stavros.

He found Mehmet in the midst of the orange orchard. After wandering through the old man's farm, Loukis was shocked by its disorderly appearance.

'It's too much for me now,' Mehmet admitted when Loukis broached the subject. 'I'm old and, if I'm truthful, I no longer have the heart for hard work. These days, I only trouble myself with enough to get by.'

'Then let me help you,' Loukis urged.

Mehmet smiled in appreciation, but he shook his head. 'I can't afford you, son. The coffers have dwindled along with my strength.'

Loukis understood, but he refused to give up; he needed the distraction and the honesty of hard toil more than he desired the money. If Mehmet agreed to it, he would harvest the old man's orchards and fix the tired fences and do anything else that was required. In return, the farmer could give him a small corner of land on which to build a home, plus permission to hunt for rabbits and birds that he could sell in the village.

Mehmet chewed over the offer, nodding his head.

'You know, that's not a bad idea,' he admitted. 'I'll have to talk it over with the wife, mind. But maybe we can come to a percentage arrangement with what we make at the market.'

The two men shook hands on the deal. As Loukis stepped back, Mehmet held on to him. His face was serious.

'I have to ask you something,' he said. 'You were in EOKA, right?'

Loukis nodded warily. It wasn't something he'd much spoken about since he'd returned home.

'I thought so,' the old man confessed. 'And tell me; during your time away did you kill any Turks?'

'No, I didn't,' Loukis assured him, and Mehmet loosened his grip.

'I never killed any British either,' he continued. 'In fact, my only casualty was a Greek church, but that's a long story.'

Mehmet snorted merrily at the confession, and Loukis glimpsed some of the man he used to know. 'Well, as long as you keep your military know-how away from our mosque then I'm sure this arrangement will work out just fine. A church, you say? I can't wait to tell the little woman that.'

The next morning, having talked to Pembe, Mehmet offered Loukis a square of land in sight of the couple's own home; not out of any suspicion at what the boy might get up to but rather because they believed his closeness might

171

bring them security. The events of the past few years had left scars on the both of them, and their increasing age brought a vulnerability they had never counted on.

At first, Loukis argued against the couple's generosity, but Mehmet told him to take it or leave it, so he took it with a grin.

During the summer days that followed, Loukis grafted on his home with a single-minded intensity, and with his hands busy he was able to resist the urge to visit Keryneia. He knew he would see her eventually, but he knew he could wait. Right now, he needed the space offered by Mehmet's fields to free his anger and allow his reason to return. He would build his home and rebuild his life, and by the time the last door had been hung he would know what to do.

While Loukis toiled alone through the day, in the evenings his father and brothers would arrive to lend their considerable strength to his cause and, together, the four of them bonded again under the weight of bricks and beams and over the puzzle of connecting water pipes and waste channels. The building was to be nothing grand, just an L-shaped one-storey dwelling made up of two rooms and a bathroom, but the men toasted every advance with a bottle of wine and Dhespina cooed with encouragement whenever she came to assess their handiwork. Although she was in no rush to see her son leave again, she was comforted by the proximity of his emerging home, and as she watched her men at work her only regret was that Nicos wasn't with them.

Since Loukis's return, Dhespina had lost count of the number of times she had been on the verge of revealing what she knew to be true. However, Georgios always sensed when her lips were about to fail them and pulled her back with a look of caution. And maybe he was correct; if the truth needed to come out, it would find a way. It might even be better if their son remained in the dark. God knows, he needed the freedom to seek a new life away from the pain of his old one. Not that he was ready to accept another yet – nowhere near it, in fact – but Dhespina spied Maria waiting in the wings and, more sadly, Michalakis did too.

After being so fired up by his few walks with the girl, Michalakis had retreated to the capital to hide his disappointment in work, which would later be given pride of place in the family home. Among the cuttings already pinned to the walls were four front-page articles covering Makarios's grand return; the official EOKA ceasefire; Grivas's departure to Greece; and the handing in of weapons. However, Dhespina knew all of her sons backwards, and though she appreciated that Michalakis was truly very busy, she recognized he had been bruised by his encounter with Maria. She also realized that Loukis was oblivious to that fact.

As the bricks and rocks taking up space on Mehmet's land began to take the shape of Loukis's new home, Cyprus busied herself with the political necessities of independence.

People began to believe in a future away from the foreign oppression they had always known and the community conflicts they had so recently suffered. And as if in blessing of all that was to come, that summer Lenya gave easy birth to a baby girl. She named her daughter Niki in memory of Nicos and Dhespina wept with joy and gratitude at the gesture.

'She's adorable,' she told Lenya, lifting the baby in

her arms to kiss at the soft white curls crowning her head.

'I told you blondes ran in your side of the family,' Georgios joked, taking his turn after his wife.

'Lenya, you best take care Mamma doesn't shave your child's head when you're not looking,' Loukis joined in. 'Come on, Papa, hand her over.'

As Loukis took hold of the baby, Dhespina felt sadness prick at her eyes. In a matter of weeks his own child would be three years old, and she silently grieved for his loss. Dhespina felt Georgios's hand land on her shoulder, and she reached for it and kissed him. Two weeks ago they had both seen their granddaughter playing along the cobbles of the harbour. She was growing into a striking little girl, and the fringe her mother had recently cut into her dark hair accentuated the night in her eyes – an unwitting gift from her father.

Praxi slipped herself out of her dress and leaned over the sink to wet her head. Yiannis and Elpida – as well as her ever-present mother – had gone to the store to buy supplies, and Praxi took the opportunity to wash the sweat and the dust from her hair before they returned. Time was a rare luxury now that her daughter was of an age where she was intent on testing her own agility and, coupled with the growing popularity of the café, she barely had a moment's peace. Not that she was complaining; the less time she had to think the better.

After towelling her hair dry, Praxi brushed it straight. Behind her, the door opened.

'What have you forgotten now?' she asked, turning around with some annoyance.

'What have *I* forgotten?'

Praxi's heart lurched to her mouth. Where she had expected to see the apologetic form of her husband, there stood a man, impossibly tall, whose dark eyes flashed pain and fury at her from under heavy black brows. For a full two minutes, neither of them moved, stunned into stillness by their own confused emotions.

Loukis was the first to wake, and he reached Praxi in two strides to grab her roughly by the back of her wet hair. He closed his mouth upon hers before she could speak and Praxi responded to his touch with a violence of her own. As they kissed she tasted blood.

Finally released from their dreams and fading memories, their longing was desperate and naturally ferocious, and they fell on to the bed in a frenzy of greedy hands and ravenous lips. Without a word, Praxi tore at Loukis's shirt until she felt the warmth and the hardness of his chest on her palms. He took what was left of her clothes and they lost themselves in the way they had always been meant to. In the tangle of their limbs, they were flesh and blood, rock and water, and they crashed and melted, took and gave, with the certainty of knowing that their very existence depended on the other – and of the two of them becoming one.

By the time their madness took leave of them, the light of the room was dimming with dusk and the reality of what they had done hit Praxi with a jolt.

'Oh God,' she muttered, jumping out of the bed and dressing herself hurriedly. 'Yiannis will be home soon. He can't . . . my God . . . Loukis . . . it's not . . .'

Loukis swung his legs out of the bed to pull on his trousers. His voice was hoarse with emotion. 'How could you?' he asked simply.

'I know . . . I'm sorry . . .' Praxi stumbled, hardly knowing where to start, 'but when you left I was alone and . . .'

'You were lonely?' Loukis jeered. 'My bed had hardly grown cold and you were lonely?'

'It's not what you think,' Praxi tried, blinking back tears.

'Isn't it?' Loukis demanded. He was now dressed, and the anger he had strived to tame returned with a vengeance. 'Why didn't you wait, Praxi? I was there for you. I never left you!'

'You did leave me!' she screamed back. 'You walked out of my life without a word!'

'You knew I would come back!'

'But when, Loukis? When? Three years you were gone!'

'And for three years I thought of no one but you. It has always been you!'

'And don't you think I felt – and feel – the same way? Every night I held you in my dreams, every day I prayed you would return to me, but I didn't have the time, Loukis, I had . . .'

'Praxi?'

The two of them span around to face the door. Yiannis stood there, his face colourless.

'Oh God,' Praxi moaned, dropping defeated on to the bed.

'What are you doing in my house?' he demanded of Loukis. His voice sounded braver than he felt, and his hands shook with indignation and fear. The boy he had known had been replaced by a man who towered above him.

'What do you think I'm doing in your house?' Loukis sneered and, regrettably, Yiannis realized he had to make a stand.

'Get out!' he ordered. 'Get out of my house!'

Before he had time to think about the possible repercussions, Yiannis pushed Loukis hard in the chest. Loukis barely moved, and he grabbed Praxi's husband by the throat and pinned him against the wall.

'And now what are you going to do about it?' he shouted, but Yiannis no longer had the power of speech and, as he struggled, his face grew swollen and red.

'You chose this over me?' Loukis spat back at Praxi.

She sprang to her feet and pulled at his arm, but he refused to release his hold. 'Please,' she shouted, 'don't hurt him. Please, it's not his fault.'

'Are you serious?' Loukis asked incredulously. 'You actually give a damn about this apology of a man?' He relaxed his grip and Yiannis slid to the floor, choking. 'Then have him, Praxi. Have him and be happy. I won't be troubling you again.'

With that, Loukis strode out of the room, slamming the door loudly behind him. Although every inch of her wanted to give chase, Praxi bent to her husband and placed a hand on his shoulder. Yiannis flinched in response and turned away.

'Don't touch me,' he mumbled.

She could not see his face, but Praxi heard the hurt in his tremulous voice. She stood up to assess the foetus-shaped form that was the man she had married. With his body curled against the door frame, he looked pathetic and, may God forgive her, but at that moment his weakness disgusted her.

'Where's Elpida?' she asked.

'She's downstairs with your mother.'

As Praxi moved to pass him, he grabbed at her ankle.

'Praxi, I don't care what you do. I don't care that you don't love me. But please, I'm begging you, don't take my daughter from me.'

'We're not going anywhere,' she replied coolly, and disappeared downstairs.

In the café, her mother somehow managed to stay her tongue as she handed over her granddaughter. Praxi was grateful for the silence, and she took Elpida to the far end of the room. Holding her closely, she cried into the child's hair. Although the smell of love still clung to her body, she had never felt more alone.

As the summer sun cooled into autumn and froze into winter, Praxi waited for Loukis to return, convinced he would be unable to resist her, but, true to his word, he never troubled her again. Meanwhile, her husband spent his nights in his office and his days in denial, and Praxi filled the space he'd left in their bed with the ghostly image of the man she loved.

When the spring arrived to stir the romance still nesting in her breast, Praxi toyed with the idea of going to Loukis, but whenever she built up the nerve something would come to make her see reason; often it was the giggle of her daughter in the arms of the only father she knew, on other occasions, her mother's look of disapproval, sometimes just the fact that she knew what was right.

By the time summer returned, and with it Elpida's fourth birthday, Praxi had distanced herself enough to accept the half-life she lived, and she managed to take the late gift Dhespina brought her daughter and not ask after the health of her son. In turn, Dhespina offered no hints as to Loukis's state of mind, but she was quietly pleased to see the truth of their situation showing more than ever in the child that had been denied him. Elpida was an astonishingly pretty little girl and though she had her mother's ready smile from childhood, Dhespina also saw an unknown quality that was the mark of her son. On her way home, she passed by Loukis's new home to check on the chamomile bushes she had planted a few months earlier. They were in good shape, and she was pleasantly surprised.

'Maria,' Loukis confessed when his mother voiced her astonishment. 'She's been tending them. I'm not sure why she bothers.'

Dhespina knew full well why the young woman wasted her time seeing to her son's plants and she was damn sure he did too. In a way she felt sorry for the girl, but she couldn't entirely forgive her for the unhappiness she had caused another of her sons.

Since Loukis had returned, Michalakis was a fleeting presence at their home. Of course, Dhespina accepted that he was needed in the capital; he had his job to do and it was an important one, now more so than ever because, that night, her son would be writing history.

'Will you be joining us back at the house this evening?' Dhespina asked Loukis.

'I wouldn't miss it for the world,' he smiled.

'Well, make sure you don't, and bring Mehmet and Pembe with you.'

Loukis said he would and that evening, along with Christakis and Yianoulla and their three little boys, the family and their two Turkish guests ate in the garden. A slight breeze eased the strangling heat of high summer and it mingled with the smell of kebabs and the cigarette smoke of the men. In a matter of hours, the crate of Keo Marios had carried from town had been demolished and the talk turned lively and loud. As it grew late, Georgios brought out the radio and they fell silent. It was 15 August 1960, and at the stroke of midnight a broadcaster announced that the Union Jack above Government House was being lowered.

From his place on the press bench, Michalakis heard the fanfare of military trumpets followed by a twenty-one-gun salute. As the sound of the last shot echoed across Lefkosia, the Independent Republic of Cyprus was born and Michalakis found himself swept away by an uncommon rush of emotion – the island was free.

During the EOKA campaign, six hundred people had died, most of them Greeks. Another 1,260 had been wounded, and 156 British had also lost their lives. Independence had come at a terrible cost and, though he was proud to bear witness to the moment, Michalakis wondered whether the bereaved would agree the price had been worth it.

Ten hours after the British flag came down, the first Parliament in the country's three-thousand-year history met for the formal investiture of President Makarios and Vice-president Fazil Küçük – and the Cyprus flag was raised. The island was a gold silhouette on a white background, with two crossed olive branches to symbolize peace and unity. The president was Greek, his vice-president Turkish. Political power was shared to give one community the right to fight for their dreams through democratic process, and the other the right to a respect they believed had long been denied them. Meanwhile, the British retreated to their sovereign bases in Dhekelia and Akrotiri. On the Cyprus Broadcasting Service, the former British governor sent a final message to the people he had hoped to tame.

In the clipped tones of his British accent, Sir Hugh Foot told them: 'What of the future? It is for you to answer that question. A few dismal commentators say that the people of Cyprus will destroy each other. They say that you will tear yourselves to bits – Greek against Turks and Left against Right. There are a few who say that the island will go down in a sea of blood and hate. It could be . . . but I don't believe it. People who have been to the brink of hell don't want to go over the edge.'

PART TWO
1963

In the event of a breach of the provisions of the present Treaty, Greece, Turkey and the United Kingdom undertake to consult together with respect to the representations or measures necessary to ensure observance of those provisions.

In so far as common or concerted action may not prove possible, each of the three guaranteeing Powers reserves the right to take action with the sole aim of re-establishing the state of affairs created by the present Treaty.

The Treaty of Guarantee Article IV, 1960

11

She reached a good age, everyone said so – not that her longevity made it any easier to accept the end when it came. But death is rarely a welcome visitor, no matter how tardy the knock on the door. With the benefit of hindsight, Dhespina recognized the tell-tale signs – the creeping melancholy, the untouched food – but she had held seasonal change responsible; with the spring breeze stilled by the heat of another summer, it sapped the appetite of everyone. To her shame, Dhespina had denied the truth of her own eyes and, when she woke that morning to find the old girl still sleeping, the realization hit her like a brick in the chest.

'She was a good goat, Mamma.'

'Yes, she was, Marios. Yes, she was.'

Dhespina leaned the spade against the orange tree and took a handful of dried rose petals from the pocket of her apron. She scattered them across the grave – a small gesture to show Athena that she had been appreciated and very much loved.

'We'll get you a new goat,' Georgios offered. 'Once you feel ready, of course.'

Dhespina smiled because she saw her husband meant to

comfort, but they both knew there would be no replace-
ment, just as they had never had the heart to bring another
dog into their lives. And besides, Dhespina was tired of
creating mounds of earth. Under her dark clothes, she ached
for the happiness of her youth.

After a dispirited breakfast of grilled halloumi and ham,
Georgios drifted off to his den with an apologetic look and
Marios left for his brother's workshop. Dhespina walked up
the lane to find her youngest son. When she spied Loukis,
he was sat on a large rock in front of his home, skinning a
rabbit. His hands were streaked red and the scene gripped
her by the throat. Her baby had grown into a man. The fat
of youth had long fallen from his face, and even at a distance
she saw the determined twitch in his jaw as he pulled fur
from muscle. As ever, he was dressed carelessly, in black
trousers and a grey shirt frayed at the sleeves. Behind him
the white walls of his home served to accentuate the darkness of his clothes. Compared to the modest building, he
also looked freakishly large, so much so that, following the
agiasmos blessing, the priest jokingly insisted on returning
once the house had been expanded to accommodate the size
of its owner. Stepping quietly behind Loukis, Dhespina
swept her hands under his chin and pulled back his head to
place a kiss upon his forehead.

'What's wrong with your face? You look miserable.'

'Athena's dead.'

Loukis tore his gaze away from the near-furless corpse to
meet his mamma's eyes. 'Shame, but she was a good age.'

'Yes, she was,' Dhespina agreed. Looking to her right, she
waved at Pembe, who was sitting on her porch weaving date
leaves into baskets. The old woman shouted a cheery *salaam*

and continued stabbing with the large packing needle her people called *cuvaldiz*.

'Have you thought any more about what we spoke about?' Dhespina asked, returning her attention to her son.

'Not much,' he admitted, trying to ignore the weary shake of his mother's head.

'It's not fair on the girl, Loukis. You ought to marry her or let her go.'

'Not much of a choice there, Mamma . . .'

'This is no laughing matter, son. For more than two years you've allowed that girl to run after you. You can't keep her dangling on your belt like another dead rabbit. It's time to make up your mind, Loukis. It's getting embarrassing. I hardly know where to look when I come across her poor parents.'

'OK, I'll think about it.'

'Don't just say it, mean it,' Dhespina demanded, reaching to take Loukis's chin in her hand.

He knocked his head away.

'I said I'll think about it. Now could you leave me in peace? I've got a stew to prepare.'

Loukis got to his feet. As he walked into the dimness of his house, the easy smile he had gifted his mother slipped from his lips.

Elpida looked at the plate in front of her and dropped her head to the table, smacking her forehead on the wood with a bang.

'Not more apples . . .'

'They're good for you.'

'They're boring!'

Praxi pursed her lips and continued picking the seeds from the abandoned core, placing them in a small bowl by her side.

'*Yiayia* says I have to eat meat to make my blood strong,' Elpida protested.

Well, your grandmother isn't trying to kill her husband, Praxi responded silently.

'Just eat your apple, Elpida.'

Praxi couldn't be sure at what point she had decided she wanted to poison her husband. It was a plan that seemed to appear out of nowhere, before fading into fantasy days later. But as she had few pleasures in life, she was damned if reason and her daughter's grumblings were going to rob her of the satisfaction of pretence.

Praxi had no idea how many seeds it might take to fell Yiannis, but the simple act of transporting pip from core to bowl somehow added fresh purpose to her life, and for hours she was able to lose herself in vile imaginings; pulverizing pips into a marinade for his meat; lacing his salad dressing; decorating his bread with tiny beads of poison. Even with Yiannis's expanding girth, Praxi was confident she could finish him in one meal. Naturally, a whisper of conscience occasionally shamed her out of these dreamy acts of assassination, but the discomfort she felt largely sat in the realization that she hadn't the courage to carry out the crime. Rather like divorce, murder was a sin against God and society, and Praxi hadn't the disposition for hell or for prison. Unquestionably, she needed a miracle. Unfortunately, divine intervention was rarely bestowed upon the malefactor, the knowledge of which had sent Praxi scurrying to the Church, much to her mamma's brief relief.

As the town's bishop was fond of saying, 'The nearer a person comes to the light, the more light he gets, the closer he draws to the fire, the warmer he is, and the nearer he approaches sanctity, the more saintly he becomes.' Suitably encouraged, Praxi energetically gave herself to the Lord in the hope that she would receive a little of His glory, heat and holiness. Regrettably, and try as she might to keep her mind on the script, all too often her lips betrayed her as they whispered prayers to a Merciful God that mainly involved her husband being struck down with a fatal illness, a tragic accident or at the very least a bolt of lightning. As Praxi had been to church enough times to realize that no good could come to the sinner who uttered such entreaties, it therefore came as a blessing when her mamma's proud encouragement started to falter. Because Praxi was taking communion with such uncommon regularity, the rest of the congregation had turned suspicious, with a hardcore believing a heinous crime must have been committed to warrant such devotion, such as murder or adultery. Therefore, following the embarrassed but firm instructions of her mamma, Praxi slid back into her original haphazard method of worship – and right back to where she started, with a husband she was desperate to be rid of.

Praxi couldn't leave Yiannis – that much was clear. Perhaps if he had raised his fists to her like any other man would have done faced with his wife's infidelity, she could have used her bruises as a ticket out. Of course, the injuries would have needed to be severe. It might even have been necessary to lose a few teeth, or a limb. But Yiannis never did hit her – he barely raised his voice in anger – which was why only his passing could ever release her. If only God would send him some terrible disease! Or smash a thunderbolt upon his bulbous head! With an untimely death, there could be no recriminations, no disgrace to carry on her shoulders, no blame darting from the eyes of her own flesh and blood. In fact, the more Praxi thought about it, the fewer repercussions she saw, save Elpida's tears of mourning, and even they would cease in time. However, the Lord remained oblivious to the living hell of Praxi's life. To her increasing annoyance, Yiannis appeared to have the constitution of an ox; and he rarely ventured out in bad weather on account of the adverse effect it had on his hair.

With a sigh, Praxi left the table to place the bowl in the cupboard above the sink, next to the condiments and out of her daughter's reach. As she hooked the latch she knew she would have to throw the seeds away at some point and the thought of it made her nauseous. In the emptiness of her days, Praxi had grown to rely on the pips to pep up her life. She wasn't really heartless; she recognized it was a desperate and even sad fixation. It wasn't as if she hated Yiannis in any great way. If anything, she felt indifferent. All the love she could physically give was swallowed by her daughter; the rest she emptied into the hole left by Loukis. But it wasn't enough. She couldn't rest. In the early days, when Loukis was missing, and even for a while once he'd returned, Praxi believed that time would allow the situation to become more tolerable, but if anything the passing years had only increased her torment. She had no life she wanted to live that didn't include Loukis, and the only way she could think of to rectify such injustice was to bury the man who stood in her way. As a widow, she would be released from the obligations that tied her to the wrong husband. And after a

190

decent period of time, society would allow her to begin again.

After nearly six years of marriage, the gratitude Praxi had once felt towards her husband had steadily shifted until she was left with little more than resentment. No longer maintaining the private facade of husband and wife, they were but two residents of a house and the genial hosts of a popular café-bar. And to Praxi's growing fury, it was apparent that Yiannis was content to carry on with the farce until the day they died. His public displays of affection and the clumsy grab of her waist in front of his Greek army friends made her physically ill. And though she was grateful for his distance when the doors of their business slammed shut, she knew beyond doubt that she had to change her destiny – and that transformation lay in a casket she had opened in her mind and in which she had already laid her husband.

As Praxi continued to fill the bowl hidden in the cupboard, she seasoned the charade with the rationale of destiny. As sure as Cyprus would be delivered to Greece, Praxi would again lie in the arms of Loukis – which is why, when she bumped into Maria shopping in the stores of Keryneia, her world slipped from beneath her feet.

With a thin smile and barely disguised triumph, Maria gleefully revealed she was searching for a new dress, in readiness for the priest's blessing – Loukis had proposed and Maria was going to marry him.

Michalakis sipped at his coffee, checked his watch, drank from the glass of water, lit a cigarette and strained to keep his irritation in check. Kyriakos was late. He was always late.

191

And knowing this, Michalakis was annoyed only with himself, because he should have known better than to arrive on time at one of Lefkosia's busiest bars. Already he had disappointed a number of customers coveting the empty chair in front of him, and he was starting to feel like an abandoned suitor stubbornly guarding the seat of his missing sweetheart.

By the second cup of coffee – and having resisted the temptation to order a beer – his contact landed heavily on the chair in front of him. His bald head dripped beads of sweat and the short-sleeved shirt he wore accentuated the stumpy hairiness of his arms. It was fair to say that Kyriakos was not the kind of man that women might swoon over, yet he had managed to achieve what Michalakis had so far failed to do – he had recently snared himself a wife.

'Recovered from the wedding?' Michalakis asked, waving at the *kafetzi* as he spoke.

'Marriage, as I am finding out, is a constant state of recovery,' Kyriakos laughed. '*Sketto!*' he told the *kafetzi*, and Michalakis raised an eyebrow in question.

'The wife,' Kyriakos explained. 'After two months of marriage, she now thinks I'm fat. Luckily for her, I'm still blinded by her nakedness, so I've agreed to forego the sugar in my coffee. Take my advice, friend, never marry a thin girl, especially if they have good breasts. They will only make you crazy.'

Michalakis took the advice with a smile, but it meant nothing. Following his promotion to political editor, the only company he kept nowadays came with large moustaches, varying degrees of body hair and ever deeper frowns etched along their foreheads.

Crawling into its third year, the government was un-ravelling. The complex structure of power-sharing had given disproportionate rights to an 18 per cent minority. The vice-president had the right of veto, and the Turkish Cypriots protected their privileges with an even greater intensity than they guarded their daughters' virginities. As a result, the government machine was cranking to a halt.

'We are not partners in government, we are partners in suffering,' Kyriakos had commented during their first meeting, more than a year earlier. Michalakis had contacted the Makarios loyalist following the condemnation coming from Grivas in Athens. The exiled colonel had denounced the 1960 deal as a sell-out. And with only *enosis* being acceptable to EOKA hardliners, the former fighters had once again begun littering the towns and villages with leaflets.

Kyriakos clicked his tongue in irritation. 'It's mindless to think the president has betrayed *enosis*. Any fool can see he is playing the long game. The people will get their time at the ballot box and they will vote for union with the motherland.'

'But the treaties safeguard against both *enosis* and *taksim* . . .'

'Yes, yes, yes, but there's a plan,' Kyriakos casually admitted. 'An off-the-record plan, that is.'

'Go on.'

Kyriakos shifted in his seat to bring his face nearer. His voice fell low, and Michalakis smelled garlic on his breath. 'Makarios is working to abolish, stage by stage, the excessive rights granted to the Turkish Cypriots, thereby reducing their position to that of a minority, enjoying such minority rights as are generally in use internationally. The first stage is to introduce amendments to the constitution . . . with the backing of the international community, of course.'

'There's no way Küçük and his men will allow that.'

'No, we don't expect they will. But if the Turks resort to force, the security forces will be called on to maintain law and order. If they're not up to the job, the paramilitaries will take over, with orders to use as much force as necessary to put down a revolt – albeit with enough restraint to avoid Turkish mainland intervention.'

'Christ, that's a hell of a risk.'

Kyriakos shook his head. 'Not if the amendments are given the chance to breathe. Right now, the republic is in deadlock. We can't move forward. We can't move back. We can't even agree on taxation, for God's sake. The government of this country is being strangled by rules created by foreigners. It's a fiasco. It's unworkable. No one can agree on anything and the majority cannot overrule the minority because of the power of veto awarded to Küçük. The treaties have brought a battalion of Greek *and* Turkish troops on to our soil; we have two British bases on land which is no longer deemed to be ours; and our government finds itself unable to govern. It is a staggering aberration that no other country on earth would accept. Our only hope is that the president will wrestle back enough political clout to give this island its right to self-determination. Granted, this would be at the short-term expense of the minority but, ultimately, it would be for the benefit of all.'

The mosque was uncharacteristically packed, even for Friday prayers, and it made Mehmet uneasy. In front of them, standing to the left of the imam, was a man who looked familiar but whom he couldn't place. He was dressed like a townsman, but when he spoke his voice carried the words of a fighter.

'Brothers,' he cried in welcome, opening his arms to the gathering of men, some barely past their thirteenth year. 'I address you at a time of great urgency, and it is no exaggeration when I say all our lives depend upon your discretion and honour. Because of the nature of what you are about to be told, I have to insist that no word you hear today shall be uttered outside of these holy walls, neither at home, nor in the workplace nor the coffee house. And though it pains me, I swear by the holy Quran, here in my hand, that any one of you who breaks this silence will be severely punished – in this life and the next.'

As the man paused for breath, Mehmet glanced at the faithful closest to him, but their gazes were unflinchingly concentrated on the stranger before them.

'Brothers,' the fighter continued, 'I ask you to take your lead from your *hodja*.'

The imam stepped forward to kiss the holy book. His face was flushed and serious. In a loud, clear voice he stated, 'I swear by Allah and on the holy Quran that what I see and hear today will go to the death with me. If I break this oath I know I'll be killed in return and I consent to this punishment.'

As the Quran slowly passed among them, Mehmet watched stupefied as boys who were still children repeated the words of men, and grandfathers responded to their commitment with proud tears. When it came to his own turn, Mehmet swore on the holy book, knowing he would honour the oath but trembling at the thought of the coming secret he was being asked to keep.

As the Quran made its way back into the fighter's hands, and he was satisfied he had the command of his audience, he continued.

'Brothers, this island is a breath away from falling into the clutches of Greece. Your Greek neighbours, believe it or not, resent our legitimate presence in the government of the republic, and I tell you they will work to fulfil their dreams of *enosis* whatever the cost, even if that includes the murder of our people.'

The man paused to allow the full weight of his words to sink in, letting his gaze drift along the rows of eyes before him. Mehmet felt the man's scrutiny and coloured.

'Yes,' he accepted, as if reading the thoughts of a silent few, 'I know the villages here have escaped the blood that has been shed elsewhere on the island, but there are those among you who have been forced to give up your vineyards and gardens for Greek bases. You have seen your children intimidated, found your animals poisoned and your donkeys shot dead. Oh brothers! If the Greeks have done no more than this we only have Allah to thank for this mercy. But I tell you, with purity of heart, there are plans ahead that will make what we have so far endured a time of paradise. We have intelligence coming from the capital that EOKA plans to take up arms again in order to take this island by force and deliver her to Greece. Should you survive that day, can you even imagine what will become of your lives? Ousted from meaningful government; silenced by the iron fist of Athens; and demoted to peasants when you are rightfully kings! I tell you in all seriousness: it is only a matter of time before these blood-drinking beasts descend upon your villages. You have to act now. From here on in you must be

196

on your guard, and I urge you to support your brothers. We are here for you, and I promise in the coming days we will call on you.'

When the man finished, the mosque echoed with murmurs of appreciation and defiance.

'It's right what he said,' an elderly gentleman remarked to no one. Catching Mehmet's eye, he continued. 'Last week the bus driver refused to open his doors to my wife though she was stood at the Keryneia stop and it was clear she was waiting. What kind of man would take out his hate on an old woman, I ask you? A Greek, that's who. A damn Greek.'

Mehmet gave the man's shoulder a gentle press and walked on. Outside the mosque, he remembered Aphrodite and the fright that death had locked in her eyes. And he pondered the hostility he was encountering more frequently at the marketplace. There was a definite change in the air. But would it pass? Above him a rumble of thunder signalled the start of the autumn storms, and Mehmet shivered, not from cold but from apprehension.

It was the first sky-breaking crack that woke her.

Stirred from sleep, Praxi touched the damp sheet, crumpled by the twists and turns of unwanted dreams and patchy with sweat now quickly cooling against her skin. Her head pounded out of rhythm to her heart, and she felt the wind pulling at her. She walked from her room and descended the outside staircase.

Underneath her feet the cobbles were hard but comforting, and the wind circling in the trap of the harbour snatched at her hair as the first drops of rain fell. Praxi's nerves were numb. She felt immune to the cold and she chased the wind that led her away from the street's light into the dark. As she ran, smooth stone turned to gravel. She felt the sharpness of the stones stabbing her soles, and the nightdress she wore clung wetly to her legs. She picked up speed, intent on fleeing the life behind her. As she ran, her ears drummed to the beat of her breaths.

Praxi knew where she was heading right from the moment her bare feet touched the ground, and above her the thunder roared its encouragement after lightning broke through the clouds to show her the way. She felt the force of the world at her back, pushing her on, demanding she fight.

As Praxi neared the house, she slowed at the light of a candle glowing in the window. The glass was hazy and she could feel his breath on it. Although she had never visited, she had listened to the idle chatter between the emptying of coffee cups and it had helped her imagine the place he had built, to the very last stone. In her mind she had walked a million times among the rooms they ought to have shared.

Praxi inched towards the light. Before she had a chance to raise her hand to the door, it swung open and their eyes met. Behind him, Maria was buttoning her coat.

'Loukis . . .'

'What in God's name?'

Loukis looked at the tiny creature in front of him. She was soaked to the bone and her bare legs were muddied and scratched. Maria moved to his side, shock and anger written in ugly lines across her face.

'Shut the door!' she ordered, and reached to pull Loukis away. He shrugged free of her touch and moved for Praxi's hands to bring her out of the cold.

'I had to see you,' she told him in a whisper.

'Shut the door!' screeched Maria. Loukis shot her a look and pulled the door to – leaving her alone inside.

Before him, Praxi stood shivering, and her chest heaved with effort.

'We need to get you home,' he stated flatly, but Praxi squirmed from his touch and, with a wildness that came from her genes, she grabbed hard at his face. Her eyes were fierce and Loukis struggled to avoid them.

'You have to promise me!' she demanded, pulling him towards her. 'Swear upon everything we have ever been that you will never betray me!'

'Praxi, stop . . .'

'You cannot marry Maria! If you do, you might as well take that gun of yours and shoot me in the head, because I tell you it will kill me. Promise me, Loukis! Promise me you won't do this!'

Loukis fell to his knees.

'How can you even ask me this?' he pleaded.

'Because you belong to me!' Praxi screamed back at him. 'You have always belonged to me, and on my life I swear I will never let you go. Not ever! Not until the moment we are both within our graves and the world has stopped turning! That's how I can ask you, Loukis! That's how I can ask you!'

And having done so, Praxi fell at his feet, unconscious.

12

In the years to come, when pragmatism allowed for moments of reflection, Michalakis would privately claim that the beginning of the end came with the rise and fall of a whore's drawers.

In November 1963, President Makarios unveiled his proposals for constitutional change. The thirteen amendments would abolish the vice-president's power of veto and the island's separate municipalities. They were presented as a genuine attempt to overcome the difficulties paralysing the government and standing in the way of unity, but the archbishop was unable to conceal the fact that they also worked to the advantage of the majority.

The following month Turkey rejected the amendments and within days the island was again looking down the barrel of a gun. An EOKA monument was blown up and Greek Cypriots readied their arms. The Muslim fighters of the TMT mounted machine guns on top of mosques and districts were sealed off. Then, on 16 December, the police were called to investigate a quarrel over a prostitute in Lefkosia's Turkish quarter. An angry crowd gathered, guns were fired, and the hostility that had lain dormant for three years exploded.

Six people died in the first two days of fighting and, as Greek Cypriot forces mobilized, Turkish Cypriots in the gendarmerie and police force abandoned their posts. By the third day, seventeen Turkish Cypriots and eleven Greek Cypriots lay dead, and the sniping had spread from the capital to Larnaka, Ammochostos, Lemesos, Pafos and Keryneia. Private armies were unleashed and armed with mortars, rifles, automatic weapons and armoured bulldozers. Telephone lines to Muslim areas were cut and whole villages were taken hostage on either side. As the violence escalated, the bells of Christmas Day battled against the noise of Turkish jets roaring threats of invasion across the capital. As panic took hold, three troop carriers were said to have entered Cyprus's territorial waters. President Makarios ordered a ceasefire. The British, who had sought to extricate themselves from the island's problems, hurriedly scrambled a Truce Force in order to pacify both communities and calm the international concerns that the violence would drag two NATO allies, Greece and Turkey, into major conflict. The day after the ceasefire, hostages were exchanged, but the damage was done. Cooperation between the two communities ceased, and the Turkish Cypriots withdrew from government, never to return.

As the tense stand-off stretched the island's nerves, Michalakis joined a group of foreign journalists invited to tour the destruction in one of Lefkosia's suburbs. In Kumsal, they were led to a house whose floors crunched with broken glass. In the corner of one room lay a child's bicycle. In another lay the body of a woman, her head shattered by a bullet. One reporter, a British man, murmured his disgust, but as the group moved to the bathroom he was silenced by the scene that met their eyes. In a blood-stained tub were three dead children, piled on top of their murdered mother. The stunned journalists were informed that the house belonged to a Turkish major. The bodies were all that was left of his family – and a neighbour who found herself in the wrong place at the worst possible time.

As they left the house, Michalakis excused himself from the group. He turned the corner and, leaning against a wall, he brought up his breakfast. The horror of what he had seen would remain with him for the rest of his days and colour every account he would go on to hear. The massacre not only triggered his revulsion at the inhumanity of man, but also his incomprehension, because the dead had been left on display like rotting exhibits in a kangaroo court – some five days after their murders had taken place.

'Show me the animal that has more faces than a Turk!'

Victor threw his jacket on to a stool and reached for the bottle of brandy behind the bar. Yiannis collected two glasses from the sink and locked the door. He placed the tumblers on the table nearest the fire. The lights were off, and the candles had burned to the wick.

When Victor pulled up a chair, the flames from the hearth danced light and shadow upon his brow and Yiannis found himself mesmerized; the young officer's nose had the strength of a real Greek and it complemented his sharp, handsome face.

'Tough day?' he asked, extending a cigarette.

'Is there any other?' Victor replied. He touched the bandage on his forearm that hid the burn of a bullet from the previous day's skirmish. Following the fights in the capital, the Turkish soldiers had moved out of their barracks to take control of the pass leading from Keryneia to Lefkosia. The Greek Cypriots led by Victor and his fellow Greek officers had fought hard to regain control, but they had spectacularly failed, and the Turks remained in place, enabling snipers to take pot shots at will.

'You know, it kills me to say this, but we've been skilfully outmanoeuvred by the Turks,' Victor told Yiannis. 'While your president has been playing politics, the Turkish Cypriots have been busy arming themselves with shipments from the mainland. They've retreated into their strongholds, practically bringing *taksim* to the island right under your noses, and they've engineered an excuse for Mother Turkey to intervene with shouts of murder and persecution committed by their own hands!'

'They're a devious lot, all right,' Yiannis muttered. The inanity of his contribution echoed around his head, but he couldn't help it; his mind was distracted.

'All this propaganda,' Victor continued, 'the so-called murders. You want to find the real killers? I tell you, go look in the Turkish slums. That's where you'll find the guns with blood on their barrels. We all know the barbarians wouldn't think twice about sacrificing their own if it meant achieving their goals.'

Yiannis nodded and poured more brandy into their glasses. His own face was flushed from the alcohol he had drunk in anticipation of Victor's return and he was battling to pull his thoughts away from the moist traces of saliva resting on the officer's bottom lip.

'Do you still have the police?' Yiannis asked.

Victor gave a short, humourless laugh. 'For now, but I

doubt it will remain that way for much longer. Even as your country lies in jeopardy, your leaders have no stomach for the fight.'

'We can't give them up!' Yiannis yelped with genuine concern. 'We need them for the bargaining and all that.'

Victor knocked the bottom of his glass against the rim of Yiannis's, signalling his agreement. Although the Turkish battalion had wrested control of the pass, the Greek Cypriots had acted quickly to secure Keryneia and, on Christmas Day, they had arrested a number of Turkish Cypriot police. They were now hostages that would be killed should Turkey invade.

'The trouble is,' Victor said as he roughly swept the hair from his face in frustration, 'we're being seen as the aggressors here. Forget that Turkey will do anything in its power to stop the breath of Greece from warming her backside when Cyprus rejoins the motherland. Forget that Turkey has persecuted our people for centuries. Forget the genocide of the First World War! Oh, I tell you, Yiannis, the Turks and their bastard offspring have played it well. The Turkish Cypriots turn their back on the government over a few minor constitutional amendments; they pull their people out of jobs, claiming they've been threatened; they order families into enclaves to shore up their positions; they take control of the road most strategic to their invasion plans; and then – and this is the real genius – they cry victim, to ensure that Greece and Makarios get slapped by the foreigners. And your president's courting of the Soviets isn't helping. America and her allies won't endanger their precious spy bases. Believe me, Makarios is playing this all wrong.'

'We need Grivas,' Yiannis agreed, refilling Victor's empty glass for the fourth time that night.

'Perhaps,' Victor admitted. 'We certainly need a man with his eye fixed on the prize if we're to bring Cyprus back into the arms of the motherland.' Pausing to give Yiannis a confident smile, he added, 'Our people belong together.'

And with that he leaned forward and delivered the promise Yiannis had been waiting for.

For three weeks, Praxi had drifted in and out of consciousness, trapped by a fever that turned her cheeks scarlet and tangled her hair into knots. The doctor had come, but offered no remedy, and in desperation Elena called on Dhespina, who brought wet herbs to heal Praxi's feet and two buckets, which she immediately filled with water – one warm and wafting rosemary; the other cold as ice.

As they worked to rid Praxi of the illness Dhespina insisted on calling 'the Terror', Elpida danced between their feet, and Elena's heart dipped at the flashes of joy it brought to her friend's gentle face. But when Elpida called her to the window to take a look at the black-eyed man waiting outside, Elena thanked Dhespina for all the help she had given and said she could continue her daughter's care alone.

'Who is he, *yiayia*?' Elpida asked as Dhespina closed the door behind her.

To her eternal shame, Elena told her grandchild the stranger she had seen was the village crazy man.

For years, Yiannis had spent his nights waiting for the sun to rise so that he might escape his own bed but now, as he felt his warm breath drift to the base of Victor's spine, he couldn't think of a more heavenly place to be. These times, when the morning was new and his eyes remained sticky with sleep, were the closest he had come to knowing peace, and he wished with all of his heart that the waking day would never arrive – and his wife would remain at her mother's for ever.

In a typically awkward encounter, Elena had told Yiannis that Praxi had been sleepwalking when she escaped to the village in the dead of night. As Yiannis had witnessed his wife's nocturnal wanderings, he could have easily accepted the tale – if he hadn't also witnessed her adultery. And though three years had passed with no evidence of a repeat, he couldn't shake the feeling that he was again being duped. Even so, to his surprise and slight consternation, he realized that he didn't particularly care what Praxi got up to, as long as his child and neighbours remained ignorant of it. Of course it irked to think that she was lying in the arms of a half-feral farming hand, but he felt nothing resembling jealousy. His feelings came closer to exoneration.

A little over a year ago, he had been more agitated. He had suspected his wife was resuming her affair when she began sloping off to church at every given opportunity. But in those days he was still needled by the humiliation he had experienced in the sanctity of his own home. And of course it turned out that Praxi really was going to church, which began to calm the rage he felt, as he assumed guilt must have finally got the better of her. Then, once Praxi's fad of repentance appeared to be over, Yiannis found he was able to move on by doing nothing, and the more he did nothing, the more detached he became from the woman he had married. Not to say that he didn't miss his daughter. In fact, the first week Praxi spent in convalescence, he was close to dragging her back to the bar because he couldn't stand the quiet left by Elpida. But then, as the fates would have it, Victor came by.

The two men had known each other for three months. Mother Greece was furtively pouring her troops on to the island and, to Yiannis's secret delight, Victor was stationed in one of the camps lying west of Keryneia. After his first visit to the café with a handful of other officers, he became a regular face, and on occasion he even talked to Praxi about his own wife on the mainland and their two little boys. And yet Yiannis thought he saw something he recognized in the officer's off-hand glances.

Then, eight days after Praxi had run barefoot to the village, Victor had offered his help as the last of the café's customers took to their homes. When Yiannis thanked him, he sensed the mood turn in an instant and he could barely stop his hands from shaking as he brought the stained coffee cups and froth-lined glasses to the sink. As the water poured, Victor stepped behind him, leaning for a cloth, and Yiannis felt the man's stomach trace the shape of his spine. He turned towards the officer and never looked back.

After their first night together, Victor stayed away from the café for three days, and Yiannis began to feel a prickle of shame creep along the nape of his neck when he thought about what they had done. But then, when he was close to giving up hope, the door opened wide and Victor's smile told him he had nothing to fear but his own insecurities.

Yiannis had never dared hope he would come to know such joy, and the thrill of it consumed his every thought. Not that it was always easy. Victor was a proud man, whose opinions bounced off the walls hard as facts, and when Yiannis opened up about his own loveless marriage, he was felled by the swift condemnation that met his account of the day he had found Loukis in his home.

'If it was my wife I'd have killed her . . . or him . . . probably the both of them.'

Victor turned on the bed to rest his head on his hand. 'There are times to be a man,' he said simply, and the words hit like daggers in Yiannis's heart.

Unsurprisingly, Yiannis was loath to mention his wife again, not least because he was enjoying the pretence of living alone, but Victor remained curious. When it eventually came to light that the man she had slept with also lived with two Turks, the Greek officer almost spat his disgust in Yiannis's face.

'Allowing your wife to cavort with a traitor is a stain on your reputation that will last a lifetime,' Victor sneered.

Now, in the dim light of the barely born morning and confronted by the beauty of Victor's naked back, the insult ate at Yiannis's insides.

Pembe was dragging a basket of logs into the house when she saw the car pull up. She stretched upright to welcome the visitors, but they ignored her and headed straight for Loukis's home. She shrugged at the men's ill manners and bent to take up her basket again, but as she turned towards the door, a last look set her hairs standing on end. From under their long coats, the three men pulled out metal chains and heavy sticks. As they neared Loukis's house, she watched them lift the scarves from around their throats to cover their faces.

Two of them stood either side of the door, and the third knocked.

'Loukis, no!' Pembe screamed. As the door pulled open, the surprise hardly reached his face before a baton struck him hard in the gut. Two of the men grabbed Loukis by the arms and hauled him to the apple tree. As Pembe went running for her husband, she saw them tying him to the trunk. They called him a 'Turk-loving traitor', and she heard it as clearly as if she had been bound to the tree herself.

Although Pembe hadn't run for the best part of a decade, she flew through the olive grove with a fleetness of foot that instantly alarmed her husband when she found him.

'It's Loukis!' she screamed. 'They've come to kill him!'

Mehmet dropped the scythe he was holding and took his wife by the shoulders.

'Where is he?'

'At the house. At the tree. Oh merciful Allah, help him, Mehmet!'

'Stay here!'

Mehmet ran to the tractor standing idle by the grove. Cranking the machine into action, he thundered down the lane that curved around his property. Under his breath, he uttered prayers that he wouldn't be too late. He felt no fear, only a desperate need to save the boy, but as he turned towards his home he was shocked beyond words at the savagery taking place. Loukis's chin was bouncing on his chest, and even from a distance Mehmet could see blood pouring from his mouth and the ugly welts of chains that had ripped through the sleeves of his jumper. The farmer crashed through the gate, sending splinters of wood flying before him.

'Get off him, you bastards!'

Mehmet lurched towards the men, bumping the small tractor over the white rocks Marios had placed on the ground to create a pathway to Loukis's front door. Swerving right, Mehmet headed straight for the apple tree.

'Get off him!' he yelled again, the force of his words tearing at his throat.

As he neared, the men moved to face him. Charging past, he clipped one of them on the leg, bringing a yelp of surprise. Mehmet span the tractor, kicking up stones and grass in his fury, and squared up to them. As the three assailants readied themselves, from behind him Mehmet heard a crack of gunshot. He turned in his seat to see his wife, old and frail as she was, calmly reloading another cartridge into a hunting gun.

The three men swapped looks, and with one last kick at Loukis's face they fled, running back to the Chevrolet in which they had come.

Dhespina was brewing celery tea for Mandalena, the baker's daughter, when Mehmet came haring around the bend on his tractor to tell her her son had been attacked. As she hurriedly filled her bag with everything she might need, the young woman arrived and found herself directed to the teapot, with apologies that she'd have to deal with her cystitis on her own. Dhespina then ran to Loukis, while Mehmet continued to the village phone box to summon the doctor.

As soon as she saw her son lying on his bed – bruised, battered and barely resembling the boy she loved – Dhespina got to work. Running her fingers over his blood-soaked head and quickly swelling body, she found four angry lumps on his skull; his nose was misshapen and clearly broken; two of his back teeth were cracked; he had a number of broken ribs; ugly rips running along his arms, chest and thighs; and a puncture hole in his left knee.

'Did they stab you as well?' she asked, as she placed a bucket of water on the stove.

Loukis attempted to respond, but his words were lost in the devastation of his mouth.

'Did they stab you?' Dhespina repeated, fury rising in her chest.

'Tree root!' Loukis spat, and he closed his eyes in a fruit-less effort to shut out the pain.

By the time the doctor arrived, Dhespina had washed her son's wounds with drops from the Shepherd's Purse tincture she had brought with her. The doctor smiled encouragingly and took out his own tools.

'Four broken,' he concluded after checking Loukis's ribs. 'Breathing OK.'

Once he'd bandaged Loukis's chest, the doctor moved his experienced hands up to the boy's face.

'This may hurt,' he told him softly. He took hold of Loukis's nose and snapped it back into position with a sickening crack. Water sprang immediately to Loukis's eyes and an expletive leapt from his lips. Given the circum-stances, Dhespina let it pass.

After the doctor had finished his examination, he prescribed painkillers and rest. And even though Dhespina was far from comfortable with the potions of science, she accepted the medication because she simply wanted her boy's hurting to stop.

When the doctor left, with promises to return the next day, Dhespina stripped the bed and replaced the sheets. Helping Loukis back on to the mattress, she kissed his brow and drew the curtains. As the first sob welled inside her, she went outside. Waiting for her were Mehmet and Pembe. The old woman's face was stained with tears of her own, and Dhespina moved forward to stroke them away, while expressing her gratitude.

'Don't thank us,' Pembe sobbed. 'If it wasn't for us . . . if Loukis wasn't here . . . if . . .'

Pembe fell into her husband's soft chest, unable to go on.

'Allah help us, Dhespo,' Mehmet continued for her, 'Pembe is right. She heard those thugs as they attacked your boy. It was because of us; because he lives with us – two Turkish Cypriots. They called him a traitor.'

Dhespina raised her hands to her face and angrily shook her head. 'My son is no traitor! And don't you dare carry the blame for this vermin – they are the ones betraying the island. Bad characters, that's what they are. What you two did today was . . . my God . . . Mehmet . . . Pembe . . . you saved my boy's life.'

Realizing it was neither the place nor the time to argue the point, the old couple muttered their appreciation at Dhespina's kind words, but the fact was they felt degradingly culpable, and this belief only hardened with the arrival of the rest of Loukis's family.

When Georgios saw the swollen, discoloured form of his son, rage flared in his chest and he demanded the police be called. Loukis grunted his disapproval, and Dhespina firmly told her husband she didn't want the whole village knowing their business. Unsurprisingly, when Marios came to see what had happened, he burst into tears. Christakis tried to shake off his own feelings of helplessness by interrogating Mehmet and Pembe.

Over the following days, as Loukis slowly mended, and he moved from soup to soft lentil stew, he remained stubbornly unwilling to discuss the attack.

'How's Praxi?' was the first coherent question he asked, and Dhespina despaired.

'The girl's fine, and back in Keryneia,' she lied. At her words, Loukis looked as though he'd been kicked again in the face, but, as his mother, Dhespina only cared for his health. His feelings could be nursed at a later date.

By the time Loukis was able to dress himself without the help of his parents' hands, Christakis came to talk to him.

'Pembe said your attackers came in a Chevrolet,' he told his brother. They both knew of only one such car in the area, and the big man waited for a response. Loukis gave none.

'I'm going to see him,' Christakis said finally.

'And do what?' Loukis asked.

'Smash his face into a pulp, what do you think?'

Loukis looked at his brother's huge fists and managed a smile. He had been on the receiving end of them enough times as a boy to appreciate the power they packed. He shook his head. 'It's not your fight.'

'Loukis, if you touch one of us you touch us all.' As Christakis spoke, a fat tear rolled down his face, losing its way in the thick ends of his moustache.

'I need to think,' Loukis told him.

Christakis opened his mouth to protest, but his brother cut him off.

'I'll tell you when,' Loukis promised, 'but not now. I'm not ready.'

Christakis nodded begrudgingly. Although every inch of him stood ready to match like with like, it wasn't his call to make. When the carpenter left, Pembe and Mehmet came to spend the evening with Loukis. They brought with them a bowl of seasoned meat and potatoes, which helped fill the pauses that littered their awkward conversation.

After making sure Loukis had enough wood to keep his fire burning through the start of the night, Mehmet grabbed him in a gentle hug and Pembe kissed him lightly along the grazes of his cheek. Later, when the moon hung heavy in the sky and the world had fallen to sleep, the elderly couple closed the door of their home and carried two suitcases to a Bedford bus waiting on the edges of the village. As they boarded, they nodded to the other passengers. Every last one of them was a Turkish Cypriot, and none of them spoke because their eyes said it all. The driver pulled the door closed and they travelled southwards.

The following morning, Dhespina called on her son and found herself troubled by the stillness around her. Pembe's front door was shut, but not locked, and when she went inside she saw everything was in its place. The dishes were washed, the beds were made and the scene was one of un-accustomed order. It made Dhespina uneasy. When she returned home, she was about to tell Georgios of her concerns, but he beat her to it.

'Have you seen Mehmet and Pembe?' he asked. She shook her head.

'May God help us,' her husband replied, slumping to the table and running his trembling fingers through his hair.

'They've left, Dhespo. The Turks have fled the village; every last one of them.'

Praxi pulled at the shutters, but they wouldn't budge. She cocked her head to investigate, and her eyebrows lifted in surprise.

'Mamma?' she asked. 'Why have you nailed the windows shut?'

Elena stopped making the bed and turned to face her daughter. After quickly sifting through the options, she realized there was no good way to say it.

'To stop you getting out and to stop him getting in.'

Praxi leaned against the wall, slid to her bum and shook her head. She told her mother she was acting insane, but Elena ignored her.

For two months Praxi had been convalescing from illness, both real and affected, and Elena was stung by her in-gratitude. Day and night, she had been a prisoner in her own home – tied to a child who refused to get well and besieged by a wolf at the door who refused to give up. Her nerves were in shreds; she hadn't been able to attend the women's coffee mornings; she hadn't been to church; she hadn't even been to the store. Instead she had handed out shopping lists and coins to any visitor who happened to pass by. Elena doubted that any other mother would have been so patient. After the fever had loosened its grip and Dhespina's poultices had worked their magic, Praxi had resisted the truth of her recovery and twisted and squirmed her way into more fitful madness. As her energy waned, she had lost her appetite, and Elena had to push her meals down the girl's throat. A form of depression then took hold, and when Praxi's eyes weren't weeping they were fixed on the wall in a way Elena found creepy. In fact, it wasn't until Mrs Televantos came calling that Elena started to notice any improvement in her daughter's health at all.

Unlike the wiry and haemorrhoid-plagued form of her husband, Mrs Televantos was blessed with regular bowel movements and a full stomach protruding above black-stockinged legs that made her look rather like an egg on sticks. She was quick-witted, an amiable host when it suited and, above all else, the most terrible gossip – which is what brought her to Elena's home.

Having spent the past few months trapped by maternal devotion on the outskirts of the village, Elena felt starved of the daily updates that made village life both so comforting and unbearable. The men had the coffee shop, but the women had the convenience store and the bakery, and there was nothing worth knowing that didn't pass over both counters. Yet, as accustomed as she was to village intrigue, what Elena heard as she served up her syrup-dipped doughnuts made her hair stand on end, much to Mrs Televantos's delight. Struggling to put the details into any coherent order due to the excitement of being first with the news, the elderly woman revealed that the Turks in the village had disappeared overnight, all sixty-eight of them, leaving their homes without a backward glance. Shamefully, some of the 'bad ones' in their own community had been quick to take advantage of the exodus, furnishing their homes with fridge freezers, double beds and other such furniture they had no right to, and in one case they hadn't only ransacked the house but set it alight.

'The fire didn't take hold because that nice Mr

Panayiotou – Lambros not Elias, he's a swine – well, he beat the flames out with his own jacket, right until it fell to pieces in his hands. It was a good jacket as well. Kostas later suggested he take one of the coats left by the Turks, as it would be a fair and right exchange, but Mr Panayiotou wasn't having any of it. He said he'd rather walk naked than steal another man's jacket, and Mrs Miltiadous laughed that she wouldn't mind seeing that! Of course, it wasn't really a laughing matter. It's a damn shame what happened; losing your neighbours and burning their homes.'

Mrs Televantos clicked her teeth in disgust before hurriedly moving on to other topics of interest. Apparently, the village chief was in a fury. Doros had run over Eleftherios's dog and had been told to hand over a goat in recompense, but was refusing to do so; Takis the butcher had sliced through the tip of his finger and now everyone was afraid of buying his sausagemeat in case the fingertip turned up on their plates; Costas Charalambous had raised his fist to his wife again after getting drunk with Fotis the farmer; and it was said that the Germanos girl, Maria, was recovering in a Lefkosia hospital after slicing her wrists with broken glass.

'Her mother is calling it an accident, but there are some who say it was attempted suicide,' Mrs Televantos whispered, crossing herself and casting a sideways glance at Elpida, who was playing with a doll in the corner. Uncertain whether the child was listening, the old woman raised her eyebrows, to show she thought there to be some truth to the story.

'Oh, that's awful,' commented Elena, genuinely upset for the Germanos family. 'Is there no end to a mother's suffering?'

'Not in my lifetime,' Mrs Televantos replied, and grabbed for her bag.

When the old woman left, promising to return the next day with spuds and canned meat, Elena saw Praxi watching. She hadn't stepped out of her room since the day she arrived, and Elpida flew up the stairs when she saw her mother finally out of bed.

Later that evening, and displaying the kind of recovery that was close to miraculous, Praxi managed to bathe, dress and eat her meal without help. As she leant across the table to cut the meat on Elpida's plate, Elena felt the weight of responsibility begin to shift from her shoulders. The constant effort of trying to keep Elpida indoors had brought a dozen or more grey hairs to her scalp and she was quite seriously exhausted. Of course, the next morning the first thing Praxi did – even before she had had the decency to dress – was to open the door and free her child.

'Why do I even bother?' Elena muttered, and Praxi brought her lips to her own mother's hair and told her not to worry.

'She won't come to any harm in the village,' Praxi assured her, but they both knew why Elena had been so intent on keeping her grandchild indoors.

Encouraged by her mother's laughter, Elpida ran through the garden, jumping to swing on the branches of the nearest apple tree. In a frenzy of pent-up energy, she leapt for the almond pods hanging at the end of the pathway. Then, casting a glance back at her mamma, who was cheering her on, Elpida ran through the gate and into the village.

Walking back into the house, Praxi found her mother sat on a chair by the stove, disapproval written all over her face.

Dhespina wiped the edges of the sink before moving to the wooden cabinet. On her knees, she banished the cobwebs forming under the arches of Pembe's small dresser then, coming back to her feet, she let her gaze fall upon the row of black and white photos given pride of place upon the shelves. Carefully, she flicked the dust from the frames which held faces she had known and some she could only guess at. One of the oldest pictures showed a proud-looking man dressed in baggy white trousers tucked into dark leather boots. He wore a white belted shirt, and a tasselled fez crowned his head. Was he Pembe's father? Or perhaps Mehmet's? Dhespina could only imagine, and she wondered what had become of him. As her daydreams threatened to take hold, Marios walked in on her thoughts.

'I've done the work,' he informed her. 'Now I need a drink.'

Marios had been helping on the farm, with Christakis's blessing, from the day of the attack.

'Go and see your brother and get yourself some juice,' Dhespina told him. 'I'm nearly done here.'

Marios left his mamma to her cleaning. Fifty-three steps away, because he had been counting, he found Loukis sitting in a chair, already dressed and fiddling with his boots. Marios bent to help him with his laces.

'I need to get out of here,' Loukis said. 'I'm suffocating.'

'Where do you want to go?'

'I don't know – anywhere.'

'Do you want to come and see Nicos with me?'

Loukis saw the expectation in his brother's eyes, and he couldn't refuse him.

219

It took an extraordinarily long time to walk to the church given Loukis's sore limbs and broken ribs, and when they reached Nicos's grave he sat on the grass with a grimace. Marios placed his bag behind his brother to give him some support, and began pulling at the weeds struggling for life around Nicos's headstone. He discarded them roughly with a tut.

'How often do you come here?' Loukis asked. He could only remember visiting his dead brother a handful of times, and it shamed him.

'I come every day,' Marios said.

'And do what?'

'Talk . . . clean the ground, because these weeds come back so fast . . . whatever I like, really.'

'And what do you talk about?' Loukis asked.

'I don't know; everything, I guess. At the moment it's mainly about you and the men who beat you up. I was saying we should go to the police, but Nicos said it would be better to get a big stick and beat them into the next life.'

Loukis laughed, and winced. He was oddly comforted by the thought of his dead brother's anger – even if it did come from his living twin's imagination. He leaned gingerly back on the bag Marios had given him. As he did so a flash of dark hair caught his eye. He jerked his head towards the gates of the cemetery. 'I think we're being spied on.'

Marios looked up, and a broad smile lit his face.

'Elpida! Come here and say hello.' He got up to usher the child away from the gate and urged her to join them. As her curiosity got the better of her, Loukis saw that she was tiny, but then all children looked impossibly small to him. He moved his head to catch her face, but she kept hiding behind his brother's legs.

'Come on, Elpida *mou*, come forward, don't be shy, come and say hello.'

Slowly, the child came out of Marios's shadow. In the sunlight she stood with her legs apart, ready to sprint.

'Do you know who this is?' Marios asked, pointing to his brother. Elpida slowly nodded her head.

'Who is it?'

The child took a deep breath. 'He's the village crazy man.'

At her words, Loukis laughed loudly and pain darted through his body, causing him to finish with a wince. Marios was puzzled.

'He's not the crazy man, Elpida. He's my brother Loukis.'

Elpida's eyes turned wide. Throwing a glance to Marios, who smiled his encouragement, she inched forwards. Within reach of Loukis, she slowly extended her right hand to his face.

'Loukis?' she asked and, a little stupefied by the child's attention, he nodded slowly so as not to scare her hand away.

'Loukis,' Elpida stated again, but more firmly. 'Loukis the wolf.'

Marios felt his chest swell with pride, remembering the present he had carved the girl when she was a baby.

'Yes!' he affirmed. 'Yes, Elpida. Loukis is the wolf.'

'You're the wolf,' Elpida giggled, smiling into Loukis's face. 'And you're always here to protect me.'

13

Cyprus was at her most charming in the spring, which was partly why Loukis took to walking. It wasn't a conscious decision; he woke up willing to work, but by the time he'd slipped on his boots he felt less inclined to do the chores his injuries allowed for and hit the road instead – timing his travels with waves of anemones that opened with the sun and closed at dusk. When hungry, he bought lunch from farmers he didn't know, and he satisfied his thirst at fresh water springs. He wandered along the slipping banks skirting the sea, through white gravel lanes hijacked by billowing bushes, up mountains unspoilt by booby traps and snipers, and basically went anywhere that allowed him to avoid people.

Occasionally, a motor car would pass carrying tourists from the south, but it would be gone within seconds and the raucous calls and arguments of birds would return to break up the noise of his thoughts.

Everywhere he turned he fell into colour: fields were vivid with carmine cyclamens and white and yellow narcissi; black tulips peeked from among green shoots of wheat; and along grey ragged rocks the sun rose glowed from atop of purple buds. His mother called Keryneia the jewel of Cyprus. But to Loukis, spring opened up a treasure chest of gems with flowers in full bloom spraying blue, violet and purple in his path and Cleopatra butterflies rising before him like painted clouds. On days like this, Cyprus could steal a man's breath away, yet nature's colourful dance heightened Loukis's longing, and the acrobatic swallows tending to their young only served to amplify his suspicions.

The summer of 1957, that's what Marios had said.

Although his brother couldn't be more exact, despite being present at the birth, his insistence that the child had come early was enough to shake Loukis's certainty of betrayal. And if his suspicions were correct nearly seven years had passed; seven long, irretrievable years in which a baby had become a girl and he had played no part in her life beyond conception. If there was a god for Loukis to blame, he would have swung his fists at the heavens; instead he could only rail at his own stupidity.

By the time Loukis returned home, having exhausted his mind enough to rest, his mother was usually waiting for him. As Dhespina dished out her meals, seasoned with herbs picked for their medicinal value, she sensed a change in her son that she couldn't quite fix. Nothing was said, but she felt his eyes following her. When she told Georgios, he dismissed her concerns as 'the fevered imagination of an overly protective mother'.

'Calm down, Dhespo. Don't you think the boy has enough problems without you creating more for him?'

Although Dhespina thought her husband possessed all the sensitivity of a plank and wouldn't recognize a problem unless it collapsed at his feet coughing up blood, she let the moment pass. However, the following day she had a quiet word with Marios and asked him to keep an eye on his younger brother.

'In case he does what?'

'I don't know . . . anything unusual.'

'This is Loukis we're talking about,' Marios groaned, 'when doesn't he do something unusual?'

'You know what I mean,' Dhespina responded tartly, but Marios really didn't.

'For how long do I have to watch him?'

'For as long as it takes.'

Marios looked at his mamma, wondering whether he should ask her to be more precise, but her back was turned to him and he guessed she'd had enough conversation. Privately, he prayed Loukis would do something pretty damn quick, because he was tired of being at the farm. It was nice spending time with his younger brother and he was glad he could help Mr Mehmet and his wife, but he missed the light of Christakis's workroom and the gentle taps of his brother's carvings. What's more, he was sure the chairs for the new hotel would be finished and he was excited to see them. They were extra grand, and his papa had helped in their making by cutting dyed leather for the seats. They were family-made chairs and Marios loved that fact. Of course, he also loved Loukis, who was more important than chairs, even leather ones, and if his mamma wanted an eye kept on his brother into forever, he would. But Marios couldn't be in two places at once, and when Loukis asked why he was following him as he made his daily walk instead of working on the farm, Marios confessed that their mamma had given him orders to do so because she was worried.

'About what?' Loukis asked.

'To be honest with you, I'm not that sure,' Marios replied. 'Maybe she thinks you're going to run off again.'

'I'm not going anywhere,' Loukis responded.

'Or you'll drop down dead.'

Loukis stopped in his tracks. 'Why would I drop down dead?'

'I don't know,' Marios confessed. 'But it would be unusual, especially as you're not even close to dying now.'

'I guess . . .' Loukis replied.

Whatever their mamma's reason, Loukis was confident it wasn't due to any fear that he was about to keel over. However, Marios's confession pulled him out of his idleness, and for the next week he permitted his older brother to keep an eye on him as they packed oranges for market and checked the olive trees for disease – the only aspect of farm work that appeared to genuinely interest Marios.

'There was a writer who lived in the old days who used to call olives liquid gold,' Marios informed his brother. 'Of course, it's not true – it's poetry – because if it was true every Cypriot farmer would be rich as a king, and no one is.'

'It must be poetry then,' Loukis agreed. 'You know, they say olive trees were brought to the island by the Romans?'

'No, I didn't know that,' Marios admitted, shaking his head. He looked around the orchard in amazement. 'It must have taken for ever to plant them all.'

As Loukis stifled his laughter, Marios got to work checking for fungus. He investigated branches and trunks for signs of olive knot and scrutinized the undersides of leaves to see if they had fallen to the black-dust disease. Afterwards he agreed with Loukis that the diagnosis was good. It was a huge relief. Marios didn't think he could ever forgive himself if Mr Mehmet's trees died while he was away with his wife.

The next day, after they returned from the morning market, Loukis gave Marios 20 shillings to reward his hard work. His brother then told him he was going into town, and Marios looked at him uncomfortably.

'Fine,' Loukis said, throwing his hands into the air. 'Come if it makes you and our mamma happy, but I'm only going to the bank.'

By the time they reached the town, having walked there on foot, the sun was beating hard on their necks, as if it was summer, and the streets were crowded with people taking drinks under the umbrellas of new cafés and restaurants along the port's twisting roads. Everyone looked so happy, and Marios couldn't believe there was a better place on earth than Keryneia.

At the bank, the brothers were relieved to find only one, hot-looking, customer in front of them. He was halfway through counting a hefty bag of coins at the desk and a dark line of sweat ran down the back of his shirt. When it came to Loukis's turn, he emptied his pockets of notes and told the teller he wanted to make a deposit.

'Excellent, Loukis,' the woman replied, and Marios wondered when his brother had made friends with her, because she wasn't from the village. She bent under the desk. 'Now, if you could fill out the forms, we'll open an account for you straight away.'

'I said I wanted to make a deposit not open an account,' Loukis corrected the woman firmly, and she blushed in response.

'Sorry, my mistake,' she smiled, putting the forms to one

side. 'Let's start again. Into whose account are you putting your funds?'

'Mehmet Kadir's,' Loukis replied, and the woman's smile slipped from her lips.

'The Turk?'

'Yes. The Turk.'

The woman looked behind her and rolled her seat away to speak to a man sat at one of the desks. He bent his head so she could talk into his ear and, after casting a curious look in Loukis's direction, he shrugged. The woman returned with the smile painted back on her face.

'OK, that's fine,' she said.

Marios wasn't sure what was going on, or why the woman had to go and talk to the man, but once Loukis had finalized his business and they walked out into the sunshine he still felt the bank people's eyes on them. It made him wonder whether Loukis had done something unusual and whether it needed mentioning to their mamma.

'They probably think we're going to rob them,' Loukis grunted.

'But we've just put money *in* the bank!'

'Bank people are paranoid. They're also mean, which is why they find jobs guarding money. Now why don't you disappear and go say hello to Christakis?'

'Why? What are you going to do?'

'Take a walk, get some sea air and go home. I'll see you tomorrow.'

'But Mamma . . .'

'Marios! I know you're doing your best to help Mamma, but really, what trouble do you think I can get into?'

Marios actually thought Loukis could get into trouble

just by sitting in his house, but he stopped short of answering.

'I'll see you tomorrow,' Loukis repeated, and strode down the next lane.

Unhappily, Marios continued along the main street, until he was halted by an overwhelming surge of guilt. When he turned around, Loukis was gone. Breaking into a run, he reached the end of the cobbled lane just in time to spot his brother walking into the café owned by Yiannis and Praxi.

'OK then,' Marios muttered and continued to the workshop, excited at the prospect of seeing Christakis and Yianoulla again, as well as his four little nephews, especially as he had yet to fix the latest baby's face in his head. When he arrived some three minutes later, he was surprised to see not only his papa in town but also Michalakis.

'What are you doing here?' he asked, moving to hug his brother.

'Oh, that's a nice welcome, isn't it?' Michalakis noted, playfully ruffling his younger brother's hair.

'Your brother's come to show off his new car,' their papa informed him.

'Really? Wow! The chairs look great.' Marios stepped forward to take a look at his father and Christakis's handiwork.

Georgios beamed. 'Much better than some old motor car, eh?'

'You're all jealous,' Michalakis retorted.

'Ooh, listen to the city boy!' Christakis jeered, before turning to Marios. 'And to what do we owe this pleasure?'

Marios explained that he'd come to say hello after visiting the bank with Loukis. Christakis frowned with disappointment.

'You know, it wouldn't kill him to come and say hello himself sometimes.'

'Oh, I don't think he means anything by it,' Marios added hurriedly. 'It's devilish hot out there and he must have really needed a drink because when he left me he went to Praxi's coffee shop.'

'He did what?' his father asked abruptly, dropping hold of the leather seat to help himself up from his knees.

'He went to Praxi's,' Marios repeated.

'Mother of Mary!' Christakis shouted, causing Marios to jump. He had no idea why everyone was so angry, but when his father and older brothers went running from the shop he naturally followed.

Despite his age, and the length of their strides, Georgios kept up well with his boys, and when they burst into the café he was only seconds behind them. Inside, Loukis was stood with his back to the door. He held a broken chair leg in his hands, there was a man on the floor and two others were holding batons of wood and a poker. As Marios, Michalakis, Christakis and Georgios moved into unspoken positions either side of Loukis, the men faltered.

Yiannis looked at the wall of flesh in front of him and lowered the poker. His heart hammered in his chest and his head scrambled to make sense of the confrontation. He recalled playing cards, the door opened, Loukis walked in, Yiannis whispered to Victor and then, well, all hell broke loose. To his right, his lover was frantically shuffling along the floor to be out of harm's way. The officer next to him was sweating profusely along the top of his lip. Yiannis was struck by their feebleness.

'Now,' said Loukis carefully, 'I asked you for a beer.'

'Make that five,' interrupted Christakis, and Loukis turned to him with the smallest trace of a smile.

Yiannis gave a questioning look to the men beside him. When they offered no response he slouched to the bar and the Economidou men took a table outside. Seconds later, Yiannis appeared with two half-litre bottles of Keo and five glasses. Georgios dismissively handed over his coins.

'On the house,' Yiannis muttered with embarrassment.

'I wouldn't hear of it,' Georgios insisted, and the man walked away with his neck burning.

'Do you think he spat in it?' Marios asked as his father poured.

'Unlikely,' Michalakis replied, 'his mouth will be dry from all the piss in his pants.'

The five men sniggered, and banged their glasses together with a small cry of *yiamas*.

'Now then,' Georgios said, turning his attention to his youngest son, 'what the hell did you think you were doing?'

'Why didn't you come for me?' Christakis hissed accusingly.

Loukis took a cigarette from the packet Michalakis had placed on the table.

'I didn't come for a fight. I was looking for Praxi. I had something to ask her. Before I even opened my mouth some mainlander went for me.'

'The man on the floor with the bloody nose?' Marios asked.

'Yes.' Loukis glanced at his knuckles before looking at the upstairs window of the café. 'Anyway it would appear that Praxi's not here.'

'I could have told you that!' Marios revealed with a shake

of his head. 'She hasn't left the village since she got there.'

'But Mamma said . . .'

Georgios closed his eyes with a weary sigh. He raised a glass to his four sons.

'Let's just finish our beers and get home before those bastards bring in reinforcements.'

Loukis sat at the kitchen table and waited for his mother to join him. The air was still, as if time itself was holding its breath.

'I'm off to see Nicos,' Marios declared.

'Me too,' muttered Michalakis.

And Georgios watched them go with barely disguised envy.

'Do you have any idea what's going on?' Marios asked his brother as they made their way to the church.

'I've as much idea as you,' Michalakis admitted.

'And you call yourself a journalist?'

'Sometimes,' Michalakis responded.

After paying his respects at Nicos's grave, Michalakis left Marios to perform whatever ritual he had devised for himself and headed for the shore in search of a breeze to blow away the despair of living in Lefkosia. A few months ago, a British general had sought to contain the capital's warring factions by slicing the city in two, separating twenty thousand Turkish Cypriots from forty thousand Greek.

'First it was divide and rule, now it's divide and hope for the best,' Michalakis's editor said of the Green Line, and the journalist thought it was the first honest assessment he had heard in a long time.

Although *The Voice* largely fell into line with the rest of the Greek press, the newspaper maintained a semblance of integrity by questioning the portrayal of a Turkish revolt against the republic via opinion pieces penned by academics and communists. The violence engulfing the island was perpetrated by both sides, yet the media largely provided one-sided accounts for their own biased audiences and, though *The Voice* wasn't as guilty as some, Michalakis could feel the blood dripping from his fingers.

Over the past few months he had witnessed Turkish homes being looted and torched; he had watched armoured vehicles draped with Union Jacks race to restore order; he had heard, but not written about, an imam murdered in his bed, along with his blind, paralysed son; he had reported at length on the Greeks abducted and slain; and, due to the unequivocal evidence paraded before international cameras, he had been gifted a few column inches to describe the mass grave found at Ayios Vasilios. The next day Michalakis received twelve hate letters.

Throughout Lefkosia and her village suburbs, pitched battles were taking place, with private militias acting as judge, jury and executioner. Hundreds had fled their homes and, as the flames of hatred leapt from one district to another, the Truce Force found itself woefully overstretched. From the sidelines of yet another bloody incident, Michalakis overheard a British officer remark that it was like 'medieval times, with every village armed against the other, each fearing the other will attack'. Meanwhile, as Turkish homes burned, tens of thousands of soldiers amassed on Turkey's southern shores, and the UN felt compelled to organize a peacekeeping force to keep them at bay. Even then, the atrocities continued: shoppers were taken hostage;

neighbourhoods were besieged; and young idealists died beside warmongers. When peacekeepers finally arrived on the island, their presence proved to be little deterrent; the blue berets could only fire in self-defence, so if one community wanted to blast the other to kingdom come, the international troops could do little more than stand back and observe.

When Michalakis drove from the capital that morning he passed a number of Finnish troops manning a checkpoint at the mouth of Keryneia Pass. They politely asked for his details and wished him farewell. After that he was on his own. It was a situation he was all too sadly getting used to. But then he saw Maria – although he didn't recognize her at the time, as she was two hundred yards from dry land and face down in the water.

Tearing off his shoes, Michalakis plunged into the waves crashing against the shore, not knowing who he was attempting to save. He had only glimpsed the red of a dress and the tentacle arms of a woman's black hair, so when he reached the floating body and pulled her head to the surface he was astonished.

'Maria! What the hell?'

Amid her coughs and splutters, Michalakis saw confusion turn to recognition before a new despair crept along the girl's gaunt face and she plunged herself back into the icy waters, dragging Michalakis down with her. Grabbing her by the stomach, he heaved her upwards. As he struggled to tread water and keep them both afloat, Maria fought him every inch of the way. But Michalakis was too strong, and he managed to bring her to the shore, where she collapsed, exhausted.

As Maria vomited salt water she slammed an angry fist on to the ground. The force of it brought blood.

'Will no one let me die?' she screamed.

'Why did you tell me Praxi had returned to Keryneia?'

Dhespina tried hard to match her son's gaze, but she hadn't the support of truth at her back.

After a short while, she whispered, 'I wanted you to get well,' and Georgios reached for her hand.

Slowly, Loukis shook his head. He wasn't angry. He was surprised. He had never known his mother to lie to him, but now that she had he wondered 'how often?'

'I've seen Elpida,' he stated, and he let the weight of his words hang in the room. The sharp look that darted between his parents did not go unnoticed. 'When was she born?'

'In the summer after you left,' Dhespina replied.

'Yes,' Loukis encouraged in a soft, patient tone, 'when in the summer?'

'Eight months after you left, seven months after Praxi married.'

'And the child is mine?'

'We believe so, yes.'

Loukis nodded his head.

'Thank you,' he said.

Michalakis praised the wonderful coffee Mrs Germanos had made, and the small woman stroked the back of his hair in appreciation as she walked back to the kitchen to deal with her tears.

Before him, Maria sat in fresh clothes. Her face was pale

and her eyes were listless, yet Michalakis still thought her extraordinarily beautiful.

'You've lost weight,' he remarked, and Maria pulled at the shawl around her shoulders.

'I've not been hungry,' she replied. And it was true. When she tried to eat she gagged. Forkfuls of food, no matter how small, felt impossibly huge and intrusive. And now, with the sun hitting her face through the window and Michalakis looking at her with pity swimming in his eyes, she realized she'd lost not only her appetite but also any sense of dignity she once possessed. Michalakis glanced at the scratches she had torn into her arms.

'I know,' she acknowledged. 'I've made myself ugly.'

'That's impossible, Maria *mou*. You're more beautiful than I even remembered.'

At the unexpected kindness of his words, all the hurt, anger and humiliation Maria had so recently suffered poured out from her. Michalakis gave her a tissue and waited for the moment to pass. Twenty minutes later and with his arms now around her shoulders, he tried to make sense of her pain.

'Has your life become that unbearable, Maria?'

Meeting his gaze, she struggled for a moment with the enormity of his question, until she gave up and released all the words that had lain trapped inside her since Loukis had broken her heart. She spoke of his devastating dismissal; of how her loyalty had been thrown back in her face; of her horror at the thought of being alone – of being known as the village reject, the woman who had devoted her life to a man who didn't want her. Scratching at the scabbing lines running along her arms, she described the laughter of her peers and the hollow sympathy of mothers only grateful that their own daughters hadn't been so shamed. The truth was she hated herself; she despised her own weakness and her stupidity. She had allowed herself to become a joke – she, the girl who could have had any boy in Cyprus, let alone Keryneia. And she wished – oh yes she did, with all of her heart – she wished for death to come and swallow her; to take her away and save her from the rot of humiliation eating at her insides.

When she had finished – exhausted and dazed by her own confession – Michalakis found himself torn between sympathy, jealousy and desire. Awkwardly, he reached for her hand. When she didn't pull away he gained courage.

'You should leave here,' he said.

Maria laughed bitterly. 'And go where?'

'To Lefkosia,' he told her. 'With me.'

Maria looked at him sharply, scarcely able to believe what she was hearing. Michalakis had experienced a similar sensation as the invitation leapt from his mouth, but the next day he paid Loukis a visit.

He found his youngest brother picking the last of the spring oranges from the trees on Mehmet's farm. From a distance he was struck by how similar they looked, and for a second it troubled him.

As Michalakis approached, Loukis gave him an easy smile.

'Great timing,' he said. 'I could do with a beer.'

'At this hour? It's barely ten o'clock.'

'Brother, the city has made you soft.'

'Oh Christ, don't you start.'

With their arms around each other, the men headed to

Loukis's home, where they took a couple of Keos from the fridge. Choosing to sit in the sun, they shared a cigarette as they discussed Michalakis's work, the troubles panning out from Lefkosia and Loukis's interesting encounter at the café.

'You should be careful,' Michalakis added. 'Memories run long here, and forgiveness is a rare concept.'

'I'm expecting to find that out in due course,' Loukis replied honestly.

If Michalakis suspected his brother was afraid he found no trace of it in his face or the easy shrug of his shoulders. He lit another cigarette. As the smoke curled between them, Michalakis knew he couldn't delay the reason for his coming much longer. Watching for a shift in Loukis's face, he revealed that he was taking Maria, with her parents' blessing, to Lefkosia.

Loukis didn't even flinch.

'There's a secretarial position at the newspaper, and she'll be staying at one of the ladies' boarding houses.'

Loukis acknowledged the move would be good for her, but Michalakis hadn't finished.

'There's no gentle way of saying this, Loukis . . . I hope one day to make Maria my wife.'

Loukis lifted his eyebrows in surprise, but offered no comment.

'Of course, there's nothing to say that she will agree to this,' Michalakis continued, 'but if she does, and I hope one day that happens, I want to know how you might feel about it.'

'Feel?'

'Yes. I need to know if this is going to be a problem for you.'

'Not unless it's a problem for you,' Loukis replied, and Michalakis was both pleased and shocked by the easiness of his response.

He touched his glass gently against his brother's.

'*Yiamas.*'

'*Yiamas.*'

Loukis didn't react immediately. Instead he gave himself room to wonder how best to handle the situation. After a week had passed he was still no nearer to forming a clear plan of action and, weary of deliberation, he shaved, put on his best clothes and walked to Praxi's mother's house.

In the garden, Elpida was playing on a swing attached to the old apple tree – just as he and her mother had done so many years before.

'The wolf!' she yelled as he walked up the pathway. Jumping from the swing, she ran to take him by the hand and lead him into the house. When Elena saw Loukis walk through the door she dropped the glass she was drying and Praxi, who was sewing a tiny dress, looked up in surprise. Slowly a smile crept over her face, and she told Loukis to take a seat while she helped her mother collect herself.

Following an awkward hour of forced niceties and sticky *baklava*, Praxi finally told her mother that she and Loukis were going for a walk.

'Can I come?' Elpida asked, and when Praxi agreed her mother clutched at her chest.

'Are you having a heart attack?' Praxi asked.

'Would it make any difference?' her mother grumbled.

'It might delay matters for a time.'

Elena clicked her teeth. 'I'm not having a heart attack.'

'Good. Then we'll see you in a little while.'

Freed from Elena's dramatics, the three of them ambled towards the sea. Some years ago, Loukis and Praxi would have made their way to St Hilarion's, but Turkish troops had taken that joy from them.

As they walked, Elpida skipped in excited circles around the adults until she felt the pull of the Mediterranean and ran ahead. Coming to sit on a patch of grass, Loukis and Praxi watched the child pick pebbles from the sea bed to carry in her skirt. The air hung heavy between them, sticky with conversations that should have taken place long ago, and it was Loukis who finally broke their silence as they watched Elpida play.

'Is she mine?'

'Yes, she is,' admitted Praxi.

'Good,' he said softly.

With the smallest of movements, Loukis reached to cover Praxi's fingers. Together they watched their daughter collect rocks in the sunshine.

14

They had been talking for more than an hour – thick as thieves, their heads almost touching – and when the man placed a calming hand on Victor's arm, Yiannis felt nauseous. Taking orders he could barely hear over the taunts of his own jealousy, his eyes continually drifted to the table by the window where he felt the stranger's warm fingers caressing Victor's skin. Yiannis's lips curled at the dirt he saw lying beneath the man's nails.

It was irrational, he was aware of that – not least because the Cypriot was missing a leg – but he couldn't keep the bile from his mouth. He was worried. Since the fight in the café Victor had been moody and withdrawn, as if Yiannis were somehow responsible for their humiliation, and when the officer finally relented and returned to their bed, his touch was hard and violence seeped from his pores. But while Victor was consumed by vengeful thoughts, Yiannis only wanted peace. Something had shifted inside of him; in Loukis's clenched fist he had recognized the force that propelled the man, because Yiannis felt the same heat racing through his own veins whenever he thought of Victor.

Yiannis was not naturally inclined to aggression and the

memory of what happened at the Turks' farm, when adrenalin had conquered reason, persisted in haunting him. He had walked away from the encounter a lesser man. It hadn't been a fair fight, it was an ambush, and it was shameful in every way, which perhaps explained why he accepted the embarrassment Loukis had brought to them: it eased his own guilt. Praxi, however, was a different matter. His wife, such as she was, could rot in the dark hovel of her mother's home for all Yiannis cared. She had never loved him, and though he had tried, he had failed to love her also. The night she ran from their home to bring dishonour to his door had finally emptied his patience, to be filled by something unexpected and all-consuming. Although he missed his daughter, he was content with the twice-weekly visits engineered by his mother-in-law. But Praxi, he didn't miss her at all, and his relief at her departure was only increased by the opening of a kitchen cupboard. It was Victor who discovered the seeds.

'Crazy,' the officer remarked. 'What if your kid got hold of them?'

'They're only apple pips.'

Yiannis ran his fingers through the bowl, completely at a loss as to why Praxi had felt the need to keep them.

'They're poisonous, you fool. This bowl contains enough cyanide to kill a horse.'

Yiannis quickly set the bowl aside and washed his hands. When Victor left for the base, he bent to investigate the rest of the cupboards. He found death staring back at him with every examination: bottles of bleach, pesticides bearing cross and bones, jars of paint stripper, canisters of lighter fluid and a drawerful of glinting knives. That morning, Yiannis saw

241

his life flash before his eyes, and he saw himself prostrate on the floor of his own kitchen – felled by poison, burnt by chemicals and punctured by four blades still resting in the small of his back.

Behind him, Yiannis sensed movement and he turned from the sink to watch Victor's crippled friend take his leave. The man tucked his crutches under his arms and shook hands before heading out of the door, where he was assisted into a car by a driver.

'Who was that?' Yiannis asked.

'A colleague,' Victor replied.

'Ugly bugger, isn't he?'

Victor slammed the glasses he had brought from the table on the counter with such force that one of them cracked. Yiannis held his stare until his eyes could no longer take the challenge. He returned to the sink.

'That *ugly bugger* is one of the bravest men I know.'

'Sorry, I . . .'

'Save it, Yiannis – just wash your dirty cups like the little woman you are.'

Loukis picked up the pebble and placed it in the wooden bowl Marios had carved him. So far he had collected fourteen of them, all white, all carefully washed and all of them left at his door. It had taken him three weeks to discover the identity of the pebble fairy, but the cramp in his legs as he squatted by Mehmet and Pembe's porch had been worth every painful minute. They were secret gifts from his secret daughter.

Loukis wasn't sure why Elpida felt compelled to award him in such a manner, given that she was no nearer to knowing the truth than she was a month ago, or what significance the stones held, but every time he found a new pebble he knew that whatever frustrations he faced, they were worth it. Hell, they were even worth the tedious hour he had just spent at his mother's. He had been cornered by old Mrs Televantos after dropping off two skinned rabbits. She was fishing for information about Maria's sudden departure to the city and Praxi's seemingly indefinite return to her mother's. When her careful probing failed to net any results, she consoled herself by pinning Loukis and Dhespina to their seats with a verbal onslaught that offered no pause for breath – or opportunity to leave.

Showing an uncommon enthusiasm for politics, Mrs Televantos recounted radio reports of the National Guard's assault on Kokkina; the latest attempt to wrest the Keryneia Pass from the 'infidel dogs of Turkey'; and how Makarios had agreed to an amnesty, even offering to settle the 'so-called refugees' for the sake of peace on the island.

'The man's an absolute saint,' Mrs Televantos clucked, crossing her breast as she did so. Loukis took the moment of piety to rise from his seat. He was too slow.

'Oh Loukis, you'll love this,' the old woman cackled, before breaking into another monologue, this time covering the unfortunate complaint of her neighbour Christos, who had pulled a tick from his scrotum only to watch it swell to the size of an orange – 'that's his testicle not the tick, Loukis'; the good fortune of builder Costas, the man who had once charged her a king's ransom to grout her back wall, who had recently landed a lucrative contract with the army – 'You wash a dog, you bathe a dog, it still smells like a dog';

and the latest misfortune to befall the butcher, who had apparently severed another finger.

'He needs glasses,' Mrs Televantos declared. 'His wife has begged him to get some, but will he listen? No, of course not. Stubborn old fool. I tell you, the whole village will be forced to eat through his six remaining fingers before he sees sense.'

'He should eat more fruit and vegetables,' Dhespina advised, but the old woman laughed at the suggestion.

'Some butcher he would look!'

As the two women settled into the topic of medicinal herbs – discussing the double benefits of a decoction of nettles to stimulate the old woman's hair growth and ease her husband's enlarged prostate – Loukis took his leave, unable to cope any longer with the increasingly intimate details of neighbours he hardly passed the time of day with.

Back at home, and warmed by the pebble on his doorstep, he was surprised half an hour later by the visit of a ghost.

Arriving by car, the apparition approached on two crutches.

'My God,' cried Loukis, striding forward to greet him. 'Antoniou, I thought you were dead!'

'I nearly was, lad!' Releasing himself from Loukis's fierce embrace, Antoniou shook his head in disbelief. 'Mother of Mary, I wouldn't have believed it if I hadn't seen you with my own eyes; you're even bigger than I remember!'

'Save your surprise for when you meet my brothers,' Loukis laughed.

'After the conversation I had this morning I almost feel like I have. Your family has a few bridges to mend in the town, it seems. But don't let it worry you. You're one of us.

Now come on and show me that house of yours, my one foot is killing me.'

Loukis stooped to pick up Antoniou's crutches and led the former EOKA man into his home. Over coffee and his mother's syrupy *baklava*, Loukis listened quietly as Antoniou recounted the story of his survival. The leanness that once hardened his face had been lost to time and inactivity, and as he spoke his full cheeks trembled with emotion.

'After Stelios's bomb went off, I was found, arrested and taken to a military hospital,' he started. 'When I gained consciousness I found my leg gone, but my freedom reinstated.'

Loukis thought back to his own dream-like stay at Havva's home. He could still taste the despair in his mouth on learning that independence had come too late to save his friends. He shook his head. He hoped the old woman was well.

'It was tough going,' Antoniou continued, running his bony fingers along the shrapnel scars pitting his face. 'In fact, for a long time I couldn't see the point in going on. I'd lost my leg, and it felt like my right hand with Harris gone. And even though Cyprus was supposedly free, I was appalled by the deals that were made behind our backs. Makarios betrayed us. We fought for *enosis* and he compromised our ideals for the power of presidency. Your old friend Demetris, as blind as the British made him, saw all of this mess coming. He said the government would be unworkable and we had merely opened the door to Turkey. Jesus, Loukis, was there ever a daughter more betrayed by her own father?'

Loukis shifted uneasily in his seat. He knew he ought to

say something, but he had never carried the conviction of the same dream on his shoulders.

'It's a mess,' he conceded.

'Damn right it's a mess.' Antoniou took a cigarette and lit it impatiently. 'Right now, the Turkish Cypriots are developing their own civil and military administrations. In Ammochostos, they kill three of our people and nobody bats an eyelid, and there's barely a month goes by that the Turks don't threaten invasion. As for Makarios and his romancing of the communists and the Czechs – well, he simply has to go. He sold us down the river and now it's time for someone else to take back the paddle.'

'Like Grivas?' Loukis asked. Although he was even less interested in politics than he was in his mother's fanciful herbs, he supported his brother Michalakis by reading *The Voice*, and the newspaper was full of the EOKA leader's return to the island to command the Greek army.

'Exactly Grivas,' Antoniou admitted.

'He's hardly the most unifying presence,' Loukis commented. It was no secret that the newly promoted general was fiercely anti-Turkish and, despite his recent – laughable – rally calling for the two communities to come together, no one believed him.

'Look, I know you're a . . .' Antoniou stopped to search for the right word. With an exasperated wave of his hand he gave up. 'You're something of a sympathizer, Loukis. But despite your situation here, on this farm, I know you're one of us. That's what I've been telling the men this morning. You lived with Turks. OK. It's done, but they've gone. You're on their land. You're making your money. We all need to earn a living – although it would help if you would stop with the bank deposits. Anyway, the point is, the Turks aren't the enemy but they have become – what should I say? – the misguided thorn in our side. They took advantage of the extraordinary powers we handed them to cry and bitch their way to some form of partition. In a way, it's our own fault. We should have been less charitable. But hindsight is a wonderful thing.'

'Isn't it just,' Loukis agreed, thinking of circumstances altogether different. He got to his feet and fetched two more beers from the fridge. As he moved, Antoniou paused from his speech to look around.

'Small place you got here,' he noted. 'Not found the love of a good woman yet?'

'I'm working on it,' Loukis admitted.

'I bet you are,' Antoniou replied jovially. 'You know, I always thought young Toulla had the hots for you.'

Loukis laughed, shaking his head. 'She only used me to get to Stelios.' Despite his lack of faith, he couldn't help protecting his friend's feelings, even in death. 'But what about you? Have you found a woman to wash the lice from your clothes?'

Antoniou gave Loukis a sly grin. 'I may have lost my leg, son, but I'm back in the game and back in the saddle. Rather fortuitously, my nurse turned out to be a big fan of the resistance. We've agreed that once the island is back on course, we'll celebrate by heading down the aisle.'

'Can she wait that long?' Loukis asked, only half joking.

'I think our problems will be solved sooner than you think,' Antoniou replied, and he crashed his glass against Loukis's with a wink.

*

It hadn't been so bad in the village, where fear was largely the product of their own insecurities. But here in Gönyeli they were witness to nightmares.

Mehmet handed over his best, and final, pair of trousers to the teenager rocking at his feet. He was little more than a child, and his thin arms hugged his body in a primeval act of self-protection. The mind was broken, the eyes were lost.

'Here you go, son.' Mehmet placed the trousers at the boy's feet. He saw they were too large, but the pants were all he had left to give.

Around them, men were busy constructing walls and a rooftop out of any scraps they could find. Supplies had dwindled since the Greeks put up their blockades, yet the needy kept coming. Some came to sleep in cars rendered useless by empty petrol tanks and rusting engines; the luckier ones relied on the charity of relatives who still possessed floor space. The latest family seeking sanctuary were the flotsam and jetsam of Erenköy, the place the Greeks called Kokkina. There were four of them: father, mother, grandfather and son. A week earlier they had been five.

Sevket Osman and his family had arrived at night, tired, hungry and traumatized. The village was not ignorant – the reports from Radio Bayrak had kept them abreast of the horrors at Erenköy – but the siege took place more than thirty miles away, in the north-west of the island, so when the realities of the conflict appeared on their doorstep they were speechless.

The Greeks' bombardment had been relentless.

It was no secret that Turkish arms were being smuggled in through the enclave as well as trained volunteers from the mainland, but it was also a lifeline for food and medicines.

Even so, the National Guard launched a full-scale assault on the port. As the Greeks descended, the UN withdrew, unable to stop the attacks, leaving the enclave to defend itself. Surrounded by mountains, its back against the sea, there was no escape, and no quarter given.

'It started with a battle for the highway,' explained Sevket. 'Then there was a ceasefire arranged by the Blue Berets, and they brought in their troops to enforce it. But it meant nothing. When the Greeks came with their mortars and heavy artillery, the foreigners left us to it. For days we were attacked, there was nothing but night; houses were blown apart, boys were snapped like twigs and fell broken at our feet, and those bastards kept on coming, even though we were left with nothing. They forced us backwards until we were up to our knees in the sea – where their navy waited like sharks to blow us out of the water. We were completely overpowered, we were slaughtered. Yusuf, my beautiful son, was murdered as he fought to save us. And the children, I saw them, torn and shredded, tiny innocents that will never walk again, never throw a ball. Children, I tell you! What had they done? What crime could they possibly have committed?'

As Sevket's tears fell, Mehmet could take no more, and he retreated from the wooden shack the man's family would now call home. Outside, he found the village imam weeping into his hands.

'What can I do?' he pleaded when he felt Mehmet's hand rest on his shoulder. 'I can only give them faith, and what use is that against men intent on massacre?'

'Faith is the best gift you can give them,' Mehmet said gently.

'And if I find it slipping from my own grasp? May Allah forgive my weakness, but I am failing them all.'

Mehmet looked into the holy man's reddened eyes. There was nothing he could say. The man had his own battles to fight, like the rest of them.

Although Gönyeli was Turkish to its last stone, the stronghold was of no value to the Greeks and, as a consequence, it escaped the attacks occurring elsewhere. Even so, the men remained vigilant, and the barrels of guns peered from trenches dug around the village. All able-bodied males were required for patrols, earning two pounds a month from the mainland, and they took their orders from former police officers and members of the now defunct Cyprus Army. On one occasion not long after Mehmet had arrived, a Greek Cypriot drove through the village – perhaps unaware of the territory he had entered, perhaps too drunk to care – and he was taken from his vehicle and beaten to death. Although some in the village were shocked by the murder, the majority were more alarmed by thoughts of retribution. However, after a month passed and no armoured mob descended, the panic subsided and the man was forgotten – at least in the village. Not so long ago, Mehmet would have demanded the perpetrators be brought to justice, now he was simply grateful he hadn't witnessed the crime and, lying by Pembe's side, he mourned the probity that once made him a better man.

'You know the child was a twin?'

Mehmet turned to his wife. 'No, I didn't. Just brothers.'

'Well, they were twins, and they were inseparable, their mother said.'

While Mehmet had been listening to Sevket's story,

Pembe had spent the evening in the company of the man's wife.

'The surviving boy, Ali, was the youngest by half a day,' Pembe continued in a whisper, so as not to disturb their nephew's children, sleeping beyond the curtain that separated them. 'Their mother said he hadn't eaten since the attack, and even when they force food into his mouth he just coughs it back up again. He'll only take water, but he can't wash away the taste, you see. His mother said he was next to his brother when they shot him. The bullet exploded in his head and the boy ate his brother's brains.'

'Oh, that child.'

In the dark, two silent tears slipped from the corners of Mehmet's eyes as he imagined the boy's torment, and he wondered how the young man would ever find the strength to carry on. The next day, before the cock had even crowed, Mehmet got his answer in the frantic screams of the child's mother.

Ali, son of Sevket and twin brother of Yusuf, killed himself while the rest of the village was sleeping. The method was battery acid. The child had burned the taste of his brother's death from his throat.

Almost a year ago, Dhespina had taken a sharp knife to a hundred peeled walnuts and sliced the ends off each and every one of them. She soaked them for seven days, changing the water daily, and on the eighth she added a handful of limestone. She then washed the walnuts and placed them in a large saucepan of water, which she brought to the boil. Ten minutes later she drained the walnuts and, with fresh water, brought them to the boil again, letting them cook for a further twenty minutes. After this she took a skewer and pierced two holes in each one before boiling them a third time for another twenty minutes. Once they had been drained and cooled in cold water, she added the juice of two lemons. Then she drained them again and stuffed an almond into the ends of each walnut. She put them back into another saucepan, poured sugar over them and cooked them on a low heat until the syrup thickened. Adding the juice of half a lemon she cooled them, placed them in jars, turned the lids tight and hid them away in a cupboard until a suitable occasion came calling. It was a long and punishing process – not least on the walnuts – and as a consequence, Dhespina now felt that neither they nor she were being given their due respect.

'Eat!' she commanded, and everyone in the room hurriedly picked up a small silver fork to nibble at the sticky balls oozing syrup on their plates. As they ate in silence, Dhespina handed around glasses of water.

'I don't like them,' Elpida muttered.

'Sh!' Praxi admonished.

'It's like wood in my mouth.'

'I don't like them either,' Loukis confessed with a wink.

'Well, I think they're lovely,' interrupted Lenya, throwing a smile in her sister's direction.

'I love them!' agreed Marios.

'Yes, very good,' added Georgios.

'They need more cloves,' Mrs Televantos said with a grimace.

'You've food on your chin hairs,' Elpida informed their neighbour, eliciting another shush from her mother. 'What now?' the child asked in frustration, and Dhespina broke into a thankful smile at the timely reminder of why everyone appeared to be taking up space in her front room. This was about her granddaughter.

As Georgios had once predicted, the truth had finally found its own way, bursting into the open like a gasp of delight only to be buried again beneath the petticoats of propriety. Loukis had been rightfully named as Elpida's father, Dhespina had been proved correct, Georgios was merely grateful that his wife had played no role in the drama and Elena believed that Praxi had chiselled the first cracks in a dam that was destined to break and destroy them all.

In light of their new circumstances, Dhespina had invited Praxi and her daughter to visit after a chance meeting at the bakery two days earlier. On hearing of Praxi's plans, Elena had insisted on tagging along – no doubt to clamp Praxi's mouth shut should she be taken to any more sudden confessions. However, no sooner had the door closed behind them than Loukis arrived, displaying once again an almost supernatural attachment to the mother of his child by turning up unannounced and at a time that was wholly out of character. Just when Dhespina thought the afternoon couldn't get any less intimate, or more crowded, Lenya and Andreas turned up with their daughter, Niki, to share the news that they had another child on the way. Soon after, Marios arrived home from work. And then, like the icing on a plate of *loukoumia*, the unscheduled party was completed by the arrival of Mrs Televantos, who had 'been passing by' and assumed the gathering was some sort of wake to honour the dead of Kokkina.

'The animals used napalm!' she screeched. 'Our sons try to stop them smuggling in guns that kill Greeks and the Turkish send their jets to pour hell on our faces!'

Georgios handed the old woman a nip of brandy to calm her nerves.

'You know, I shouldn't,' she reasoned before swallowing and handing the glass back for 'another small one'. To her left, Praxi was watching Loukis with a smirk on her lips and a glint in her eye. Dhespina noticed Lenya look quizzically at the pair of them.

'So, Praxi *mou*,' Mrs Televantos said as she gamely chomped through the clove-light walnuts on her plate, 'when will you be returning to that husband of yours?'

Beside her daughter, Elena almost choked on the water she was sipping.

'Mrs Televantos, it's impossible to say,' Praxi replied coolly, tearing her eyes from Loukis and allowing a look of sadness to flicker across her face. 'As you know, we have a busy bar, which is a blessing, but it's not the right environment for a young girl, as I'm sure you can appreciate – all those beer smells and noisy men. Yiannis and I have talked about it and we agree that Elpida's health and well-being must always come first.'

'I quite like beer,' Elpida remarked, and Praxi shot Mrs Televantos a knowing look, which was returned by a nod of sympathy.

'Quite right, young Praxi, you must think of the child and put your own needs second.'

'And what with the troubles and Turkey threatening to invade . . .' Praxi continued.

'No, absolutely right,' confirmed Mrs Televantos. 'There is no time for romance in the shadow of war.'

Loukis and Praxi shared a look, and Elena felt her skin go

clammy. 'I haven't the stomach for this,' she mumbled and took the plate to the sink.

'You know, I think I could do with some fresh air,' Praxi announced, rising from her chair.

'Can I come?' asked Elpida.

'Yes, of course.'

'I'll come with you,' stated Loukis.

'Me too!' cried Elena, stung into action by the thought of Mrs Televantos's loose tongue.

'I'll come as far as the cemetery,' Marios said.

'I might as well join you then,' added Georgios.

'Count me in,' mumbled Andreas.

'Papa, can I come?' asked Niki.

'Of course you can, *mikri mou.*'

And everyone left, leaving a puzzled Mrs Televantos to suck bits of walnuts from the gap in her dentures. Dhespina and her sister collected the abandoned plates. As they approached the sink they watched the trail of guests leave the garden.

'Do you think Loukis and Praxi are . . .?' Lenya let the whispered question hang.

'No, of course not,' Dhespina replied firmly, 'they never would. They're just . . . Oh, for goodness sake, they've only just begun talking again. Besides, when would they even find the time? Loukis might have the freedom to come and go as he pleases, but Elena watches Praxi like a hawk.'

'Yes, of course. Sorry. You know, I thought Elena would die of embarrassment when Mrs Televantos asked about Yiannis.' Lenya reached for a towel to dry the day's plates. 'I mean, it is odd, staying at your mother's house when your husband is only ten minutes up the road – and what with

Praxi's history with Loukis . . . Really, they must be careful, Dhespo. People will talk, rightly or wrongly. Praxi is a married woman.'

'I hear what you're saying, Lenya, but isn't there a part of you that thinks the world has swung back to its natural order?'

'Why? Because the two of them are friends again?'

'I guess.'

'Mother Mary, Dhespo! You're more impossible than they are. No, I don't think the world has shifted for the better. Loukis and Praxi are no longer children. They are adults with responsibilities. And should they go any further than talking – not that I'm saying they will, but there's bound to be temptation – they will be committing the most terrible sin. So please, keep your eye on them, because as sure as I'm carrying my second child, everyone else will be.'

15

A flash of blond hair caught Loukis's attention. The child was travelling at a furious speed.

'Is that Niki?'

Elpida looked over the fence and nodded in reply.

'Where's she running to?'

'I don't think she's exactly running to anything,' Elpida mused. 'She's more running from something.'

Loukis stopped cleaning his hunting rifle and waited for an explanation. Elpida shrugged and dipped the corners of her mouth in a way he recognized.

'I told her there were snakes here.'

'There are,' Loukis confirmed.

'Yes, but I told her they were devil hungry for little girls and they would try to eat her.'

'You're also a little girl.'

'Hardly, Loukis the Wolf, I'll be eight in a few months. Niki isn't even six yet.'

'Oh, then she really is a little girl. Not like you.' Loukis picked up the barrel of his gun and continued cleaning it, vaguely wondering how he felt about his own daughter persecuting his young cousin. He decided it showed character and imagination, and let it pass.

'I had that dream again last night.' Elpida came to sit on the rocks next to Loukis, where she tied his soot-blackened rags into a chain.

'Which one?'

'The one where the clouds come down on my face and try to steal my breathing.'

'And what did you do?'

'I blew them away – like you told me to do.'

'Did it work?'

'Yes. But I had to do some fierce hard blowing. It quite tired me out actually.'

'Well, some of those clouds can be hellishly tough.'

A smile crept over Loukis's face as he imagined his daughter blowing herself back to sleep. It was hard to believe that a year ago he had been lost in thought and winding country lanes, unable to make sense of the world around him. Now, sitting in the same warm sunshine, his life had purpose, and it centred on a little girl, not quite eight but much older than six.

Despite calling Yiannis 'Papa', it was now Loukis Elpida came running to – for fun, out of boredom, or whenever she was spooked by nightmares. And that Christmas she visited his mamma's house with Praxi and handed him a small box, carefully wrapped in gold paper. Inside, nesting in a bed of cotton wool, was a perfectly smooth white stone. As she handed it over, Elpida squinted with interest at the coming response. Loukis's eyes told her everything she needed to know.

'A pebble?' Praxi asked on seeing her daughter's gift.

'It's a moonstone, Mamma – a moonstone for a wolf.'

Elpida pulled roughly at the back of her socks and stood up to check the stick Loukis had stabbed into the soil.

'The shadow's nearly gone,' she said. 'I suppose I better go home. *Yiayia*'s making *psito* and I'm seeing Papa this afternoon.'

In an instant, Loukis felt the warmth vanish from his world. His child's words were a reminder of a reality he was choosing to ignore.

Twenty minutes earlier, Michalakis had been taking notes in the heat of the new sun outside one of Lefkosia's busy café-bars. Now he was inside, jostling for space as a sheet of rain caught everyone by surprise. As his mamma often warned, 'Don't put the wood away until the end of May.'

Kyriakos barged his way to a free table by the slot machine and ordered two coffees. Sudden weight loss had caused his cheeks to crash, and they hung in folds either side of his face. Michalakis couldn't be sure whether it was due to the demands of the politician's wife or the pressures of government. In the past year, Cyprus had been a whisper away from war with Turkey. Five threats of intervention had left the island bitterly disunited, and nine months of fighting had made ghost towns of a hundred and three Turkish Cypriot villages. People had died on both sides, and though the storm had subsided, the situation remained as volatile as the spring weather and nobody was any closer to a solution.

'Right now, we're standing at the edge of a political abyss,' Kyriakos informed Michalakis. 'Turkey has flexed her muscles, mother Greece has revealed her inability to match like with like, and our own armed forces are led by a man who holds the president in barely concealed contempt.'

259

'Why doesn't Makarios simply take General Grivas out of the equation?'

Kyriakos emitted a short volley of humourless laughter. 'And how do you suppose he does that? Grivas has the backing of Greece – and he holds all of the guns.'

'I guess when you put it that way . . .' Michalakis slurped the last of his coffee away and gave Kyriakos a look which he hoped might come across as more ambitious than desperate. 'Do you think you could get me in to see the president?'

'With your newspaper's reputation? Not likely!' Kyriakos balked. 'You haven't been the staunchest of allies over the past few years.'

'Maybe not, but we've always tried to be fair.'

'I can't fault you there.' The politician sighed, and he gave Michalakis a look he hoped was sympathetic rather than pitying. 'Look, leave it with me and I'll see what I can do. Perhaps with the president depending more on the communists for support, you may have a glimmer of a chance.'

Michalakis thanked him. He checked his watch and rose from his seat. He was going to be late.

'Keeping you from something, am I?' Kyriakos asked.

'Yes, you are,' Michalakis replied. 'Good to see you, old friend.'

'The pleasure, as always, is mine – just like the bill, I see.'

Outside the café, the earlier torrent of rain had petered out to a few heavy drops. Michalakis walked briskly to his car and drove to the Ledra Palace Hotel. There he found his mother and Maria drinking Coca-Cola by the new swimming pool. Dhespina looked awkward and out of place in her black headscarf and thick tights, whereas Maria shone like a goddess. Michalakis noted with pleasure that she was wearing the blue cotton dress he had bought her the week before.

'And how are my two most favourite ladies?' he asked, coming to join them. He placed a gentle hand on his mother's knee. Dhespina rarely ventured to the city – she said it made her itch – and he appreciated the effort she had made at his request. Following Maria's move to Lefkosia, Michalakis had trodden a careful and achingly slow path of courtship, and it was time for his family, and in particular his mother, to reconsider their associations with the girl.

'Did you get what you needed from your government friend?' Dhespina asked.

'Time will tell, but I hope so. Have you two been sun-bathing by the pool all day?'

'Hardly! Didn't you see the downpour?' cried Maria, pulling at the ends of her hair, which had curled in the wet.

'We went shopping,' Dhespina told her son.

'Why aren't I surprised?'

Maria playfully kicked Michalakis under the table, and Dhespina smiled at their games. It was an odd situation they found themselves in, and as a mother she was trying hard to shake the picture of Maria looking longingly at another of her sons. However, even a blind man could see the sparkle in Michalakis's eyes, and Dhespina prayed that the same tell of devotion would appear in Maria's face at some point in their future. It was not impossible. Nothing was. A quick look around the pool at the cocktail-drinking guests in various states of undress told her that.

Subconsciously, she scratched at the insides of her upper arms.

Praxi loved the unpredictability of spring, when the sun would be beaten by storms only to rally and win back the skies. As the last of the rain fell, she felt energized and as playful as the air. For so long she had languished in the dark of winter, but a new day was breaking and it brought the tantalizing presence of possibility. Finally, Loukis knew all there was to know: that she had betrayed him out of necessity not out of spite; and that the daughter she had born carried his blood. And though she was no nearer to feeling his breath on her face, hounded and shadowed as she was by her mother and the suspicious eyes of uncharitable neighbours, she knew no one else would warm to his touch either. Maria had run bleeding to the city, rejected by a man who had no wish for her in the first place. Praxi was unashamedly pleased by the development. If it hadn't been for Maria, she would have been pushed down the aisle and into the arms of Loukis eight years ago – and it would have been the happiest day of their lives. Instead, they had been victim to the whims of fate. Yet Praxi was hopeful. Somehow they had squirmed out of the clutches of inter-lopers and they were again in the same village. Surely more good would come their way. God and the island would see to it. They were His children and they were Cyprus; they were rain and sunshine; bitter wind and soothing breeze; they were everything and nothing and Praxi felt every flutter of nature within her soul as she skipped and twirled her way back to her mother's house, swinging two inert rabbits around her hips. The butcher had charged her a king's ransom for the corpses, but she felt the hand of Loukis in their deaths and she parted with her money because she yearned for the ghost of his touch.

By the time Praxi arrived home Elpida had returned from her afternoon with Yiannis. As Praxi waltzed through the door, Elena threw her a suspicious look, which Praxi dutifully ignored. She danced towards Elpida, who was laying the table for dinner. Her talk was full of the wedding she had seen in Keryneia.

'It was made by the *proxenitra* and it was a good match, wasn't it, *yiayia*?'

Relieving Praxi of the dead rabbits, Elena nodded and smiled in agreement.

'There were so many people there!' Elpida cried. 'It was like the most brilliant party. *Yiayia* told me that before the wedding there are loads of other parties before the big one, like the bed-laying. That's when the women put sheets on the bed and sing and dance while they do it. Afterwards, family guests put money on the bed, as well as a small baby boy. I'm not sure why they would do that, but it's called tradition.'

Elena and Praxi shared an amused look, knowing full well the reason for the fertility ritual.

'Anyway, the bride was just so beautiful, like an angel, and she wore this amazing white dress. And when she gets home she will have to take her bed sheets and hang them over the veranda – I guess to show everyone that she enjoyed her wedding so much she can't sleep.'

Unable to contain themselves, Elena and Praxi burst out laughing.

'What? What's so funny?'

Praxi rushed to her daughter's side, seeing the confusion and stress in her eyes. She hugged her hard.

'Elpida *mou*, we're delighted that's all – delighted by your wonderful story of the wedding.'

'Really?'

'Yes, really. And I tell you, I cannot wait for the day when you grow up and get married and another little girl your age runs to her own mamma to tell her about the beautiful angel she has seen.'

Elpida's face broke into a fierce smile that reached all the way to the back of her black eyes.

'That would be good, wouldn't it? And even though my own wedding is still a million miles away, I know exactly who I'm going to marry.'

'Do you now?' Praxi laughed getting to her feet. 'And who might that be?'

'Why, Loukis the Wolf, of course!'

Behind her Praxi heard the crash of plates. When she turned she found Elena unconscious on the floor.

16

Everywhere she looked, Elena saw problems. In the village, her daughter was hiding from her vows while her grand-daughter was planning a wedding to her own father, and in Keryneia, peeking out from under a little-used marital bed, was a pair of men's briefs much too snug to belong to her son-in-law. Elena kicked them out of sight to lessen their impact. Her nerves simply weren't up to the questions men's underpants might arouse.

She needed to talk to someone, but to whom? Dhespina, who for so many years had been her voice of reason and part-time physician, seemed content to bury her head, and there was no one else she could think of to trust. Her husband was long dead, the Lord seemingly deaf to her prayers, the saints unhelpful and the priest – well, she would be better off asking Mrs Televantos to announce her troubles from a loud speaker in the square for all the discretion that man showed. No, she was on her own – scrabbling to retain her principles and her mind, and failing at every corner. Throughout the summer and into autumn she had done her utmost to pull her family back on to the path of normality. She had chased Praxi home whenever she disappeared to

265

Dhespina's for longer than was neighbourly, and she had encouraged her granddaughter to play with Lenya's child rather than scurry off at every given opportunity to the Turks' farm. But Niki never stood still, and Elpida possessed neither the patience nor the legs for such a friendship. And when Elena tried to speak to Praxi about her concerns she rudely dismissed the unholy mess of her own daughter's affections as 'a childhood crush'.

'And what about you?' Elena asked.

'Me, Mamma? I'm over my crush and waiting to fulfil my destiny.'

Elena conceded that her daughter might have a point – if destiny was a turd in a date-leaf basket. No, it was abundantly clear that her family had fallen under the gaze of the Evil Eye.

To counter the curse, Elena had taken to cleansing her house daily, moving from room to room with a burner of smoking olive leaves, and when Elpida dragged the devil himself into her home, she threw salt on his seat to prevent him from returning. Begrudgingly, she noticed that Loukis had enough grace to wear an apology on his face whenever he walked into her parlour, but a sheepish look wasn't enough to protect them from ruin. Elena was truly at a loss. Not so long ago, she had believed her home was her castle – an impenetrable fortress to keep them all safe – but in recent years it had become her Constantinople. They said the great city would never fall until the day ships sailed on the land. A thousand years later, the Ottoman Turks built a pathway from the Bosphorus to the Golden Horn and they pulled their vessels across the dirt as Constantinople watched in dismay.

Elena spat on herself to ward off the ill omen of her own meanderings. As she did so, Yiannis entered the room, pausing to look around with theatrical amazement, as he always did.

'You've done a grand job, Elena!' He clapped his hands in appreciation.

The woman blushed, convinced that, as ineffectual as her son-in-law might be, he could somehow read her mind. She rinsed out the cloth and placed it in the cupboard.

'I'll drive you back to the village. I've bought you a gift and it's fairly heavy,' he said, and he disappeared downstairs, leaving Elena to worry about the new intrigue set to befall them – Yiannis hadn't been this considerate even over Christmas.

In the car, Elpida sat on her father's knee pretending to drive. It was a game they continued in the house, until the child became impatient and demanded they unpack the box Yiannis had brought with them. Inside was a television. No one was more surprised – or suspicious – than Elena. By the time they found a picture, the winter sun had gone and Praxi was tapping her fingers upon the table with undisguised boredom.

Yiannis hadn't laid eyes on his wife for more than a year, and when he first saw her he wasn't sure whether to kiss her or shake her hand. In the end he did neither. Everything felt too awkward. He had abandoned his visits to Elena's home soon after he had made love to Victor, convinced that Praxi could somehow smell the sin on his clothes, and when she didn't protest he allowed time to let them drift further apart, until their only contact came via messages from his daughter or mother-in-law. Naturally he was curious to know what his wife had been up to, because no whispers had crept to him from the village. He had also been cornered in the post office by Mrs Televantos, who congratulated him on the sacrifice he had made to protect his daughter from the vices inherent in the hospitality trade. Yiannis had blushed at the old woman's words. He had no idea what she was talking about, but his hair stood on end in the mistaken belief that she suspected the level of degeneracy taking place under his roof.

Yiannis rose from his knees, having located the best picture he could on the box in front of him. He turned to his estranged wife.

'It's time to pack your bags, Praxi. You're coming home.'

In front of Elena, the television flickered black and white images in a visual display of the machinations occurring in her stomach. With trepidation, she watched Praxi's eyes narrow, but in the end her daughter voiced no objection; she simply collected her clothes, gathered her make-up and creams and kissed her mother goodbye. May God forgive her, but Elena felt nothing but relief when the door closed behind the three of them.

Yiannis backed the Chevrolet out on to the street. As he had half expected, the journey to the harbour was quiet and tense. No one spoke, and the stares were unforgiving. Every time he looked in the mirror he was unnerved. It was the oddest sensation. He couldn't say he was scared – it was his daughter he saw gazing back at him – but all the same it made his neck itch.

In the house, Praxi dropped her bags in the middle of the floor and passed her eyes around the place.

'My mother's been busy.'

'Where's my room?' Elpida demanded. 'I'm not sleeping with Mamma again.'

'You'll have my room,' Yiannis stated. Seeing the panic fly into Praxi's eyes, he added, 'Don't have a cow, I won't be staying here. Until I go, I'll make do with the bar. I'll also cook my own meals . . .'

'Where are you going, Papa?'

'To serve my country, Elpida *mou*. The message came on the radio. I've been called up to the National Guard and I'll be gone in two days.'

Dhespina left Georgios snoring in their bed. It was uncommonly cold. All the fires were out and patterns of frost decorated the windows. She looked at her husband with envy. He always slept well. But Dhespina's mind had woken and the light was too bright to deny it. She slipped on her shoes to fetch the wood from the shed. As she stepped outside, her heart jolted in shock. He was huddled by the door and his nose dripped with cold and tears.

'Mr Televantos, whatever are you doing here?'

The old man lifted his head and strained to get to his feet. Dhespina bent to help him.

'Dhespo, please come. My dear wife, you must do something.'

'What is it, what's wrong?'

Dhespina shouted for her husband, and Georgios came quickly, his eyes heavy with sleep. Marios followed soon after.

'Fix Mr Televantos a warm drink,' Dhespina told her husband. 'Marios, you come with me.'

'No, Dhespo, let me come too,' the old man said, and how could she deny him?

Grabbing their coats, they set off for the small stone house in the centre of the village. Mr Televantos held on to Dhespina's arm. Their speed was slower than the urgency she felt. As they entered the house, Mr Televantos led them to the bedroom. The air was still and, under heavy pastel blankets, the old woman lay unmoving. As Dhespina stepped closer, she saw that her eyes were open, but the light was gone.

'Give her something, Dhespo,' Mr Televantos pleaded. 'Make her wake, let her get up again.'

The old man sat on the wicker stool by the bed and reached for his wife's hand. Dhespina looked at her husband.

'I'll get the priest,' he whispered.

Dhespina told Marios to return to their house and bring a bottle of jasmine from the den. She couldn't make the old woman wake, they all realized that, even the old man, but she could wipe the smell of death from his wife's skin as they waited for the priest.

Dhespina moved behind Mr Televantos and wrapped her arms around him.

Michalakis collected his uniform, stood in line, took in the speech, stored his tin can and gave silent thanks to Kyriakos.

'Before you go, get yourself a short back and sides,' he had ordered. 'While you're there, don't disagree but don't be a pussy, don't get into politics but be sure to play the patriot card and, most important of all, grab yourself a top bunk – you'd be surprised how many men forget to wake up when they need to go piss.'

It was sound advice. The army shears were brutal, the

level of ignorance astounding and the barracks overcrowded. There were fifty men to a room and the beds were stacked in threes. Having spent much of his life surrounded by four brothers, Michalakis had grown to value his own space, and he'd almost forgotten the irritation of another's flatulence.

After announcing their year of birth on the radio and television, the government had given a window of ten days for the new conscripts to present themselves at the old British Military Hospital. Michalakis was as furious as he had ever been, not least because Kyriakos had suggested during their last chat that the beleaguered archbishop was on the verge of granting him an interview for the paper. It would be a journalistic coup and it made his current situation even more galling. In fact, the only positive to come out of the call-up was Maria's sudden interest in him. Although they had grown close, and their lips were no longer strangers, the road to intimacy had remained closed, and it was only when Michalakis revealed that he was on his way to the military that he felt the first taste of urgency in Maria's kiss. The surprise of it blinded him. It also set his mind. When he had done his duty he would propose, and he was sure she would agree to marry him.

It would be eighteen months before Michalakis finished his service, and after the first night he spent in the barracks amidst the snores, creaking springs, moans and, in one case, screams of other men, the period of his confinement promised to be an unholy exercise in sleep deprivation. In his mind he heard Christakis chuckling at his womanly sensibilities. Michalakis pulled the scratchy blanket over his head and attempted to find sleep – as a man.

By the time morning arrived, Michalakis had accepted

that his life was no longer his own, along with every other bleary-eyed resident of the dormitory, and the general air of apathy gave him cause to believe the experience might not be as painful as he had first envisaged. From what he had overheard, no one else seemed to be that keen on performing their patriotic duty either, bar a few achingly earnest brothers of Hellenism. 'Cheerleaders for imperialism,' Savvas muttered in the bunk next to him, and Michalakis smiled in agreement.

Savvas was a trade unionist from Pafos. He was a working man's intellectual, with a dry wit and a deck of playing cards, and Michalakis quickly warmed to him over games of *pilotta*. He came from a long line of illustrious communists; his grandfather fought in the Spanish civil war; his father was pistol-whipped by EOKA fascists; and Savvas had followed in their ideological footsteps to become an active member of AKEL, the Progressive Party for the Working People.

'I'm the black sheep of the family,' he revealed one evening during a game of cards. 'I've yet to be shot or beaten for the cause.'

'Don't be too downhearted,' Michalakis replied, 'it's bound to happen sooner or later. You're in the army now. If the enemy don't get you, the squad leader's certain to.'

'That is no laughing matter,' Savvas replied grimly. Earlier that week, and following a three-day exercise in the forests of Troodos, the conscripts had packed their tents, covered their latrines and thrown their weary bodies into the backs of four trucks, ready for a return to barracks. As the convoy rumbled into action, the squad leader jumped on board with a flare gun in the holster at his side. One unexpected lurch later the gun went off and a rocket shot through the floor, right between Savvas's legs.

'I was a whisker away from joining the sisters,' Savvas recalled. Absent-mindedly, he dropped a hand to check on his wares.

'Perhaps it was no accident,' Michalakis mused. 'We all know how Grivas feels about the communists.'

'You jest, I know, but we're living in dangerous times, and the testicles of a few brave men are all that stands between our people and servitude,' Savvas quipped. 'The Greeks are undermining the republic from within, and we currently find ourselves at the heart of this fascist machine, comrade.'

Looking around him, Michalakis reflected on his friend's statement. It was hard to believe that their largely mono-syllabic brothers in arms might have the wherewithal to subvert what shred of democracy they still enjoyed on the island. The National Guard, now in its second year, was made up of labourers, farmers, carpenters, plumbers, electricians, cooks, idlers, businessmen, teachers and a couple of other journalists. No one was exempt from con-scription unless they were medically unfit, or they were Maronites, Armenians, Latins, or wearing the robes of the clergy. Perhaps unsurprisingly then, intellectual debate was an uncommon concept within the barracks. Even less of a surprise to Michalakis was the moment he came into contact with Yiannis again, seeing as they had once shared the same classroom.

Though they used to be friends of sorts, Michalakis had no wish to relive the moment and so he did his best to avoid Yiannis. He wasn't sure why. Maybe it was out of loyalty to Loukis. Perhaps it was simply that the man made him uncomfortable. And with no reasonable excuse to call on, Michalakis often felt guilty. From idle chatter in the barracks he knew that Yiannis spent his free evenings in the city rather than venture home, and the thought of the man's loneliness tugged at him. A better man would have extended his hand.

Every Wednesday evening, the soldiers were free to leave the BMH to visit loved ones and make merry with their wages – all of three Cyprus pounds. Most of the recruits journeyed home for a few snatched hours with their wives and girlfriends, others such as Yiannis headed deeper into the city – not that there was anything to do there: the Military Police kept a regular eye on the bars, which were prohibited to them. Those from further afield lived for Saturdays when they were released until the following morning. And somehow it made the rest of their days tolerable.

With Maria being but a bus journey away, Michalakis returned to her twice a week, unable to resist the heat of her wet lips, and once he had spotted the way her eyes dilated at the sight of his uniform, he always made sure he was impeccably dressed. If he had been in possession of his senses, he would have taken advantage of this momentary attraction and be done. But in those days, he was still foolish enough to mistake his lust for love. For all his condescension, Michalakis wasn't so far removed from any other soldier in his dormitory.

For most of the men, army life was only as punishing as their boredom made it and, to his surprise, Michalakis actually enjoyed the training. He had the good fortune to be gifted an unusually reliable Martini-Henry, and the endless laps and push-ups sculpted grooves of muscle in his arms and thighs, which he rather liked, never having been the athletic type. He wondered whether Maria would notice under his uniform. However, the most quizzical aspect of military life came when he wore his beret adorned with the emblem of the two-headed eagle. The mythical bird was said to have been the protector of Zeus, and Michalakis was quite unprepared for the surge of pride that welled in his chest. Of course, it was debatable as to which god the new recruits were protecting – Greece, Cyprus, Makarios or Grivas? The conscripts were divided.

Within the first few weeks of training, Michalakis witnessed Grivas in action. It was a blisteringly hot day and rumour of the general's arrival spread like wildfire around the camp.

Surrounded by bodyguards, Grivas descended on the BMH with the swagger of a rock star and stepped up to address the new recruits with a power in his voice that belied his small stature. He was in his sixties and the black of his broad moustache had grown grey, but his words had lost none of the fabled fire of his youth and, when he declared that the soldiers would push the Turks into the sea, a great roar of approval rose from the crowd. By Michalakis's side, Savvas dryly commented that the Turks would have to wait in line for the communists to go first.

Forty minutes after he took to the stage, General Grivas left the camp with the sound of adulation and support ringing in his ears. Released from the line-up, the men headed for the canteen, where Michalakis found a worm in his stew.

The anti-Turk rhetoric was the staple diet of army life. The 'enemy' lay only forty miles north of Cyprus and their 'sleeper cells' waited in the wings of enclaves littered around the island. Every day, for ten minutes – depending on the weather and the conviction of the speaker – this message was drummed home. The pride of Greece was at stake, the destiny of Cyprus in jeopardy, and all that stood between the safety of their families and the virginity of their young women was them. There was no room for argument, because to differ smacked of betrayal. The Turks would be defeated because they had no place in the Grand Idea, and their masters in Ankara would die like dogs should they interfere in the march towards the great Hellenic dream. Michalakis didn't need the insight of Savvas to come to the conclusion that they were all deluding themselves. In the five times that Turkey had threatened to invade, the wrath of Athens had acted as little deterrent. And when Turkish planes bombed the crap out of villages, blowing up brigades and charring innocents, Greece was paralysed by economics. She had neither the manpower nor the resources to come to the island's aid – no matter how slowly. And more to the point, Turkey knew that.

During one of their lessons in courage over common-sense, a local man and former fighter delivered a stirring speech that came close to moving Michalakis. There was a truth to his words that was born of experience, and the crutches by his side spoke of his own sacrifice. Then, as the applause died away and the recruits wandered off to the canteen, the oddest thing happened. The man rose from his seat and made for Michalakis with delighted surprise painted on his face. As he neared, the flicker of a mistake crept into his eyes, and he turned back with a frown to rejoin the officers.

Although the training was far from taxing, there was no

distinction made between abilities, and some of the recruits struggled. At the shooting range, a fat man, already squeezed into his ill-fitting uniform, wet his pants, as nerves and embarrassment at not being able to hit the target got the better of him. Most of the men laughed, but Michalakis felt his shame – and retreated further into his clique of intellectuals and Marxists.

Although Michalakis wasn't averse to the rough and tumble of other men, he was surprised to see Yiannis taking so well to the environment. So often the butt of jokes and playground ambushes for his loud mouth and soft chin, the man was quick to take up a leadership role, and as his confidence grew so did the level of his voice, as he spouted his beliefs like a true son of Hellenism. God knows where he had acquired his information, but he seemed well versed in the intricacies of army life and its Greek officers. Although they never once shared a conversation at BMH, Michalakis was inexplicably relieved when their training was over and they were assigned to their fields. He was sent to an infantry division in Lefkosia. Yiannis was sent to Larnaka.

The bar was a mess. The candles were gone, the table cloths lay discarded, and the lighting was a disaster. Praxi wasn't sure if a place could be depressed, but if it was possible she was standing in the middle of it. The friendly air she had envisaged had been destroyed by fluorescent light bulbs, plastic glasses and bilious men. There was no warmth, and the bar held all the charm of a military cafeteria. The Greek officers and their shady-looking companions had to go. And almost immediately, Praxi started to loosen the grip of her husband's authority on the business.

Following Mrs Televantos's funeral, which, sad as it was, gave Praxi occasion to explain her hasty departure from the village and the less disastrous effect on her life than she had originally feared, the Economidou men became a twice-weekly presence at the bar, with one of them staying a few minutes later into the night than the others. As she had half expected – and half prayed for – God and the island had engineered a way forward. Not to say it wasn't agony to have Loukis so near and yet so far from everything she wanted them to be. But thankfully, Georgios and Christakis – who could read his mamma as good as any of them – conspired to give Loukis an excuse to be at the bar and close to his daughter. Sweetly, at the shout of closing time they chatted among themselves as Loukis and Praxi bid each other good-bye with soft words and deep eyes.

'I feel like a prison guard,' Christakis muttered one night as they waited. Georgios nodded but kept his thoughts to himself. In truth, he was torn between wanting his son to move on and the need to protect him knowing he couldn't.

When Praxi's thoughts weren't consumed by Loukis and how she would ever get to be with him, she threw them into re-energizing the bar. Within a month of Yiannis's departure, she had created a menu of snacks to lure daylight tourists and hired a singer for the evenings to entice any locals look-ing for romance. As the atmosphere slowly shifted, and the army regulars decamped, she skipped across the road tothe Dome Hotel. Dressed to impress in conservative grey and a flash of red lipstick, she persuaded the manager to enter a pact of dual promotion. Visitors to the bar would be directed to the hotel and guests at the Dome would be encouraged to sate their thirst at the bar. She also hired

Christakis and Marios to paint her a new sign, which she hung proudly across the door. It read 'The Jewel of Keryneia'.

Although the troubles had all but killed tourism on the island, the times were slowly changing and a steady trickle of islanders and foreigners were creeping back to view the pretty harbour. A brave few ran the gauntlet of Keryneia Pass; others took the longer route to avoid the now sporadic attentions of snipers. As the number of visitors slowly increased, so did the port's optimism, and along the town's cobbled streets new hostelries and restaurants acted as testament to a growing confidence. Keryneia was clawing her way back to where she once was – albeit with an absence of Turks. Although the radio and television still carried reports of flaring violence, unlike previous years, the skirmishes were demoted to bit actors on the stage of world events. The Greek Cypriots had weathered the storm, and for the majority a sense of relief overrode the frustration of political impasse. And as the relative calm continued, the spirit of *enosis* found itself usurped by an entrepreneurial fervour.

As Praxi took control of the bar, her buoyancy began to soar with the takings. She had never imagined she might have a head for business, but the books didn't lie and she loved her work. Her only regret was that Loukis stood not at her side but in the shadows of her life. It maddened her. They had loved each other for twenty-four years, possibly twenty-five if Dhespina's story of her pregnancy was to be believed, yet fate had conspired to make fools of them both – with one of them now married to an idiot.

Although Yiannis only appeared twice a month, to spend

the day with Elpida, Praxi still entertained herself with fancies of his imminent demise. Sometimes the cause was a bullet – he was in the National Guard, after all; sometimes it was a car crash on his way to Keryneia; sometimes it was a heart attack brought on by his heavy smoking and even heavier frame. Praxi accepted that she would almost certainly go to hell for such thoughts, but if it meant spending this life with Loukis she considered the punishment worth it. Frustratingly, as the months passed by, Yiannis remained stubbornly unscathed and Praxi could find comfort only in the fleeting annoyance in her husband's gaze when he saw what she had done with his bar. But when she brought him the books and he saw the increase in takings, he shrugged in what she guessed was appreciation.

'Shall I fix you something to eat?' she asked.

'No, I'll take my chances elsewhere,' he replied.

17

'What's your name?'

'Jason. What's yours?'

'Artemis.'

'Like the goddess.'

'Exactly.'

Elpida sat down with a nonchalant flick of her hair. She wasn't sure what had inspired her to lie to the boy; it just came to her that it might be fun. She had been watching him for close to an hour, and she found him intriguing. He was white as a doctor's coat and still as a statue, and when she made her approach she had an overwhelming desire to push him into the sea. She could have done, easily, but almost upon him she thought better of it because *yiayia* was watching her watching him and such behaviour wouldn't have been becoming in a young woman nearly turning ten. So instead of slamming Jason in the back, Elpida joined him on the harbour wall.

'What are you looking at?' she asked.

'Nothing,' Jason replied.

'Why are you looking at nothing?'

The boy sighed and turned to face her. Astonishment widened his blue eyes. The girl was beautiful.

'My father, Jack, is out there – diving.' Jason pointed through the gap in the curving walls.

'Is he a fisherman?'

'No, he's an archaeologist.'

Elpida wasn't certain she knew what an archaeologist was, but it sounded impressive.

'There's an old boat out there,' Jason continued. 'They think it sunk about 300BC. Jack is taking a look at it for the University Museum of Pennsylvania.'

'Where's Pennsylvania?'

'It's in America.'

'Are you American then?'

'No, I'm British. Well, half Greek,' Jason corrected. 'My mother was from Athens.'

'So that's why you speak Greek so well?'

'Yes.'

'And where's your mamma?'

Jason looked at Elpida carefully. 'I usually tell people she's dead.'

'Is she?'

'No.'

'Then why do you say it?'

'I like it better than the truth.' Jason paused and Elpida waited. He instinctively recognized the futility of resistance. 'My mother ran off with a hairy-arsed painter from Bulgaria.'

Elpida leaned back and hissed through her teeth, because she hadn't yet mastered the art of whistling. It couldn't be easy losing your mamma to a monkey man.

'Where's Bulgaria?' she asked.

As Jason patiently explained, Elpida shared her chocolate bar and listened. The boy's accent was soft, with none of the heaviness of her own tongue, and it was charming; his words washed over her like music, and she bombarded him with questions to keep it humming in her ears.

Bulgaria, she was told, bordered Greece and Turkey – at least two countries she knew well – and after the Second World War it had become a communist state and a People's Republic.

'That sounds nice,' Elpida noted.

'What?'

'A People's Republic,' she repeated. 'We've got a republic here too, but it's the Republic of Cyprus and nobody wants to take care of all the people, from what I can see.'

Jason looked at her quizzically, but he let the comment pass. She really was very pretty.

'Tell me about the ship,' Elpida ordered. And Jason did as he was told.

A sponge diver had recently discovered the vessel and, when they realized it might date back to the time of Alexander the Great, everyone became incredibly excited. Jason's papa was currently in the sea with a metal detector and a team of scientists surveying the site.

'If it turns out to be what they hope it is – the oldest trading ship known to mankind – then a team of under-water archaeologists, students and technicians will come next year to record the positions of all the objects before lifting them from the sea. They will also try and lift the ship itself and probably put it in some museum – 2,300 years after she sank. It's going to take for ever.'

'So you'll be staying in Keryneia for ever?' Elpida asked.

'Looks like it,' Jason replied. And Elpida was actually quite delighted by the news. Behind her, she heard her mamma calling her in for dinner.

'I thought your name was Artemis?' Jason asked. Elpida laughed in reply and ran to the bar.

The officer took the three of them to a house in the far north of the city. No glass remained in the window frames, the electricity had been cut off and the property had clearly been abandoned some time ago. Since December 1963 was Savvas's guess.

'Where are the Turks?' asked Pieris, a farmer's son from Trimiklini.

'Over there,' directed the officer with a wave of his hand, and left them to it. As the night was pitch black, none of them was any the wiser as to where 'there' might be.

Feeling along the walls, they moved into a room offering light from the half moon. They placed their backs against the wall and kept their heads below the hole of the window. Pieris rooted in his pockets for cigarettes and matches.

'I wouldn't do that if I were you,' Michalakis advised. 'You might get your face blown off.'

'It's the third light that does for you,' Pieris replied.

'Oh I see,' Michalakis responded. 'I therefore take it you're counting on it happening to one of us as we all smoke. Nice to know you've got our backs.'

'I didn't mean it like that,' the soldier protested.

'Calm down,' Michalakis laughed. 'I'm only pulling your leg. Smoke away. We can wait.'

'Actually Pieris,' Savvas piped up, 'you have unwittingly

revealed yourself to be the victim of capitalist ingenuity.'

'Oh yeah?' Pieris lit his cigarette.

'Yes,' Savvas replied. 'You probably believe that three men taking a light from a single match is considered to be bad luck from the First World War – the notion being that one of them would be killed because when the first soldier lit up the enemy would see the light, when the second lit up the enemy would take aim, and when the third lit his cigarette the enemy would fire. However, it's all nonsense. There was in fact no such superstition during the First World War. The falsity was invented almost a decade later by the Swedish match tycoon Ivar Kreuger in an attempt to get people like you to use more matches.'

'God, that's sick,' declared Pieris.

'That's business,' Savvas replied, and Michalakis could almost see the mischief spreading across the AKEL man's face. The moment brought a pang of loss to his chest. In a few months, all three of them would be back in civilian clothes and, to his surprise, Michalakis found himself bordering on the nostalgic whenever he thought of the life he had yet to put behind him. Despite his initial irritation, he had enjoyed playing the soldier. His body was stronger, his attitude more tolerant and thus far he hadn't had to kill anyone. When all was said and done, he would genuinely miss the bond he had formed with some of the men.

'Oh come on, this is dumb,' declared Michalakis, getting to his feet. 'Let's go and see where the so-called enemy is so at least we know which direction to fire in.'

'I'm hearing you, brother.' Savvas heaved himself from the floor and Pieris reluctantly followed.

With their guns pointing forwards, the three soldiers tip-toed their way around the winding streets that used to be home to a bustling Turkish Cypriot community. The silence was eerie, and the evidence of conflict unnerving and sad.

'This is stupid, there's no one here!' Pieris grumbled as they lost sight of the forgotten house that had been designated their 'base'.

'Well, someone's here,' Savvas whispered ahead of them. Michalakis joined him at the corner of two narrow streets. Before them, a flicker of light danced from an open doorway, obviously from a candle.

Taking a firm grip of their weapons, the soldiers looked at each other and nodded in silent agreement. They inched across the cobbles, employing the hand gestures of their training. Michalakis took the lead, with Savvas at his back. Across the road, Pieris covered them both. Suddenly a shout broke the silence.

'I can hear you!'

The soldiers were startled to a standstill. They had been rumbled by the enemy, and the enemy spoke Greek. Michalakis looked at Savvas, who readied his gun. Leaping into the light with his Martini-Henry positioned for contact, Michalakis was confronted by the withered form of a man hunched over a Formica table, eating a meal. He was as old as Methuselah.

'Uncle, what are you doing here?' Michalakis asked in exasperation as his heart steadied to a more regular beat.

'What does it look like?' the old man grumbled. Michalakis heard Savvas chuckle behind him.

'Are you alone?'

'I am.'

'Aren't you scared?' shouted Pieris, still covering the road outside.

'Of what?' the old man shouted back. 'I've only my own shadow for company, unless you count the cats and rats.'

'What about the Turks?'

The old man clicked his dentures. 'There are no Turks here, son. Look around you! And even if there were, why would they bother with me? I'm not hurting anyone.' He rose from his seat and took the candle into another room. When he re-emerged he brought with him three small glasses, into which he poured a drop of brandy. Michalakis took the gift with thanks and passed the glasses to Savvas and Pieris.

'Where's your family?' Michalakis asked.

'Long gone.'

'Is there nowhere you can go?'

'Why would I leave?' the old man asked in genuine surprise. 'It's quiet here. I have my home. I have my life. And, touch wood, I still have my health. Every day I walk to the neighbouring village to pick up my cucumbers and tomatoes, and once a month I take a bottle of brandy. I don't harm anyone and I mind my own business. If everyone else did the same, perhaps you'd also be in your homes tonight instead of here . . . patrolling for ghosts.'

On 21 April 1967, Greece was rocked by a military coup instigated by colonels and senior officers from the intelligence service. The head of the junta was Colonel George Papadopoulos, and Yiannis wasn't sure what to make of the development – until Victor directed his thoughts.

'Now we'll start to see some progress,' the officer

confidently predicted as they tucked into a meat meze, reasonably priced, in a picturesque tavern on the coast of Ammochostos.

Yiannis bit into a spicy sausage and nodded in agreement before hitting his chest with the thick of his palm to dislodge the heartburn building. Victor winced at the thunderous expulsion of gas and Yiannis coloured at his own vulgarity.

'I don't think the end of your service can come soon enough,' Victor laughed, and Yiannis relaxed, choosing to take the gentle ribbing as a sign that he had been missed.

For sixteen months the lovers had restricted themselves to meeting every other Saturday in hotels and hostelries dotted around the island, always being careful to book two rooms to avoid suspicion. When the weather allowed they camped under the stars. And when Victor disappeared to the mainland on leave, Yiannis revisited all the places where he had loved him. It was foolish, he was shamefully conscious of that fact, and he should have taken the opportunity to visit his daughter, but he couldn't face the pretence that accompanied the journey, and it merely heightened his own sense of loss. While Victor was away, Yiannis was struck by a desperate detachment. At times, when his insecurities got the better of him, he effectively lost the will to speak. And if it hadn't been for the army, he most certainly would have spent the duration of Victor's vacations in bed. Typically, the only person to understand any of this was Yiannis. Although he ached to discuss the extremities of sadness and exhilaration that Victor aroused in him, he was unable to do so because he was paralysed by his own prejudices. He was still a man, no matter his leanings, and only women examined their emotions.

Although Yiannis knew beyond doubt that he loved Victor, he didn't possess the same measure of certainty that his feelings were reciprocated. He prayed that Victor felt even a fraction of his own devotion. Despite the years they had laid together, love was never mentioned. They talked about politics and little else. They no longer even discussed their families or the lie of their marriages. Sometimes they met to find they had nothing to say at all. But tonight, a second jug of *kokinelli* and the news of the coup had brought the easiness back to Victor's eyes, and Yiannis didn't think he would ever find the strength of feeling for another human being as he had for the man sitting across the table from him.

'You watch,' Victor told him between mouthfuls of pork kebab and pita bread. 'The junta will come out fighting for Cyprus. Right now we've got ten thousand of our troops on the island, and the age of kowtowing to the cassocked Castro is over. The colonels will back Grivas over Makarios in a heartbeat. It's time to take the war to the Turks.'

'Some of the officers in Larnaka have been talking of Kophinou,' Yiannis revealed. Victor grinned.

'That's definitely where it will start,' he confirmed. 'The dogs there have been laughing at us too long.'

The roads from Lefkosia, Larnaka and Lemesos all met under the gaze of Kophinou, and the Turkish Cypriots had erected roadblocks to prevent the police from passing through. It was no secret that Grivas wanted to break the village's resistance and, with the new junta in place, he would have the confidence to proceed, with or without the consent of the president.

'You never know, what with you being based in Larnaka,

289

you might actually find yourself playing a part in history,' Victor grinned.

Yiannis returned the smile, warmed by the possibility that such heroics might bring to their relationship. He raised his glass.

'*Enosis!*'

'*Enosis!*' Victor responded. Pointing with his fork, he added: 'You might want to clear that parsley from your teeth.'

Loukis sat far enough away to avoid any lapses in concentration that might bring his hand to rest on Praxi's knee. As a result she was holding court under a sign reading 'The Jewel of Keryneia' and he was stuck in the glare of the sun surrounded by men discussing the humiliation of football. Earlier in the year, the national side had got off to a dismal start in the UEFA EURO qualifiers, losing 2–0 to Italy and 7–0 to Romania. Now the team would have to redeem itself in November, first against Italy and then against the Swiss.

'Shame it's away from home, the lads could do with some support,' lamented Andreas.

'Asprou will come good, don't you worry about that,' Georgios predicted.

'Not on your life,' Marios laughed. 'If anyone, it will be Papadopoulos who will score. I'd bet a month's wages on it.'

'And I'll bet both your year's wages that we come home with nothing,' muttered Christakis. 'We haven't a hope with Gavalas as manager. That man wouldn't know how to split a bale of hay between two donkeys.'

At the top of the table Elena leaned towards Dhespina. 'Are they talking football again?'

'Well, it's preferable to politics,' her friend replied.

'Mamma, can you pass the potatoes?' Niki stretched a pleading hand towards Lenya. She was squatting on the seat of her chair, convinced that Keryneia's snakes were on a mission to seek and destroy even during mealtimes.

'Don't you think you've had enough, Niki?' Lenya asked.

'Nearly,' her daughter replied, and Elena raised an eyebrow.

'That child has the appetite of a lion,' she commented to no one in particular, but the thread was picked up by Niki's father at the other end of the table.

'She has the appetite of a champion, Elena!' Turning to the men, Andreas revealed that his daughter had been selected to represent her school's Under 11s in the 400m at the national competition. 'She'll be the youngest on the field,' he added proudly.

'If she continues to show promise, the school says we should think about getting her a professional trainer,' Lenya told the women. 'Of course, Andreas thinks it's simply a ploy to bring the games teacher more cash.'

'We don't need a trainer do we, Niki *mou*?' Her father shouted in reply. 'Just remember the snakes are on your tail!'

'Papa!' the girl shrieked, and Lenya rolled her eyes at the other women, who all instantly responded with examples of their own manmade exasperation – all of them apart from Praxi, who wasn't really in any position to discuss such matters. She glanced at Loukis and found him looking back. Even now, after all these years, his stare thrilled her to the bone. It was a look that stripped her bare and, more scandalously, she felt his nakedness in the gaze. Without warning, the bubble of excitement rising in her stomach erupted in a giggle.

'What's the matter with you?' her mother asked.

'Nothing at all,' Praxi replied, dragging her into a hug. 'I'm just happy to have you all here!'

'*Yiamas* to that!' Christakis shouted from his place with the men, and everyone lifted from their seats to knock their glasses together.

It was the third time they had all gathered at the bar, the first occasion having been to test out the new cook Praxi had hired. It was such a success they vowed to repeat the exercise every second Sunday of every new month and, looking around her, Praxi didn't think she had ever been happier. Even her mother had managed to shake off the misery of her moral anxieties amidst the chatter of Dhespina, Lenya and Yianoulla. And towards the end of the table, Loukis slipped comfortably into his role as the unspoken head of the party, making sure the glasses of the men were constantly refreshed, and playfully guarding the bottles of Keo from Christakis's four boys. In fact, the only cloud to cast a shadow over the proceedings came in the form of their daughter, who had taken herself away from the table to sulk. It had been two days, but she was still sore from the tongue-lashing Praxi had given her after the incident with the foreign boy.

Earlier in the week, Elpida and Jason had been searching for coins in the harbour when their conversation had turned to hair colour. Jason's was not so much blond as white, even though he was half Greek, but as he pointed out, both Niki and Christakis were also very fair.

'It's unlucky,' Elpida insisted. 'The only reason they didn't shave Niki's head every day like they did with Christakis is because she's a girl.'

'Actually, it's a sign of nobility,' Jason replied. Although he was only twelve years old, his vocabulary amazed Elpida. He sounded like an adult. He also called his papa by his proper name, Jack, which helped Elpida to make sense of why his mamma had run off. No one was playing by the normal rules.

'What's nobility?' she asked.

'It's the top classes, the rich people,' Jason explained. 'And look at the ancient gods, a lot of them were blond, such as your own Aphrodite.'

'The goddess of love,' Elpida sighed, looking mischievously at Jason, who immediately turned pink.

'Actually, Aphrodite wasn't as loving as you Cypriots make her out to be,' Jason replied. 'She was quite cruel to those who displeased her. She punished Glaucus for not wanting to breed his mares by making his horses rip him apart. She forced six of Poseidon's sons to gang-rape their own mother, and when Aegus refused to worship her she made him child-less. And she was always at it. Even though she was married to the crippled smith god Hephaestus, she had loads of affairs: she went to bed with Ares, and Hermes, Dionysus, and Adonis – and too many mortal men even to count. But what do you expect from a goddess who was created from the severed genitals of Uranus?'

Elpida was astonished. She had never heard such stories, or such language.

'How do you even know all of this?' she asked.

'I told you, Jack's an archaeologist, it's his job to know this stuff, and he tells me about it too. In fact, in the old, old days there used to be a cult that worshipped Aphrodite here on the island and they basically had sex with anyone and

293

everyone in her shrines and temples – her priests were nothing more than pimps.'

That evening, Elpida was so suitably troubled by Jason's revelations that when she returned home she spoke to her mamma, who was busy with *yiayia* getting the bar ready for the night's customers.

'Aphrodite was the most beautiful creature ever created and she had the ability to make any man fall in love with her,' Praxi informed her daughter. 'She was born from the sea and carried to Cyprus on a shell, which is why she is so very loved on the island.'

'Oh Mamma, we've got it all wrong. Aphrodite was a terrible goddess!'

'Why would you say that?' Praxi asked.

Elpida sat heavily on a chair and shook her head. 'Mamma, Aphrodite was a slut who was worshipped by prostitutes and who was made from a man's plums.'

For once, Praxi's face mirrored her mother's. When Loukis later arrived at the bar, chaperoned by his father and Christakis, she told him of Elpida's outburst, and his laughter forced tears from his eyes.

'That's probably the most accurate description I've ever heard of our most beloved deity,' he roared. Praxi, out of sight of their daughter, agreed.

'We've really made something special, haven't we?' she whispered across the counter that separated them.

'Yes, we have, Praxi – we've created a little girl with her mother's startling beauty and her father's searing intellect.'

'Do you really think I'm beautiful?'

'Yes, I do,' Loukis confirmed. 'There's not a woman in the world that could hold a candle to you.'

Praxi's eyes welled at the compliment, and she quickly turned away, fearing her hands would reach out and betray them. Two days later, Loukis's words remained powerful enough to flush her face once again as she rose from her seat to clear the table. The sun was resting on the sea and the left-over *souvlaki* had grown cold on their plates. The other women followed Praxi's lead and rose from their chairs to remove the meal's debris. They disappeared into the bar, emerging minutes later with trays laden with coffee and desserts. As Praxi rejoined the party with two bowls of fruit, her face suddenly fell pale as Elpida bolted from her seat.

'Papa!'

Yiannis swung Elpida high in his arms and kissed her roughly on the cheeks and forehead. As he neared, his hold became territorial and his eyes hardened. Loukis felt his muscles tense and Dhespina moved to his side, to support and tether him.

'Come on, we'd best return to the village,' she whispered.

Loukis stepped forwards, and Yiannis instinctively inched back. As Elpida turned in his arms, Loukis saw the question in her eyes. He stopped himself and walked away.

In her chest, Praxi felt her heart break.

18

In a village almost halfway between Larnaka and Lemesos, a young mother shovelled loaves of dough into an earthen oven. Her husband would be home in an hour, wearing a rifle slung over his shoulder and a weary smile that hinted at the beauty of his youth. Her eldest son would rise from his bed to take his father's place at the southern gate. Only when the sun set would the rest of their children return from play. As they slammed the door on the bite of a coming winter, the woman would be minded of the tired sweaters piling up in the boys' bedroom in need of attention. In every way, it was a normal day, indistinguishable from any that had passed before it in recent years – until ten to three when the gates of hell flew open.

Equipped with guns, mortars and bazookas, three thousand soldiers descended on Kophinou and unleashed everything they had. Within fifteen minutes of the first explosion, UN peacekeepers capitulated and pulled back, and the gunfire spread to every corner of the village. As bullets bounced off walls and tore through flesh, mothers ran screaming for their children, cut off and stranded in fields, while their fathers and older siblings reinforced wooden barricades with antiquated rifles that could only spit in the face of the inferno that had come to eat them. Kophinou was pounded with mortars and heavy artillery until every street crackled with flames and every mother was stunned into silence. At 9 p.m. the village fell – exhausted, depleted and defeated. Boys and men lay dead; bodies burned like torches on doorsteps; and in the heart of the Turkish village Greek voices barked their victory.

The soldiers marched from house to house, gathering their spoils of war. They herded the shell-shocked villagers into the clinic and bar, where they were guarded at gunpoint through the night. Then, at dawn, as suddenly as they had come, the Greeks withdrew.

'We were free to bury our dead,' the woman quietly told Michalakis. Her nails were scabbed and there were scratches at her throat. 'But for days afterwards, I was worse than dead. The grief was too big. I couldn't make sense of what you had done to us. It was only later that fire engulfed me. What is done is done, but I will never forgive and I will never forget. My husband and son died defending their village. They are martyrs now, they are heroes. You people sought to destroy us, but instead you brought us only honour and pride.'

When the woman had finished, Michalakis put his notebook away and thanked her. Her eyes didn't attempt to mask her contempt, and Michalakis shrank in her presence. He walked away, relieved to have played no part in the massacre but painfully aware that providence had saved him rather than choice. Had he still been in the National Guard, would he have found the courage to say no when the order came? He couldn't be sure. All he was able to do was recount the woman's story faithfully. A few weeks ago, such an idea would have been unthinkable but, in the blink of an eye, everything had changed.

In his haste to conquer Kophinou, Grivas had made a catastrophic error of judgement. The swiftness of the operation caught Turkey by surprise, but the speed of its conclusion failed to temper her fury. Ankara's patience had run out, and the call was not only for intervention in Cyprus but also conflict with Greece. Huge demonstrations echoed the war cry, and Turkish jets once again buzzed their intent over the island. The threat was deemed to be so serious that Britain moved her subjects on to Dhekelia airbase ready for evacuation. As the world's governments span themselves into a frenzy and Greece recoiled at the prospect of all-out war, Turkey demanded that Grivas be banished from the island and left to fester in his own hatred in Athens. They further insisted that all Greek personnel above and beyond the 950-strong battalion allowed by the Treaty of Guarantee be withdrawn, they called for the National Guard to be disbanded, illegal Czech arms to be put in custody and compensation paid to Turkish Cypriots. There was no room to manoeuvre: the Turkish threat was very real and the capability to repel it slim. Reluctantly, the Greeks brought their soldiers home, the contraband weapons were stored away, sanctions against Turkish Cypriots were lifted, and Grivas was exiled a second time and put under house arrest in Athens. Only the National Guard survived the mauling. And though Turkey also withdrew troops that had infiltrated the island, the price paid by the Greeks for Grivas's rashness was heavy. The junta recalled more than ten thousand soldiers; it lost its foothold and influence on the island; and above all else it was deeply humiliated. The only winner was Makarios, who saw the threat to his power annulled by the deportation of his former ally.

Yiannis hadn't worked out how he was going to make Praxi move back to her mother's, but he suspected she might be amenable whatever excuse he devised. She enjoyed managing the bar, that much was clear from the takings, but he also knew she liked running the business when he played no part in it. So the biggest problem he faced was Elpida – and her curious attachment to the British boy.

'I don't think so, Papa,' she retorted when he casually mentioned a return to the village.

'You'll do as you're told, young lady.'

'You think so?' Elpida asked, and the scorn in her voice floored him.

In his absence, his daughter had grown moody. Being ten years old, there could be no hormonal justification for such insolence, and only his guilt prevented Yiannis from taking a father's hand to her. To his horror, he saw his weakness reflected in Elpida's flinty stare. Even so, he couldn't deny his hunger. But just as he struggled to find a way to satisfy both his daughter and lover, the youthful distraction that had captured Elpida's heart was whisked away to the safety of Dhekelia airbase, and there was no longer any advantage in Yiannis having his house back, because Victor was taken away too.

The news came in a painfully short phone call and, to Yiannis's dismay, it was distant in every possible way. He heard anger, he heard irritation, but there was no hint of any greater loss behind the words. And by the time he had recovered enough to find the courage to ask, Victor was gone.

'When will I see you again?' he rasped. Only pips replied before the line went dead.

A week later he received a letter in the post.

Well, old friend, this is it. My plane leaves in an hour, and there will be an ocean between us and our greater dreams of *enosis*. Can you believe it has come to this? I think I'm still in the midst of what the medics might call shock, and I see it mirrored in the eyes of each and every man around me. No matter what the world might throw at us, we were fighting for what we believe in; for the glory of Greece and the protection of Cyprus and our people. I know that you, perhaps more than most, will feel our collective pain and sadness at the situation we now find ourselves in. Together and apart we marched on the same path, only to see it fall away at our feet. We have lost everything, and I don't think I have ever felt more miserable or betrayed in my entire life. So, where do we go from here? Where can we go? These are questions I have no answers to. Not now. We have been bloodied, but we are not broken. The day will come, Yiannis, when we will again be joined as brothers and Greeks. For now, as terrible as the reality may be, we must return to our lives and wait out this devastating moment in both of our histories. Trust me, we will pick up the pieces and we will be victorious. Don't lose faith. Both Greece and I are here for you. As I write, I imagine that frown forming a line between your eyebrows. Perhaps you find my words hard to believe, as I haven't always treated you as you might have expected or wanted, and I realize you have been on occasion hurt by the harshness of my words, but you have to understand that I spent my time with you because I wanted to.

You are the greatest source of happiness I take away from this island. Yours, Victor.

Yiannis carefully folded the letter, placed it in the shirt pocket covering his heart, gave it an affectionate pat and attempted to get back to his work. Seconds later, the words pulled at him, and within three days the folds had become worn creases that threatened to rip in his indelicate hands. However, with each reading, his determination increased until eventually he joined Praxi and his daughter at the dining table. To their utter dismay he told them they would be moving to Greece.

That night, after Elpida had cried herself to sleep and Yiannis had followed suit, albeit in silent isolation, Praxi took her red shawl from the back of the door and left the Jewel of Keryneia via the outside staircase. In the street, the cold hit her like a wall and she pulled the scarf closer. The soft wool smelled of her perfume and she felt it catching in her hair, which she purposely wore loose.

Unlike before, her steps were slow but sure. This time there was no storm urging her on. There was no fear. And, remarkably, she couldn't recall a moment of greater clarity. The accusations that had previously nagged at her had grown quiet and shame no longer seemed to hold the same terrifying power it once had. If it was to be a choice between nothing or everything tainted by disgrace, she would take the latter.

Coming to the door, she turned the handle, knowing it would be unlocked. As she entered the room she saw his shadow shift violently upon the metal bed against the far wall. She heard rather than saw his hand reach for his gun.

'Praxi?'

A match scratched to life. As the flame shuddered and died in his fingers he stepped forward. As he neared she smelled the musky scent of sleep upon his bare chest, and her teeth pulled at her lips. In the dark his face took shape and his black eyes promised time without end. She let the shawl fall from her shoulders. Quickly, her hands worked at the top buttons of her dress before she reached for his face.

'I don't care any more,' she whispered. 'Whatever you want, I will do it.'

Dhespina raised her son's head so that their eyes were level. The colour had vanished from his cheeks and his jaw pulsed with effort. She brought her lips to his forehead. 'Breathe, Loukis, breathe with me. I am here for you. I will always be here.'

And Loukis groaned in response.

An hour earlier, Dhespina had been chasing the dust from Mehmet and Pembe's porch, lazily wondering how Maria would fit into their family now that Michalakis had proposed, when Loukis came staggering towards her.

'We have to stop it,' he told her simply. And instead of running for her buckets and herbs, Dhespina guided her son to his home, drew the curtains and tried to find a way.

In the dimness of his room, they sat upon the floor and she asked him to explain. Forced to voice his fears, his breaths softened and his eyes focussed. Dhespina was little surprised when the story started with Praxi.

'All my life I have loved her,' Loukis murmured. 'I would gladly live in her shadow as long as it kept her with me.'

'And when she goes to Greece?'

'She won't go.'

'She must, Loukis.'

'I'd kill him first.'

Dhespina looked at her son. There was no anger beneath the contortions of his face. He spoke with certainty and clarity. And she believed him.

'You can't murder Yiannis,' she said.

'Why, do you want to do it?'

'Loukis! You can't kill a man simply because he stands in your way. Do you want to spend the rest of your life behind bars?'

'This is Cyprus, Mamma. Killers escape prison every day.' Dhespina angrily shook her son's shoulders. 'For mercy's sake, of course I know I can't kill Yiannis,' Loukis admitted with a snarl. 'But I can't live without Praxi. I don't want to live without her. If she went – if they went – it would destroy me.'

'So what will you do?'

'Leave.'

At his words, Dhespina's heart fell through the floor. To her private shame, she was affected in a way that she hadn't been when Loukis spoke of murder. She battled the tears stinging her eyes.

'Yes,' she agreed, 'you could leave. But where would you go?'

'England?'

'I suppose it could be arranged,' she admitted. Despite the turbulent history between the islands, thousands of Cypriots had made the journey in recent years, including Georgios's cousin.

In her hands, Loukis became very still. Slowly he raised

his head. He looked at her with such intensity that she thought she heard the words before they formed in his mouth. It was the moment she realized the Terror had not been stirred by Praxi after all.

'I can't imagine my life without you, Mamma.'

'Nor mine without you, son.'

Her heart breaking, Dhespina took Loukis's head and placed it upon her lap, where she stroked his hair and rocked away his worries until she saw the Terror creep by and leave him. Unable to tear herself away, she stayed until she knew he was asleep. He looked exhausted, and much older than his twenty-six years. But he was still her boy. Oh God! He was her boy! Dhespina grabbed at her headscarf and bit on it to still her tongue.

When the moment had passed, she gently removed herself. She placed Loukis's head on a pillow and brought the blanket from his bed to cover him on the floor where he lay. As fresh tears threatened to take her, she left for home.

Outside, the moon was up, and she was startled to see a light shining from Mehmet and Pembe's house. She knew she couldn't have left it on, because it had been daylight when Loukis came looking for her. Quietly, her heart hammering, she crept on to the porch. Through the window, she saw an old man seated on a chair staring at a framed photograph. It was Mehmet. And he was alone.

19

Mehmet stirred as he heard Pembe catch her breath.

'See the horse,' she mumbled, and shifting a little closer she drifted back to sleep.

It was the first time since leaving the village that she had mentioned the animal that had played such a magnificent role in their wedding. And when he awoke, Mehmet was distraught to find that the white horse of his wife's dreams had returned only to carry her away. There was no illness, no torturous preamble of pain. Pembe died in her sleep with a smile on her lips. Her passing was as gentle as her spirit, and it was the ending Mehmet would have wished for his wife – if only she hadn't left him so far behind.

For the next month, Mehmet remained in Gönyeli to complete the rituals of death. Their daughter, Ayse, arrived from Leymosun with her four children, and their two sons travelled by boat from the mainland. Their grief and sense of guilt was claustrophobic, and Mehmet felt relief when they reluctantly returned to their own homes, unable to convince him to move with them. Once they had left, the men who gathered daily at Uncle Çavuş's coffee shop stepped up to distract him with long games of *tavli*, and he was even persuaded to take in a film at one of the two small cinemas. It was a love story, and he found it painful to watch, not so much because of his loss but because the flickering images left him with a headache.

As his own life emptied, around him the world steadied. Barricades built to protect and imprison were slowly dismantled, and though Turkish soldiers retained their barracks at the old school, the air of fear and defiance waned. Predictably, with Pembe gone, Mehmet yearned more than ever for his home. And so it was that, when all was done that needed to be done, he began walking. Unable to dissuade him from leaving, his nephew offered to arrange transport, but Mehmet shook his head, saying he needed to feel the journey in his feet. Taking no more than the clothes on his back, and with Pembe's favourite scarf tied about his throat, he left Gönyeli. Seven hours later, he walked into his own home. From the moment he turned the door handle he felt his wife with him and his shoulders straightened with the memory of real happiness – as well as with surprise. After so many years away, their house remained intact and immaculate. Everything was in its place, just as he half expected it would be, but there was no dust to show the passage of time. In their absence the house had been cared for, and when he turned towards the footsteps sounding behind him the miracle revealed its face. He took Dhespina into his arms and cried his grief and gratitude into her hair.

The next day, Mehmet sat on his porch and patiently waited for Loukis to emerge from his bed. A brief tour had revealed the farm to be in good order, and he wanted to thank him. When Loukis finally walked into the sun, the strains of a difficult sleep were evident on his face, and Mehmet felt a glimmer of sadness at missing the boy's transition to a man. He was huge, and somewhat stern-looking, but Loukis had always been dark, even as a child. Typically, Loukis showed little emotion at Mehmet's sudden presence save a small smile that pulled at the side of his mouth. Without a word, he headed back into his home, to return seconds later with a small booklet. He handed it to Mehmet. It was from the bank, and the farmer's name was written on the first page. A long list of numbers followed.

'I've only taken for my wages and some expenses for upkeep,' Loukis explained.

'There was no guarantee I was coming back.'

'I knew you would return.'

Touched beyond words, Mehmet struggled to voice his thanks before Loukis turned on his heel to save them both any further embarrassment.

From the house, Mehmet was certain he heard his wife's delighted laughter.

The coach belched its way through back streets littered with plastic bags spilling household waste, and passed tired houses dripping rust from ageing pipes. From his seat, the people below were shabbily dressed and the pervading air was one of decline. Only when Yiannis caught a fleeting glimpse of the most perfect building built by the world's most advanced civilization did he find his pride in the motherland restored. The Acropolis was stunning. Despite everything he had read, he was unprepared for the sight, and part of him ached to climb the hill and immerse himself in its white-stone glow. But Yiannis didn't have the time – and he felt unworthy. From his books he knew the ancient city was also called Cecropia, after the legendary Athenian king Cecrops, who was said to have been half man, half serpent. At that moment, on a coach heading southwards, Yiannis felt all snake.

After three hours twitching in and out of a fitful sleep that saw the passenger next to him seek rest elsewhere, Yiannis arrived in Tolo, on the Peloponnese peninsula.

First mentioned by Homer in his account of the Trojan War, the picturesque bay had since been the port of call for many an empirical battle and, following the Greek revolution, a number of Cretan refugees had resettled there. In 1916, the fishing village became known as Tolo and, as the years passed by, dwellings tumbled out of the bay to line the beach and take advantage of the northern Europeans flocking to the area in search of warm seas, fine sands and the district's many archaeological sites. Collecting his one bag from the belly of the coach, Yiannis paused to catch his breath and light a cigarette. A protective circle of mountains gave the bay a secluded but open feel and Yiannis was imbued with a sense of safety. It really was very pretty – just like Victor had described it.

After checking out the two hotels on the seafront, Yiannis retreated further up the hill and away from the wallet-draining views. Eventually he found a faded, three-storey establishment offering basic comfort and a free breakfast at a reasonable price. He changed his shirt and headed back to the shore, passing hand-painted signs for boat trips to the islands of Hydra, Spetses or Poros. After finding his bearings, he settled into a lively establishment called the Paradise

Bar which gave a panoramic view of the bay – and its residents.

The next morning, following a lonely but hearty meal of halloumi, olives and stale village bread, Yiannis began looking for potential business premises. Buying a newspaper, he struck up a conversation with a large, affable man called Panos. It transpired that Panos's brother's sister-in-law had an uncle who knew somebody in the property game. The two men shook hands and arranged to meet up again the following Monday. With no other plan to engage him, Yiannis returned to the Paradise. By the time the fourth night of his stay had gone in another blur of *metaxa*, he cursed his stupidity at never having got an address.

Although Victor had frequently talked of his home, Yiannis had paid little attention, because it suited his purposes not to believe that his lover led another life away from him. Now, he racked his brain for any detail Victor might have given: a tree-lined street; a porch decked with roses; a sight of the sea; a popular shop – anything. But there was nothing to be dragged from the slurry of his memory. Yiannis couldn't even recall the name of a bar in which he could hunker down and wait, and he didn't have the stomach to visit them all asking if anyone knew Victor. Even for Yiannis it was a step too shameful. And his mood wasn't lifted by the wizened form of his landlady.

'How long are you staying?' she croaked.

'I don't know. A few weeks.'

'Why don't you know?'

'Do you want my money or not?'

The old woman eyed him with suspicion, but it didn't stop her grasping fingers from snatching his notes for that night's stay and burying them in her pocket.

'Do you want your sheets washing?' she asked. 'You've been in them for more than a week.'

'Will it cost me more money?'

'Do I look like a saint?'

'In that case I'll leave it.' Yiannis headed back to the Paradise.

The following morning, he met the man who knew the uncle of Panos's brother's sister-in-law. His name also happened to be Panos, and he took Yiannis to a rundown building that appeared to have all the tourist-pulling power of a pig shed.

'It doesn't look much now,' the man admitted, with an enviable degree of honesty, 'but you have to see the potential.'

Yiannis squinted, but the potential appeared to be lurking around a corner he couldn't yet negotiate.

'Firstly, it's in a prime location close to the town, but with room to expand,' Panos cajoled. 'And once the farmer moves his pigs, the land here will be full of hotels. The deal's almost done and in a couple of years this place will be buzzing with tourists. Trust me, you're buying into a goldmine and you could find yourself with a thriving business, if you have the mind for it.'

Yiannis told Panos II that he would set his mind to sleeping on it and they agreed to meet up again the following Monday. He headed back to the Paradise, and in an all too frequent fit of despair he bought a bottle of *metaxa* rather than paying by the glass. When he came to, the following morning, his head pounded to the rhythm of the previous night's brandy, and there was blood on his sheets. With a start, Yiannis ran his hands over his chest, convinced he had somehow been stabbed during his sleep. As his heart slowed and his memory kicked in, he recalled missing a step leading up from the square and falling heavily on his face.

Embarrassed but relieved, he heaved himself from the lumpy mattress and stumbled to the bathroom. Splashing himself with cold water, he looked up into the mirror. In the place where his two front teeth used to sit was a dark, torn hole. He vomited noisily into the sink.

With no stomach – or teeth – to face breakfast, Yiannis managed to still his trembling fingers long enough to button a clean shirt. Nimbly avoiding the landlady waiting for his rent on the stairs, he climbed from his window and went in search of assistance. After two hours of indescribable humiliation, Yiannis found a dentist in the centre of the village who whistled a little at the mess, laughed a little more at the story and promised to fix his teeth to the very best of his ability the next day. Mightily relieved, Yiannis wandered back to his digs. On the way, he stopped by the 7-Eleven for bread and cheese. After missing his one free meal of the day, he was as hungry as a horse – and in dire need of aspirin. As he handed over his coins, a young child screamed in fury at the door of the store and Yiannis turned with pain and annoyance. The mother slapped the boy into silence and Yiannis's heart quickened. Before he knew what he was doing, he was stood in front of the family with his arm outstretched. Victor's face paled in surprise, and his throat convulsed in shock and genuine horror. Belatedly, Yiannis clamped shut his mouth.

After an awkward introduction, Victor's wife insisted Yiannis come to their home the following evening. He arrived with a bottle of wine and an ill-fitting dental plate, which made him self-conscious and sibilant. The night was agony in every perceivable way. The enjoyment of the glorious spread of *souvlaki*, village salad and roast potatoes was severely impeded by the difficulty of his dentures and the acrobatics of his stomach. He realized even before the food hit the table that he had made the most terrible mistake, and to his great distress Victor was abrupt and unconscionably rude for most of the evening. His wife wasn't much better. A tall and imposing woman, she appeared to suffer her husband with the same intolerance she showed to her kids. Her inquisition of their guest bordered on the hostile, and Yiannis turned to politics to try to explain his relationship with her husband. As he spoke it sounded like an apology. Victor did nothing to ease his predicament. In fact he seemed bored and unable, or unwilling, to appreciate the enormous effort Yiannis had made on his behalf. By the time coffee arrived, Yiannis was exhausted, his gums were sore and he felt impossibly foolish. When he shook hands with Victor at the end of the night he knew it would be the last time they would ever touch, and the thought of it killed him.

The next day he caught the early bus to Athens. Because he was angry, he exacted revenge on his landlady by flitting with the last of the rent he owed still in his pocket. He also left his bloody clothes and dirty sheets in a heap on the bed. As the bus ambled its way through the picturesque village, it came close to the shed that could have possibly made his fortune. The farmer still had his pigs in the field.

*

312

'Did you love her?'

'Did you ever love Yiannis?'

'Oh Loukis, that's a ridiculous question!'

'In that case, you may appreciate the stupidity of your own.'

Praxi smiled and nudged herself deeper into the dip between his shoulder and chest. In truth, she knew the limitations of Loukis's heart, but her own was jealous and her mind unrelenting. Maria must surely have slept with him, despite the sin, just as she had once done and was doing again. And even if Maria was little more than a vessel to Loukis, tipped out of bed once the moment had passed, surely there was some tenderness, times when he allowed her to lay in his arms listening to him breathe – and the thought of it gnawed at her insides.

'Do you ever think of her?' Praxi felt the rise of irritation in Loukis's chest. 'Come on, it's a fair question.'

'OK, yes, sometimes I do,' he admitted, sitting up and lighting a cigarette. 'But not in the way you think.'

Praxi raised herself from the grass to read him, but his eyes were concentrating on the ring of smoke breaking above them.

'Did you care for her?' she persisted.

'No. I can't say I did. But that doesn't mean I don't wish her well.'

'I can't say I wish Yiannis well at all,' Praxi confessed. 'Isn't that terrible?'

'Only if you don't mean it.'

Praxi laughed, and Loukis took the jacket they had been lying on to place it around her shoulders.

'God, I love it here,' she sighed.

'Me too.'

'So how can you leave?'

'Because I love you more.' Loukis turned his head so she could see the truth of it in his eyes.

'But will you love me for ever and never leave me?'

'Praxi!' Loukis grabbed her about her waist to swallow her in his arms. 'I will never leave you.'

'If you mean it – promise me.'

'I promise.'

'Swear on the Bible!'

Loukis raised his arms in exasperation, taking in the scenery around them.

'OK,' Praxi conceded. 'Then swear on my life!'

'OK, I swear on your life, and on my life, and on the life of anyone you ask me to.'

'Swear that you will never leave me even if the whole world catches fire.'

'I will never leave you even if the whole world catches fire and you're nothing but burnt toast. There, are you satisfied?'

'Yes. I am. Thank you. I love you, Loukis.'

'I love you too, Praxi.'

Hand in hand, they gazed at the grey and white clouds drifting over them, moving southwards on a gentle breeze. The sun was warm, and around the pistachio tree spring flowers sprayed their colour like a welcome-home parade. Far below, the sea glinted in the distance; brilliant blue waves kissed by golden rays. Intermittently, tiny raindrops soaked into their clothes, but it didn't detract from the beauty of the day, and they sat in silence, desperately endeavouring to catch every sound, smell and breath of their island, not knowing when they would see her again.

For more than a decade they had kept themselves from Saint Hilarion's, but nothing had changed. Although Turkish soldiers remained close by, they no longer shielded snipers or posed any danger. The menace of fear and mistrust had died in the aftermath of the National Guard's assault on Kophinou, and the huge military withdrawals had left Cyprus buoyant. It made the prospect of leaving her all the more tragic.

'We'll be back one day,' Loukis whispered, as if reading her thoughts. But Praxi wasn't so sure. They both knew it was hard to return once you'd run away.

'I never thought I'd say it, but I'll miss my mamma,' Praxi said.

'I never thought I'd say it, but I'll miss her too,' Loukis laughed.

With Yiannis in Greece, Praxi and Loukis had taken the opportunity to plan their escape to the last detail. They would leave in a few weeks, after the Easter break. They had chosen the festival to gather one last time with their families without arousing suspicion. Only Dhespina knew of their impending departure; the rest would find out in time. Elpida would travel with them, believing she was on holiday until they had the safety of distance to explain the truth of their journey. Praxi expected all hell to break loose, but Loukis assured her that their daughter would adjust quicker than they would. Although Praxi told him he was probably right, she wasn't so sure. Furthermore, she hated the fact that they were sneaking away like thieves in the night when their only crime was to love each other. Loukis had no such qualms. Whether Cyprus or England, he didn't care. It was only a different-coloured earth to tread on. However, to ease

Praxi's pain, he said they would call Elena to join them once they had settled.

'Won't you miss your mamma?' Praxi asked.

'Of course,' he answered, and before she could delve any further he planted a kiss on her lips. From the moment Loukis had made up his mind to leave, a pain had needled his thoughts, and the faster Easter approached, the more he struggled to ignore it. He could scarcely conceive of a life devoid of his mother's presence, and each time that prospect tried to take shape he felt himself wither.

'It sounds nice, doesn't it? Angel Islington?'

Loukis agreed that it sounded very nice indeed – despite having spoken to his father's cousin, who had given a description of the London borough that was far from heavenly.

'They'll have to rename it the Two Angels of Islington when you get there,' he smiled, and Praxi laughed in delight. She was still so easily charmed by him it was ridiculous, and she told him so.

Christakis's three older boys had tied the youngest to the fence. Elpida thought about saving him, but he seemed quite content to sit where he was, so she watched him from the swing on the apple tree. Beyond the gate, Niki sprinted back and forth along the road, propelled by the medals she had won and the glories, predicted by others, to come. Everyone appeared to be very proud of her. Personally, Elpida thought the girl was unstable.

Inside the house, the scene was one of organized chaos. Dhespina was commanding the main meal, aided by Lenya, who juggled pots and pans while balancing her brown-haired toddler, Erado, on her hip; Elena and Yianoùlla were fussing with desserts; and Praxi and Maria were attempting to chop salad without turning their knives on each other. In the sitting room, Michalakis and Andreas filled emptying glasses with beer as Georgios and Marios demanded a year's wages from Christakis. Getting nowhere, they loudly implored Loukis to referee the decision, as he had also been witness to the bet. Despite everyone's hopes, Cyprus had finished bottom of their group, acquiring only two points in the UEFA EURO qualifiers. It was heart-breaking, with the only light coming at the GPS Stadium in Lefkosia when Asprou and Papadopoulos both snatched a goal from the visiting Swiss – goals that Georgios and Marios claimed to have predicted. However, Christakis was in no position to honour the wager and he insisted the bet was made on successful qualification. As the national squad had watched eighteen goals slip past their net, he argued that the campaign could not, under any circumstance, be described as a success.

'What are they arguing about?' Mr Televantos asked Mehmet.

'Whether a wager's void.'

'I've had a few of them in my time,' the old man shouted. 'Tell them to get some cream from Dhespo.'

'Not haemorrhoid!' Mehmet shouted back. 'They're arguing over a bet.'

'I can't see a vet helping,' Mr Televantos grumbled and shook his head in wonder at the people of today. Mehmet let the conversation go and silently prayed that his own hearing wouldn't pass away with the departure of his wife. Oblivious to his mistake, Mr Televantos continued eating his way

317

through the mountain of eggs he had won. Although the ritual of cracking dyed eggs was usually left to the children, this Easter everyone had been involved, with the old man emerging victorious. Mehmet left him to it and moved to the table to savour the *flaounes*, *koulouria* and *tyropittes* that the women had baked earlier in the week. Despite having his own religion, Mehmet always enjoyed the Greeks' Easter. From the kitchen, he caught the smell of warm meat wafting his way. It promised to be a fine spread, and Praxi and Maria silently stepped forward to ready the long table. Dhespina rolled her eyes as she walked past them to rally the children from their play. Ordinarily, they would have eaten in the garden, but the skies threatened rain.

'Inside, children!' cried Dhespina from the doorway. To her horror, she saw her youngest grandchild tied to a fence.

'Elpida, help free the boy,' she ordered, and the girl lazily slipped from her swing to do as she was told. Dhespina clipped the heads of Christakis's older boys as they hurriedly ran past her to get into the house.

'Where's Niki?'

'Running up and down the road, as usual,' Elpida revealed, and Dhespina went to find her. As she came to the corner she almost collided with the child. Jogging on the spot, her blond hair bouncing like string around her pretty face, Niki asked why Elpida's father was crying in his car.

'What do you mean?' Dhespina asked, and the child waved towards the road leading to the village. As Niki ran to the house, Dhespina went to investigate.

With his head buried in his hands, Yiannis didn't see her approach, and when she gently opened the door and slipped in beside him, he only showed the slightest concern. Tears and the slimy excretions of his nose wetted his face, and there was something strange going on with his teeth. Dhespina dug into her jumper to hand him a clean hanky. To her dismay, Yiannis blew on it and passed it back.

'It's over,' he snuffled, as she held the offending tissue by the edges.

'What's over?' she asked, surprised he knew and dreading the coming answer, given her own guilty part in the boy's downfall.

'My life!' he cried, and he unleashed another torrent of tears. Dhespina handed the hanky back.

'Come on, Yiannis. No one wants to hurt you . . .'

'What would you know?' he angrily interrupted, and Dhespina flinched in response. 'You haven't got a clue what I'm going through. None of you has. And you! Sitting in your nice pretty house, surrounded by your big, strong boys, with a husband who loves you and people who want to be with you, what would you ever know about my life?'

Dhespina sat still, unable to answer. Yiannis's pain was difficult to watch. After everything was said and done, he was only a man caught up in the wrong love affair. He wasn't bad. He didn't deserve to be sat in his car, crying alone, during Easter.

'I love him,' Yiannis sniffed.

'I'm sure she loves you too, in her own way,' Dhespina lied. Yiannis looked at her, puzzled.

'Not her. Him! I don't love Praxi. I love Victor.'

Around them, the very air seemed to pause at the enormity of Yiannis's confession. Dhespina wasn't sure what to say.

'I've shocked you,' he stated flatly.

'Well, yes you have, a little,' Dhespina admitted, and she looked at Yiannis with fresh eyes. He didn't look like a homosexual, not that she had ever met one before. Casting an eye over his thick neck and drab clothing, she found herself strangely disappointed; she had expected a homosexual to be more flamboyant. However, now that he had revealed himself, it did make some kind of sense: the lack of children from his marriage – knowingly conceived or not – and the blind eye he must have turned all those years while his wife stayed in the same village as her childhood love. It must have been horrible for the boy, and indescribably lonely.

'Tell me about this Victor,' she whispered, and because Yiannis had ached for an opportunity to do so, he did.

As Yiannis unburdened himself, he spoke honestly and unashamedly of his love for another man, and to her surprise Dhespina managed to see past the sin of his confession. Yiannis was a young man, the same age as Michalakis, and he was a homosexual; a homosexual with a lover who no longer wanted him.

'Oh Yiannis, what can I say to you? It's not easy to find the courage to go on when your heart is broken. But you have to find the strength. You have to move on.'

'Like your Loukis did?' Yiannis sneered. When he saw Dhespina's fallen face, he immediately regretted his harshness. 'I'm sorry,' he muttered. 'That was uncalled for.'

Dhespina said nothing, because there was nothing truthful she could say.

'You know, for a long time, I hated your son,' Yiannis continued. 'And then I became scared of him. But slowly I think I began to understand him. I can't say I like your

Loukis, never have done, but in a way I respect him. He's never let go of the woman he loved – even though that woman happened to be my wife. And maybe if I had ever loved her I wouldn't be here talking to you like this. But I've never loved Praxi. The thought of touching her made me ill. And I'm sick of pretending otherwise and having people think I'm stupid. All of us have spent the best part of our lives lying to each other. And are any of us any happier for it? You know, I would gladly let Praxi go. I don't care if she ends her days with Loukis or not. I really don't. But this isn't America. We can't just go and get one of those divorces. And then there's my daughter to consider . . .'

Yiannis paused, and Dhespina saw the question in his eyes. She kept her face still, but her conscience grated at the gratitude that swept fleetingly across the man's face.

'. . . My daughter is the most important thing in my life,' he continued. 'She is all I have.'

'But you're taking her to Greece.'

'I was,' Yiannis corrected, 'but I was chasing a dream, and the dream didn't want me. So, my life is here – with my daughter.'

Once again, Dhespina was lost for words. But, for the first time in weeks, she felt happiness flutter inside her chest.

'Come,' she said finally, patting her lap to convey her determination. 'Join us for dinner. It's Easter – a time to let go of the past and old quarrels. Yiannis, son, it's time for us all to move forward. And if I can help you, I will.'

Lamblike, and floundering for any olive branch, Yiannis followed Dhespina from the car. In truth, he was ravenous, and his stomach and heartache left little room for reasoned thinking. Therefore, he was quite unprepared for the sea of stunned faces that greeted him as he walked through the door of the Economidous' home. Mercifully, Elpida's delighted squeal broke the heavy silence. As he lifted the child high in his arms he felt the weight of the world slip from his shoulders, and he smiled for the first time since he had left Athens.

'Good God!' Mr Televantos shouted. 'What the hell have you done to your mouth?'

20

A pre-wedding drink lured them to the Jewel of Keryneia but, at the sight of a white bikini, the brothers decamped to the harbour wall. Side by side, they lined up their chairs. A packet of cigarettes traded hands, and with a clink of glasses they settled down for the show. The woman noticed them watching – how could she not? They were four uncommonly tall, extremely handsome men dressed to kill in dark suits, pressed shirts, polished shoes and slicked-back hair. She held in her stomach and dived gracefully into the water. The brothers raised their eyebrows in appreciation.

Behind them, Angelis came running.

'Mamma says you've got to come home now. We'll be late and she's getting angry.'

Christakis grabbed his eldest son and pulled him on to his lap. 'Your mamma would be the first to agree that nothing should come before your education. Sit and learn.'

As the boy was at an age where the secrets of men were of substantially more interest than a roomful of women, he did as he was bid. 'What are we looking at?'

'The woman,' Loukis replied, pointing a lazy finger out to the bay.

'Why? She's only swimming.'

'Watch,' his father teased.

Some seventy yards away, the woman glided through the water, occasionally disappearing behind wooden fishing boats and rolling waves. Her long graceful arms swept over her head in an arc and her lean legs caused only the slightest of spray. Her bikini shimmered.

'Won't be long now,' Michalakis commented, glad of the distraction on his big day.

'Seconds away,' agreed Christakis.

Although the May sun burned hot, the sea remained icy, and experience told them the woman would soon retreat from the cold. After circling an orange buoy, she headed for land. The brothers nodded slowly, as one. Approaching the rocks, the woman momentarily trod water, looking for a suitable foothold. As she reached to climb out, she fell backwards with a scream, slapping furiously at her left breast, which was now in the tentacle clutches of a fiercely determined octopus.

'Off you go, Marios!' ordered Christakis, and his brother ran to the rescue.

Reaching the jetty, he gestured to the panicked woman to come nearer. She was still flailing wildly, but he grabbed her hand and in one fluid movement hoisted her upwards, grabbed the octopus by its head, and pierced its brain with the tip of his thumb. The unlucky creature released its grip and the woman's legs gave way in gratitude and embarrassment.

Christakis turned to his son, 'Octopuses are attracted to light colours, and in the old days fishermen would drop white hankies into the sea to lure them from their holes between the rocks. So you see, the woman was asking for trouble in that bikini.'

As the men laughed at their good fortune, Marios rejoined them, victory lighting up his face.

'Well?' asked Michalakis.

'We're meeting tomorrow at eight,' he confessed with a grin.

'Excellent!' Christakis applauded. He rose from his seat to ruffle Angelis's hair. 'And that, my son, concludes today's lesson. Now, let's go and watch your uncle get married.'

As the brothers dragged their chairs back to the bar, a battered Ford Cortina rattled to a halt in front of them. The door opened with a kick, and Savvas emerged with a smile.

'I was beginning to think you wouldn't make it!' Michalakis greeted him.

'And miss the opportunity to turn a journalist into an honest man? You've got to be kidding.'

Michalakis introduced his best man. If circumstances had been different, and he hadn't had the sensitivities of his bride and other brothers to consider, he might have asked Loukis to be his *koumbaro*. Instead, he could think of no more capable person to perform the honour than his former army colleague.

'Nervous?' Savvas asked. Michalakis replied that he was, which shocked him a little, because it was so unexpected, and when he arrived at the church he was even more astonished to find his hands shaking as he took the posy of flowers from his mother.

'Nervous?' she asked, and he tried to reply that he was, but his tongue was now glued to the roof of his mouth and he was afraid he might vomit. Silently, he took his place by

325

the entrance. Some fifteen minutes later, Maria arrived in a glorious creation of billowing white satin with her long hair curled and tumbling over a shining tiara.

'My God, you look amazing,' Michalakis managed as he handed over his mother's flowers. Maria smiled coyly, confident that she did indeed look fabulous, but conscious of the good impression a trace of modesty makes. Michalakis felt a pinch at his arm.

'You're a lucky man,' Christakis told him. And Michalakis agreed that he was.

As the bride and groom entered the church, their guests dutifully followed, chattering loudly and critiquing Maria's luscious gown. Inside, they found Mr Televantos already planted in the best seat, having sneaked in early. Some moved to join him, others chose to stand, and around their feet hordes of children ran wild, bored before the priest had even begun the Service of Betrothal.

'This is the weirdest wedding I've ever been to,' whispered Jason. He had returned shortly after Easter with his father Jack after the British had declared Cyprus safe from imminent invasion.

'Why is it weird?' Elpida asked.

'Look around you,' he said with a flourish of hands. 'Everyone sits where they want, some don't sit at all, kids are running all over the place and everyone's talking so loudly you can hardly hear the priest. I wouldn't be surprised if that old man in the front row gets out a bag of sandwiches soon.'

'But why is it weird?' Elpida insisted, casting a look in Mr Televantos's direction.

'All right, maybe it's not weird, just different. In England, we sit where we're told and no one speaks apart from the bride and groom and the vicar. Here just about everyone speaks apart from the bride and groom!'

'God, how dull – it doesn't sound like much of a celebration in England,' Elpida noted.

'No, I suppose not,' Jason admitted. 'Actually, Jack says marriage is a crime against man and a form of legalized castration.'

'What's "legalized"?' Elpida asked.

'It's when something is allowed by law.'

'And what's a castration?'

'It's the act of cutting a man's knob off.'

Startled beyond belief, Elpida moved her eyes to the altar and tried to concentrate on the ceremony, praying her cheeks wouldn't betray her embarrassment and the merciful Lord wouldn't punish Jason's sin with killer bolts of lightning. Michalakis's friend from the army was performing the ritual of the rings with the bride and groom.

Savvas kept his face solemn as he swapped the gold bands three times to symbolize the Holy Trinity. As he finished, the priest raised his voice in prayer and brought Michalakis and Maria's hands together. Above their heads, *stefana* crowns linked by the white ribbon of unity were exchanged three times. The priest spoke of the marriage of Cana at Galilee, when Jesus performed his first miracle by turning water into wine. Michalakis then drank from a goblet, three times, after which the priest led the couple three times around the altar, shadowed by Savvas, who was carefully endeavouring to hold their crowns in place while avoiding tripping over the chasing children. For Michalakis and Maria, it was their first steps as a married couple. When they came to a halt, the rice came out and the priest casually lifted his Bible to protect his face.

When a semblance of calm had returned, the priest finally separated the couple's hands using the holy book, reminding them that only God had the power to break the union they had just entered into. At the back of the church, Praxi dipped her head, Yiannis developed a slight twitch, and Loukis watched on dispassionately.

With the service over, the congregation poured out of the church, blinked in the sunlight and scurried off to the village hall. Shaking hands with the newlyweds, guests scrambled for seats on tables nearest the raised stage and waited for the kitchen's hatches to open. Georgios and his sons took their turn behind the counter, shovelling food on to plates and spinning *souvla* on a spit. The women, who had spent the previous day peeling spuds, slicing onions, cutting vegetables, and preparing salads, were given the evening off. As bellies filled, and the room buzzed with happy drunken chatter, the music began and Michalakis and his bride stepped on to the stage. Taking their lead from the parents of the happy couple, the guests lined up to pin rows of money upon Maria's beautiful dress, with a degree of showmanship directly corresponding to the denomination of notes.

After Kyriakos had pinned his own generous gift upon the bride, he shook Michalakis's hand and whispered in his ear. 'I've another present for you; the archbishop will grant your newspaper an interview early next month. Call me when you've recovered from your husbandly exertions and we'll set up a time.'

Michalakis didn't know what to say. Swept away with the happiness of the day, he kissed Kyriakos roughly on both cheeks and picked up his bride. He swung her playfully in

328

his arms as the appreciative crowd roared their encouragement. Infected by the joy in their son's face, and the strains
of the *bouzouki*, Georgios and Dhespina walked back on to
the stage, arm in arm. One by one, other couples came
to join them, as young men begged theatrically reluctant
girls to also play their part. A large circle was gradually
formed to begin the traditional *syrtos* dance. As the music
gained tempo, Christakis placed his cigarette between his
teeth, ripped open his shirt and entered the circle.
Michalakis, Marios and Savvas came to join him, bending to
rub their fingers along the soles of their shoes. To the shouts
and claps of the other dancers, they battled each other with
arms outstretched and fingers clicking for the loudest cheer
from an already enthusiastic crowd. Meanwhile, looking
distinctly out of place among the geriatric spectators,
Loukis, Praxi and Yiannis remained seated.

Since Easter's scandalous revelations, the three of them
had come to an unspoken agreement whereby Praxi and
Elpida were again spending their nights at Elena's and their
days in Keryneia. On his return from Greece, Yiannis had
lost the will to dislike his wife. For all her faults, and he
thought they were many, she had never broken his heart.
She had turned his stomach, reduced him to tears and made
him fear for his life, but she had never broken him. In
turn, Praxi saw her husband in a new, more sympathetic
light. She had always imagined that she had been the one
trapped, but really Yiannis had been more caged than any
of them, contained behind the bars of her lies and his
sexuality.

'I actually feel sorry for him,' she told Loukis. 'What do
you think of it all?'

'What do I think?' asked Loukis, imagining all the nights that Yiannis had spent in the arms of his Greek officer while he had been crawling up the walls of his own home. 'I think he owes us a few more tumbles, that's what I think.'

Although none of them could say their situation was even remotely satisfactory, none of them wanted to leave the only home they had ever known. So they had come to a truce of sorts; a dignified compromise that allowed for the love of two, the respect of three, and the pretence of conformity for the sake of Elena and the rest of society. The accord was not enough, however, to allow them to take to the wedding-hall floor with the gay abandon of other guests, and therefore they clapped along with the pensioners and hoped people would have the good grace not to comment.

Elpida lifted the spoon and dropped it again. Her hair ached from *yiayia*'s mauling and her head felt impossibly heavy. She placed her cheek on the table and closed her eyes.

'Hurry up, you'll be late for school,' Praxi scolded.

Elpida stretched her arms and released an affected yawn. 'I don't think I'll go to school today.'

'Are you ill?' Elena asked, reaching for the child's forehead.

'No, I'm fine.'

'Then why don't you think you're going to school?' her mother inquired.

'Because it's unnecessary,' Elpida answered.

'I beg your pardon?'

'Jason doesn't go to school, and he's the most intelligent person I've ever met.'

'You're only ten years old, Elpida. You've not met enough people to qualify that statement.'

'Mamma, school isn't a place of learning, it's a place of repetition.'

'And I suppose Jason told you that, did he?'

Elpida shut her mouth. She knew when her mamma was trying to trick her.

'What's she talking about?' Elena asked her daughter.

'Elpida doesn't want to go to school today because Jason doesn't go.'

'The British boy?'

'Yes.'

'Is he one of those drop-outs?' Elena asked. 'I saw it on the television news. Hoppies they call themselves.'

'Hippies,' Praxi corrected.

'Hippies, hoppies. It's the hand of the devil, all that long hair and free love.'

'What's free love?'

'Elpida! I won't tell you again – get up those stairs and get ready for school before I tan your hide.'

'Oh honestly, you are so . . . bourgeois!' The child ran from the table before her mamma's hand could reach her.

'What the hell's bourgeois?' Elena asked. Praxi ignored her, a little because she could feel her temper rising but mainly because she wasn't overly sure herself.

'I blame the schools,' Elena continued. 'In my day we learned about Mother Greece and God the Father. Now it's the Mamas and the Papas and Uncle Sam.'

'Where do you get this stuff?' Praxi asked incredulously.

'I told you – the television – although I only watch it for Archbishop Makarios, may God bless him and keep him safe from harm.'

'Of course you do, Mamma. Of course you do.'

*

Michalakis was shown to a sparse room devoid of any presidential trappings of office save for a gilt-edged seat glinting behind a sturdy wooden desk. His hands were wet with anticipation, and he was rubbing them on his trousers just as Archbishop Makarios arrived, followed by a small man with an impossibly large bundle of papers. Michalakis moved to kiss the back of the archbishop's hand. To his surprise, Makarios responded by congratulating him on his marriage. Unprepared for such pleasantries, Michalakis gave rambling thanks which bordered on the incoherent before unleashing a stream of consciousness about the day itself; curious details that fell unbidden from his lips and that he seemed incapable of stopping. The archbishop smiled patiently before urging Michalakis to retake his seat with an apology that time was not on their side and he had other business to attend to. Michalakis found himself taking up more time by apologizing.

It wasn't the first occasion Michalakis had laid eyes on Makarios: he had attended numerous political rallies in Lefkosia; he had watched the president pick through the ruins of intercommunity conflict; and he had once felt the brush of his black cassocks as they passed in a ministerial corridor. Even so, in the intimacy of this room, Michalakis was struck by an awe that came from years of conditioning. The archbishop was the political and spiritual leader of the island. He was statesman and father. And Michalakis was taken aback by the man's presence. Behind the flecks of grey in the full black beard was a smile bordering on the mischievous, and the eyes, dark and hooded, sparkled with wit and gentility. Under the cylinder-like *kalimafi* hat, the president oozed confidence – as he should: four months earlier he had been re-elected with a majority of 96 per cent over his opponent.

'Were you surprised the Enosis Front fared so badly in the election?' Michalakis asked.

Makarios allowed time for measured thought, but his answer was an easy no.

'The people, at this stage in time, understand the need to preserve the republic as an indivisible unitary state. We have to find solutions to the constitutional problems we face through peaceful means that will afford safeguards to the Turkish Cypriot community while ensuring effective government in accordance with democratic principles. It is my belief that Athens stands ready to sacrifice a part of this island to Turkey in exchange for union of the remainder with Greece. Clearly, this is unacceptable, not only to me, but to the Greek Cypriots of this island. It is a price for *enosis* that none of us is willing to pay. And if *enosis* is only attainable with the risk of partition, it is a goal we must put aside, for now.'

'There are some who say you have abandoned your commitment to *enosis* in favour of an independent Cyprus with you at its helm as president.'

'Meaning that I put my own ambitions before my country?' Makarios asked. His face was still and serious, but his eyes laughed at the question.

'That has been an accusation levelled at you,' Michalakis said carefully.

'From Cyprus or Athens?' Makarios inquired, before casting aside his own query with a wave of his hand. 'I'm not deaf to the claims of other, shall we say, interested parties, but I have a responsibility to Cyprus that cannot be manipulated to please the expectations of a disgruntled power or minority. At this precise moment in history, we need to make a courageous compromise. We must be willing to accept a feasible solution, and yes, it's true, that solution might not fulfil all of our desires, but right now, this is the right path for Cyprus and for Greek Cypriots.'

Although it was abundantly clear that much of the archbishop's willingness to compromise stemmed from a lack of enthusiasm for political union with a military dictatorship, neither man voiced it.

'So, where do you go from here?' Michalakis asked.

'We walk down a long and difficult path. To show my own faith, and to herald this new dawn in our history, I have ordered all Greek Cypriot forces to pull down their fortifications and to abandon roadblocks around the Turkish quarter of Lefkosia. In a little over a week we will begin negotiations for a settlement. I truly believe there is goodwill on both sides, despite the tragedies suffered by both our communities, and we need to build on it to find a real and lasting solution so we can move forward without fear of intervention by a third party.'

21

Shortly after the Americans put a man on the moon, Elena joined a hardcore group of doomsayers in daily prayers. In contrast, Christakis's boys took to wearing buckets on their heads as they stalked the town in slow motion – serving to accentuate Niki's own supersonic skills – and Yiannis bought a Ford Torino Cobra with fastback hardtop, bucket seats and high-level trim. The Chevrolet he decided to give to Praxi, which meant driving lessons.

'One small step for woman, one giant leap out of the way for mankind,' Yiannis joked as they took their positions.

'Very funny,' Praxi scowled, but her ill humour came from nerves; she meant no malice. Despite their differences – and the uncared-for vows that tied and once strangled them – Praxi and Yiannis had stumbled upon a friendship that neither could quite believe. Resentment had been cast adrift in a wave of partial honesty – the truth of their daughter's blood remained unsaid – and they were living their lives instead of railing against their pasts. Praxi had Loukis, and Yiannis had his once-weekly visits to the city. Praxi didn't inquire as to what her husband got up to in Lefkosia but, whatever he did, it had had an effect on the length of his hair and the leg width of his jeans. He seemed close to being happy and Praxi was glad, even though she had to blank the physical image of what might lie behind that happiness.

In a mess of stalled engines and kangaroo starts, the couple laboured their way out of the harbour, passing Elpida en route. Praxi failed to see her daughter through the tunnel vision of fear that kept her eyes glued to the road, but Yiannis threw her a cheery wave, followed by a mock grimace. Elpida turned her back, appalled at the spectacle being created by her parents.

'This is so embarrassing,' she moaned, and Jason laughed at her discomfort.

'I think it's pretty cool, your mother learning to drive.'

'Well, I'd expect you to say that,' Elpida replied. 'You've got no sense of what is proper.'

'Is that right?'

Jason suddenly swooped and flicked Elpida's skirt high, revealing her knickers to all and sundry and causing the girl to shriek with mortification. Instinct told the teenager to run, and he sprinted down the cobbled street with Elpida screaming fury behind him. Dodging pedestrians, tourists and the occasional cat, the two of them burst on to the high street, screeched around the square and came to an exhausted stop by the church.

'When I catch my breath you'll pay for what you did,' Elpida gasped.

'I don't doubt it,' Jason replied, and he shot her a smile that melted her insides to butter. Lazily, he stretched his legs in front of him. To Elpida's eyes, he looked impossibly long. Last year, she had thought she was close to matching him, but when he returned from his mother's spring 'retreat' in Crete he was a head taller than she remembered, with stories to match.

'We stayed in a place called Matala,' Jason told her. 'There were a couple of British rock stars hanging around, smoking dope and talking bullshit, but it was pretty cool. You know, legend says that when Zeus seduced the princess Europa in the form of a white bull he crossed the sea and brought her to Matala's beach. He then changed into an eagle and flew her to Gortys, where he had sex with her.'

Elpida blushed at her friend's typically shocking revelations, but even in her embarrassment she felt herself taken by unformed desires in which she sparkled beneath a setting sun as a guitar strummed close by and a meta-morphic boy with a crown of soft white hair stared at her longingly.

'Why do all your stories have sex in them?' she asked.

'Because it's all I tend to think about,' Jason replied, and Elpida squirmed at his teasing.

'It's not healthy,' she said, echoing her grandmother's condemnation of all things bodily.

'How can it not be healthy?' Jason challenged. 'It's as natural as eating, and one day you're going to have to do it whether you like it or not. Hopefully with me.'

'Jason!'

'Elpida!' the boy mimicked, and he punched her playfully in the arm to reassure her that that time was not quite upon them.

From the churchyard, they saw Marios walking hand in hand with a short woman with long red hair into which she had braided a number of tiny flowers.

'She's new,' Jason commented. Elpida agreed, and waved when Marios spotted them.

'Who's that?' the woman by his side asked in English.

'Elpida,' Marios replied. He would have said more, but his English was lacking, not that it seemed to hinder his friendships with the foreign girls. With the fighting no longer tearing the island apart, tourists were descending in their droves, and Marios was finding his time increasingly taken up by female attention. None of the Greek girls he met showed much interest in him, but the foreign ones, with their burnt skin and pale eyes, were always happy to hang on his arm. And to his great relief, none of them seemed that interested in talking. Marios recognized he was different. He didn't possess the intellect of his brothers, or indeed of most men his age, and his conversation often bored people. When he spoke to the local girls, he registered the disappointment in their eyes before they collected themselves and turned into his mother. But the foreign women, with their holiday spirit and differing language, retained the sparkle of immediate appreciation.

'You're heading for trouble,' his mamma sternly informed him, but his papa warmly encouraged his friendships, despite their difficulties. Over the past two years, Marios had grown experienced enough to understand that girls were more complicated than they looked, even the foreign ones. And if you were friends with too many at one time, they fell into the most fearful strop. During one confusing encounter at Praxi's bar, when two of his girlfriends came face to face, there was a baffling display of shouting, which led to thrown drinks and pulled hair. Despite his slow learning, Marios quickly cottoned on to the fact that the only way to keep all his girlfriends happy was to keep them away from each other. Therefore, every two weeks, he limited himself to one new friend. When they returned to their own country he kissed them goodbye, promised to write, and went looking for another. For Marios, life was pretty sweet, and the latest girl on his arm was just as pleasing. Her name was Carina and she lived in Germany with her parents and a cat called Remo. She was ten years younger than Marios, but her ways were older and, despite the flowers in her hair, she was stricter than a schoolteacher. Unlike the other girls, she hadn't progressed beyond holding hands and they were well into her second week. Although Marios felt some frustration at her coldness, he found Carina strangely comforting, and he believed that he might even miss her when she left. Therefore when she reappeared a month later, Marios was not only surprised but delighted. It was midday, and he was eating a kebab with Virginie when Carina materialized before him. Wordlessly, she pulled a handkerchief from her pocket and wiped the grease from the corners of his mouth before chasing the French girl away with a scowl. As she settled into Virginie's vacant seat, Marios sensed that this was perhaps the way his life would be from now on, and he halved his lunch and handed it over.

With her parents' blessing, Carina had found a job at a small hotel on the outskirts of Keryneia, helping in the restaurant in the evenings and with the accounts during the day, as she had graduated from business school. She had brought most of her clothes with her, and she later bought a bicycle. On Tuesday and Thursday evenings, she took lessons in Greek. As her language skills increased, Marios waited for the girl to grow bored, but to his amazement she didn't. In fact, the more they were able to speak, the better their time together became until eventually – three months after Carina returned to Keryneia and when the hotel was closing for the season – he asked her to stay and to marry him. To his surprise, she agreed to both requests.

Somewhat nervously, Marios took Carina to meet his parents the very next day. Dhespina was thrilled by the visit and she plied the girl with hip-fattening cakes as Georgios batted easy questions around the table. They both seemed genuinely taken with Carina, and Dhespina made a frightful fuss of her red hair before Marios managed to still the conversation with the bombshell of their engagement.

Dhespina threw Georgios a look and he rose from his chair.

'Marios, son, let's go and tell Nicos the news.'

As the men left, Dhespina continued smiling at their guest in a way she hoped would come across as patient rather than patronizing. Coughing slightly, she then did her best to approach the subject with as much delicacy as their limited conversation allowed.

'First of all, let me say how pleased I am that you have made Marios so happy,' Dhespina started.

Carina held her stare, unblinking, and replied that Marios made her just as happy. Dhespina nodded calmly.

'It is clear that you like our son,' she continued. 'It is a big step to leave your home and come to Keryneia, but real life is a world away from a holiday and the truth is, you hardly know each other.'

'I know this,' Carina responded. Two small creases lined the top of her nose as she looked for further words to explain. 'I am friend with Marios for five months. I am not in holiday. I am living.'

Dhespina smiled in encouragement, but the truth still needed saying.

'Carina, I worry that it is maybe too soon for you to speak of marriage until you get to know each other a little better. Marios is . . .'

'A retard?' the girl finished for her.

'Well, I was going to say "different",' Dhespina replied, flustered but relieved at not having to voice her son's short-comings herself.

'Mrs Economidou, I am not a little girl. I had boyfriends, some with big brain, some with little brain. See this ear?' Carina pointed to her right lobe. 'This ear not hear. This is what a man with big brain gave me. But Marios. I see Marios is little boy in big man, but he is a good man. He is gentle and sympathetic and he makes me happy in heart and mind . . . like . . .' The girl scrunched her nose in concentration. 'He is like a wall of a castle. He is much kind, much strong, much beautiful, much funny, and I love Marios. We will make a good and happy and safe life together.'

Dhespina threw the girl another soft smile – somewhat reassured but not yet convinced that with the onset of a greater vocabulary she would remain so attached. However, the girl obviously knew her own mind. Since the day Dhespina had understood the nature of her boy, she had agonized about his future. Now, sat before her, was a young woman with a good head on her shoulders, asking to take away that worry.

'Well, if you are certain this is what you both want, we had better prepare for the celebrations,' Dhespina said, and she moved from the table to gather the girl in a deep hug.

Not so far away, sat in front of a small headstone etched with love and dedicated to the memory of Nicos Economidou, Georgios lifted an arm to Marios's shoulders.

'She's a beautiful girl, Marios. But are you ready for marriage?'

Marios turned to look at his father. His eyes were gentle and accepting.

'I know that you all think I'm too stupid for a wife . . .'

'No, son, that's not what I'm saying at all . . .'

'It's fine, Papa. Really, I don't mind. I know I'm not clever. But I have a good job with Christakis, I make my own money, I can take care of myself, and I know I can take care of Carina too. I know, deep down, we will be happy. I want you to know that too.'

Georgios nodded and brushed a small tear away with the back of his hand.

'I'm proud of you, son. And I think you've made a grand choice.' He paused for a moment and raised an eyebrow. 'Carina's not pregnant, is she?'

Marios answered with a grin. 'Not yet, Papa.'

22

'Do you want to see it?'

Before Michalakis could say, 'Well, actually, it's the last thing I'd like to see,' Savvas had picked at the plasters holding the dressing in place. Carefully, he peeled back the bandage. Michalakis whistled in response.

'Because the barrel contacted the skin, the gases released by the fired round caused the star-shaped laceration at the entrance wound. Note also the grey-black discoloration from the soot, as well as the faint abrasion ring.'

Michalakis duly noted the discoloration and abrasion ring. 'Does it hurt?'

'Does the archbishop wear black? Of course it hurts; I've been shot in the leg.'

'Yes, of course. Sorry.'

The AKEL man had been surprised – and then shot – while working late at his office. The can of petrol abandoned by the intruders pointed to a planned arson attack, but they hadn't counted on dealing with a furious Savvas. In the ensuing scuffle, a gun went off and the trade unionist fell bleeding to the floor with the office still intact. Although he lost a pool of blood, the wound looked worse than it was, and though Savvas would never admit it, the confrontation had elevated him to the heroic status of his politically tenacious ancestors. In contrast, Michalakis was appalled at the shooting; it made him uneasy. The attack was symptomatic of a new wave of violence sweeping the island, and the columns of his newspaper were once again filled with reports of bombings, beatings and shootings – only this time it wasn't Greek against Turk, but Greek against Greek.

Michalakis offered his arm as his friend eased himself from the hospital bed to take up the offer of a slow stroll around the grounds. As Savvas passed the matron, he winked in mischief, and the middle-aged woman rolled her eyes. But Michalakis also noticed the self-conscious pat of her hair as they exited the ward.

'Does the hero have an admirer?' Michalakis inquired, and Savvas grinned.

'I'm doing my best to convert her to the cause.'

'I'm sure you are. I only hope her husband isn't another gun-wielding *enosis* cheerleader.'

'Knowing my luck, he's probably a fully-fledged member of the junta with his own tank.'

As the two friends left behind the sterile fumes of Ward Three to walk along the paths skirting the hospital's tidy lawns, a woman approached them with a cheerful smile. Varnavia was Savvas's sister. She was wearing a bright yellow dress with green shoes and a blue ribbon tied into her carelessly curled hair. Michalakis could almost hear Maria's scornful laugh as the young woman neared – and it made him feel oddly protective.

'Brother of mine,' Varnavia greeted Savvas, planting a kiss on his cheek before throwing a brilliant smile towards his friend. 'Michalakis.'

'Varnavia,' he responded. 'Good to see you again.'

'You're rather like some angel of death, aren't you?'

Savvas gasped at his sister's daring, but Michalakis could see she was joking. At least he hoped she was. They had met five months earlier, following an assassination attempt on the president. The archbishop's helicopter had been showered with bullets as it took off from the palace destined for a memorial service. The pilot was critically wounded but, unbelievably, Makarios walked away from the attack unscathed. Police later found a Sten gun and two rifles abandoned on a school rooftop. Varnavia was a teacher at the school and, with Savvas's encouragement, she had furnished the journalist with some wonderfully vivid quotes.

'Still housing assassins?' Michalakis asked her.

'Not any more,' she laughed. 'We're subverting from within.'

The previous month, and despite the public being massively sympathetic to the president following the attempt on his life, the left-wingers had romped home with 30 per cent of the vote in the parliamentary elections, so it was now conceivable that the communists could one day go on to win. Savvas and the bullet hole in his leg were proof of the upset the result had caused among the island's more trigger-happy factions, who feared Cyprus might one day be delivered into the hands of Moscow rather than Greece.

'The mother we aspired to be reunited with has turned into a vicious, amoral bitch,' Savvas declared in typically uncompromising fashion after admitting it was unlikely the Left would consent to union with the unelected fascists governing Greece.

'Democracy not autocracy,' Varnavia cheered, and Michalakis warmed to her enthusiasm.

That night, amid the chintz and crystal of his home furnishings, he asked his wife what she might prefer, democracy or autocracy. Maria looked up from her magazine, with its models sporting knife-blade nails and lacquer-stiff hair, almost surprised to find her husband in the same room as her let alone addressing her. She paused to consider his question before discarding it as a trifle not worth answering. If Michalakis had pursued the subject, he would have discovered that his wife feared her husband was having a laugh at her expense. She might then have discovered that in actual fact he wasn't, he was merely trying to strike up a conversation. However, neither of them could see beyond the other's perceived insults, and Maria returned to her beauty magazine, leaving Michalakis to pick up a newspaper.

Fifteen minutes later, watching his wife get up and leave the room, Michalakis glanced at the trim form of her back-side and waited to feel the usual response. To his horror, there was nothing, and the discovery sent shivers running down his spine. Both of them were so young, they had a lifetime to spend together, but without the basest level of attraction that prospect threatened to turn into an eternity.

Reeling from the chill of his wife's frostiness, and the shock of his own disinterest, Michalakis couldn't imagine surviving the roll call of years to come. As a consequence, he threw himself into his job like a man drowning. The following year, his dedication was rewarded with a press trip to Moscow, where Makarios spent eight days romancing the

Russians and Michalakis spent two of them wooing his translator.

Naturally, the guilt Michalakis felt on his return led him to seek ever more absurd reasons to stay away from his wife, which merely increased his sense of shame. Surprisingly, it was General Grivas who came to his rescue, by escaping from house arrest in Athens, thereby legitimizing Michalakis's working hours with a flurry of front-page bylines. According to the journalist's impeccable sources, the disgraced general had returned to Cyprus in the dead of night disguised as a priest. He had quickly begun to organize a number of armed groups into a new version of EOKA which he named EOKA-B. The aim of the militia was to overthrow the president.

There was blood on the tissue, and its presence brought both relief and great sadness. Praxi's period was only a few days late, but it had been time enough to produce sudden panic attacks and lazy oneiric musings. The palpitations came from the certainty that another unplanned baby would ruin them all. The daydreams were led by her heart, which silently ached for a second child.

Deep in the emptiness of her stomach, Praxi mourned for a baby that didn't exist. She longed to bear Loukis a family as big as his own, but the dream was impractical and she knew she should be grateful for the happiness fate had mercifully given her. Yet, as the toilet flushed noisily behind her, she felt completely and utterly wretched. In an attempt to shake off her malaise, she went to check on the blessing she already possessed.

Elpida was in her bedroom, gazing listlessly out of the

window. Her face was pale and her eyes glassy. It had been a week since Jason had left the island to finish his unconventional education at an examination-board-friendly public school in Edinburgh, and the heart he had left behind was distraught. Other parents might have dismissed the girl's tears as the passing dramatics of a childish crush, but Praxi had been little more than a year older than her daughter when she had first made love to Loukis. She understood Elpida's pain, and she could taste her devotion.

'He'll be back in the holidays,' Praxi comforted, coming to stroke her daughter's thick black hair.

'Unless he finds someone else,' Elpida stated, and the tears rolled down her cheeks, as they had done for much of the week.

'Jason won't find anyone else, Elpida *mou*. The boy adores you.'

'Do you really think so?'

'I know so. In fact, I'd bet your grandmother's telly on it.'

Elpida managed a small smile. Over the past year, they had been driven half mad by a volume button that raised a notch with every new outrage committed against Elena's beloved archbishop. And as the attacks on the island occurred with greater frequency, the black and white pictures became a constant presence in their home, with commentators blaring warnings and accusations throughout the house and halfway into the village. Some of their neighbours, who had yet to acquire such technology, had even taken to walking up and down the street, in apparent exercise, solely to keep up with the events screaming from Elena's open windows.

'Do you think you might manage a little something to eat tonight?' Praxi asked her daughter.

'What are we having?'

'*Kleftiko*.'

'Could you leave it in the oven? I'll come and take it later.'

'OK, but mind that you come before it dries out.'

Elpida nodded, and Praxi left her to her sadness.

When the evening turned into night, Praxi took some food to her daughter's room. The child was already curled in her bed and so she gently placed the plate on the floor in case she should wake hungry in the night. Gathering her coat, she left to join Loukis.

Turning the door handle to his home, she found him already in bed, and she quietly undressed to creep in beside him. At her touch, Loukis stirred and turned to hold her. On the windowsill a single candle burned next to a bowl of pretty white moonstones.

'Elpida's still very upset,' Praxi whispered.

'Over the boy?'

'Yes.'

Loukis sighed and raised himself up. Scratching at his eyes, he dragged a tired hand down his face before reaching for a cigarette. 'She'll get over it.'

'Perhaps not,' Praxi differed. 'I think she's truly in love with Jason.'

'Oh good grief,' Loukis laughed. 'They're little more than children.'

'Children they may be, but we weren't much older when . . .'

'You don't think they're . . .'

'No! No!' Praxi hurriedly replied. 'God, I'd kill her! I'm just saying that the feelings we have for each other remain as strong today as they were when we were their age, that's all.'

'True,' Loukis acknowledged. 'I suppose that means I'll have to keep an eye on the boy when he comes back next summer.'

'Make that the two of us,' Praxi replied. 'I swear, we're going to be more exhausted than ever.'

'Don't remind me,' Loukis grunted. 'What I'd give for a proper night's rest with you instead of always hiding in the dark.'

At his words, Praxi hugged Loukis with all the strength she could muster. She cherished the few hours the moon gifted them but, like him, she ached to have the morning sun wake her rather than having to flee with the first cock crow of dawn. The world was turning so fast and robbing them of time. Around her thickening waist, Praxi felt the weight of passing years gather and she saw it in the broadness of Loukis's shoulders and the square of his chin. They were no longer young but inching towards middle age. In a matter of weeks, Praxi would turn thirty, and their daughter was well on the road to becoming a young woman.

'I hate getting old,' Praxi grumbled, and she felt Loukis's chest jerk in a half laugh.

'You're not old.'

'But I feel old.'

'Well, you don't look it.'

Praxi playfully dug her elbow into his stomach in reply, and Loukis kissed the top of her head. For him, the passing years only made Praxi more beautiful. He loved the creeping softness that plumped her thighs and gently curved her stomach; he loved the lines that the harsh daylight now showed along her eyes, faint grooves that had been crafted by her smile; and he loved every exhausting effort she made to run to his bed when she could have easily slept elsewhere.

'It doesn't bother me growing old,' Loukis confessed. 'What does concern me is the future.'

Praxi tilted her head to better concentrate on his words. It was rare for Loukis to voice his worries, and she wanted him to know that she was listening.

'Our daughter is growing up,' he continued. 'She's in love with a boy who seems to share the same feelings for her, and one day they might marry. Even if their affection doesn't last, and I hope for her sake it does, we both know that Elpida will end up marrying someone at some point in her future, and when that day comes I know it's going to kill me. I'll watch her walk into church, in her spectacular dress, with her beautiful smile, and I'll have to stand by while another man takes my rightful place as father of the bride.'

'Oh God, I hadn't even begun to think that far ahead,' Praxi admitted.

'Well, when I lie here waiting for you, I do, and a lot more besides.'

'Oh Loukis . . .' Praxi buried her face deep into his neck, embarrassed by her own selfishness. While she had been searching for more hours in the day, he had been praying for the time to rush by, and while she flitted between Keryneia and the village, between her mother's house and his bed, Loukis filled his days working and waiting. With no other option, he had fitted himself into her life when he should have been living his own, and Praxi felt ashamed of having been the one to force him into the dead end he now inhabited. If she truly loved him, she should have let him go. Wasn't that the way love was meant to be – the one power strong enough to overshadow the self? But she couldn't even think of loving anyone more, and to hand him to another – to give up his touch and let him walk away – well, it was beyond contemplation. She would never leave Loukis. Never. And with nothing to be said that could take away his concerns, Praxi closed her eyes and attempted to sleep.

The next morning, after a night of sad dreams, Praxi rose late and ran home fast, praying her daughter had not emerged from her own bed. On the way she was forced to duck behind a hedge as Niki raced into view, followed by her father, who was pacing his daughter in the family motor car. Two months ago, the girl had been selected to train with the national squad, and there was even talk of her taking part in a future Olympics. Realizing his daughter was even more gifted than anyone had thought, Andreas had started taking her running more seriously, which meant saving for a private trainer and rising before the sun was up to show his support. As girl and machine flew past her, Praxi was, not for the first time, staggered by the speed of the child.

Belatedly arriving home, Praxi saw her mother angrily grabbing at leaflets caught in the hedge. 'Is Elpida awake?'

'No,' Elena assured her with a scowl. 'Have you seen these?' A handful of papers were thrust into Praxi's face. She took them in her hands to get a proper look. The printing was primitive, but the message was clear. Above the signature 'EOKA-B', the text was a call to arms. The leaflets urged all former heroes of the British resistance to join once more the battle for *enosis*.

'EOKA-B!' Elena spat. 'Whatever next? I've a good mind to grab a gun and start calling myself EOKA-C!'

Praxi couldn't help laughing at her mother's fiery words – but they were nothing compared to the catalogue of obscenities Elena unleashed four months later when three pro-*enosis* bishops stepped forward to demand the archbishop's resignation.

At a session of the Holy Synod, the bishops of Kition, Keryneia and Pafos tabled a motion proposing that their brother Makarios give up the presidency, as the holding of secular office was actually against the canons of the Church. Some seventeen days later, Makarios accused the bishops of having conspired among themselves and with others outside of the Church. He added that should he be obliged to step down, it could only lead to national disaster.

Elena was, as ever, unwavering in her support of the archbishop. Shaking an angry fist at the TV screen, she railed, 'First they try and shoot him out of office and now the bloody bastards are trying to stage an ecclesiastical coup!'

Outside the window, the faint applause of curious neighbours echoed her cry.

23

The office was a symphony of tapping fingers, ringing telephones, barked orders and ripping paper. The pasty-faced reporters were living on coffee, cigarettes and adrenalin, and Michalakis hadn't been this enthused about his work since the milestone of independence. Cyprus was in the grip of presidential election fever.

Under fire from every quarter, Makarios had called the faithful to the ballot box to shore up his position, and front-page stories were leaking from every orifice of the palace. With the tacit endorsement of the government, the media was finally baring its teeth and turning on Athens. Headlines railed against the junta's authority, and commentators clamoured for the expulsion of its officers. *The Voice* upped the stakes with editorials calling on the ousted Greek premier to set up a government in exile. It was a risky strategy, which made a target of every member of the reporting team, but there was not a murmur of dissent. For Michalakis and his colleagues, the shackles were off.

'Desperate bastards.'

The editor slammed the press release on Michalakis's

desk. It was another demand by the *enosis* lobby to swap the presidential vote for a plebiscite on union with Greece.

'A bit late in the day, isn't it?' Michalakis observed. The election would take place in less than twenty-four hours and, short of the junta rolling its tanks into the capital, the vote would almost certainly go ahead. At the desk next to him, the crime reporter Tassos banged down his phone. The floor gave him the attention he sought.

'More raids!' he bellowed.

'Where?' the editor demanded.

'Two in Pafos, one in Lemesos and three around Larnaka.'

His boss whistled through the gap in his teeth. 'OK, get writing. Michalakis get confirmation and a comment from the palace. Production – redraw the front page!'

At the editor's command, the office whirred into action. Over a crackling telephone line, Michalakis quickly verified the crime reporter's latest tally of eighteen raids. The targets had been police stations, and an estimated 150 gunmen were involved, some wielding dynamite. Michalakis relayed the appropriate comment of condemnation from the palace, and Tassos slipped it into the third paragraph, above the catalogue of spoils taken by the attackers. The insurgents had come away with uniforms, arms and ammunition – all destined to be used on their own people.

The following day, *The Voice* hit the streets screaming the headline 'Gunmen Target Democracy' – and Makarios marched unopposed to a third election victory.

Georgios glanced at Mehmet, who was deep in concentration. Around them, tables hummed with mundane conversations and playful teasing, and the late afternoon was

355

just like it used to be, except he now drank his coffee *sade* instead of *sketto*.

With the horrors of the sixties fading into sad memory, half of the village's Turks had returned to reclaim their lives. To the shame of a few, a handful had left again after seeing their pilfered homes, but the majority remained, stoical if not always forgiving. And with just enough customers for a viable business, the Turks' coffee shop, which had been abandoned in the exodus, quietly reopened.

When Georgios had first invited Mehmet to join him for a drink, the old man had reluctantly agreed, unsure where the boundaries of betrayal might lie between past insults and present-day reconciliation. Therefore, with his mind set elsewhere, his surprise had been evident when Georgios walked not through the door of the Greek coffee house but across the road to his own. The reaction on both sides of the tarmac divide was one of quiet disapproval, followed by disinterest – by and large, the villagers were tired of petty grievances. Rising to the occasion, the café owner had joined them at a table, bringing a small cup with him.

'To drink one cup of coffee together guarantees forty years of friendship,' he stated. Georgios had relaxed at the sentiment. Mehmet rolled his eyes.

Today, more than four years later, Georgios mused that he had drunk so much coffee in the company of his new friends he'd need to follow them into the next life to fulfil their prophesy. He hated to admit it, but they were getting old. His joints ached in the mornings, his breath was worryingly short and his hairline was on the retreat. Meanwhile, Mehmet was steadily galloping towards his sunset.

Having initially been his father's friend, Mehmet had

always seemed old to Georgios, but with his shrunken frame and gently trembling fingers, he had in recent times become elderly. Mehmet was probably the oldest man Georgios had ever met, easily having passed into his nineties, and the farmer revelled in the miracle of his longevity, joking that he would gift his body to science if it weren't against the rules of his religion. Remarkably, and in spite of his advancing years, he retained the wit and intellect of the man Georgios had always known, which was at times rather annoying, especially when they were engaged in a game of chess. With a nod, Mehmet moved his queen to face Georgios's last remaining bishop.

'Checkmate.' After examining the board, Georgios knocked his king to the deck in defeat.

'Mehmet got you there, Papa.' Marios grinned. Georgios resisted the urge to reprimand his son for stating the obvious.

'Now tell me,' Mehmet wheezed, returning to the conversation victorious, 'how's married life suiting you?'

Marios shrugged. 'It's different.'

'It's certainly that,' the old man laughed. 'Does she cook?'

'Yes.'

'Does she wash your clothes?'

'Yes.'

'Does she keep your bed warm?'

Marios chuckled in response before confirming that Carina did indeed keep his bed warm.

'Then you've picked the right woman,' Mehmet concluded.

'Yes. I guess I have,' Marios agreed. And it was true: Carina did cook, she did wash and she was very warm, but she also had a lot more about her – and most of it involved planning. After only a few months of marriage, Marios was exhausted. No sooner had he finished at the workshop than Carina had him looking at tables of numbers. More often than not, she held a book in her hands that paraded fresh orders and, though he was a slow and precise worker, he had been forced to somehow find the speed to match his wife's ideas.

Carina was a bubbling pot of baffling proposals. Right now, she was back at the house bending Christakis's ears with designs for a leaflet. Unlike himself, Christakis was equally as passionate when it came to Carina's big talk. But Marios yearned for peace and the nocturnal warmth Mehmet spoke of. Unfortunately, even with the lights out, Carina's mouth remained in constant motion, and she was forever working on ways to enable them to move out of his parents' house. Marios felt none of his wife's urgency because he was happy where he was, but Carina needed her space and, after visiting her parents' home, he understood why; the place was bigger than a palace, with a large motor car on the drive and a horse in a paddock. Next year they would spend the summer in Germany, and he was looking forward to losing himself in the space of his in-laws more than he could say. Beside him, Christakis pulled up a chair.

'You managed to escape from my wife, then?' Marios asked.

'Just about!' he laughed. 'I tell you what, Carina has some big ideas!'

'Tell me about it.'

Georgios ruffled Marios's hair and ordered a coffee for his oldest son. Having his boys with him, on the wrong side of the road, made him ridiculously proud. He had raised his sons well.

'Have you heard the news?' Christakis asked. 'It's bedlam out there.'

Mehmet moved his head to take a look.

'Not there.' Christakis half grinned. He waved his arm in a large circle. 'Out there. It said on the radio that there were thirty-two explosions in Pafos, Lemesos and Larnaka today.'

'Good God!' Georgios exclaimed.

'Grivas?' Mehmet inquired. Christakis nodded.

'Little surprise there, then,' the old man muttered.

Following the election, the disgraced general had warned Makarios that he would experience the same terror as the British if he betrayed *enosis*. But Grivas clearly didn't possess the patience to wait for betrayal, and he was now employing the guerrilla tactics that made his name eighteen years ago, with armed raids on police stations and bomb attacks on politicians. Incensed, Makarios set up a new auxiliary force, the Tactical Police Reserve, to thwart him.

'You know, we'd have more sympathy for your archbishop if he actually wrote off *enosis* as a legitimate goal,' Mehmet grumbled.

'Impossible,' Christakis whispered, keeping his voice low so as not to offend the other customers. 'The Greek Cypriots have a problem with the junta, not with Greece herself. She is still our mother.'

'So you keep saying,' Mehmet replied. 'But sometimes a child needs to walk its own path.'

Elpida read the letter again, but the news didn't get any better as the words flew from their pages to crash in her brain. Jason was staying with his mother for the summer. It wasn't his decision, he was at pains to point out, but rather at his father's insistence. Jack was concerned at the growing violence in Cyprus and he couldn't, in all good conscience, allow his son to be placed in such danger. Therefore, there would be no visit that year and none in the near future if the situation failed to improve.

In his angry scrawl, Elpida could see Jason's frustration as he railed against his father, employing typically inappropriate adjectives in his four-page diatribe. She felt his despair, and she thought she would burst every time her eyes fell on the few passages devoted to their love. In Keryneia Jason had been tough and teasing, but with distance his heart had grown sweet and she pined to hear the words that he wrote fall from his lips. In desperation she turned to her mother.

'Let me get this right,' Praxi replied. 'You want me to allow you to go abroad, on your own, to stay with a seventeen-year-old boy and a bunch of dope-smoking hippies? You must have finally lost your mind.'

'Papa said he'd think about it.'

'He's humouring you, Elpida.'

'But . . .'

'Not another word. You're not going, so get used to it.'

Elpida frowned. She got up from her seat and made herself useful, washing the potatoes and peeling the carrots. When she felt she had given it enough time, she tried again.

'You could come with me.'

'I have a business to run,' Praxi replied, already waiting and more than prepared for the second wave of reasoned appeal, before her daughter turned to dramatics and emotional blackmail.

'Then *yiayia* can come,' Elpida declared.

'You're not dragging me into that den of sin,' the old woman shrieked.

'Oh come on, *yiayia*, it's not that bad . . .'

Elena raised a sceptical eyebrow. 'Bad is bad, child. And besides, I'm needed here.'

'For what? All you do is watch television!'

'Elpida!' Praxi reprimanded.

'Well . . .' the girl grumbled. 'It's true.'

'I'm watching the back of our archbishop, that's what I'm doing,' Elena defended.

'But he's won now!' Elpida protested.

'The devil never gives up, and neither will I.'

As Elena turned her attention back to the TV screen, Elpida fell to the floor with pounding fists, announcing that if no one stepped in to help her she would surely die. Praxi smiled. Elena turned the volume a touch louder.

With her spiritual leader in mortal and political danger, Elena had rigorously performed her prayers at church, done her civic duty at the ballot box and glued pictures of the great man in the windows of her home. Makarios had been up against not only Turkey, Turkish Cypriots, Greece, Grivas, the pro-*enosis* lobby, elements of the National Guard, his own police force and two out of three private militias, but also members of his own church. Thankfully, the archbishop was wily. When his fellow brothers demanded his resignation he called a Supreme Synod, which easily outclassed a holy one. The rebel bishops were accused of causing a schism in the Church and promptly defrocked.

'In the good old days, they'd have been stoned as well,' Elena declared.

'Like the hippies?' Praxi asked. Elena didn't dignify the joke with a response. The future of the archbishop was no laughing matter.

Unable to get a rise out of her mother, and assured that everyone in the house was suitably distracted, Praxi announced she was going out for some air. As she reached the door, Elpida looked sadly up from her letter. 'I'd come with you, Mamma, but it's hard to walk when your heart is broken.'

Praxi rolled her eyes. Her daughter really did remind her of herself sometimes. Free from the theatrics of her family, she drifted away from the village and headed for Loukis's house. When she arrived, he was poring over an article in his brother's newspaper.

'Well, they got him,' he stated matter-of-factly.

'Who?'

'Antoniou Charalambous.'

'Your friend with one leg?' she asked, and Loukis nodded.

'Well, you said it might only be a matter of time,' Praxi stated, belatedly aware of how unsympathetic she sounded. 'By the way, Elpida wants to visit Jason in Crete.'

'And you said?'

'No, of course.'

Loukis smiled as he pictured his daughter's brow creasing in frustration at what must appear an impossibly unfair response to her request. 'Under normal circumstances, I'd agree with you, but this place is going to hell. Maybe she'd be better off abroad.'

'Oh come on, Loukis, it's not that bad,' Praxi retorted.

'We've been through worse. And besides, two weeks is hardly going to be time enough to turn the island around for our daughter's safety.'

'True,' Loukis acknowledged. He folded the paper away. The way the troubles were escalating, the violence would be unlikely to pass any time soon.

Although Loukis could never condone the path Antoniou had taken, he understood it to a certain degree, and he felt desperately sorry for him. Antoniou wasn't a bad man. He was governed by grief and an unshakeable belief in a cause that had cost him a leg. However, the under-pressure president had acted decisively. When EOKA-B fighters stepped up their game, the Tactical Police Reserve was dispatched on search-and-destroy missions. One of their raids netted Grivas's deputy, along with twenty other senior figures. Antoniou was among them.

According to the newspaper, the men had been charged with conspiracy to overthrow the government. There was a quote from the Pro-Enosis Party refuting the claims, but Loukis accepted the truth of the indictment. It wasn't so long ago that Antoniou had appeared on his own doorstep to whip up loyalty for the fledgling rebel movement, and with the raids uncovering another plot to assassinate the president, Loukis felt mildly dirtied by his friend's visit.

Michalakis was at the doctor's surgery with Maria, trying to work out why she was failing to fall pregnant, when a stunned receptionist revealed the latest attempt to kill the president. Michalakis asked to use the woman's telephone to call his office. The news-desk secretary answered. He could hear the pandemonium in the background. There had been four mines, she said, and they had detonated on a road just minutes before Makarios was scheduled to pass in his car, on the way to conduct a service near Ammochostos.

'The big man's got more lives than a cat,' Michalakis responded and, with apologies to his wife, he left for the office. Once he had gone, Maria calmly rose from her seat and told the receptionist the appointment would no longer be necessary.

Back home, she put a coffee pot on the stove and cried bitter tears for the chance she had lost. God knew it had taken superhuman strength to hang on to her virginity until her wedding night, and He also knew how hurt she had been when the proof of her honour brought delighted surprise to her husband's face. And though she had tried hard to forget that sting of humiliation, the wound had festered, until she could no longer think of making love without conjuring up the face of another. Now it was abundantly clear in the harsh light of the kitchen, with its empty table and sterile work surfaces, that their inability to conceive was due to one fundamental flaw – Maria's husband was not the man his brother was.

Later that evening, when the newspaper had been put to bed, Michalakis returned home to find his wife asleep. There were dark spots of dried blood on the sheet and scratches along her arms. Michalakis didn't know what to think, never mind what to say. Silently, he crept into bed beside her. He could tell from her breathing that she wasn't asleep, but he hadn't the courage to challenge her or even put his arm round her. The next morning, Michalakis awoke to find Maria already up and making breakfast. Her arms were covered by long sleeves, and he pretended not to notice. As casually as he was able to, he asked how the appointment had gone, and his wife assured him they had nothing to worry about.

'Some couples take longer than others,' she explained, 'especially when sex is so unpredictable.'

Michalakis ignored the dig. 'Lenya and Andreas took a while, and they've now got a future Olympic champion on their hands.'

'Maybe I should take one of your mother's potions and slip on a pair of big knickers, then.'

'What, bigger than the ones you wear already?'

Maria placed her fruit salad on the table and took a fork to it in silence. Michalakis sighed. He had meant the question as a joke, but he was barely able to raise a smile on his wife's face these days. Maria was tetchy and miserable, and Michalakis was unaccustomed to the level of attention one person could require. After their wedding, he had thought it would be impossible to be any happier – and he was right. Once they moved into their small house on the outskirts of the capital heading towards Larnaka, Maria gave up her job to concentrate on creating a home. Her taste was delicate and expensive, and there had been quarrels as Michalakis's wage failed to keep up with his wife's demands. When the house had finally been beautified to his wife's precise requirements, she turned her attention to the ladies' coffee mornings, which consequently led to personal inquiries about her slim figure and motherless status. Maria seized on the women's concerns as the reason for her marital problems and set about rectifying the situation with the same concentration she gave to all her projects. As a result, their love-making had evolved into an act of procreation devoid of all sensuality. Michalakis had come to realize beyond any doubt that he had made the most enormous mistake in getting married – at least to Maria. He had succumbed to the falsities of infatuation. Behind the obvious beauty of their union, there lay a bare canvas: they simply had nothing in common.

Some time after coming to this sad conclusion, Michalakis had been losing himself in cold coffee and cigarettes at Zach's Café, close to the office, when he saw his newspaper slapped on the table in front of him. Expecting a disgruntled parliamentarian, he looked up and into the soft brown eyes of Savvas's sister.

'Nice to see you read a quality newspaper,' he remarked coolly, even as a long-forgotten knot formed in his stomach.

'I use it to line the vegetable rack,' Varnavia replied, coming to sit with him, despite no invitation having been extended. 'If nothing else, *The Voice* is printed on good-quality paper.'

Michalakis raised an eyebrow, hoping it looked something close to debonair. He wasn't prickly about his newspaper; he knew it had grown into a trusted journal offering a largely impartial view of the world's complexities. Still, he felt a small thrill that Varnavia felt it necessary to try and needle him. And because he felt energized by the woman's company, he invited her to join him for coffee the following week. After a couple more impromptu meetings, their chats at Zach's became a weekly occurrence that allowed for ferocious political sparring and a pinch of careful flirtation. They both knew what drew them, but neither of them possessed the nerve to voice their longing or the discipline to break the spell. And so it was that, when the

Greek junta leader was thrown out of power by the head of the Greek Military Police, Michalakis was sat with Varnavia.

Together they listened with wide eyes as the café radio reported that Brigadier Ioannides had installed Phaedon Gizikis as the new President of Greece.

'Installed is the right word,' muttered Michalakis.

'Is this the same police chief who approached Makarios with a plan to eliminate our Turkish community?' Varnavia asked.

'I think so,' Michalakis replied, vaguely remembering an incident involving Brigadier Ioannides and the local militia leader Nicos Sampson in 1964. 'If memory serves, Makarios showed the Greek the door.'

'That bodes well then,' Varnavia said with a whistle.

24

On 27 January 1974, Georgios Grivas died. To some he embodied the dreams of an estranged nation. To others he was a fallen hero; a divisive leader embittered by a thwarted destiny who died not in battle, but of heart failure while hiding in Lemesos.

Two days after his death, Grivas's funeral was held in the garden of the house that had been his last hideout during the campaign against the British. Tens of thousands turned out to pay their respects and, bowing to public sentiment, the government declared three days of mourning. Makarios did not attend his former ally's funeral, but Michalakis did, and he watched in disbelief as Nicos Sampson stepped forward to hijack the event.

The brutally ambitious leader of his own private army, Sampson wrapped himself in the Greek flag and banged his apparent rage and grief upon Grivas's closed coffin. He called on the mourners to continue the fight for *enosis* and to avenge the death of their leader, seemingly oblivious to the fact that natural causes were to blame for the diminutive general's passing. Back in his office, Michalakis filed his report with the metallic taste of rage heavy on his tongue.

Grivas's death could have signalled the end of an era – a heroic time, grown shabby with disappointment. Instead, he felt it a portent of worse to come.

Dhespina instinctively ducked under the onslaught of two nesting swallows that clapped their wings above her head as they divebombed her into retreat. Their angry attentions were irritating but understandable, and so the saplings would have to wait for their pruning. Inside the house, far from finding peace, she found the place insufferably quiet. It seemed only a heartbeat ago that she had five noisy sons shouting their youth from the kitchen to the living room, along the stairs to the bedrooms. Now her children were memories. Christakis was middle-aged and battling the chaos created by his own boisterous boys; Michalakis was lost to his work; Nicos, God rest his soul, was lying in the cemetery; Marios had flown to Germany to spend the summer with his wife's parents; and Loukis was, as usual, immersed in his own private world. As Dhespina waited in uncomfortable silence for Georgios to return she was almost tempted to send for old Televantos, but the pensioner had recently become bed-bound and she doubted his daughter, who had temporarily left her own children in Pissouri to nurse him through his dying days, would consider Dhespina's loneliness reason enough to uproot her father. How Loukis lived such a solitary life was beyond Dhespina's comprehension. Although she understood his ways more than most, there remained aspects of his character that left her puzzled and sad for him. Behind her, the door opened. To her great relief, her husband strolled through it with a smile on his face.

'How was it?' she asked.

'Bloody terrible,' he informed her. 'I could hardly believe my eyes. Painted along the church wall – the *church wall,* Dhespina – was some crap castigating Makarios. I'm no God-fearing Bible-basher, but I tell you, if I find the little bastards responsible I'll wring their bloody necks.'

Although Dhespina was as shocked as her husband at the act of vandalism, this paled into insignificance compared to her worry about her husband's health.

'What did the doctor say, Georgios?'

Her husband kicked away his best shoes, pulled off his socks and rolled them into a ball.

'Not much,' he admitted.

'Georgios!' Dhespina warned. Her husband gave her a gentle smile. He walked over in his bare feet, took hold of her hands and held them close to his chest as if they were about to take up a slow dance.

'My sweet beautiful Dhespo, everything is going to be all right.'

'Oh, thank God,' she muttered.

'At least the doctor hopes so, he hasn't got a clue,' he continued, laughing. 'He's passing the buck to Lefkosia, and I've an appointment with a heart specialist in July.'

At his words, Dhespina burst into tears.

Mehmet watched Loukis load the oranges on to the tractor. Not so long ago, his arms would have possessed the strength to help him. Had she been alive, Pembe would have arrived with chilled melon juice to sate their thirst and protect their kidneys, and the tractor would have been a donkey called Aphrodite. Sad to say, the years had flown by quickly and, looking around him, Mehmet could hardly believe he had so little to show for them. It appeared the longer you lived, the more death took from you.

Across the field, he spied Praxi coming their way. Her long hair was released from its elastic band and the wind played with the ends of her tresses. Loukis lifted his head, as if scenting her arrival, and Mehmet shook his head. So some things didn't change after all. He was glad of at least that small mercy.

Although not everyone in the village would be so accepting of the pair's friendship, Mehmet couldn't imagine things being any other way, and he struggled to think of either of them as individuals; they were Loukis and Praxi, two names, one being. All their lives he had watched the two of them chase each other's shadow in the sun, had seen them fight like rabid dogs and care for each other with an almost religious devotion. And despite their journey into adulthood, they remained but children to Mehmet, hopelessly – and some might say foolishly – in love with each other with the same degree of certainty that had fired them in their youth. Although Praxi had married another, Mehmet was not as blind as he was old, and he knew the girl came to Loukis's bed in the dead of night. And Loukis, who had grown strong and handsome and who was therefore a prize of masculinity for any young woman on the prowl, had never sought a life away from her. Their relationship was conducted in the shadow of sin, and yet Mehmet had rarely observed a love that made greater sense. And though he didn't say anything, when he looked at Praxi's daughter, he had his suspicions that all was not quite as had been said.

'Off you go then, lad,' Mehmet ordered. Loukis placed

the last load of oranges upon the tractor and promised to return within the hour. As he reached Praxi, he checked for prying eyes, kissed her lightly on her lips and asked why she wasn't at the bar.

'The car's broken,' Praxi replied. 'Yiannis has given me the day off.'

'That's good of him. What's wrong with the car?'

'Do I look like a mechanic?'

Loukis stopped to scrutinize the woman before him. She wore a light-blue dress that hinted at the contours of her curves. Her hair was long and thick, her lashes dark and pretty. The only mechanic Loukis knew was Theoris Moustakas, and he had to agree that Praxi looked nothing like him.

'So where do you want to go?' he asked.

'I'm feeling dry as a bone.'

'The sea?'

'A delightful idea.'

'Did you bring your swimwear?'

'No, I didn't,' Praxi confessed with a wink, and she ran to the shore with Loukis chasing behind her. As they reached the shingle, they tore away their clothes, giggling like children.

Meanwhile, a few miles away in the Jewel of Keryneia, Yiannis was slowly recovering from a dressing-down of his own. Behind him, a Greek flag graced the back wall of the bar, and the two men who had been so insistent that it be raised were drinking cool beers – on the house – under an umbrella outside.

Typically gutless without the backing of other men, or even of his wife, Yiannis had acquiesced to the ordered request despite having long ago lost his fervour for the motherland. Although no direct threats were made, and there was no sinister bulge of metal hidden under clothing, the intimation of trouble to come was achingly clear when the men had approached him to suggest he might want to fly the blue and white banner of Greece.

'Times are changing,' the larger of the men told him. 'And you ought to be on the right side, don't you think?'

The newsreader spoke in a calm and measured voice, and Elena could only marvel at his self-control as he read out the letter written by the archbishop to the President of Greece. In all her days, she never thought she would live to see such a thing.

'. . . *It is with the deepest regret that I am obliged to report to you certain intolerable developments in Cyprus for which I must hold responsible the Greek government . . .*'

'Do we have to listen to this?' Elpida moaned.
'Yes we do,' Elena informed her granddaughter.

'. . . *Ever since the clandestine arrival of General Grivas in September 1971, there have been rumours supported by tangible evidence that he came at the instigation and encouragement of certain circles in Athens, and he formed the criminal organization EOKA-B, which has been a constant source of grievous troubles for the island. The National Guard, staffed and controlled by Greek officers, has been from the very outset the main supplier in men and materials for EOKA-B. You appreciate, Mr President, the bitter thoughts that have been constantly tormenting me since the realization that members of the Athens government are persistently conspiring against me and, what is even worse, are dividing the Greek Cypriots and driving them to destruction through fraternal bloodshed. More than once have I felt, and in some instances almost touched, an invisible hand stretching all the way from Athens seeking to extinguish my earthly existence . . .'*

'I need a cold drink,' Elpida moaned.

'You know where the fridge is,' Elena retorted.

'Do you want anything?'

'Child, please!' Elena begged. 'You have no comprehension of the enormity of what we're hearing!'

Elpida sighed but remained seated. Satisfied, Elena turned her attention back to the screen, unwilling to miss a word of the president's cannonball missive to the motherland.

'. . . I regret, Mr President, that I find it necessary to say many unpleasant things in order to describe in these lines and in a language of raw sincerity the lamentable situation which has existed for a long time. This, however, is dictated by national interest . . . I do not wish to interrupt my co-operation with the Greek government. It must, however, be kept in mind that I am not an appointed commissioner of the Greek government in Cyprus, but an elected leader of a large section of Hellenism, and I demand analogous behaviour towards me from the National Centre. The contents of this letter are not secret.'

Thirteen days later, the Greek colonels responded with gunfire.

*

374

Maria shook Michalakis awake and, with a detached sense of the inevitable, flatly revealed their latest failure. Inwardly Michalakis groaned at the prospect of yet another month of loveless exertions.

'And unlike me,' Maria informed him, 'you are late.'

Michalakis grabbed the bedside clock and then released it with a forceful expletive. He ran to the bathroom, but found it occupied by his father, who had arrived the previous evening in readiness for his appointment at the capital's best cardiology department.

'Two minutes!' Georgios cried, and Michalakis didn't have the heart to hurry him, given his possible medical condition. He headed to the kitchen in search of coffee. To his surprise, and immense gratitude, his mamma had been busy paying for her keep and, instead of cooling toast thrown unceremoniously on a plate in front of the marmalade, the table wafted with grilled halloumi and warm bacon. Maria came po-faced to the table, where she picked at a fruit salad.

'All yours,' Georgios told his son as he joined them for breakfast, and Michalakis took a mouthful of bacon to chew on during his own ablutions. When he emerged seven minutes later in a clean shirt and with only the smallest of nicks drying under a tear of tissue on his chin, he moved to kiss his wife and then his mother.

'I'll see you at two,' he told them.

'Don't be late,' his mamma begged, and Michalakis assured her that the job at the palace would take only an hour and he'd be back in plenty of time to drive them to the hospital.

'Don't worry,' he ordered.

'I'm not worried,' Dhespina lied, before a solitary tear gave her away. Georgios raised an eyebrow to his son and moved his hand to cover his wife's. Maria busied herself with clearing the table.

Arriving at the palace, Michalakis was hurriedly ushered down a series of bare corridors into a reception room that shone bright with the morning sun, and a group of excited children. The archbishop was already seated, having arrived punctually at his desk at 7.45 a.m., and he playfully nodded towards the clock on the wall. Michalakis gave a sheepish smile of apology and reached for his notebook. It was 8.20.

He unfolded the press release hiding in his shirt pocket. The children were from a school in Cairo, and they had come to the island at the personal invitation of the archbishop. They were his first visitors of the day, and they had dressed for the occasion in smart uniforms and clean faces, which were polished off with impeccable manners. Michalakis, late and belatedly tearing the dried tissue from his chin, felt horribly grubby in their presence. Although the assignment was clearly not of the greatest importance, it was a small gift from the president to thank *The Voice* for its continued support amid the rising tensions on the island, and further afield in Athens – events which, Michalakis noted, had taken their toll on Makarios's beard, which was a greater shade of grey than the dense black it used to be. He settled himself into a seat at the side of the gathering. In front of him a young boy fought back tears, sweetly overwhelmed by the occasion, and a woman, he presumed a teacher, leaned over to comfort him. With a self-conscious cough, the leader of the group rose from his seat to address the archbishop. Michalakis scrawled a reminder on his pad to get the man's name once the formalities were over.

With a slight tremor wobbling his voice, the man started by offering his sincere thanks for the invitation, which meant so much to the youngsters, to the school and to the children's parents. Makarios nodded in encouragement. As he did so, the first sounds of gunfire echoed in the distance. The speaker lowered his papers and the children twisted nervously in their seats, whispering to each other and reaching to tap the elbows of their chaperones with questions. In front of them, Makarios remained still. Only his eyes moved, following a member of his staff who was disappearing through the door.

'Please, continue,' he calmly told the children's representative.

The man held aloft his papers, his fingers noticeably shaking, and restarted his speech, but the echo of gunfire continued, growing ever louder and more frequent until he was soon shouting to be heard above the noise. When the first rocket exploded, the man abandoned his script altogether and screamed at the children to get down. The terrified youngsters immediately fell to the floor in panic. As they cowered under chairs, a presidential guard burst through the door to reveal that there were tanks at the gates of the palace. Michalakis ran to the window. The courtyards were empty. Turning back to the room, he saw members of staff imploring the president to run, but Makarios appeared stupefied, almost dazed by the reality of what was taking place. The Greek colonels were executing a coup.

Outside, more rockets shook the air, and Michalakis returned to the window, where he began to see the strength of the threat almost upon them. V-shaped holes had been blasted through walls, and a number of tanks were bull-dozing their way towards them, crunching over rubble and churning their way on noisy tracks into the heart of the palace grounds in search of Makarios. With no other choice, and amid the increasingly desperate entreaties of his staff, the archbishop walked quickly towards the west doors, issuing calming words to the children as he went. Three guards accompanied him, one leading the way, the other two covering the president's back. All of them had their guns drawn, and their faces were tense but controlled.

Michalakis was by now on the floor along with the rest of the archbishop's petrified guests. Easing his head above the windowsill, he counted several tanks and as many armoured cars, and they were closing in. Black smoke billowed from burning buildings, and the rapid return of gunfire ricocheted around the courtyard as the presidential guard did their utmost to resist. The blood pounded in Michalakis's veins, and though he was scared beyond any fear he had ever known, he was still conscious of his responsibilities: this might be the last time he saw his president alive. At the other end of the room, a bullet smashed through one of the tall windows, and the room screamed in response as Michalakis leapt to his feet to chase Makarios and his bodyguards through the west doors.

As Michalakis emerged in the sunlight, he saw the four men ahead of him, disappearing out of a small gate. They scrambled down the slope before bolting across a sparse orchard of new saplings. Reaching the road, they flagged down a passing car. Michalakis saw the driver scramble out with his hands held high, and the guards and their president jumped in. Makarios slipped into the back seat, where his head swiftly slipped from view and, though Michalakis was tempted to keep on running, he turned back to the palace.

Inside the reception room, he joined the adults in trying to calm the terrified children. As he did so, he straightened the press pass hanging around his neck. He then waited for the rebels to arrive and release them.

Elena wailed with grief and fury. Spittle shone from her chin as she violently resisted the attempts of both her daughter and granddaughter to calm her. Fighting against their arms with scratches and bites, she cried for herself and for the whole of Cyprus. All was lost, her heart was broken. Makarios was dead.

Over martial music, Cyprus Radio had broadcast its message repeatedly from 9.15 a.m. After only the second repetition, Elena knew the treacherous script by heart, and it echoed around her head, mockingly triumphant:

We stress this is a purely internal affair between Greeks and Greeks. Makarios is dead. Firearms should be surrendered. All movement in the streets is forbidden. Anyone who puts up resistance will be executed at once.

By 2.50 p.m., Nicos Sampson had been sworn in as President of the Republic.

As Praxi and her daughter helped Elena to bed, less than a mile away, Loukis and Mehmet were listening to the developments over a bottle of Keo on the farmer's porch. As Sampson declared that Cyprus would remain independent and non-aligned, the two friends read the scepticism in each other's eyes. Sampson was a former EOKA member, the leader of an execution squad, and a pal of Greece's latest military dictator. More damningly, he had headed a private militia that had carried out a series of despicable attacks against Turkish Cypriots in 1963. Such a man could never bring peace to the island, and everything Loukis and Mehmet had endured, and everything their people had gained, seemed to fly from their grasp, snatched within seconds by the winds of the most terrible change. As the men opened another bottle, an hour's drive away Michalakis was making his way home.

The gun battle at the palace had lasted three painful hours. The children and their guardians had been released, but Michalakis was kept for a further four hours as the uniformed assailants secured their hold and disarmed Makarios's loyal staff. Kept in a corner, bent on his knees, his hands atop his head, Michalakis heard the efforts of Greek officers working to discover the whereabouts of the missing president in the screams and tears of captured palace minions. Although Michalakis still wore his press card, it offered little respite from the angry fists of their captors, who failed to appreciate the newspaper he worked for. He noted that the Cypriot soldiers retained enough decency to turn their backs as the Greeks pummelled their outrage on his chest and face. Finally, and after they had dropped the bombshell that Makarios had been killed, Michalakis was free to go. He drove home in tears, shocked and racked with guilt that he should have done more to protect the president; that he should have taken up arms; that he should have done at least something other than watch.

In the car, he caught a glimpse of himself in the rear-view mirror. His right eye was swollen, his bottom lip was split in two places, and he looked abhorrent, so much so he could scarcely believe it was his own face staring back at him. But nothing seemed real and, throughout the journey, he had to keep reminding himself that his country's spiritual and political leader had been hunted down and destroyed by military agents of the motherland. Unable to fully register the enormity of the moment, Michalakis's most overriding concern as he drove through the deserted streets of the capital was that he had missed his father's appointment with the heart specialist.

Arriving home, he was little surprised that it was his mamma, not his wife, who was the first to rush into his arms weeping tears and questions. Behind her stood his papa, the relief evident on his face. Hovering in the background was Maria. She was too far away, and his eyesight too blurred to be able to read her.

'What have those monsters done to you?' Dhespina wept, dragging him into the kitchen to clean his battered face. 'When we heard the archbishop was dead we thought, oh God . . .'

'I can't believe it,' Michalakis mumbled. 'Makarios is dead.' His heart dropped as the news finally sunk in.

'The archbishop was dead,' Georgios clarified, and he gave his son a moment to properly hear the words. 'He was the late Archbishop Makarios III up until two hours ago. The old guy outran them all, first fleeing to Troodos and then on to Pafos, where he broadcast a message.'

'My God,' gasped Michalakis. 'Are you sure?'

'It was Makarios all right.'

A broad smile slowly crept along Michalakis's face, causing him to wince in pain. The man in black had foiled them again and, after his mother was done with her fussing, and apologizing for not being able to do more without the benefit of her herbs, Michalakis called his office. As he tried to extract some sense from the news-desk secretary, her high-pitched squeal was suddenly replaced by the reassuring boom of his editor's voice. Michalakis hurriedly reported his account of the coup at the palace and asked to be put over to the copytaker. To his dismay, the editor told him to save his energy; there would be no newspaper tomorrow. *The Voice* was out of business, on the new government's orders – until further notice.

'Our time will come,' the editor rasped. 'Makarios loyalists are fighting in all major cities. The people are rising. Those bastards . . . the dogs who have done this . . . their blood isn't Greek. Write up your words, and in a few days . . .' Without warning, the line went dead.

Yiannis put down the telephone, undecided and perplexed by the request. Dhespina had called the bar hoping to find Praxi or Elpida but instead had to implore Yiannis to tell Christakis and Loukis that she and Georgios were safe at Michalakis's house in Lefkosia. It was a liberty really, asking him to run around reassuring his wife's lover and his wife's lover's brother that their parents were unharmed, but Yiannis reasoned that they were living in extraordinary times. As he prepared to deliver the message, the telephone rang a second time. It was Jason, calling for Elpida. He assured the boy his daughter was safe, and he took a number so that she might call him. As he walked to the car, he wondered whether anyone would feel so moved to check if he himself were still alive.

Revving the Torino, Yiannis put aside his peevishness to play the heroic messenger. His apparently selfless bravado was somewhat fuelled by the earlier sounds of Greek tanks and other military paraphernalia rumbling out of the area in hot pursuit of Makarios. Yiannis was quietly proud that their archbishop had given the Greeks a run for their money, although he hadn't yet mustered the courage to pull down their blue and white flag from the back of his bar. One shouldn't be too hasty.

After relaying Dhespina's words to Christakis, who awkwardly thanked him with a generous pouring of brandy, he drove to the village to deliver Jason's message to Elpida. Elena's house was locked and, on peering through the window, seemingly empty. His chest stirred with a creeping sense of unease. But to his relief, and mild embarrassment, he soon found his daughter, her mother and grandmother with Loukis at the Turks' farm. They were seated on Mehmet's porch listening to the old man translate the broadcasts of Radio Bayrak.

'We couldn't trust Cyprus Radio,' Praxi apologized self-consciously as Elpida clutched the devotion of Jason's words to her chest. Yiannis accepted the glass of beer offered by Loukis.

'The National Guard closed in on Makarios in Pafos,' Mehmet revealed. 'Sampson moved his men into the area and gunships shelled loyalist positions. The British then acted. In the midst of the fighting they sent in a helicopter. It was fired on but not hit. The chopper flew your archbishop to the base in Akrotiri. The radio believes he has now been taken to Malta, with the feeling being that he'll go on to London.'

With a shriek of gratitude, Elena rose from her seat to throw her arms around Mehmet. 'Thank you,' she said, and he patted her hand.

'I can't believe it,' Praxi murmured, clinging tightly to her daughter's hand. 'To think the Greeks could do this to us.'

'Like a daughter being slapped in the face by her own mother,' Elena agreed, and she placed a kiss on Praxi's hair to demonstrate the strength of the betrayal they all felt.

'Will Turkey react?' Yiannis asked Mehmet, and the old man replied that it was certainly a possibility.

'God help us all,' Elena prayed. And perhaps because they felt a certain safety in numbers, none of them made a move as the night descended.

Driven by hunger, the women took over Mehmet's kitchen to cook a simple, but comforting, lentil stew. Once their bellies were full, and the night air had grown quiet, they drifted off to sleep, still on the porch, as the radio stood guard in the background. The next morning, Yiannis and Loukis returned to Elena's home to collect her television so that they might also watch the Greeks' version of events. The pictures made for unpleasant viewing, as scores of Makarios loyalists were paraded in chains before the cameras. Elena wept for them as the men around her muttered uneasily.

'Turn it off,' Praxi appealed, and for once Elena agreed. Elpida hit the button, and the picture shrank to a white spot before the screen fell black with idleness. None of them said a word, but all of them shared the same nagging fear of a future they had yet to know.

With uncertainty rattling around their chests, sleep seemed an almost impossible dream as the group settled together for a second night. Yiannis couldn't help but notice that Loukis and Praxi were inching closer with every passing hour, and he got to his feet, wondering whether he should demand his wife and daughter accompany him home. But then Mehmet asked him to stay, and he felt it would be churlish, given the circumstances, to drag his family away from the comfort they seemed to find on the old man's porch. Personally, he found the peculiar set-up un-comfortable, and he returned to Keryneia with promises to his daughter that he'd be back in a few days. Loukis shook his hand before he left, and Yiannis again wondered at the extraordinary times they were living in.

Three days after the coup, Elena, Praxi and Elpida con-sidered it safe enough – and themselves dirty enough – to warrant a return home. Some twenty-four hours later, Makarios took to the world stage. In no uncertain terms, he told the UN Security Council that Greece's military junta had extended its dictatorship to Cyprus without a trace of respect for the independence and sovereignty of the republic. The coup was not an internal matter, he railed, but an invasion from outside.

As the world debated the appropriate response, all eyes turned to Britain, one of the few countries legally permitted to act in the event of a breach of the Treaty of Guarantee. To growing outrage, she dispatched her commandos to help evacuate British subjects and defend the Queen's bases. Other than that, her politicians sat idly by as Turkey amassed 90,000 troops on its southern shores.

Niki pulled her blond hair into an elastic band and got to work on the bends and lunges designed to warm her muscles and protect her future. Last year, when her body had begun to develop, there had been a worry that puberty might hinder her pace but, thankfully, the upper curves she had inherited from her mother hadn't slackened the speed of her legs. Given this godsend, Niki became more determined than ever to look after the body she had been gifted, and Lenya often joked that it made her tired just watching her daughter prepare for a run.

As the teenager reached for the door latch, she was startled by a hacking cough.

'Why didn't you wake me?' Andreas asked, after dislodging the tar of the previous night's cigarettes.

Niki looked at the bags dragging at her papa's eyes and what was left of his hair. She shrugged in response, because it was easier than telling him the truth: that he was too old to be up so early.

For as far back as she could remember, her papa had been at her side, cheering her on and paying for a better coach than he could ever hope to be. But when she had taken to running before dawn, attracted by the ghostly quiet and empty roads, he had insisted on coming with her. She wasn't a selfish child, and his efforts made her feel guilty. Her papa had sacrificed so much, not only his wages but also his sleep, so that she might chase her dreams.

'I was going to stay around the village,' Niki fibbed. 'I thought you could lie in.'

Andreas rubbed the top of his balding pate. 'Well, I'm up now. Give me a minute to splash the sleep from my face.'

'Papa, please don't worry, I . . .'

'Tsk, Niki.' He cut her short. 'You're my daughter, and I'll not have you running around in the dark on your own, whether you're in the village or not.'

Less than three minutes later, the keys were in the ignition of the car, and Andreas was following his daughter to the main road leading to Keryneia. As he trailed Niki – the Datsun's lights illuminating her like a ballerina in the spotlight – he lit his first cigarette of the day and rested his arm along the open window. The cool air blew the last of the sleep from his eyes, and he watched her pounding the road ahead of him, as ever amazed by her natural ability and, more recently, by how tall she was getting. It seemed only yesterday that Niki had been a much-longed-for baby girl. Now she was a whisper away from becoming a woman and a household name. Could a father be more proud?

To his surprise – and, it had to be admitted, to his initial horror – his daughter had always been a morning runner. She said she loved the quiet. She also confessed that, when dawn burst through the night, she imagined it was the moment she broke through the tape of an Olympic finishing line. Andreas thought it romantic nonsense, but he never said so, and after a while he too began to imagine the cheers of an appreciative crowd as the sun came up and his own daughter smashed another world record.

Ahead of him, Niki played with her pace, jogging and bursting into a sprint whenever the fancy took her. As they hit the slope downwards, Andreas killed the engine and let the car roll silently behind her. To his left, he saw the black of night begin to lose its density along the horizon, and he flicked the butt of his second cigarette out of the window to concentrate on the coming ovation stirring in his imagination. Naturally, as the sun's rays cut into the world there was no deafening applause. Instead there came the crack of a fighter jet tearing through the sky. A series of explosions followed and, before Andreas had time to wonder, he saw the road tear up behind him. Under his feet, the Datsun flipped like a coin from a ruler and he lost consciousness.

An hour later, Andreas saw the hands of strangers working to free him from the wreckage. He screamed for his daughter before the world turned black. The next time he would wake he would be lying in a hospital bed in the south of the country. His wife and youngest child would be missing and he would find out that Niki was dead. Mercifully, he would never know that it was his own car that killed her; that the Datsun had landed on top of his daughter, pulping her head and body into an unrecognizable mess while her slim legs remained intact, peeking out from under the crumpled roof, twitching but unscathed.

When he felt the ground tremble beneath his bed, Yiannis's first thought was to rip the Greek flag from the bar. His second was to get to his family.

In the half-light of dawn, people emerged from their homes groggy with sleep to gauge the extent of the danger they might be in. In answer, another jet roared overhead and, somewhere, a woman screamed. Everyone turned to the sea. A wall of troop carriers was heading for land, and behind them floated the shadowy forms of a dozen warships. The town erupted in panic.

'Mother Mary,' Yiannis muttered, and ran to his car. Stamping on the clutch, his leg shuddered as his fingers struggled to fit the key into the ignition. Finally, the Torino purred into action and Yiannis put his foot down. As he sped along the cobbles, turning right into the narrow lane leading to the main road, people ran in all directions, clutching children and hastily packed suitcases. As he hit the brake to avoid a young girl, a hand pulled at the passenger door and he leaned over to slam it shut again. The fear-filled eyes of an old woman floored him.

'My family! I've got to get my family!' he yelled in apology.

Screeching on to the highway, another jet strafed the road ahead, sending concrete and tarmac hurtling in his direction. Yiannis pulled at the steering wheel and careered into a field, ripping up rows of aubergines in his wake. He cleared the vegetation with his wipers to see a fiery ball blast into a derelict building. It crumbled to the ground in a pile of rubble and twisted girders. To his right a garage belched angry flames into the sky, and above the rooftops of Keryneia columns of black smoke rose, twisting and mushrooming into the blue as if in unspeakable agony. Above him, the squadron of jets continued to swoop and strafe the area, like carrion crows feeding on the crippled.

In the village, the residents were far enough away from the destruction engulfing the harbour to gather their thoughts as well as their belongings. Every house had its radio turned on, and the Cyprus Broadcasting Corporation acted swiftly to dismiss rumours of an invasion, calling them 'irresponsible'. However, within thirty minutes of the first explosion, a line of cars began snaking westwards, away from the war the villagers patently saw which threatened to swallow them.

In ten-minute intervals, the jets split the sky overhead, and Loukis smelled death in the air. Grabbing his

389

hunting rifle, he checked on Mehmet, who told him to run.

'It's started,' the old man told him. 'Radio Bayrak is calling it a peace operation, but I don't know, son. I'd feel better having you away.'

Loukis hated to leave, but he knew the old man's chances of survival were considerably better than his own, should the Turks enter the village, and they would increase still further if he weren't there. He felt he should have said more, but he simply grabbed the old man in a hug and uttered 'Thanks'. Loukis ran for Praxi. By the time he reached her his lungs were on fire. She was dragging her mother out of the front door. Elena was grappling to keep hold of an armful of icons she had snatched from the wall.

'We haven't time!' Praxi shouted.

'I can't leave them!' Elena insisted, and her daughter threw up her arms in frustration as Loukis approached. He took hold of Praxi's face and kissed her hard but fleetingly on the mouth. He strode into the house to take a leather bag hanging on a hook by the door and placed Elena's religious keepsakes inside it. Elpida emerged behind him carrying a small suitcase and a wad of letters in her hands.

'Letters?' Praxi yelled.

'They're from Jason,' the girl replied, and Loukis took them from her and put them inside the bag, along with Elena's precious icons.

'I should lock the door,' Elena muttered.

'I don't think it will matter,' Loukis replied honestly.

From around the corner, Yiannis's Ford Torino squealed its arrival, coming to a halt in the hedge. He jumped out to grab the one suitcase his daughter held and threw it in the boot, shouting orders for everyone to get into the car. Elena and Elpida immediately climbed on to the back seat, but there was a second of confusion as Praxi looked at Loukis and they both looked at her husband.

'Jesus! Just get in,' he cried, and Praxi joined her daughter and mother in the rear as Loukis took the passenger seat. He rolled down the window. His shirt was drenched in sweat. His hands gripped his gun. His knuckles were white.

As they turned into the main road leading through the village, they found their path suddenly blocked by the huge form of Mr Televantos's daughter. Her face and hefty arms wobbled with fear and disbelief as she banged on the panels of passing cars beseeching her father's neighbours to help them as they fled in panic.

'Please!' she cried. 'For the love of God, please someone help us!' In desperation, she threw herself on to the bonnet of Yiannis's car, forcing him to stop. Before anyone could prevent her, Praxi jumped out.

'Where's your father?' she demanded.

'He's in the house. Please God, you have to help us.'

'Of course we'll help you.'

Praxi turned to Loukis, who was already out of his seat. Yiannis, at the insistence of his daughter, also ran to assist. Inside the stone cottage, they found Mr Televantos upstairs. Loukis gently eased him out from under the bed sheets.

'I don't want to go!' the old man cried, tears streaming down his anguished face. 'Let me die in my house! Don't take me away. This is my home! I don't want to leave! I beg you, let me be!'

Because they had no time to convince him otherwise, no one offered any argument as to why Mr Televantos should leave the home he was born in and that his father had built. Loukis simply carried him to the car. He placed him carefully in the front seat and strapped him in. The old man's daughter had already staked her place in the back, with Elena squashed in the middle next to her granddaughter. Loukis opened the boot and told Yiannis to get in.

'You'll have to drive,' he informed Praxi.

'What about you?'

'I'll make my own way,' he said, and grabbed the gun lying at Mr Televantos's feet.

'No, Loukis,' Praxi whispered. 'I won't leave without you.'

'You will, Praxi,' Loukis insisted.

'I won't.'

'You will.'

As they argued, Yiannis sheepishly climbed into the boot.

'Please, Praxi, I can make my own way. I'll head straight for Michalakis's house in Lefkosia. When you can, call his office, and he'll tell you where I am. I'll be waiting for you.'

Before Praxi could say another word, Loukis grabbed her by the back of her hair and forced her mouth to his. He drank the tears falling from her eyes and swallowed her breath as he pulled away. In the boot of the car, Yiannis closed his eyes in shame. On the back seat, Elpida looked on, astonished. Loukis tore himself from Praxi's arms and ran.

'Praxi, drive!' Elena shrieked, and her daughter beat at her chest to control the sobs that threatened to take her as she slid into the front seat.

'I don't want to go,' Mr Televantos whimpered at her side.

'None of us do,' Praxi answered harshly. She turned the key in the ignition and checked the rear-view mirror, but it was blocked by the lid of the boot. Carefully, Praxi reversed the car before completing a three-point turn to take up the rear of the convoy of cars moving west.

'I've got to get back,' Dhespina muttered.

'Let Michalakis do his job,' Georgios replied. He kept his voice calm, but his chest was tight in a different way than it had been for the past year. Although he didn't say so, he was grateful that Marios was abroad and safely out of harm's way. Although the radio insisted that talk of an invasion was nothing short of scandalous, his hands grew clammier with every report seeping out of the capital. If the rumours were correct, the National Guard was heading northwards; ten thousand Makarios loyalists had been freed from jail; and the skies above the Pentadactylos mountain range were black with Turkish paratroopers.

'There's still no answer,' Michalakis told his parents. He had been calling Kyriakos for the best part of an hour, and Dhespina understood his frustration – she had received the same silence from the Jewel of Keryneia and Lenya's house.

'Drive me home,' Dhespina begged her son. With an apology, Michalakis said he couldn't grant her request.

'We'd be arrested before we reached the plains,' he told her.

'Or shot,' Maria muttered behind him. Michalakis threw his wife a warning glance, and she walked off to their bedroom to worry about the fate of her own parents. By the time the afternoon came around, none of them were any longer in doubt as to what was happening. Turkish jets had buzzed the capital, and in the north of the city they dropped bombs that turned Greek homes into craters and children into orphans.

*

'Do you know where you're going?' Elena asked anxiously. She leaned forward in her seat to allow her body to breathe, away from the suffocating folds of Mr Televantos's daughter.

'I guess we'll loop north after reaching Panagra and Myrtou,' Praxi told her mother.

'What do you mean, "you guess"?' Elena demanded.

'Mamma! I'm just following the other cars.'

'Well, you'll be in trouble if you fall much further behind. We're losing sight of the red car already.'

Elena pointed at the disappearing rear of the Nissan ahead of them, but her grumbles were quickly silenced by the rattle of gunfire.

'Snipers!' Mr Televantos screamed. In response, his daughter emitted a moan of lament, no doubt aware that she made a particularly large target. On the roadside bullets kicked up dirt.

'Oh Mother Mary!' Elena prayed as the glass shattered by Mr Televantos's head, causing everyone to start screaming. At the back of the car, Yiannis frantically banged his fists on the boot lid, and Praxi put her foot down, more scared of being shot than of losing control of the car. More heavy thuds sounded from the boot.

'OK! OK!' Praxi shouted. 'Tell your father I'm going as fast as I can!'

Elpida pushed her head out of the window. 'Mamma's going as fast as she can, Papa!'

'Did he hear you?' Praxi asked as her daughter pulled her head back inside, breathless and flushed.

'How do I know?' Elpida snapped. 'You can see as much as me!'

'We're going to die!' Mr Televantos's daughter suddenly cried.

'I told you to leave me,' her father angrily retorted. 'I could have ended my days in my own bed.'

'Shush now!' Praxi ordered. 'No one's going to die!' And to everyone's amazement, they ran the gauntlet of gunfire with a burst tyre which they managed to ignore, in spite of the smoke and the sparks, until they reached the safety of Myrtou.

Coming to a halt close to a handful of cars taking shade at the edge of an orchard, everyone but Mr Televantos left their seats to stretch the terror from their legs. Over the sea, the dark forms of Turkish jets still circled, but the noise of their engines had been silenced by distance. Praxi breathed her relief as she held on to her shaking knees. Her mother hobbled to a tree, reaching for oranges to put the sugar back into their blood. As Mr Televantos's daughter begged for water from the other refugees who had parked up, Elpida screamed in alarm. Praxi ran to her side. Crumpled in the boot of the car, Yiannis lay bleeding, his chest rising and falling in great tortured breaths. His eyes flickered in pain, and they looked to Praxi for help.

'Oh God, Yiannis. Oh dear God . . .' She pulled him roughly from the car, ordering Elpida to help with his feet. Yiannis tried to speak, but he no longer possessed the power.

'Find help!' Praxi ordered her daughter before turning to Elena. 'Mamma, I need water!'

As they raced away, Praxi cradled her husband's head in her lap. She took her skirt to wipe the blood from his face. His skin was white, and he shivered despite the searing heat.

'Oh Yiannis,' Praxi cooed, rocking him gently. 'Oh my

poor Yiannis. How can this be? Don't worry, help is coming, sweetheart. Help is coming.'

In response, Yiannis reached for his wife's hand, and a tear fell from her eyes as he did so.

'May God forgive me,' Praxi whispered into his hair. 'I have wished you dead on so many occasions. But Yiannis, I swear I never truly wanted to see you like this. Not ever. Not even when I collected pips to poison you and spent the days in between fantasizing about the Turks shooting you. And now here you are, with a Turkish bullet in your chest, and I can't bear it, I promise you, I can't bear it.' Praxi burst into tears, a very real and wholly unexpected grief tearing at her insides. When Elpida returned with a man carrying a First-aid kit the only papa she had ever known had breathed his last, and his eyes were standing open in stunned surprise.

Kyriakos looked like death. He hadn't slept since taking his wife and baby to stay with relatives in the south. He hadn't eaten either, and fear and hunger had plunged his sugar levels so low his hands constantly shook. Ushering Michalakis into his office, he apologized for his absence, and the journalist told him there was no need. Michalakis then waited patiently for his friend to gather himself as the stress of the past twenty-four hours released itself in sobs that racked the length and breadth of his body.

'It's worse than you can imagine,' Kyriakos revealed, and Michalakis took out his notepad. 'The fighting has been bitter. We've taken small victories and the Turkish Cypriots have surrendered in Pafos and Lemesos, but Keryneia has fallen. Earlier today the Turks reached the beachhead and unloaded their battle tanks. Our forces had no choice.

They had to retreat. There was simply no other option.'

On the politician's desk a telephone rattled its urgency. Two seconds after it fell quiet, Kyriakos's secretary appeared, her face pinched with the strain of duty.

'It's Glafkos Clerides,' she whispered.

Michalakis got to his feet and gestured his thanks as Kyriakos swiftly reached for the telephone. He quickly made his way to *The Voice*, which had been granted a reprieve following news of the invasion. At the entrance he leaned heavily against the wall, feeling sick to his stomach. Kyriakos had made no attempt to soften the shock. Keryneia had fallen. And there was still no word from either of his brothers. In the dead of night, Yianoulla and her two youngest boys had arrived on his doorstep. They had come by bus while Christakis and the older boys remained behind to defend their business and their island. At the news, Georgios had slammed his fist on to the dining table, but Dhespina remained quiet. She ushered the family into the last of Michalakis and Maria's spare beds, where she watched over them until the new day broke.

'The boys will be here soon,' Dhespina stated defiantly over breakfast, and no one had the courage to argue otherwise. But now Michalakis would have to return home and tell her Keryneia had been taken. A hand fell gently on his shoulder. It was the editor.

'Come on, Michalakis, we've got a paper to get out.' He lit a cigarette and carried it upstairs. Michalakis followed, not knowing what else he should do.

Inside the newsroom, reporters were ripping slips of papers from their typewriters and handing them to the news editor. Sitting at Michalakis's desk, a college volunteer was attempting to write up words shouted over a telephone line by one of the staff men. The teenager looked increasingly flustered as he tried to rectify his mistakes and apologize at the same time. Michalakis gently urged the boy to shift over and took the phone from him.

'This is Michalakis,' he informed the reporter on the other end of the line. 'Take it from the top.'

'Greetings, Michalakis. This is Yiannakis. Ready?'

'Ready.'

'Cypriot forces backed up by two hundred Greek commandos have so far managed to repel Turkish efforts to take Lefkosia airport. Point new par. The fighting has been fierce with both sides reporting heavy casualties. Point new par. Meanwhile on this the second day of the illegal Turkish invasion, the British have secured a ceasefire so as to evacuate the four thousand foreigners stranded in the city. Point new par. They left in a thousand trucks, buses and cars draped with the Union Jack. Point new par. Greek Cypriot civilians have been offered no such salvation and they continue to lose their lives under the Turkish rampage. Point. Ends.'

Michalakis thanked the reporter for his patience and handed the typed copy to the work-experience boy to take to the news desk. Behind him, Sotiris was translating the latest bulletin from Radio Bayrak to the editor.

'They say the National Guard has forced Turkish Cypriots out of villages and quarters in Larnaka, Pafos and Ammochostos,' Sotiris revealed. 'They claim fleeing refugees have been taken hostage and that women and children have been shot.'

'What about our women and children?' Tassos angrily

inquired. The editor ignored the crime reporter and asked Sotiris to continue.

'The Turkish premier says, "This is not an invasion but an act against invasion. This is not aggression but an act to end aggression. The operations of peace will bring an end to the darkest period in the history of Cyprus".'

'Bullshit!' Tassos shouted again. Beside him, Michalakis's telephone rang. It was Kyriakos.

'I've a couple of leads for you,' he said. Michalakis grabbed his pencil. 'The first is napalm. We're being told the Turkish have dropped napalm on villages in the north, and on fleeing refugees. Secondly, we're hearing that Turkey has vowed to continue its onslaught until the northern half of the island has been seized, including Keryneia, parts of Lefkosia and Ammochostos.'

'*Taksim*,' Michalakis uttered.

'You said it. I'll bring you more as I get it.'

Michalakis thanked Kyriakos for the second time that day and typed up the article. When he returned home in the small hours, his parents and Yianoulla were sat waiting for him. He shook his head in answer to the question he found in their eyes. His mamma nodded and informed him that Maria's mother and father had arrived safely and were sleeping in his bed, with their daughter lying on the floor by their side. Michalakis was happy for his wife, and he went to tell her so.

The next morning, when he arrived at the office, he found Praxi waiting in the lobby. Michalakis couldn't hide the truth, and Praxi burst into tears. Ushering her into one of the interview rooms, he asked the news-desk secretary to bring them coffee. He then listened to her story. It started with a kiss from Loukis and, after a change of tyres at Myrtou, it ended in Pissouri, with Yiannis's body wrapped in an old bed sheet in the boot of his car.

'Irene insisted we stay, which was very good of her,' Praxi said.

'Irene?'

'Mr Televantos's daughter.'

Michalakis agreed it was indeed kind of Irene, but he still offered what floor space he had in his own house. Praxi shook her head and said they would stay where they were until Loukis arrived. She handed him a phone number in Pissouri and said that, if he didn't mind, she would come to his office tomorrow, just in case.

'If there's anything you need,' Michalakis told her as he accompanied her downstairs.

'I only need Loukis,' she insisted, and left him to his work.

Back in the newsroom, the floor was buzzing with news of Nicos Sampson's resignation. The 'president' had stepped down at 4 a.m. Hours later, the Greek military government collapsed and Turkey agreed to a ceasefire.

Ten days after the invasion, peace talks convened in Geneva, attended by the foreign ministers of Greece, Turkey and Britain. There were no representatives from Cyprus and the revelation caused Georgios to condemn the process as a sham.

'An autopsy conducted by criminals with the corpse left outside,' he muttered. Mr Germanos conceded he had a point, but Maria's mother flinched at the vulgarity of the analogy. However, and in spite of his verbal scepticism,

Georgios inwardly prayed that the diplomats would hammer out a solution. He was tired of living in his son's house like a sardine in a can. He wanted to go home. He wanted to find his boys.

Irritated by the paralysis of his confinement, he left the dining table and wandered to the window. Sitting on the kerb outside, his wife comforted Praxi. Every morning, she came to the capital hoping for news of Loukis and every evening she returned to her temporary home empty-handed. She had lost weight, and her colourful dresses had been exchanged for the black of mourning. Georgios couldn't be sure who she was grieving for, her husband or his son.

'Do you still feel him?' Praxi asked Dhespina.

'Yes, I do,' his mother replied, but it sounded like a lie. God help her, but death had been clawing at her throat from the very first day of the invasion. The silence coming from the north was deafening. There was no word from Christakis or Loukis, and there was no news of her sister. Dhespina didn't know how long she could stem the worry welling within her. But while she had breath she had hope. Whatever the Turks took from her – whether it be her home, her dignity or her life – they would not take Loukis, and they would not take Christakis. Her sons would find a way. They would return to her.

As the peace talks rumbled on, Turkey continued to move her soldiers and tanks on to the island, quietly increasing her creeping hold on the north. Under the cover of ceasefire, her troops fanned out from the corridor they had taken to occupy villages, suburbs and highways. And under the weight of destruction, Aphrodite's Island sank into squalor.

On the first morning of the invasion, Lenya and her youngest daughter were flushed from their home by the sound of gunfire and the panic of others. Turkish boots marched on Cypriot soil and her neighbours screamed at them to run. Unable to withstand the terror everyone felt, Lenya grabbed Erado's tiny hand and together they fled to safety, chased by tales of bloody murder and rape. As they ran, Lenya felt her heart crushing under the weight of shame. But Erado was only six years old and she needed a mother's protection. Somewhere, Niki had Andreas, and she was certain they had escaped ahead of them. The two would be safe together. It was just a case of waiting, and as Lenya gazed around their tent – at the widowed woman weeping in the cot next to them and the listless old man chewing over the memory of his sons – she knew they were lucky. But when she looked at her youngest daughter she couldn't find the words to explain why.

From the day they arrived at the refugee camp, Lenya had trodden the baked earth calling for her first child and her husband, shouting to be heard above the wails of the lost while avoiding the stares of children haunting the wasteland with large eyes and wordless mouths. All around her were widows and waifs – and those waiting to find out. Now and again TV cameras would come to capture their pain and the Red Cross would take names and check for others on their lists. As the sun rested overhead, Lenya would temporarily give up her search to join the tattered queue waiting in line for food, which was slopped into plastic containers and buckets. For women who had spent their whole lives protecting their families from the kitchen it was a cruel humiliation and Lenya would have dropped to her knees and cried for pity had everyone around her not been in the same position.

More than three weeks after the invasion, representatives from the Greek and Turkish communities finally joined the negotiating table in Geneva, where they took the opportunity to hurl accusations of atrocities and hostage-taking at each other. As the talks limped on, Turkish troops broke out of their bridgehead to advance east, west and south. The Turkish foreign minister then told reporters, 'Diplomacy is silent, the guns are now talking.'

From dawn, Turkish Phantoms swept over Cyprus, concentrating their attacks on Lefkosia and Ammochostos. More than three hundred tanks headed south from Keryneia, capturing Mia Milea, Kythrea and Chatos. And under the cover of ceaseless air raids, artillery bombardment and shelling by warships, the Turks moved their forces to cut off the northern third of the island. By midday, Greek Cypriot forces had pulled back from the capital and Ammochostos, tanks blasting holes in their defences. Homes and factories burned as the Turks pushed ever south-wards. Huge plumes of smoke billowed over the island, and queues of cars laden with mattresses and suitcases stretched for six miles as more refugees sought sanctuary at the Brits' Dhekelia airbase. Still the Turks ploughed on. Their jets dropped 500lb bombs on National Guard positions, and warships pounded coastal towns throughout the night. Within two days, the island lay scorched and broken, and Dhespina screamed with uncontrolled fury.

For weeks she had remained calm in the face of the catastrophe that had come to take them. She had waited, she had prayed, and she had watched at the window. But now the war was all-consuming and she could see no way of return, no hope of escape, and she smashed anything she could grab hold of to vent her rage. As Georgios fought to restrain her, she ripped at her hair before grabbing an ornamental teapot, sending it flying against the wall, narrowly missing Mrs Germanos's head. Maria instinctively sprang forward and slapped her mother-in-law in the face. Michalakis reacted by delivering a stinging riposte on the right cheek of his wife. Everyone was stunned into silence and Dhespina fell quiet.

Seconds later the tears fell and she began to rock on her heels and keen. What had her sons done? One was a carpenter, the other a farm worker. They were good men with good hearts and they deserved to live, to be with those they loved and who missed them so very much. But in this tiny house that wasn't her home she didn't know who to tell, or who to reason with. She had no way of reaching out to protect her family, and as desperation surged again in her chest she opened her mouth and howled. She tore the silence she had worn like a veil; she ripped at the fabric of failed reason. Dhespina howled because she could do nothing else, and this time no one tried to stop her.

By the time his mother's fit had passed, Michalakis had rung a doctor, who prescribed rest with the aid of sleeping pills. The medic further promised to contact the Red Cross, who might have knowledge of his brothers' whereabouts. Thousands had been swallowed by refugee camps, hospitals and prisons on the Turkish mainland. He would check the growing lists of names, he said, and Michalakis thanked him.

The next morning, Andreas woke from his coma and Red Cross volunteers were able to track down his wife and guide her to his hospital bed. Taking care not to aggravate his injuries, Lenya gently held her husband's hand as they grieved for the daughter they had lost. By their side, Erado remained quiet, struggling to understand how a sister could simply disappear. Twenty-four hours later, Ankara declared another ceasefire and the military campaign was officially over.

Cyprus was divided, with the Turks occupying a third of the island from Ammochostos to Kato Pyrgos, displacing a third of the population in the process. As the boundary was marked, thousands remained missing, including Loukis and Christakis.

It took a further two months for one of them to return.

PART THREE

'For the Greek race, it is the greatest disaster since that of Asia Minor in 1922. Our casualties amount to about 6,500 – 3,500 are dead, 3,000 are missing. Of the latter, I doubt whether more than a few survive. According to the evidence we have, most of the missing have been executed in cold blood. If we draw a parallel with other countries, the proportion of our losses would be: for the United States, about 2,800,000; for England or France, over 700,000; for the Soviet Union, more than 3,000,000; for Greece, around 120,000.'

Archbishop Makarios III, 1974

Pissouri, 2007

The Englishwoman had been giggling and deliberating with her husband for close to twenty minutes, and Praxi was fast losing patience. How much debate could a small figurine with a gargantuan penis provoke? Eventually, and with a phoney gasp of shame, the woman brought the ornament to the till. Typically, her embarrassment didn't prevent her haggling over the price and nor did it stop her pointing out that the 'naughty statues' in the trinket shop around the corner were much cheaper. Praxi calmly explained that the souvenirs in that particular premises were largely made of plastic, whereas everything in her store was handmade from the finest wood.

'The little fella has impressive wood, all right,' the husband joked, and Praxi acted like it was the first time she had heard such a witty aside. When the couple left, she reached for the shutters.

Before locking up, Praxi let her gaze fall upon the collection of fruit bowls, carvings, jewellery boxes, benches and treasure chests, all lovingly created by Marios and his nephews in their workshop in Lemesos. The larger, more expensive items they saved for the furniture store in

Lefkosia. From small beginnings, and with Carina's business savvy and a generous loan from her parents, the family had built up a thriving and reputable company. Christakis would have been proud beyond words.

Praxi checked her watch. It was 7 p.m. and later than she had planned. She leaned the chalk board against the wall and walked quickly along the cobbled lane, passing rows of noisy tavernas spilling sunburnt bodies on to the crowded pathway. The younger ones were already singing.

Praxi found the tourists annoying and, more often than not, inappropriately dressed. Even so, she had to admit they had been the saviour of the Republic. When the Turks had stamped their boots on the north – stealing two thirds of the island's cultivated land and 60 per cent of the water resources, mining and quarrying – the legitimate government turned to holidaymakers. With posters of bare-chested Aphrodite superimposed upon the crystal waters of the Mediterranean, they papered over the cracks of despair to reel in the foreigners. By the mid-1980s, hundreds of apartment blocks, restaurants, bars and hotels had sprung up to cater for the influx of wallets. And the south prospered.

Although Praxi was grateful for the lifeline, like everybody else, she found it strange that most of the visitors happened to be British, given the bombing campaign that had sent them into retreat when she was a teenager. She wondered whether this showed remarkable forgiveness, collective amnesia, or simply an ignorance of history. Praxi couldn't be sure. Whatever the reason, it was none that she could fathom. Greeks knew their history like the back of their hands.

We do not forget.

A little over thirty-three years ago, her people lost everything. Homes became the floors of relatives or friends, public buildings, churches, monasteries, shacks, tents or the open skies. Small towns doubled and tripled in size. Relief agencies flew in food rations and medicine. The trail of human misery seeping from the north was astonishing. Fleeing villagers had been executed in cold blood, men were gunned down with children in their arms. Mass graves hid the murdered. Soldiers, shepherds, masons, plumbers, the decrepit, the naive – no one was spared. The captured who survived were subjected to beatings with fist, foot and electrified club. Cigarettes were extinguished on bare skin, bodies stabbed and doused with flammable liquid. Gang rapes broke women – the young and old, the pregnant and retarded – and when they carried their shame to the south, the government amended the abortion law.

A month after the north was lost, a line of buses snaked through Lefkosia. They carried home prisoners of war, and it seemed that every Greek Cypriot came out to greet them. As the coaches wheezed to a halt, Praxi held Dhespina and Yianoulla's hands.

'Come on, come on, come on,' Dhespina muttered into her handkerchief.

One by one, the men who had been shipped to Turkey's Adana prison disembarked, dazed and overwhelmed by freedom and the huge crowds that had come to welcome them. As the fourth bus opened its doors with a mechanical sigh, Dhespina threw her hands into the air and pushed herself forward, clawing through the mass of people to get to him.

'My son! Let me pass. My son has come!'

Other waiting families immediately parted, feeling her

joy even amidst their own envy and misery. As Dhespina reached the clearing, she flung herself at her boy, and he scooped her from her feet.

'Mamma . . .'

Christakis gathered Dhespina in his arms. Behind him, his two sons burst from the bus and pulled in their own mother as she battled her way through the throng.

Praxi took a tomato and the last of the ham out of the fridge. Adding a touch of salt and a splash of olive oil, she carried her dinner and a small glass of wine to the veranda. A warm breeze drifted lazily from the bay to play with the hem of her black skirt. It reminded her of home.

There were a few pleasures in life that kept Praxi thankful, and the sight of the sea was one of them. Though age had left her too ashamed to dance in the waves, the beauty of them continued to stir her spirit. The land and its hideous complications might drag at her resolve but the sea never failed her. It was life, it was soul, it was power and it was freedom. And Praxi couldn't imagine how Dhespina and her family had lasted so long away from the salty breath of the shore. It must have been a daily battle between hope and reality. Sadly, by the time they succumbed to the call of the coastline, Georgios was gone. His diseased heart expired two months before they moved to Lemesos, leaving Dhespina racked with guilt for not having left the city smog sooner. But it wasn't her fault. Georgios had been dying for years and everyone had waited – anticipating the call home. When the guns fell silent, thousands of suitcases stood at doorways and tent openings ready for the taking. Expectation thickened the air. It would only be a matter of time. Everyone agreed. Then, as the weeks turned into months, those bags were wordlessly placed under beds. When the months turned into years, they were stored away completely; hidden but not forgotten.

We do not forget.

With no money and no hope of getting any, twelve years passed before Praxi moved into her own home. The two-bedroom apartment was a gift from the government. It wasn't what she had known, but it was better than what she had managed with. Not that she didn't count her blessings: even today, Praxi's eyes misted with gratitude at the care shown to her by Mr Televantos's daughter. A single car ride had been repaid a thousand times over.

In those first few terrible months, Praxi, Elena and Elpida had sat in a bedroom belonging to Irene's children, waiting to leave. When it became apparent that Keryneia was lost to them and they were officially 'displaced', Irene's husband had cleared out the shed and made it as comfortable as possible until a solution was found. Over the years, government grants allowed for a kitchenette and bathroom, but their 'home' remained a shed that offered little space until Elpida flew the nest – winging her way to Jason and to England. Naturally, Praxi and Elena followed, but they carried return tickets in their handbags and spent only a fortnight under the country's grey, mirthless skies.

'It's no wonder they coveted our island,' Elena grumbled when the fifth day of rain dampened any holiday spirit she might have felt. 'This place is miserable.'

Praxi conceded her mamma had a point, but no amount of sunshine could have chased the misery from their hearts as they celebrated the happiest day of Elpida's life. The reality couldn't be denied; the pair's union was tainted by separation, because neither the bride's dramatics nor the gentle coaxing of her new husband could convince Praxi and Elena to stay. The women simply refused to allow the Turks to push them any further from their home, and so they buried their heartache and told the newlyweds they were content where they were. It was a lie of course, everyone knew that, and six months after Praxi was handed the keys to her new house, her mother passed away.

With a weary sigh she told her daughter, 'I'm sorry, Praxi *mou*, I just don't like it here.'

As they laid Elena to rest, Praxi prayed that, while her mother's bones were trapped in the 'here', her soul had travelled to heaven via 'there'.

The following year, Praxi found herself attending another funeral, after Christakis shocked them all by collapsing in his workshop. The medics did everything they could to save him, but Yianoulla was widowed. Although nobody voiced it, the common feeling was that the past was to blame. Christakis had never spoken about his internment, but he had been irrevocably damaged by the experience, his great stature bowed by the terrors he had witnessed and endured. His sons occasionally told of soldiers standing in double rows ready to beat them, but the most Christakis ever revealed was that 'their hatred was immense.' Over time, he had been killed by the pain of his memories.

We do not forget.

The telephone rang; it was Michalakis. Praxi settled herself on the stool in the hallway, conscious of the likelihood of a lengthy conversation. Recent retirement hadn't come easy to the man, and the frequency of phone calls suggested he needed the distraction of dialogue. Still, she appreciated the effort he made. With so many lost to the passage of time, the care of those that remained became ever more precious.

Curling the telephone cord around her fingers, Praxi assured Michalakis that she was fine and thanked him for his concern. No, she apologized, it wouldn't be possible to come that weekend, but she asked him to give little Christakis a kiss for her. When she replaced the receiver, a brief fifteen minutes later, guilt tugged at her determination. The birthday of his grandson would have been a rare pleasure after the depression of the past two months, but she had made her plans and she wouldn't be changing them. Even so, she was moved by Michalakis's thoughtfulness.

Away from Marios and his large brood of multilingual offspring, Michalakis had emerged as perhaps the happiest of them all. Opinions had changed over the years – perhaps to negate the impact of greater sufferings – and the freedom of divorce had allowed the journalist to find lasting love with the sister of Savvas, the best man at his first wedding. Although Varnavia couldn't hope to match Maria in looks, she made up for her plain features with a brain like a steel trap, and Michalakis was snared, tethered and lost before the ink had dried on the divorce papers. The last Praxi heard of Maria, she had relocated to the United States to marry a plastic surgeon. She never had children, but every five years her second husband made up for this loss with a pair of new breasts.

Without Maria menacing his home, Michalakis had learned to enjoy life away from the office. Naturally, he had remained tied to the newspaper, but he managed to find the right balance with the right companion. In 1977, his dedication had seen him promoted to editor, immediately after his boss retired and shortly after Archbishop Makarios died. Having been present at the last attempt on the president's life, it seemed somehow fitting that Michalakis's final reporting assignment was his funeral.

Archbishop Makarios III had been the Republic's first president and, when he died, half the island's Greeks filed past his coffin, along with 182 dignitaries from 52 countries. Although medics took away his heart to test it for poison, Elena predicted that they would find it clean but irreparably broken. Praxi never said so at the time, but she knew it was nonsense. For thirty-three years she had endured the cracks of her own wretchedness. She knew from bitter experience that the heart never gave up as long as it had hope – be it a slither, a spit, a breath or an idle thought – the body keeps breathing. And, four years earlier, it was this whisper of possibility that had sent her back to Keryneia.

After much discussion, delay and disappointment, in April 2003 the border was opened. It was the first time in nearly thirty years that those either side of the buffer zone were able to swap places. And when Michalakis drove his mother, Marios and Praxi to the crossing in Agios Dometios, the scene was one of happiness, anger and frustration.

Dhespina, greyed and bent by age, kept her eyes open and her mouth closed. The emotions seizing her chest were varied and oppressive, and at times she struggled for breath. Finally, when the seal of the Turkish Republic of Northern

Cyprus was stamped into her passport, she felt only betrayal; as if she had somehow legitimized the criminal. In front of her, an old man wept with shame. Blinded by tears, he had to be guided back to his car by a woman she assumed was his daughter.

Driving from the checkpoint, Dhespina's dismay was exacerbated by the scene that met her eyes. Upon dry, yellow fields stood charmless, rectangular blocks of flats. Large boards advertising casinos lined the route north. Old cars stopped at antiquated traffic lights. Poverty drifted across the parched landscape and, fluttering above it all, were the red and white flags of Turkey and the reverse, white and red, images representing the north.

'The Turks may have taken our country, but they have failed to take care of her,' Praxi noted glumly. Nobody in the car responded, but Marios gently squeezed her hand.

As they moved onwards, through the mountains skirting St Hilarion's Castle, Michalakis glanced warily above him, out of habit rather than fear. He knew the snipers were long gone, but old habits die hard.

We do not forget.

Coming out of the bend, the car was greeted by an expanse of blue skies and sparkling sea. Dhespina moaned with sudden, unspoken longing, and Michalakis pressed on the brake as his vision blurred. For decades they had waited for this moment, and though the buildings had sprawled along the coastline – and the Turkish sign pointed to Girne – it was still Keryneia, the Jewel of Cyprus.

They bypassed the port and continued their journey to where the long shadow of the castle fell. Turning right off the main road, they entered the village and slowed to a crawl. Remarkably, everything appeared almost as they had left it, but smaller. As expected, the Greeks' coffee house had gone, lost to a convenience store. But the bakery remained, as did the butcher's. In fact, very little had changed, apart from the faces they saw, which now displayed largely Anatolian features.

Coming to a halt, they all held their breath. Despite her age, Dhespina was the first to take courage. She stepped gingerly from the car and wiped a handkerchief across her cheeks. Glancing around, she noted the plants were dry from the summer rather than neglect, but she still had to fight the need to find a bucket and nurse them. Self-consciously, she walked up the pathway. The crunch of gravel was achingly familiar and the front door was open. A woman, smartly dressed and clean-looking, watched them approach.

'I've been expecting you,' she said simply. She spoke Greek, and Dhespina felt some relief that her home had been taken by another islander.

There was no smile of welcome, but the woman none-theless invited them in, urging them to sit on chairs that they used to own. She left the four of them alone to make coffee, using the pot that had once belonged to Dhespina. In the corner sat a large television facing a bright-red sofa and along the wall stood a cheap dresser displaying decorated plates. Everything else remained unaltered. And it aggravated the feeling of theft.

Over coffee and cakes, the Turkish Cypriot inquired about their journey and asked where they had come from. Being a refugee herself, she mirrored the sorrow she saw in the eyes of those now sitting as guests in their own home, but she didn't apologize. And she made it clear she wouldn't be making the same pilgrimage south.

'Some things are better left behind,' she grumbled, sad and embarrassed.

When the five of them ran out of anything more to say, the woman moved to a cupboard, from which she pulled out a small case. She passed it to Dhespina. Inside were the icons and pictures that used to adorn the walls, plus the articles written by Michalakis, all carefully folded away and pre-served for a time when they would be reclaimed. At the top of the collection was the photo of Dhespina's mother that had once guarded the back door of her den. With trembling fingers, Dhespina picked through the collection of memories until she found a grainy picture of Loukis. It had been taken in Mehmet's olive grove, and a small, slightly irritated grin played on Loukis's face as he used his forearm to wipe the sweat from his forehead. Dhespina held it out to the woman.

'Have you seen my son?' she asked.

'Have you seen my father?' the woman retorted.

The two women looked at each other, seeing the folly of their situation in each other's eyes. Dhespina sighed and handed the photograph to Praxi. Loukis's face was quickly lost in the wet of her tears; he was more beautiful than she even remembered.

When all was said that could be said without causing offence or further upset, the family thanked the woman for her time and for taking care of their memories. Wordlessly, they continued their journey.

Less than a mile away, they stopped at Mehmet's farm. The old man's house had been extended and built upon, and two cars cluttered a new driveway while his tractor stood rusting by a shed. As they approached, the door to Loukis's home suddenly opened and Dhespina stumbled. However, the man that emerged was a teenager, much younger than Loukis when they had last seen him and much smaller and slimmer. He shouted something in Turkish. When he received no reply, he walked to Mehmet's house. Seconds later, a large elderly woman appeared.

'Mrs Economidou?' she asked, and Dhespina nodded her head. The woman flashed them a friendly smile.

'My father was a friend of your family's,' she explained.

Although the four of them had expected it, the woman's use of the past tense stung them all. Praxi could bear it no longer. Too much had changed, and she felt time slipping from her fingers. She grabbed the woman's hands and begged for news of Loukis. Puzzled and visibly shaken, Mehmet's daughter bowed her head.

'We thought – we hoped – you were all in the south,' she managed, before Praxi turned on her heel and demanded Michalakis drive her to the port.

'It's not you, it's . . .' Praxi tried to apologize, but she couldn't find the words. As she walked from the door, Dhespina patted her arm.

A little way from the harbour, Michalakis parked the car. The route ahead was paved and saved for pedestrians.

'Makes sense,' he muttered to Praxi, but she was beyond sense and reason, and she could barely hear over the blood crashing through her veins.

She was so close she felt strangled by the fear of coming disappointment. Cut off in the south, it had been easier to believe that Loukis might still be alive; trapped in a world he couldn't escape from, perhaps numbed by amnesia or disabled by an injury he didn't want to share. But now, standing in front of a fish restaurant that used to be her bar, the sun scrutinizing the deep lines on her face as she watched people living in the present rather than the past, Praxi realized it was near hopeless. Yet still that slither remained, that spit, that breath, that idle thought that taunted her, and so she took the photograph Dhespina had relinquished and held it before a sea of passing faces that simply didn't care. As Praxi beseeched every stranger to take a look, their eyes slipped away, either out of embarrassment or disinterest. Sometimes her efforts extracted a mumble of apology, sometimes an angry stare of defiance. At one point a youth spat on her sleeve and Praxi had to hold Michalakis back. Wiping away the young man's hate, she understood his revulsion, because she felt it herself. And the more she was ignored, the stronger it grew, until she crumbled under the weight of it and Michalakis had to help her back to the car.

They returned to the village in silence. The sun was beginning its descent to the sea, and they found Dhespina and Marios at the cemetery, cleaning the neglect from Nicos's grave. Michalakis shook his head at his mother's questions and, with a last prayer, the four of them carried their frustration and grief back to the south before the border closed.

On the journey home, Dhespina handed Praxi a letter from Mehmet. She hadn't brought her glasses and she was anxious to hear the words his daughter had written for him as he lay dying. Despite her fatigue, Praxi took the yellowed pages and tried to decipher the fading ink.

To Dhespina, Georgios and the boys,

As I lie here eaten by age and disappointment, I pray that you are all safe. Even though I feel your sadness within my own heart, if you are reading this letter it must mean you have returned, and that gives me some cause for peace.

It is hard to believe that we could have lost so much in what can only be described as seconds within our island's long history. I sincerely wish that in the following moments of time there will come greater men than those who have served us before and that they will somehow manage to undo the terrible mistakes of our past. How this will be possible I cannot imagine, or even dare hope, although I remain confident that humanity will win the day.

Without you here – Georgios in your workshop, Dhespina in your den and the boys always around, with your reassuring strength and goodwill – it is as if a cavern has opened in my chest, swallowing every sense of belonging I have ever known. Thankfully, and also regrettably, into this great hole has poured my own family. They didn't arrive at once; they came in dribs and drabs, all of them fleeing the chaos in the south. I assume their tales, and the tales of my people, mirror those of your own and that you therefore have no need to hear of the murders, rapes and brutality the Turkish Cypriots were subjected to. But let me tell you one story about my granddaughter. It is only a tiny upset within the well of desolation we are suffering, but it is no less tragic for that. My sweet Ayse was playing at the seaside when the peace operation started. When she reached our village some three days later she was still dressed in the swimming costume she fled in. She is, or was, a thirteen-year-old girl, a beautiful child teetering on the edge of womanhood. And she was forced to flee in a state of near nakedness. For any young girl this must count as a humiliating experience, but for a Muslim girl like my Ayse it is a torment that has no words. Awkward and ashamed, she was lifted on to a bus that ran a gauntlet of hate on her journey to safety. People hurled stones and insults in their path. They scarcely believed they would get out alive. I thank the man who attempted to protect Ayse's modesty with his shirt, but she was still a little girl dressed only in a swimming costume. Today, the shame and fear of those days continue to haunt her dreams, and it is all I can do to stop myself from weeping when I hear her screams. Believe me, I try to remember that no side has a monopoly on misery, but I swear as Allah is my judge, it is hard.

You have to know that the peace operation took us all by surprise. And though I can see the terror and fear that caused the Greeks to turn on their neighbours, I cannot ever forgive it. And therein lies the problem. Right now I can see no way forward to reconciliation. Your enemy from the Turkish mainland was our saviour. Our soldiers came to deliver us from the horrors of the past and the disasters of a future Greek dictatorship. And now, for the first time in almost two decades, Turkish Cypriots feel safe in their own country. Can you even begin to imagine the magnitude of that relief, even within the midst of today's sufferings and grief? What we endured we do not forget.

But I digress. This letter is not meant to be a document of justification, but a farewell to those I consider to be as much a part of me as my own family. I have known you all since you were children, and I have loved you all equally. I pray for your future happiness and continued safety. If Allah wills it, may we meet again in the next life.

Your loving neighbour and friend,

Mehmet Kadir

Praxi folded the letter and placed it in an envelope, which she sealed with a kiss. It would have been easier to phone her daughter, but she preferred the effort it took to write as well as the lasting gift that came with a letter. If Loukis had ever done the same, perhaps she wouldn't have needed to battle so hard to keep him alive all these years. Despite her best efforts, and the snatched sights and half-sounds that swept through her mind whenever she called him, the love of her life had grown flat: a two-dimensional whisper of the man Loukis used to be. For this reason, Praxi had always put pen to paper. It meant their daughter would never know the anguish of fading memory.

We do not forget.

Placing the envelope on the windowsill, Praxi unexpectedly caught sight of herself in the mirror. She was startled and horrified. In her own mind, she retained the charm of her youth, and she had no idea who the old woman who insisted on staring back at her was. Her beautiful black hair had grown grey, her eyes were shrinking under the weight of creasing lids and her cheeks were dragging. What would Loukis think of her now – this horrible old thing? Would he have called this shrivelled wreck of a woman his life? Or would he have spent his evenings fondly remembering Maria and her pneumatic breasts, which defied both age and gravity? How could she have changed so much and so quickly when the years had crawled by like a death sentence? Where was God's mercy? The world had conspired to rob her of everything, even her looks, and she didn't feel she deserved any of it.

Blowing the threatening tears – and the stench of her own taunts – from her nose, Praxi turned the mirror to the wall and set about cleaning the house. If nothing else, everything needed to be in order. It was the only way. When she was done, she took the white pebbles she had collected to the sink, where she washed them. Her daughter once called them moonstones, and tomorrow she would place them at Dhespina's graveside; a small present from a family that never really was.

Just shy of her ninetieth birthday, Dhespina had died two weeks earlier in her sleep. There had been no illness to mark her passing; it was simply her time to go. She had spent so many years waiting for Loukis, and when she finally knew where to find him she simply closed her eyes and left. She passed away less than twenty-four hours after her youngest son was laid out before her on a pristine white cloth, limb by limb, rib by rib, knuckle by knuckle; from skull to foot bone.

A team of UN investigators had been led to his grave. It was no more than a hole really, a nasty little pit dug into the earth below St Hilarion's Castle shallow enough to have been excavated by a curious dog. There were two other remains beside Loukis; both of them men. All three bore bullet holes in their cracked skulls.

Although the method was clear, the circumstances surrounding their ends remained a mystery and, unless someone came forward, they always would be. Praxi desperately wanted to believe that Loukis's death had been swift, but she tortured herself with imaginings so vile she was no longer able to sleep. Instead of a finish, the discovery brought only more questions, and they were questions without end. There would never be any answers, there would never be justice nor any attempt to make the perpetrators pay, they were left with only bones; the yellowing relics of a life stolen.

When the Missing Persons Committee contacted Dhespina, Michalakis took her to the UN's makeshift laboratory in the old Lefkosia airport. It had taken experts ten months to verify the identity of the remains. When Michalakis later told Praxi the news, she had to excuse herself for ten minutes more.

We do not forget.

After laying her moonstones and saying a short prayer, Praxi took the bus to Lemesos, where she posted Elpida's letter. After buying a litre bottle of water, she boarded another bus to the capital. It was barely 10 a.m. and the day was already blisteringly hot.

Under the soulful gaze of Dionysios Solomos, Praxi alighted at the capital's main square. She felt the poet's stony eyes follow her all the way to the no-man's land of Ledra Street. In the days of her youth, the road was dubbed Murder Mile after a series of shootings claimed the lives of British soldiers. Following independence the street was cleaved in two by the Green Line, and at least half of it became home to one of the island's finest hotels. Today, it was no more than a desolate souvenir to a troubled past, with abandoned buildings pockmarked by bullets.

Praxi walked to the booth and handed over her passport. As she returned it to her handbag, her medication rattled inside its plastic casing. She walked onwards to the currency-exchange bureau, after which she bought herself an ice cream. Hailing the first taxi she saw, Praxi settled herself into the back seat and directed the driver to take her to Keryneia. As they drove off, he wound down his window to smoke a cigarette, rendering the air conditioning useless. Praxi instantly felt herself wilt in the heat and, to her intense irritation, the man wouldn't stop talking. He was from Bulgaria, he said. Life was hard, the wages few and he missed his family. Praxi nodded in reply, but she didn't have the stomach for conversation, especially one designed to guarantee a tip; nor did she have the desire to speak English with another foreigner who didn't know Greek. This journey was meant to be about her: about her time, her people, her memories and her language. She was tired of the outside interfering in her life and in the end she simply told the taxi driver to shut up.

Reaching her destination in blissful, if awkward, silence, Praxi asked the driver to pull over. She handed him the Turkish lira she had unhappily swapped her Cyprus pounds for.

'Shall I come for you here, later time?' the driver asked.

'That won't be necessary,' Praxi replied. Registering his confusion, she repeated simply that she would find her own way back. As the car pulled away, she turned her attention to the winding track ahead of her, and prayed to God to give her strength. The rocky path seemed impossibly steep.

Grabbing a broken branch, Praxi used it to lever herself up the side of the mountain. As her breath grew heavy and her lungs burned hot, she marvelled at how strong she must have been as a girl. It used to take only twenty minutes to climb to St Hilarion's with Loukis. Now, old and alone, ninety minutes had passed before she reached the level patch of ground beneath the pistachio tree that had witnessed their first act of adult love. Praxi leaned on her walking stick and dug into her bag for the water she had brought. The air around her was still, and she longed for the breeze she had imagined.

Settling herself on the ground, she poked and prodded, twisted and turned, but she was unable to find any relief from the hard stones. The grass was dry to her touch and the old tree looked sad and defeated. Unbidden, tears began to roll from Praxi's eyes, because what she had come to wasn't what she had wanted. It wasn't the way she had remembered her time here. Everything was so hard, so uncaring and cruel. It wasn't the way it once was.

As Praxi wept, a shy movement distracted her, and she looked up to see a rabbit gazing in her direction.

'Loukis would have killed you not so long ago and had you for his dinner,' Praxi told the creature. As she spoke the rabbit ran for it, and she heard his laughter arrive on the back of a gentle breeze. Like a forgotten kiss, his memory tickled her cheeks and cooled her forehead, and in an instant everything turned that little bit easier, softer and forgiving. Praxi lifted her arms in welcome and, above her, the dry leaves of the pistachio tree sighed with lost happiness. Praxi waited for Loukis to settle on the wind.

We do not forget.

'I have loved you my whole life,' Praxi whispered. 'I will love you until the day I die and beyond, and I have come here to find you and to tell you that, because I am so very frightened there may be no other way. When I die I assume we will be together, but what if I'm wrong, Loukis, like I have been so many times in our past? What if there is nothing but the here and now and there is no eternal life waiting on the other side? So much time has been wasted and so much beauty destroyed. I can scarcely believe we spent more of our lives apart than we did together, and I regret every minute of our foolishness. If I could live my life over, I would have borne our child with pride rather than hide the truth in shame. I would have waited for you to return and I would have taken whatever insults the world threw at me, because they would have meant nothing with you by my side. I am so deeply ashamed of this weakness of mine that made you run and caused me to deny you. Oh God, Loukis. I denied you! You, of all people! The only man I have ever loved and ever wanted to be with. In my heart I know I am responsible, not only for your loneliness in this world but also for your death. If we had lived our lives together we would have left our home together and we wouldn't be here now, one person remorseful and the other a ghost. Do you remember that afternoon we spent in this place plotting our escape as Yiannis plotted our future in Greece? I do. I remember it well, and I think about it almost every day because you promised you would never leave me, that we would stay together until we were burnt toast. As silly as it seems, I believe you were true to your word, Loukis. Even though they killed you, I have always felt you with me. I have caught glimpses of you in passing mirrors and I have felt you lurking in the shadows. I have taken comfort from these moments, really I have, but God, what I wouldn't have given for just one moment to be able to reach out and touch you again. This half-life has torn me to shreds, Loukis; to have you so close and yet be so far from you. And I am tired. More than I ever thought possible. Yet maybe this is the natural order of love; confusion and division. Perhaps it is a test of our faith and our truth and we get our reward in heaven. Well, I have passed the test, Loukis, and my lonely old age has proved the truth of my devotion. There is nothing more I need do. I am ready to come home – to be with you.'

As Praxi finished, she cast aside her black scarf to let the breeze catch her hair. From her bag she pulled out the plastic bottle. Tipping a handful of white pills into her palm, she placed them in her mouth and drank the last of the water. When she lay backwards upon the hot, hard earth she felt Loukis move closer and take her in his arms.

We do not forget.

Because the woman couldn't trust her own eyes, she called the tourist guide to take a look. He leapt up the stone stairs to join her at the edge of the castle wall. His legs were lean and strong and he took the binoculars from her hands with the confidence of a man who knows his own power. Within a few seconds, the playfulness slipped from his lips as he confirmed the woman's suspicions. They descended the stairs to alert the authorities.

Although the paramedics were prompt, it made no difference. On close inspection, it was clear that the Greek woman had lain dead for more than twenty-four hours.

'It looks like the old girl is smiling,' the younger medic noted. His supervisor agreed, but he wasn't surprised: it wasn't the first suicide he'd dealt with since the border opened.

'May she be at peace now,' he muttered.

The following day, after verifying the information they had found in her handbag, Praxi's body was repatriated to the south. Elpida and Jason were notified by telephone and flew in from England. Days later, Praxi's funeral took place, attended by what was left of the family and friends she had known. And because time had flown by and nobody remembered – or those that did failed to stand up – Praxi was buried not with the man she loved but alongside her husband, Yiannis Christofi.

As the service finished, a bolt of lightning tore through the sky.

Acknowledgements

Before writing *Aphrodite's War* I consulted a number of websites, books, documentaries, articles and people. I acknowledge the most helpful here, but this should not imply that the authors or persons named accept the version of events as described within these pages. The aim is to give credit where it's due – and ideas for further reading.

Books and articles . . .
Echoes From the Dead Zone: Across the Cyprus Divide by Yiannis Papadakis (I.B. Tauris), *Healthy Living in Cyprus* by Mariam Khan (available from the Moufflon bookshop, Girne), *The Cyprus Conspiracy: America, Espionage and the Turkish Invasion* by Brendan O'Malley and Ian Craig (I.B. Tauris), *Hostage to History: Cyprus from the Ottomans to Kissinger* by Christopher Hitchens (Verso), *Imagining the Modern: The Cultures of Nationalism in Cyprus* by Rebecca Bryant (I.B. Tauris), *The Cyprus Problem: Notes to History* by Dr Latife Birgen (Rüstem), *Divided Cyprus: Modernity, History and an Island in Conflict* by Papadakis, Peristianis and Welz (Indiana), *Place of Refuge: A History of the Jews in Cyprus* by Stavros Panteli (Elliott & Thompson), *Persecution of Islam in Cyprus* by Oktay

Öksüzoğlu, *a Business of Some Heat: The United Nations Force in Cyprus Before and During the 1974 Turkish Invasion*, by Brigadier Francis Henn (Pen & Sword), *Bones Don't Speak*, article by Angelique Chrisafis (*Guardian*), *Cyprus Visitors' Guide 2008* (Cytamobile – Athk Cyta), *Cyprus* (APA Insight Guides).

Websites and the documentary . . .
www.britains-smallwars.com, www.visitcyprus.com, www.missing-cy.org, www.cyprusnet.com, www.athimedia.com, www.bbc.co.uk, www.time.com, www.cypnet.co.uk, www.akel.org.cy, www.greeknewsonline.com, www.country-data.com, www.ebos.com.cy, www.lobbyforcyprus.com, *Attila 1974* directed by Michalis Kakoyiannis.

The people and inspiration . . .
My 'second family' (Lenya, Kypros, Erato/Toulla, Marios, Kypros, Sotiris, Christos, Charis, Niki, Elena and Varnavia), Sotiris Petrakkides, the McMillan family (Honor, Ava, Sam and Steve), Tim Stear, David Carter, Mickey Burke, Mandalena and family, Mr Theofanis, Mr Charalambous, Mithat Rende, Arif Altay, Panicos Kyriacou, Marios Kyriakides, Amir, Namik and Rafet.

And finally to . . .
Mum, Dad, Lorenz, Jane Lawson, Madeline Toy, Charlie Campbell and the A-Team at Ed Victor Ltd, Varnavia (again) and my friends Hélène and Matthew – thanks for the support, the careful reading, the friendly advice and the love.